ADVANCE PRAISE FOR *DARK HOPE*

"Young people are especially vulnerable to human trafficking, in great part, because there are not enough resources focused on prevention. *Dark Hope* fills that void. It is a compelling story that will appeal to young readers while giving them critically important information on how to escape this scourge and sparking conversations among each other."

—Deborah J. Richardson, executive vice president,
National Center for Civil and Human Rights

"Monica tackles the real-world problem of human trafficking in the intriguing world of fantasy that is *Dark Hope*. Young adult readers will be turning pages quickly as the battle of good and evil unfolds before their very eyes. It is my hope that *Dark Hope* will inspire and propel another generation to action to protect children against trafficking."

—Cheryl DeLuca-Johnson, president
and CEO of Street Grace, Inc.

"An effortlessly strong narrative voice, engaging writing style, and intriguing details that make you want to read on. What's not to love?"

—Aaron Kite, author A Touch of Poison,
2012 Watty Award recipient for
Most Popular fantasy book

Dark Hope

Book One *of the*
ARCHANGEL PROPHECIES

MONICA McGURK

RIVER GROVE BOOKS

This book is a work of fiction. Names, characters, businesses, organizations, places, events, and incidents are either a product of the author's imagination or are used fictitiously. Any resemblance to actual persons, living or dead, events, or locales is entirely coincidental.

Published by River Grove Books
Austin, TX
www.rivergrovebooks.com

Distributed by River Grove Books
For ordering information or special discounts for bulk purchases, please contact River Grove Books at PO Box 91869, Austin, TX 78709, 512.891.6100.

Design and composition by Greenleaf Book Group
Cover design by Greenleaf Book Group
Cover images: [background image] ©iStockphoto.com/Rasica; [replacement girl] ©iStockphoto.com/quintanilla; [angel illustration] ©iStockphoto.com/hypergon; [birds] Copyright Background Land , 2014. Used under license from Shutterstock.com

Publisher's Cataloging-In-Publication Data

McGurk, Monica.
Dark hope / Monica McGurk.—First edition.
pages ; cm.—(Archangel prophecies ; book 1)
Interest age level: Young adult.
Issued also as an ebook.
ISBN: 978-1-938416-67-5
1. Victims of crimes—Georgia—Atlanta—Fiction. 2. Teenage girls—Georgia—Atlanta—Fiction. 3. Human trafficking—Georgia—Atlanta—Fiction. 4. Children of divorced parents—Georgia—Atlanta—Fiction. 5. Good and evil—Fiction. 6. Young adult fiction. I. Title.

PS3613.C487 D37 2014
813/.6 2013956704

First Edition

Other Editions
eBook ISBN: 978-1-938416-69-9

To my husband and children, for their love, patience, and support, and for my fan fiction readers, for their inspiration and encouragement.

A portion of the proceeds from the sale of this book will be donated to organizations that fight human trafficking, especially the sexual trafficking of minors.

PROLOGUE

When the SWAT team stormed the motel room, the first thing they saw was the little girl. She was sitting on the edge of the bed, holding her blankie and sucking her thumb, her bare legs hanging over the edge, absentmindedly kicking at the faded bedspread.

The television set blared—Wile E. Coyote getting crushed by a falling anvil, courtesy once again of the Road Runner.

The girl turned her big brown eyes and stared at the men. She didn't scream; she didn't cry; she just looked at them as if she had been expecting them all along, as if they were as natural a part of the run-down room as the peeling, speckled wallpaper and the rust-colored shag carpet.

They turned and fanned their guns around the room, looking for the man who had taken the girl, the bad man who had hurt other little girls, the man who was lurking in the corner or hiding under the bed. But he wasn't there. The door to the bathroom was closed, however, so they surrounded it.

Two of the men, who looked like bugs in their funny helmets and gas masks, began talking to her, touching her hair, her arms, as if to reassure themselves that she was there, really, really there. Was she all right? Was she hurt?

While they wrapped a blanket around her, another bug-man kicked in the bathroom door and rushed inside, brandishing his gun.

"Oh dear God," he choked out, his voice sounding tinny and far away as he backed out through the door. An acrid smell floated out with him.

The other men rushed into the bathroom to see what he had seen. Suddenly, they had to strain to move their feet, as if springs were pulling them back. The faded linoleum had melted and was sticking to their boots, stretching apart like long strings of taffy. There, in the middle of a scorched, black circle of gooey plastic, lay a pile of ash flecked with little chips of white. Teeth. Bones. The body was still smoking, its whispery tendrils rising up to leave a film of soot on the ceiling. One of the men kicked the pile, revealing a few misshapen lumps. A putrid smell washed over them as he kicked around the remains, musky sweet and tangy, like copper.

One by one the men came out, holding their hands over their faces. One rushed to the little Formica table in the corner, thrust up the front of his helmet, and vomited into the wastebasket. Walkie-talkies started buzzing and bulbs started flashing and everything seemed to get hot and loud all at once.

The first man, the man who had kicked in the bathroom door, knelt before the little girl on the bed.

"What happened? Who did this?" he asked the little girl. "Was there someone else here with you?"

The little girl just stared at him with her big brown eyes and sucked her thumb. She had no idea what he was talking about.

"Let's get you out of here," the man said, his voice rough. He swept her up in his arms, pulling the industrial blanket tightly around her. She was so tiny, almost weightless. He wound through the crowded room and headed toward the open door, trying to block the memory of what he'd seen in the bathroom.

He emerged, blinking, into the gray light. On the concrete sidewalk he paused, taking great gulps of fresh air. Emergency personnel swirled all around them while police barked at the gathering crowd, pressing them back from the caution tape where they surged, hoping for a glimpse.

The girl whimpered against his shoulder, clutching her threadbare blanket even tighter.

"It's okay," he murmured, patting her awkwardly on the back. "We'll find your mommy and your daddy. You'd like that, wouldn't you?"

He didn't wait for her answer before striding purposefully across the parking lot, moving closer and closer to the flashing lights, the cameras, and the crowd.

"Hope!"

A wild-eyed woman broke through the tape, past the restraining arms of the police officer, and then was swallowed up in the crowd.

"Mommy!"

The girl squirmed in his arms, straining toward the voice.

"Hold on now," the man cautioned, but the little girl was kicking at him now, determined to get to her mother. Carefully, he set her down on the cracked pavement. "Be careful, you're barefoot," he warned her, holding her back ever so slightly. It wouldn't do to lose her now.

A pair of EMTs fell upon her, peppering her with questions as one shone a penlight in her eyes and the other took notes. Reporters crowded around them, microphones eagerly thrusting forward like branches of trees, showering questions down upon the little girl's head.

The little girl shrank back against the SWAT leader, who instinctively wrapped her in a protective arm.

"Hope!" A desperate voice rose above the chatter of the reporters. "That's my daughter! Let me through!"

Slowly, the crowd parted for the woman who was clawing her way through.

"Hope!" she sobbed, falling on her knees before her daughter. In an instant, a man, eyes heavy with shadows, fell in behind her—the father.

The woman laughed through her sobs, running her hands over the little girl, checking that she was whole, as if she were a newborn.

"Oh my God, what did he do to you?" she choked out through her tears, clutching the little girl in her arms. Her husband wrapped them both in his embrace, weeping silently.

The SWAT leader cleared his throat, leaning in to speak to the parents. This part always made him uncomfortable, but it had to be said.

"She seems unhurt," he said steadily, low so that the reporters would not hear, "but we haven't had a physical examination yet. We don't know what he may have done to her. We need to take her in now. To be sure."

He locked eyes with the father, who blanched. He'd heard the father had been the one with her at the time she was snatched. He felt for the guy. It would be hard to live with yourself, if the worst had, indeed, happened.

The mother just kissed the top of her daughter's head. "Of course," she said. "But we go with her. I'm not leaving her side." She rose to her feet, shifting her baby girl in her arms. The girl made a little sound of protest where she rested her head against her mother's shoulder.

"Oh, poor baby, your hair is caught," the woman said. She hitched the girl up on her hip and swept the girl's cascade of silky hair around her neck.

The SWAT leader started. "What's that?" he demanded, pointing at the little girl.

"What's what?" the mother responded, confused.

"There, on her neck."

The woman turned to face her husband. "What is it, Don?"

Her husband shuddered and reached out with a tentative hand to lift up her hair and touch his little girl's neck. She flinched from the touch.

Her husband's face hardened into a mask of fury as he let her hair fall back into place.

one

Ten years.

Mona straightened the picture frame on the bookshelf. There, captured under glass, three-year-old Hope smiled up at her with big brown eyes that were untouched by fear, by danger, or by sadness.

It had been more than ten years since that portrait sitting. She remembered holding Hope's favorite stuffed animal behind the photographer, making it dance and fly around his head in an effort to get her daughter to laugh. The sound had bubbled out of her, the sound of unadulterated delight, and with a snap of a shutter the photographer had frozen that moment in time forever.

They hadn't known, then, that their carefree days were about to end.

Mona ran her finger along the edge of the frame, checking for dust. She stepped back and looked at the other photos, taking them in one by one.

There was the snapshot of her and Don graduating from Georgia Tech. A gust had threatened to lift away her mortarboard, and she'd lifted her hand to hold it down while the wind blew her long chestnut hair off her shoulders. She was laughing, and Don was turned, admiring her, the reflection of her face in his Ray-Bans and a broad, toothy grin lighting up his own.

They'd had jobs—good jobs—lined up: she as an analyst with a consulting firm and he as an engineer. They were young and crazy in love; it was there, plain to see in that simple snapshot taken by one of their friends. They were going to conquer the world. And they were unaware that at that moment a new life was already forming inside of Mona, a new life that would change everything.

So young, she thought wistfully. So young to have so much responsibility thrust upon us. But what could you do? She lingered over the wedding portrait that was tucked behind the others. Their marriage had been hastily arranged. She hadn't really cared about the fancy wedding—after all, she had no family to speak of, no one to impress or to worry about tradition—but Don had insisted.

"You deserve the whole thing," he'd stated emphatically when, after tallying up the budget for the affair, she'd suggested once again that they should simply elope to Savannah. "The big dress, the flowers—all of it. And I want it in a church," he'd said. That was the only part of the deal, she knew, that wasn't open to negotiation. "I want the holy bonds."

Mona pulled out her portrait and held it up close, peering at it with a critical eye. She'd chosen the dress wisely, she thought, always knowing what flattered her petite frame. The long column of white was elegant, the Empire waist just enough to hide the tiny bump that was beginning to show. If you didn't know it already, you'd have never been able to tell that she was already five months along in that photo. The studio had expertly wiped out the red of her eyes, eyes that had become bloodshot from the horrible morning sickness that never went away. She smiled, grimly remembering the intersection where, every morning on her way to work, she'd had to pull over and vomit, the fumes from the commute too much for her roiling stomach to bear.

She set the picture down. A mother at twenty-two. She wouldn't have believed it herself if it hadn't happened to her. It was definitely not a part of her plan. But Hope—well, Hope was worth it.

She turned back to the photo of her three-year-old daughter. There was a big gap after that: no pictures for a long, long time. Then just a trail of obligatory school pictures, her daughter in school uniform, her eyes wary, her spirit seemingly snuffed out. In each one, she seemed to shrink behind a curtain of hair, willing the camera away, hoping she could hide from it.

Ten years.

Had she done the right thing? she wondered. After Hope's abduction, she had tried to make it work with Don. She hadn't ever blamed him for what had happened. She knew how often she, herself, at the playground would sneak a glance at her mobile while her daughter played on the slide or in the dirt, trying to catch up on what was going on in the office. She knew how quickly it could have happened, and it could have happened on her watch just as easily as it had happened on his.

No, she had never blamed Don. But he had been unable to forgive himself. Even though Hope had been returned to them whole—undamaged except for that damned mark on her neck—he couldn't let go of the feeling that he was somehow responsible, and that there was more to the story. He couldn't accept that their daughter had been taken randomly by a sick, sick man, a man who had died a fiery death, a man who was no longer a threat.

Don's vow to never let it happen again had been the poison that had destroyed their marriage. His vigilance became obsession until it was the defining thing in his life, crowding out the happiness they'd once had together, crowding out even his love for her, Mona, until there was nothing left but paranoia.

She'd had no choice. She still believed that, even after all these years. She'd had to leave him, even though it had torn her apart—because, after all, she had still loved him. Or at least she had loved the memory of him: the man who had sold his beloved pickup truck to buy her a diamond ring, which she'd found inside her fortune cookie after wolfing down some kung pao chicken; the man who had gone out in the middle of the night without complaining to buy her Dutch apple pie when that had been all she craved, always coming back with an extra pint of ice cream; the man who'd cried when the doctors placed his infant daughter in his arms and whose voice, like magic, was the only thing in the world that could stop Hope's angry, newborn wailing.

Mona had made her decision, thinking that with a separation she'd be able to shield her daughter from Don's increasingly crazy rantings. On her own, she could filter Hope's exposure so that she saw only the best of her father. So while Mona couldn't bring herself to divorce him, she'd filed for a formal separation and custody, thinking that would be enough.

Instead, she'd lost her daughter when the judge deemed that her work schedule would prevent her from being a good mother. The injustice of it burned even now. The loss of custody had been bad enough. The court-ordered visitations—her tenuous link to her daughter's love—had been continuously strained by Don's insistence on keeping up security, approving every place they went, screening each site carefully for risks. Her gifts had been rejected, as if somehow the wrong blouse or dress would paint a target on their daughter, exposing her to harm. So as Hope grew older, Mona's attempts to connect with her became strained and forced, their entire relationship carefully controlled by Don's vigilance.

For ten years, Mona had mourned the loss of her husband and her daughter. She'd mourned the loss even as she soldiered on, advancing to partner in her firm, making sure that if nothing else, her broken family's material needs were met.

And now this. Hope had asked the court for a change of custody, and this time, the court had listened. This time, Hope was coming home with her.

This sudden change of events was a gift, one she was determined not to waste. She'd done everything she could to make her house ready. Hope's room had been updated to what she supposed would appeal to a young teenager. Her closet was stocked with clothing—not too much, because she still didn't know exactly what her daughter's preferences would be, but enough to see her through the start of school. She'd bought a new treadmill so her daughter could keep up with her beloved running—her only pastime, as far as Mona could tell.

No, she would not waste this opportunity. She stuffed down the pang of sympathy she felt for Don. She'd lost her daughter before. She was not going to let it happen again.

Her cell phone began ringing, the no-nonsense, anonymous tune that she'd never bothered to reset interrupting her reverie. It was Clayton Ross, the managing partner of her consulting firm and closest thing she had to a boss. And a friend.

"Checking up on me, Clay?"

"You know I'd never do that, Mona. But I did want you to reconsider my offer to drive with you to Alabama. That's a long way to drive alone."

"You'll let me fly halfway round the world to negotiate nasty mergers, but I can't handle a leisurely weekend jaunt up I-75?" she teased.

She could almost hear him smiling over the line.

"You know that's not it. But it's a big day. Thought you might like some backup if he doesn't play ball."

Clayton was referring to her husband, of course, and whether or not he would respect the order to absent himself when Mona came to pick up Hope and take her home for good.

"He wouldn't do that to me. Not now. He's been oddly cooperative since the mediator made her decision."

"If you say so. I wouldn't put anything past him." Clayton had had an up-close view of her troubles with Don over the years, and it had soured him from having any optimism. "Drive safely, then, and call me if you change your mind."

I won't, she thought to herself as she ended the call. *I've waited too long for this moment to share it with anybody else.*

two

I didn't have much to take with me from Alabama: my school, Holy Innocents, had required uniforms, so I had little clothing of my own. Dad had always deemed the things my mother kept sending me "too showy," and he'd promptly packed them up to send to Goodwill. Mom had said to leave my treadmill; she'd get me a new one. So I loaded up the backseat of her Audi convertible with my books and climbed in, ready to put my past behind me.

As Mom backed out of the long rutted driveway, I took one last look at the house in which I'd lived for almost ten years. Dad wasn't there to wave goodbye. When I'd told the judge I was afraid he'd make a scene, he'd ordered him to vacate the premises for the hour before and after my mother was supposed to collect me. He was probably down at the church, praying for a miraculous intervention to keep me from moving to Atlanta. Resentment flooded through me, and I crossed my arms, refusing to acknowledge the fluttering in my stomach.

"Ready to go?" Mom asked, looking expectantly into the backseat at me. I nodded and she accelerated. In an instant, a cloud of dust obscured my view of the house.

We rode in silence. My request for a change of custody had come as a surprise to my mom. She'd never challenged the original arrangements over the years, had never pumped me for information or probed to find his failings as a father. It was like she wanted him to be a good dad, was even rooting for him. When I'd insisted on talking in private with the court-appointed mediator, she hadn't questioned it. She'd never tried to get me to explain why I wanted to move back to live with her.

Now, as we weaved in and out of the fast lane, she kept her end of whatever unspoken agreement she had with my dad and left me to my own thoughts. But I didn't want to think. Instead, I let the steady hum of the asphalt under the tires lull me into a half-sleep.

~

"Here we are," Mom said briskly, jolting me out of my trance as she made a sharp turn. The two hours had gone swiftly, and I was surprised to see that we were in a neat subdivision, almost home.

My mom still lived in the same big house in the suburbs we'd had before my parents separated. It made no sense. She had to drive miles to get to the airport. She lived alone. The house was a massive colonial looming ahead of us at the end of a cul-de-sac: great for a family with young kids, a bit much if you were a single not-quite-divorcée.

The perfection of it was jarring after living as we did in Alabama. Even though Dad and I technically lived in a decent neighborhood (thanks to the generous check Mom sent every month), our house was pretty sad. Dad had blocked out most of the windows with aluminum foil, nailing their sashes shut, and had installed double deadbolts on every door. The yard was a dead zone with bare patches of dirt and stubby clumps of straw, all that was left of the bushes some previous owner had planted. From the mint green and plum wallpaper that looked like it came from an old Holiday Inn to the saggy garage door, the entire place looked like someone had abandoned it circa 1992. The covenants had expired on our neighborhood, so the neighbors just shook their heads and whispered among themselves about what a shame it was.

That wasn't the only thing they whispered about us. My dad had embraced an extreme religious-slash-survivalist lifestyle that was way outside the bounds of any normal church. He'd raised me like a hunted thing, always wary, pushing well-meaning neighbors away to keep me isolated from the "threat"—whatever threat it was that he imagined. We lived on the edges of social acceptability, my daily trips to school tolerated only because of the legalities and my mom's refusal to let him homeschool me. Between his erratic behavior and the story of my past, we were outcasts, tolerated at best in the small town in which he raised me. But now, all that was going to be over at last.

I felt a little twinge looking up at my new home as we pulled up the driveway. With its pretty white shutters, sparkling panes, and wide expanse of green grass, it should have been cheery, but the yawning windows looked just as sad to me. As she pulled into the spotless garage, I wondered again why Mom had lived here by herself all these years.

"You remember; your room is at the top of the stairway. I can help you carry your books up, if you'd like." The corners of her mouth contorted, as if she was either forcing a smile or trying to suppress one. I couldn't tell which.

I nodded, sitting in my seat, my hands folded in my lap, while she got out of the car and opened the door for me. I looked up at her face, uncertain. I hadn't thought about the fact that I didn't really know my mom. I hadn't really lived with her in more than ten years.

She blew out a long breath and reached in to squeeze my hands. "Welcome home, Hope."

~

Later that night, over pizza, we reviewed her plans for the week. And I mean plans.

"I'll be taking you in tomorrow for your first day of class. But I need to leave first thing in the morning on Tuesday. My secretary prepared my itinerary for you"—she passed me a glossy blue folder from a neat pile in front of her—"in case you need to reach me. I won't be back for a few days, but I asked Mrs. Bibeau down the street to check in on you after school."

I just nodded, my mouth working the cheese and pepperoni.

"The school already knows you're coming. I filed all of your papers. I made you an extra copy"—now a red folder emerged—"to keep in your backpack in case there's any confusion. We'll just need to go to the front office when we get there." Here, she frowned. "Until you get your driver's license, I am afraid you'll have to take the bus. I know that's less than ideal, but it is the best I can do right now. After you make some friends, I'm sure they'll be more than happy to pick you up. Until then, you've got to be out of the house by 7:25. Here's your bus information."

Under her breath she muttered, "For the life of me, I can't understand why your father didn't let you get your learner's permit. You're so close to being old enough to drive yourself . . . I just hope we can get you behind the wheel quickly. I'll have to sign you up for Driver's Ed."

I almost told her it wasn't necessary, but bit back my response. It probably wouldn't help her any to know that my father had been letting me drive behind the wheel of his old Honda for years. It was part of his plan for "emergency preparedness." Whatever that meant.

Without pausing, Mom turned to the pile. "I've assembled a list of emergency phone numbers for you and compiled all the information on the classes you'll be joining." *Thwack*. Another thick folder hit the table. "I wasn't sure what you'd like to eat, so just in case, I got this set of delivery menus for you for when I'm gone." She fanned them out in front of her. Her voice was starting to get a hysterical edge to it.

"Mom," I interrupted, touching her lightly on the arm. "It's okay. I've cooked for myself before. I'll be okay."

She sagged back into her chair. "Of course you will. I just feel so bad, leaving so soon after you've gotten here. If your father knew, he'd—"

"But he doesn't. And nobody's going to tell him." I leaned back in my chair and crossed my arms, pleased that an opportunity to defy him had presented itself so soon.

Mom smiled weakly. "No, I suppose not. The judge took care of that, didn't she? Unless he's assembled an army of spies, he won't be able to see you for a good three months."

I winced. I wouldn't put it past my father to have concocted some elaborate scheme to track my whereabouts 24/7. He may have even implanted a chip in me. Memo to self—check for weird bumps when you take a shower tonight.

My mom interrupted my thoughts. "Here's a cell phone for you." She set it down next to my plate. It was sleek, gunmetal gray with a cool graffiti case. "It's preprogrammed with my cell, Mrs. Bibeau's number, my secretary's number, and some emergency numbers. I'll try to call you each night to see how your day went, kiddo, but it may be late. I'm not sure how your classes at Holy Innocents compare to Dunwoody High's, so you may have some catching up to do. Or you may find them too easy. If you find you have time on your hands, you could think through your extracurriculars. I picked up this information on the ones I thought might interest you from the school. Maybe we can talk about it tomorrow night after you get home and have a sense of your class load."

I stopped playing with the stringy cheese that had dripped off of my slice and stared at her blankly as she set the list on top of the pile. "Extracurriculars?"

Mom's lips compressed into a thin line and her eyes got sad. "You're a perfectly healthy fifteen-year-old girl, Hope," she said, softly. "Your dad did what he thought best, but . . ." She stopped then, choosing her words carefully. "You should be out in the world, honey. Not locked up all day."

I picked up the page and started scanning the list. Cheerleading. Volleyball. Yearbook. Track. My heart started racing and I suddenly felt lightheaded. I wasn't prepared for the sudden sense of panic that came over me. This was what I'd dreamed of, right?

I took a deep breath, trying to calm myself, and carefully laid the page aside. As I sat there, unsure of what to say, Mom reached across the table and tucked a loose strand of hair behind my ear. "Just think about it, okay?"

Before I knew what I was doing, I blurted the words. "Mom, why did you leave Dad?"

Her face turned soft; her eyes, even more sad. "Come with me, honey."

I followed her upstairs to a little alcove she called her den. "It should be in here somewhere," she said, stretching her tiny five-foot-two frame up to reach an upper shelf. Her perfectly manicured fingers wrapped around a faded volume and pulled it down. She sat on the little love seat in the corner and patted the space beside her, beckoning me to join her. I sat down, intrigued.

"I've been saving these for when this day came," she said, setting the book down in my lap.

I opened the cover and found myself looking at a yellowed newspaper clipping. "Missing Girl Saved—But How?" screamed the headline. A grainy photo showed a police officer carrying a little girl, wrapped loosely in a blanket, in his arms. The girl gripped something in her fist, trailing it behind her.

"Is that me?" I asked, suddenly shy. I let my fingers graze over the clipping.

"Yes," my mother said. "With your blankie. Somehow you managed to hold on to that thing, even in those circumstances. I saved every one of them," she said, turning the album pages to show me newspaper story after newspaper story, carefully laid out on acid-free paper. "It was bad enough that you had been taken, Hope. But the mystery surrounding your rescue—well, that was like catnip for the press."

"What do you mean?" I asked. I had never heard about any mystery. In reality, I remembered nothing and had heard very little about my abduction. The physical consequences had been mild—except, of course, for my neck, which I didn't want to think about right now. The emotional aftermath, though? Pretty heavy. Psychologists had poked and prodded me, trying to get my fractured brain to cough up the secrets of what had happened during the horrible forty-eight hours I'd been missing. But my mind refused to cooperate, earning me the labels of "traumatized" and "victim."

I didn't like to think of myself that way, but truth be told, I wasn't eager to pry those forgotten hours out of the recesses of my memory. I liked it the way it was, with the facts about what had happened to me safely locked away where I didn't have to think about them. But now my mom had piqued my curiosity.

My mother frowned slightly, her eyes searching my face. "I know you don't remember, do you? You didn't remember even back then." She paused, seeming to gather her strength before continuing. "When the police found you, you were unharmed, thank God. But they never found the man who had snatched you. They think he was killed right there in the motel room where they found you."

"What do you mean, they think?"

"They found this in the bathroom," she said, slowly turning another page.

I stared at the dark photograph, unable to make out what it was. "What is that?"

I thought I saw her suppress a little shudder before she braced herself yet again. "It is what's left of a human being who has been burned to death."

I stared dumbly at the page, barely registering what she said as she continued to speak, carefully choosing her words.

"They confirmed it was a person through DNA testing. They were never able to match it to anyone in their crime databases, so really they had no way of knowing who it was or whether it really was the person who took you. They couldn't even tell if the person was alive or dead at the time of the burning. Presumably dead, or you'd think there'd be signs of a fight. But we really couldn't tell. All we ever knew was that this . . . person . . . was dead, and you were alive. With no memory of anything at all. Untouched . . . except for this."

She reached out to stroke the Mark on the back of my neck, and I shrank away. I didn't like anyone even knowing about that spot. I sure didn't want her reminding me of it.

"But how is that even possible?" I demanded, trying to ignore the hurt look that crossed her face as I pushed her hand away. "I mean, how could a person just go up in flames and not burn the whole room down at the same time? And me, even though I was so little, wouldn't I have remembered something?"

My mother smiled, but this time with an edge. "Therein lies the problem. You didn't. Traumatic repression, the psychologists surmised. Whatever happened was locked away in your little brain, and you were surprisingly none the worse for it. And nobody could figure it out, Hope. Not the best minds in the police department or the FBI. We finally just chalked it up to one of life's mysteries and tried to put it behind us. All of us but your father, that is."

Her hands twisted in her lap. It still pained her to talk about it. I felt a twinge of guilt for having brought up the whole subject, but not enough to make her stop.

"He could not let go of the idea that this was not a random act. It got worse when the police couldn't figure out that mark on your neck. At first they'd thought it was a brand—the sort of thing a gang would do to mark a little girl as property before putting her up for sale on the streets." I blanched, but my mom didn't slow down. "But they couldn't trace it back to any organized group and nobody would confess to having seen it before. And over time, as the rawness of it healed, it came to look less like a brand, more like a tattoo.

"They ran it through their databases for cults, looking for a connection there. They even brought in a few language experts to see if there was a word that could be deciphered, but, to tell you the truth, by that point I didn't care. They couldn't find an answer and I was tired of dwelling upon it. I was just glad you were safe.

"But not your father. To him, that mark was the key to the entire mystery. He became obsessed with the idea that you'd been singled out on purpose, that the mark was meant to show it. That maybe the person who took you was still out there, and that you were still in danger. At first, I thought it was his way of dealing with the guilt, and I was sure it would pass. But it didn't."

"Guilt?" I prompted her, my nerves now on edge.

She slumped in her seat. "He'd been the one with you at the playground the day you disappeared. He blamed himself."

I stared dumbly at the photo album. He'd never told me that. He'd never told me any of this.

My mom reached over and closed the album, and then took my hand in hers.

"I didn't want to leave you, Hope. And to tell the truth, I didn't want to leave your father, either. I still loved him, and I guess in some ways, I still do. I just couldn't live with his obsession any longer. It was stifling us. He was not the same person anymore, sweetie. His whole world had narrowed down to a paranoid focus on protecting you. He lost his job, and then he lost another, and another. He just couldn't bear to be away from you for long enough to go to work. Even normal things like going out to dinner became ordeals. What I saw as harmless fun he saw as needless security threats. So I left, fully knowing that someone had to take care of you both, and that that someone was me. I had to be strong, keep my job, and make sure you had everything you needed. I just didn't realize that he would use that against me and take you away. Or that what I was seeing was just the tip of the iceberg."

I thought about all the crazy things my dad had put me through: How he'd overwhelmed the mothers in our neighborhood with his overzealous lists of do's and don'ts until the invitations for play-dates had shriveled up. How he'd insisted on accompanying me on every field trip and social event, going so far as to sit with me on the bus, until I was so embarrassed that I didn't even want to go. The forced marches through obscure biblical texts, drilling me in preparation for God-knows-what. His odd security procedures and mock safety drills. I'd always thought my mother had willingly left me with my father so she could focus on her high-powered job as a partner in a consulting firm. In a weird way, I'd blamed her for my father's behavior and for how circumscribed my world had been. I'd never understood why any of it had happened, until now.

Mom's eyes were watery now as she hesitated, and then she reached up to tuck a stray lock of hair behind my ear. This time I didn't flinch.

"I didn't tell you this before, Hope, because I didn't want you to do anything but love your dad. I guess I kept hoping things would get better and that one day you would be old enough to understand. I just want you to know that I never, ever thought that things would turn out the way they did. And I never thought it would take so long to get you back home with me."

She gave my hand a little squeeze before continuing.

"Maybe it's just as well that whatever happened is locked away in your memory. But there's no need for you to be locked away, too. Now that you're here, maybe you can spread your wings."

The cell phone in her pocket started chirping. She pulled it out and flipped it open, frowning.

"I have to take this, Hope, I'm sorry. But it should only be a minute."

With that, she stood. She answered the phone brusquely, and I marveled at her transformation as she stepped into the hall. Her voice seemed to drop an octave as she drilled the person on the other end of the line with a sharp staccato of questions. Even though I couldn't hear what she was talking about, I could tell from the tone of her voice that she was not happy.

She slipped back into the den, her face crumpled in a frown, her long manicured nails tapping absently on the phone.

"There's been a legal challenge to the project I'm working on. My client is demanding I come out a day early." She plopped down next to me. I saw the effort she put into steeling herself. "Of course, I told him no."

I thought of all the times I'd blamed her, unfairly, for putting her job first. I needed to let her know that I understood.

"You should go, Mom."

She looked up, startled. "What?"

I launched into my reasoning before she could stop me. "It sounds really important. I mean, your client wouldn't call you on the weekend if it wasn't, right?"

She nodded her head, the grooves in her forehead growing deeper.

"You've already taken care of everything for me at school. And I really don't need you to take me in. I'm fifteen, Mom," I added, gently. "I would really prefer it if you let me go in by myself, just like any other kid."

Her eyes got a little misty again as she tucked the phone back into her pocket and folded her hands in her lap. "Like any other kid," she echoed back wistfully. "Maybe we should go over the instructions again," she said.

"Mom, I've got it. I promise."

She sighed, her shoulders sagging in acceptance. Then, she stood up, resting one hand gently on my head, stroking my hair just like she had when I was little, smiling ruefully.

"I guess I'd better let them know and go pack, then. If you need me, I'll be just down the hall."

She left me alone in the den, the clippings and pictures from my past in my lap, wondering just what else I didn't know about my past.

~

I woke up to an empty house and a note written on the back of an old grocery receipt. "Note" is actually an exaggeration; it was a list of what my mom calls "bullet points":

- *Bus at 7:30, end of cul-de-sac*
- *Wear hat*
- *Lunch money*
- *Mrs. Bibeau after school*

Love, Mom.

Mom had taped it to the bathroom door along with a twenty dollar bill. I glanced at the alarm clock. It was only seven a.m., but already my mom was long gone to catch her flight to wherever. I didn't know how I was ever going to keep track of where she was. She flew to a different city every day.

This was what I wanted, I reminded myself as I brushed my teeth. Anonymity. Space. A parent who didn't hover around me all the time, afraid I'd disappear if he looked away for even an instant. I was tired of being the girl who'd been abducted, the girl who had never been able to remember a thing that had happened to her.

I rifled through the closet to find something that would help me blend in. Everything in there was too ridiculous for words—I guess I'd have to remind Mom that I was not going out for cheerleading, nor was I planning to be an extra on some stupid teenage reality show. Besides, after years of wearing uniforms, I had no idea what went with what. I fought back a rising sense of panic and pulled out a pair of jeans and a sweatshirt, hoping it would do the trick. I fiddled with my hair, worried that my Mark would show. I settled for wrapping a chunky scarf around my neck, thanking my stars that it was still cold and that the scarf wouldn't attract attention. I glanced at the clock again and frowned. Time to catch the bus.

I walked swiftly to the end of the cul-de-sac, mowing down a granola bar on the way. Nobody else was waiting. I kicked at the pothole in the pavement and shifted my backpack, fervently hoping that the pothole would open up and swallow me before I'd have to board the bus and suffer through this day. The sound of gears grinding uphill warned me I'd have no reprieve, and then the yellow lights came into view.

I boarded the bus like a prisoner walking to the gallows. The minute I stepped on I slunk into the first seat I could find, hoping to avoid all the "new girl" stares I was sure to attract.

"Fresh meat!" Raucous laughter mocked me from the back of the bus. Something hit me in the head—a wad of paper. I sunk even lower into my seat, fiddling with my scarf and praying they'd just ignore me.

"New girl! New girl!"

I looked up at the boy demanding my attention. His long bangs fell into his eyes, which were full of undisguised curiosity and mischief. He shook his hair and darted a look into the back of the bus. His friends shouted, egging him on. I hugged my backpack more tightly and waited with a sinking feeling for him to continue.

"Watch this!" He plopped down on my seat, deliberately crashing into me, and proceeded to belch the alphabet at me. My face burned with embarrassment. The entire bus seemed to be laughing at my discomfort. I huddled next to the window, trying to make myself as small as possible. Emboldened, the boy snatched my hat and began playing keep-away with his friends. Instinctively, I felt for my scarf, making sure it was still wrapped safely around my neck, its ends tucked away where nobody could get them.

What if I'd made a mistake coming to this school? How would I ever fit in if I couldn't even handle this?

As soon as the bus lurched into its parking spot, I dashed out of my seat, climbing past the boy and into the aisle.

"New girl, wait up!" he called.

I pushed through the door, not bothering to respond to the moronic boy. Dunwoody High was bigger than I thought: two stories of gleaming glass and clean brick, surrounded by massive parking lots and playing fields. Buses were disgorging kids and a steady buzz was already building from the crowd. I squared my shoulders and walked through the set of double doors, willing my stomach to be calm.

A tide of students rushing through the hallways swept me into its current. People jostled about me, not paying me any notice as they bumped and pushed me aside. I looked around and realized with relief that I'd lost the horrible boy from the bus. It would be easy to get lost in the shuffle here, I thought, in a good way. I resisted the temptation to pull out any of the detailed lists and maps my mom had compiled for me—too conspicuous—and instead felt my way to the front office.

"What is it, sweetie? Do you need the nurse?" the bustling woman at the front counter demanded as I crossed the threshold. It was an oasis of quiet compared to the hallway, and I felt wrong interrupting it.

"Um, no, ma'am, I'm just checking in. I'm a new student starting today—Hope Carmichael?"

I braced myself for the knowing look of recognition and curiosity that always came after I announced my name, but the woman gave no sign of having heard of me. Instead she started shuffling through piles of papers. Maybe this wasn't a mistake after all.

"Carmichael . . . Carmichael . . . ah, yes, here it is, Carmichael!" She triumphantly produced a clipped set of pages from the bottom of the pile. "Your mother was in here last week. Quite a handful. Very on top of the details, shall we say." She rolled her eyes at the memory.

"That sounds like her," I said, smiling to myself.

"You probably have your entire schedule already, don't you?" she said, shaking her head disapprovingly. "Your mother wouldn't leave until she had that. All your papers were in order; she made sure of that well in advance. So just run along to your homeroom." She ran her finger down the page in front of her. "Home economics, Mrs. Raburn. Second floor."

As I was swinging my backpack over my shoulder, though, she called out, "No, wait. Note here says there's been a change. Wait over there on the bench, honey, and let me see what this is all about." She bustled away into a back room while I stood, waiting.

She came bustling back, clucking like a mother hen. "I don't know what happened, dear, but you'll just have to make the best of it. Room 107—past the gym."

"What is it?" I said, peering at the slip of paper she handed me.

"Shop, dear. Now run along, and be sure to give Mr. Reynolds that hall pass, or you will get a tardy."

Of course I got lost when I tried to find my locker. The bell had rung, sending everyone scurrying into their classrooms like cockroaches fleeing the sudden light, leaving me to wander until I accidentally found the gym and then, past it, room 107.

I stood outside the door. The smell of grease and tar wafted out to me, making me want to gag. I rewrapped my scarf, like a ritual, and pushed through the doors.

I walked right in, interrupting the lecturing teacher, who had drawn up the entire shop class in a semicircle around him. My entrance provoked a multitude of stares, hoots, and snickers. I looked around at the students. They all wore dingy denim or canvas aprons, heavily stained with greasy handprints. I was the only girl. I clutched the hall pass in my hand a little tighter, crumpling the paper.

"Can I help you?" Mr. Reynolds turned to me, annoyed that I'd interrupted his class. His eyes bugged out behind the safety glasses he wore, making him look like an overgrown insect.

"Um," I started, uncomfortably frozen in his stare. "Um. I'm a new student assigned to your class. Which is crazy, because I'm not supposed to be in here," I said, unable to stop the nervous chatter from escaping my lips. "I mean, I was supposed to be in home ec. Or AP chemistry now. Not shop."

Mr. Reynolds glowered at me from behind his safety glasses. I realized I'd inadvertently insulted him.

"Not that there's anything wrong with shop," I added lamely, thrusting my hall pass up at him.

He pushed his safety glasses up onto his forehead and read the pass. "Carmichael, eh? Nobody informed me you were joining my class. I take it you have no experience with the mechanical arts?" He pinned me down with a glare as I shook my head.

"You're just in time," he continued. "I was just about to demonstrate the proper use of a blowtorch. You can be my model."

The entire class erupted into catcalls. Over the din I heard someone shout, "New girl!" With a sinking feeling, I peered into the crowd. There, in the back of the class, I spotted the obnoxious boy from my bus.

"Come over here," Mr. Reynolds commanded, enjoying my discomfort. "What's the first rule of shop, class?"

"Safety first!" The class roared in unison, adding chest beating and more hooting to the din. Mr. Reynolds grinned and held out a big helmet, beckoning for me to come forward.

I shifted my backpack to one side and stepped to the middle of the semicircle. I stared at the big helmet. It looked like it belonged on a space suit from the 1950s.

"Go on, Miss Carmichael. Demonstrate proper safety technique to the class." Mr. Reynolds thrust the helmet at me again.

"But, I just—" I looked helplessly at the door.

"C'mon, how hard can it be?" Mr. Reynolds taunted me, tossing the helmet up in the air and catching it deftly with one hand.

I reached for it and he dramatically let it go, leaving me with the helmet's entire dead weight. It went crashing to the floor. The entire class roared with laughter as I cradled my fingers.

"Oh, is the helmet a little heavy for you?" Mr. Reynolds said solicitously. "I forgot these older models aren't quite as lightweight. Go ahead, pick it up and put it on."

I started to protest, but snapped my mouth shut. There was no way I was going to let him intimidate me. I dropped my backpack and bent over to retrieve the helmet. I heaved it up with both hands before trying to force it down over my head. When it got to my ears, I got stuck. I twisted and turned the thing around on my head but only succeeded in mangling my own ears.

"Ow!" I cried as someone banged it down, hard. I could barely see out of the tiny, dark window.

"Next time you might want to open up the helmet," Mr. Reynolds said drily as he flipped up the top, exposing my head to the foul air of the shop room. "You might want to pay attention to the rest of the safety tips."

My humiliation complete, he dismissed me. I hurried to the edge of the room, trying to be as inconspicuous as I could be with a giant tin can on top of my head.

~

From that inauspicious beginning, my day went downhill. The school itself was like a maze, and I was late for every class, instantly earning the ire of every teacher. It turned out that all my classes were wrong—nothing matched the schedule my mom had so carefully prepared for me. By the time the day ended, I was exhausted from having to explain myself to the endless parade of teachers who also had apparently never heard of me. In one class, there wasn't even a desk for me; I'd had to sit on the radiator up against the wall, and I nearly burned myself.

Everywhere I went, I could feel the blatant stares of my curious classmates. I smiled politely at their questions, giving the most minimal answers while I died inside from mortification and wished a hole would open in the floor and swallow me up. I'd almost relished my escape to the bus, hoping to forget my woes in a good book, when someone plopped down uncomfortably close to me.

"New girl! What'cha reading?" Before I could even look up, grubby hands snatched away my book.

It was the same obnoxious boy. He grinned maliciously at me and tossed the book over his shoulder toward the back of the bus. "How was your first day at school?" he asked with mock sincerity. Before I could come up with a snappy comeback, he rumpled my hair like I was a kindergartner and leapt out of my seat to join his laughing friends.

I shrank into my seat and felt my hair, comforting myself with the security of the scarf wrapped around my neck and steeling myself for the ride home.

I'd barely walked through the door after escaping the bus when there was a knock at the door. I peeked out and saw a short, trim woman with perfectly coifed blonde hair wearing a tracksuit and an apron. She held a covered tray and was rocking impatiently, a fake smile spread across her face.

Mrs. Bibeau, I realized, remembering my mother's note. The neighbor down the street whom Mom had asked to check in on me.

I swung the door open, doing my best to paste a matching smile on my face.

"You must be Hope," Mrs. Bibeau declared, stepping through the door uninvited. "Your mother felt so horrible about having to go on that business trip. I told her not to worry, that I'd be happy to come on over and check on you," she continued, her voice honeyed with a drawl I didn't quite recognize. "I had six children of my own, you know, and we had to move five times as they grew up, so I know what it's like. I thought you might like a little snack after such a big day, so I brought you my famous deviled eggs and pineapple sandwiches." She whipped the tea towel off the tray to reveal a stack big enough for an army. "Why don't we go sit down in the front room?"

Without waiting for me to answer, she steered me into the formal living room and sat us down on the sofa. I could tell my mom didn't use this room very much. The rest of the house was so neat and organized that it looked like it came out of a magazine, like no one really lived in it. But this room held my mom's entire "overflow." I saw Mrs. Bibeau take a mental note of the abandoned stack of Zappos and Amazon boxes, the pile of clothes set aside for charity, and the scattered piano books that surrounded Mom's old upright.

"Mom mentioned you'd be over," I said politely.

"Oh, it's no trouble. I just couldn't stand the thought of your mother worrying." She made a small *tsk* sound as she brought her attention back to me. "Why she keeps up that crazy schedule of hers, I'll never know. I remember when you were just a baby and she'd come home at all hours of the night. I thought she was going to drop dead one day, I truly did. Go on now," she said without stopping for a breath, "have a sandwich."

I realized with a jolt that Mrs. Bibeau had known us before my kidnapping. Before my parents split up. Suddenly on my guard, I picked up one of the dainty sandwiches and nibbled at it.

Mrs. Bibeau looked at me with curiosity. "We haven't seen your father in such a long time. Tell me, how is he doing these days?"

I took my time chewing, trying to think of the right thing to say and trying to get over the odd taste of pineapple with cream cheese.

"Okay, I guess. I haven't talked with him since I left."

"Really?" Her eyes shone with interest as she seized upon this bit of news. "He always seemed so . . . close to you. So protective. I'm surprised he didn't call you the moment you walked through the door."

He can't, I thought to myself, knowing the details of the court order were best kept to myself.

When I didn't respond, she tried again. "Billy and I were so sad when your parents split up and you moved away. Such a horrible business. But I suppose you don't remember any of that, do you?" She leaned in, unable to hide her eagerness.

"No, ma'am," I said stiffly. "Why don't I get us some sweet tea?"

I jumped from the sofa and stalked off to the kitchen. I was livid. How dare she pump me for information? There was no way I was going to give her anything to work with. Didn't she know I wanted to keep my past where it was—safely in the past? I slammed the glasses down on the counter, making a mess as I poured. My hands shaking, I set down the pitcher and took a deep breath.

No matter what, my mother would want me to be polite, I reminded myself. After all, she'd asked Mrs. Bibeau to stop by. The neighbor was doing this as a favor.

When I turned the corner back into the front room, I spied Mrs. Bibeau peeking into boxes and tallying up Mom's recent redecorating changes to discuss at her next bridge club. I swallowed my anger and cleared my throat, giving her time to settle back on the sofa before I came in.

I waited a grudging ten minutes while she continued to press me for more information, peppering her conversation with gossip about our neighbors. Time seemed to drag until finally she took my hints about studying and left me to my own devices, satisfied that she could give a good report to my mother and that she had gotten enough dirt to dish to make the visit worth her while.

I watched her march back up the cul-de-sac, her apron strings flying in the wind. As soon as I was sure she wasn't coming back, I tried my mom's cell phone, ready to bemoan my miserable day. But the phone rolled over directly to her voice mail, so I hung up. I pressed redial, pressing it over and over until I finally gave up, throwing the phone onto the sofa.

The entire day had been a study in frustration. I looked at the book I'd taken out of my backpack—a book I'd already studied two years ago at Holy Innocents—and shook my head, tossing the book aside.

"This is not what was supposed to happen," I pouted to myself out loud. "Not at all."

I was getting ready to recount my various injustices again when a little voice in my head rebuked me. *But nobody looked at you like a freak, did they?*

I shoved my books into my book bag, sullenly acknowledging to myself that I had, indeed, been treated as normally as any new kid in school would be. It dawned on me that while I'd always stood apart at Holy Innocents, my presence had been accepted. I wasn't ignored, nor was I constantly ridiculed and teased. After ten years, I was as much a part of the environment as the dusty chalkboards and smelly gym. At least until the incident that finally drove me to move in with Mom. How long would it take to become invisible in this school?

I sighed. Maybe things would seem better after I'd eaten dinner. I went to the extra freezer tucked away inside our pantry, thinking I'd heat something up. When I lifted the door, row after row of Trader Joe's eggplant parmigiana stared back at me. I dug around inside, but no matter how deeply I dug, I found nothing except eggplant. I let the freezer door fall closed and turned to the pantry shelves. Similar repetitive rows of just a few items stood at military attention on the shelves.

Sheesh. I knew my mom liked structure in her life, but this was a bit much.

I left the pantry behind and walked back through the kitchen. For a second, I thought about calling my mom one last time.

She's not here to fix things for you. The little voice in my head admonished me as I reached for the delivery menus Mom had left behind. *You're going to have to take care of it yourself. Just like you wanted.*

~

The next morning, after running the gauntlet of the bus ride, instead of going to shop class I went straight to the front office. I waved Mom's vaunted red folder in my hand and demanded to speak with the principal.

"I can't stay in these classes," I asserted, causing the nice lady behind the counter to blanch. "I took some of these when I was a freshman. I can't be stuck in them for a whole semester. My entire schedule is wrong. My mother is going to be very unhappy when she finds out, especially after all the trouble she went through to register me properly."

"We don't need to bother the principal with that, honey." The lady scurried around the counter and snatched the folder from my hands. "Why don't you take a seat here while I see what I can do?"

I parked myself on a bench inside the office and waited, proud of myself for having taken a stand. Behind me was a glass wall veiled by half-opened blinds. I could hear the voices inside. Or voice, I should say. Only one person was talking, and by the stern tone, it sounded like a serious conversation. A quick glance at the nameplate by the door informed me this was the principal's office. I strained harder, trying to hear what had gotten someone in trouble.

The door swung open and a pimply boy in saggy pants shuffled out, trailing his backpack behind him.

"This is your last warning, Ethan," the voice trailed out after him. "I don't want to see you back in here for the rest of the semester."

"I bet Ethan doesn't want to be back, either, by the looks of it," a low voice, smooth as honey, whispered to me conspiratorially.

I jumped in my seat. I'd been so intent on eavesdropping that I hadn't noticed the boy sitting down by me. But now that I had noticed him, I couldn't stop staring.

The boy sprawled out across the bench, somehow managing to fill the small space with his entire body. His outfit was odd, more California surfer boy than Georgia public school: baggy khakis bleached almost white, and a tank topped by a white linen shirt that was definitely out of season. When he shifted his position, his pants stretched across his taut thighs. Underneath all that fabric, he was lean and muscular. He didn't have the shaggy haircut I associated with most boys my age—'Bama Bangs, as my father always called them. His hair was clipped close, almost military in style. It was a contradiction to his laid-back attire. And he was tan. No, tan doesn't do it justice. He was so golden he seemed to glow.

He broke through my daydream with his chuckle, blue eyes sparkling with humor. "I think it was the smoke bombs in the boys' bathroom this time. Van Aken hates that."

"Van Aken?" I asked, aware that I was gawking and feeling strangely stupid as I tried to follow the conversation.

"The principal," he said, cocking his head to one side as he looked me up and down. "You don't look like you belong in the principal's office," he said. I felt myself flush. Flustered, my hand flew to the back of my head, smoothing my long hair over my neck, making sure my scarf was still in place.

The lady from the front desk slipped by us, cracking the door to the principal's office open to whisper something to him as she shoved in some files.

"Michael? Michael Boyd?" The principal's gruff voice cut off any response I might have made.

"That's my cue," the boy said, and with a wink, he uncoiled from the bench and slipped inside the office.

I didn't have to strain to hear their conversation; the principal's voice boomed but Michael wasn't intimidated, talking back to the principal as if he were an adult. Out of the corner of my eye, I could see the woman behind the counter hanging on to their every word.

"What's this business about you being absent again?"

"I had a written excuse. Surely this is not a problem."

"Are you just doing this to make me look like a fool, Boyd? Because I won't be made to look like a fool," the principal threatened in a thick Georgia drawl.

"Sir, this has nothing to do with you." Michael's voice was calm and conciliatory. "I just had other things to do on those days."

In the pause that followed, I could almost imagine Van Aken scowling. "It's that damned emancipation. If you had adults who could advise you, we wouldn't have to deal with all this foolishness."

"Yet I am emancipated, and I am legally able to make these decisions for myself. I promise you, I have and will continue to make good use of the guidance counselors here to avoid making any foolish mistakes."

Emancipated? What does that mean? I thought to myself.

"Well, as you say, you are legally able to make these choices for yourself." I heard a shuffle of papers as the principal apparently signed off on some form. "Just don't make a habit of it. This is a school, not a country club. I can't have you messing up my No Child Left Behind performance with a string of unexcused absences, even if you can write your own damn note."

"Thank you, Mr. Van Aken," Michael said smoothly.

The door swung open and the counter attendant scrambled to look busy. Michael came out and passed his form to her, pinning her with a wide smile. "I think this should do it, Mrs. Thompson," he grinned.

"Michael," she said, nearly blushing with pleasure as she took the paper from his outstretched hand. "You give us all fits with this emancipation business, don't you?" He laughed and shrugged. "Do me a favor, hon, and bring this new girl to her classes. We had a little mix-up yesterday, but I think we've got it all straightened out." She passed another form across the counter to him.

He scanned it quickly. "Hope?" he asked, flashing me a brilliant smile. "Let me show you to your class."

~

I still hadn't gotten into home ec, but art was a step up from shop class. All of my other classes seemed to have been magically rearranged, and oddly enough, Michael was in most of them.

"It's because we're both new," he'd replied when I asked him about it halfway through the day. "Nowhere else to go."

"That doesn't sound right," I frowned, nibbling the eraser on my pencil as I settled into the AP environmental science class we now shared.

"How about this, then: we're just smarter than everyone else, so it's natural we'd end up in the same classes." His eyes danced as he took in my puzzlement. "C'mon, Hope, I can't be your stalker. We only just met."

His choice of the term "stalker" stopped me in my tracks. Stalker is only one step away from kidnapper. Was it just a coincidence he'd used that word? What did he know about me? I was surprised—and secretly ashamed—by how easily I'd wrapped myself in the mantle of my father's paranoia, but it didn't stop me from asking my next question.

"Just how new to this school are you?" I demanded, telling myself not to be drawn in by his easy jokes.

"Just off the turnip truck three weeks ago," he smiled, putting a finger to his lips to quiet me as the teacher stepped to the front of the room.

My day was a whirlwind of new classes, but with Michael as tour guide it wasn't as overwhelming. He seemed to radiate a sense of authority, and the endless torture of being singled out as the new girl miraculously stopped. One look from him and people swallowed their questions, bit off that smart comment before it even left their lips. Everyone gave us a wide berth, and by the time we emerged from our last class, I felt like I was secure in my own little bubble.

Who could have that kind of effect on teenagers? I thought to myself. I peppered him with questions, trying to figure him out.

"Where are you from?"

"Here and there," he said vaguely, not even bothering to hide the grin that stole across his face.

"But where most recently, before Dunwoody?"

"What is this, a crime scene? Relax, Hope—there's nothing fishy about me that you have to uncover."

"If that's true, then where are you from?" I pressed him.

He turned to the locker bay and started twirling a combination absentmindedly while I fumbled with mine, waiting for his answer. "I grew up on a commune in Iowa," he finally said. "I didn't really have parents; the whole community raised me. You know—that whole 'takes a village' thing."

"A commune?" I asked, unsure of what that meant.

"Some called it a commune. Some called it a cult. It doesn't really matter."

"Oh," I said dumbly, trying to take this in. "So what happened to your parents? I mean, your commune?"

"It was shut down by a police raid last year. And because I was over sixteen, the district attorney gave me the option of staying with the community as they went through social services and the courts, or of being declared an emancipated youth."

"An 'emancipated youth'?" The term was starting to make more sense to me as I began to understand his situation.

"For all intents and purposes, I am treated as if I were eighteen. It means I operate on my own. No adults telling me what to do."

"But how—?"

"I had distant relatives here in Georgia, and apparently there was a bit of money stashed away that my real parents had never told me about. It was against the rules, you see, to have any private property or money on the commune."

"So your real parents—?" I left the question hanging in the air, afraid of what he might say.

"It was all a big mix-up. They weren't really brainwashing people or anything. So they have moved on to California. And now I'm here. I live by myself and drive myself to school and every now and then a relative checks in on me." He flashed me that brilliant smile again and shrugged. "I know it's an odd story. Probably one of the strangest you've heard."

I laughed to myself. If only he knew.

"I've heard stranger things," I said, knowing exactly how it must have felt to have such an odd upbringing. I was impressed by what he had shared with me. I'd had enough experience in the juvenile legal system to know that to be able to convince a judge to treat you like an adult was no mean feat. It seemed to explain how comfortable he was around everyone, the weird sense of authority that he just seemed to take for granted and to which everyone else succumbed. He'd been through a lot and was on his own. He *had* to come across as in charge.

Michael suddenly stiffened. A group of boys came careening around the corner, crashing into the lockers next to mine. Michael deftly maneuvered me out of the way, somehow managing to get me past the crowd without ever touching me.

"C'mon, let's get you on the way home."

Swinging my backpack, I looked over my shoulder at the knot of fighting boys. On the edge of the crowd, I saw my tormentor from the bus. He was not paying attention to the fight. Instead he was looking straight at me, pointing me out to one of his friends. The friend was tall and dark and seemed to be staring after Michael and me with a smirk. He didn't stop looking even when I started to blush. Instinctively, my hand flew up to my neck, smoothing my hair. I checked behind me, hoping that maybe the smirk was meant for someone else, but nobody else was there. Before Michael could usher me out of the school, I looked back over my shoulder. Both of them were gone.

~

We wound through the hallways, Michael unerringly charting a path through the chaos and crowds, until we emerged into the low light of the afternoon. I blinked at the light and breathed in the crisp air, for the first time really cherishing the freedom that my new school seemed to promise.

I turned to Michael and drew in my breath. The sinking winter sun was hanging low on the horizon, its glow catching Michael's hair and making it look like it was kissed by flames.

He caught me staring and grinned.

I flushed, my gaze dropping to my shoes as I fumbled for something to say. "Um, I guess I'll see you tomorrow."

"Why, are you staying after school?"

I looked up, confused by his question. He was looking at me with amusement, almost laughing at my awkwardness. I flushed more deeply before answering him.

"Uh, no. But my bus is over there," I said, gesturing weakly behind me.

"You prefer spitballs and vomit in a yellow tube of tin to a ride home with me?" he asked, mockingly stabbing himself through the heart. "Carmichael, you really know how to hurt a guy."

"No!" I said, too eagerly. "I mean, I didn't know—"

"Right this way," he said. Winking, he turned on his heel, tossing his car keys in the air and catching them deftly with one hand as he strode away, leaving me to scramble after him.

As we wound our way through the parking lot, he slowed his stride, allowing me to catch up.

"You're in the teacher's lot," I commented, surprised.

"If my life of crime is too much for you, Hope, you can always take the bus," he said, his voice dripping with sarcasm.

"Oh, no. No judgment here," I said quickly, thanking the heavens for a ride home.

"Here we go," he said, pulling up short and then gesturing broadly to the side before making a sweeping bow. "Mademoiselle, your chariot awaits."

He'd stopped in front of a car so sleek and slung so low to the ground it reminded me of a bullet. That is, it would have reminded me of a bullet if it actually looked as if it had any speed. This thing was decrepit. The panels were a dull gray, except for a few patches where the steel body had been replaced with pieces taken from other cars. The driver's side mirror was held on by duct tape and a pair of fuzzy dice hung from the rearview mirror.

"Uh, thanks?" I said, unable to suppress the questioning tone.

He swept his long, lean body upright, shielding me from the sun as he shrugged and held out his arms in a gesture of feigned hurt. "Again, Carmichael, I am not picking up the right tone of appreciation here."

"Oh, I appreciate it. I'm just wondering if this death trap has seat belts."

He ran his hand along the hood as he walked around to the passenger side. "Old cars didn't have seat belts. They're exempted."

"Really?" I asked, raising my eyebrows.

"C'mon, live a little, Hope. It's only a few miles."

I froze, every muscle in my shoulders and back tensing. "How do you know it's only a few miles?" I asked him sharply. "How do you know where I live?"

He laughed as he swung the passenger door open for me. "Everyone who goes here lives within a few miles. So what do you say? Are you coming?"

Slowly, I felt the tension draining out of my body. How could I be as paranoid as my dad? Of course I lived nearby. It was obvious. Everybody did.

I looked up at Michael standing there waiting for me and felt a pull of longing. He was the kind of guy for whom everything was easy, everything was fun. Hadn't I always wanted some of that?

"Sure, why not?" I said, giving him what I hoped was my best nonchalant smile as I walked over to his side. I ducked under his arm, uncomfortably aware of how close I was to him, before climbing into the low bucket seat. "But the instant this thing drops a muffler or anything, I'm out of here."

"Oh ye of little faith," he laughed, closing the door on my protests.

As we pulled out of the parking lot, I remained hyperaware of how close I was to Michael in the tiny front seat. I could even smell him—an earthy smell that reminded me of sweet hay and leather. I looked at my hands, which were twitching nervously in my lap, and willed them to be still.

"Left or right?" he asked me as we approached an intersection.

"Left," I said. Almost simultaneously he flicked the signal, as if he had anticipated my response.

"So what's your story, Carmichael?"

"Huh?" I darted a glance at him. He was looking at me, amusement on his face.

"It's not a trick question. You know how I came to the lovely burg of Dunwoody. What brings you here?"

He pulled up to a T stop and signaled for a right turn, not waiting for my confirmation.

"You need to go left," I said, a note of suspicion in my voice.

"Relax, Hope. It's a circle drive. I can't make a wrong turn. And don't duck the question. Why'd you transfer to Dunwoody High?"

I squirmed in my seat. "It's a long story."

"We've got some time. Go ahead."

I sighed. He was persistent, so I might as well get it over with.

"My parents have been separated for a long time. They never really divorced, but they might as well have. My dad always had custody of me because my mom travels a lot for her job. But I decided I wanted to move back with her, so here I am."

"Just like that? Here you are? Your dad didn't have anything to say about it?"

I looked at Michael. His eyes seemed full of genuine interest. I found myself wanting to trust him.

"He sort of screwed up. So no, he couldn't really do anything about it. He isn't even allowed to talk to me for a while."

Michael let out a slow whistle. "That had to be some sort of screwup. What did he do, if you don't mind me asking?"

I looked at my hands, twisting in my lap. How to explain my father without having to go through my whole past?

"Ever since I was really little, he's been very overprotective of me. He sort of controlled my every move. I guess I managed to deal with it until recently." I stopped then, unsure if I should continue.

"What happened?" Michael gently prompted me. His voice was soothing and smooth.

"There was a new kid in school. Everyone was fascinated by him—you know, that new kid thing—and for some reason he took an interest in me. I lied to my dad and snuck out of the house so I could meet him at the movies."

I closed my eyes, remembering how excited I'd been. Danny was the first new kid at Holy Innocents since I'd arrived, the only one at school who didn't know my story. He was my chance for a real friend, if I didn't screw it up. I'd been so hopeful, thinking my father would believe my story about staying after school for homework. I was desperate for him to believe it, even though it was so transparent.

"I thought I'd tricked him, but he showed up at the movie theater and made a scene."

"What kind of scene?" Michael prompted.

I could still remember the feeling of Danny's fingertips bumping into mine as we burrowed into the bucket of greasy popcorn. The angry stir of the crowd as the crazy man started spouting Bible verses at the top of his voice from the back of the theater. My horror when the crazy man started calling me by name, stalking down the aisle to claim me from my seat and pull me to his waiting car.

My embarrassment at that moment had paled in comparison to how I felt when I had to deal with the ridicule I'd later faced in school. I'd gone from tolerated misfit to ridiculed pariah in the time it took Danny to spread the story around. I couldn't blame him. He recognized the opportunity to shoot to super-popularity on the back of someone else's misfortune. It happened all the time in high school. It had just never happened to me.

"It doesn't matter," I said, trying to shrug off the feeling of hopelessness that engulfed me whenever I thought about that time. "He's just super religious and strict and kind of went too far. So that's why I wanted to come back to Atlanta. I just needed some space from my dad."

I blinked my eyes open, and realized with a start that we were parked in front of my house. I turned to Michael, startled.

"How did you—?"

He laughed and flipped up the name tag on my backpack, which I'd neatly placed on the seat between us. "Address on your tag. Easy as pie." He looked down at me, sheepishly. "I didn't want to interrupt you while you were talking. It seemed like whatever you were remembering was pretty important."

I flushed, scolding myself for how suspicious I'd become. I vowed not to let my father's craziness infect me.

"Thanks for the ride, Michael," I said, flashing him a grateful smile.

"My pleasure, Hope," he said, his own grin deepening. He reached across my lap and opened the door for me. Up close, his eyes seemed to dance, shifting into different shades of blue as the sun caught them. I felt my heart give a little *thump*. "See you tomorrow."

~

When Michael had pulled away from my driveway, Mrs. Bibeau came scurrying out of her house, nearly bursting with questions and waving at me to slow down.

"Lots of homework!" I yelled before closing the door on her. I let my back fall against the door as I clutched my bag to my chest, a silly smile stealing across my face.

Several times that afternoon as I worked on my homework I caught myself humming to myself and smiling. *So silly*, I thought to myself. *Are you really so giddy, just because someone was nice to you?*

But all the trauma of my first day at Dunwoody High seemed far behind me. As I brushed my hair out before bed, I had to admit to myself that I was, indeed, giddy with happiness. Today had turned out exactly like I'd envisioned it when I'd planned my move to Atlanta. No, it was even better. This was what I had hoped for, but I hadn't dared to acknowledge it, even to myself. Anonymity was one thing. But to have a friend, a real friend—someone who didn't know my past, someone whose picture of me wasn't skewed by looking at me through the prism of my abduction—that was another.

And he might even be able to relate, if I shared more of my past with him. After all, he'd said he'd grown up in a cult. I thought almost guiltily of my computer before giving in to the temptation and plopping down in front of it. I launched the search engine and began hunting for any news coverage of a raided cult in Iowa. Nothing. I changed the search terms and switched engines, but still only managed to come up with a bunch of raids in Texas and Utah.

How odd. My curiosity deepened. I wondered if he was telling me the whole truth. Would the fact that there were children involved mean the media had been blocked from covering the story? I frowned, frustrated, as I hammered away at the keys, launching search after search and coming up with nothing.

What had really happened in that raid? I couldn't very well come right out and ask him, could I? Annoyed, I pushed away from my desk and went back to my bathroom, grudgingly picking up the brush. As I ran the brush through my hair, I had to admit that the mystery around Michael's story only deepened my fascination with him.

But just what did Michael see when he looked at me? Was it even possible that he could be as intrigued with me as I was with him? Cautiously, almost afraid of what my appraisal would reveal, I set my brush aside and took a hard look at myself in the mirror.

I gathered the excess fabric of my old-fashioned nightgown in a ball in my fist, pulling it behind me to reveal the body that had been swallowed up by billowing folds. I had the long, lean line of a runner. I turned sideways and saw the slight rise of my breasts, the way my waist cut in over delicate hips. I knew my thighs were strong and muscular from my hours of pounding the treadmill. Thunder thighs, I thought, grimacing. I let my fist open and the gown swirled about me again, hiding my body away.

I turned forward and examined my face, leaning in to get close to the mirror. My eyes were a deep chocolate brown and almond shaped; they would have given me an almost exotic look if it hadn't been for the liberal sprinkling of freckles over my high cheekbones. My skin was pale and looked even more so when framed by my long, straight brown hair, which shielded me like a curtain from the unwelcome looks of strangers.

I ran my fingers through my hair and swept it over my shoulders. Sighing, I gathered it up in one hand and turned around, taking a mirror in my other hand.

My Mark.

If I hadn't hated it, if it hadn't symbolized everything that was wrong in my life, I would have thought it beautiful. It seemed to blossom from the base of my skull, the delicate teal markings spreading out like tendrils. I let my hair fall and traced my finger along the Mark, wondering again what it meant.

"It marks me as a misfit, that's all," I sighed to myself, drawing my hair back around me.

I shook my head. There was nothing in the mirror that could explain why someone like Michael Boyd had taken an interest in me today.

"Better not to get your hopes up. He's probably just being nice to you because he felt sorry for you," I said like a mantra. But still, in the last moments before sleep stole over me, my thoughts returned to Michael, and I fell asleep with a grin on my face.

three

I soon settled into the comforting anonymity of the large suburban high school. Even after the "new girl" smell had worn off me, Michael stayed close. I guess that since our lockers were right next to each other and since we had almost every class together and were both new, it was only natural that we should become friends. But the delight and surprise I felt every morning when the bus disgorged me and I found him standing on the sidewalk waiting for me remained strong.

I knew he didn't like me romantically. Why would he? I was plain at best, skinny and not even remotely stylish. So when I started noticing the popular girls circling him, I figured my days were numbered. The worst were the cheerleaders. They were hardly subtle, but I was impressed by their ingenuity. It had all started with Jessica Smythe, the varsity basketball cheer captain.

"Whoopsie!" she'd giggled when she "fell" off the stepladder as she was hanging banners cheering on the basketball team, ingeniously landing right in Michael's arms.

"Oh, Michael," she drawled, fanning herself dramatically, then throwing her arms around his shoulders, "you make me feel so tiny when you've got me in your arms like this."

"Maybe you should eat more," Michael said.

He peeled her arms off of his neck and unceremoniously dumped her back on the floor. She stumbled backwards, taken off guard. "Take a tip from Hope here—she can really pack it in," Michael said, tilting his head toward me.

A titter ran through the crowd that had quickly assembled to watch the scene. I blushed, horrified that he'd commented on my eating habits. Jessica's mouth hung open in astonishment as Michael resumed walking.

"C'mon, Hope," he called behind him.

I ran to catch up, looking over my shoulder at Jessica whom he'd left alone on the floor in the middle of the crowd. She screwed up her face like a spoiled child and stuck her tongue out at me.

Her failure was like a gauntlet thrown to the entire cheerleading squad. Our universe of classes didn't overlap much, so they had to squeeze their efforts into the periods between classes and before and after school, as well as lunch. But that didn't stop them from making the most of their meager opportunities. Sometimes I was witness to their efforts; sometimes I just heard about them secondhand. It started with the predictable "meet cute" bumps in the hallway, but rapidly escalated when their efforts proved to no avail. One time, they bullied the Dunwoody Wildcat mascot into giving up his post.

"Miii-chael," one overly made-up blonde wheedled over our lunch table, holding the oversized, tiger-like head of the mascot's costume on one jutted hip and pouting while the entire squad backed her up, bouncing bowed and beribboned ponytails up and down in unison. "We need your help! We can't play this Friday without our mascot—it's a tradition!"

Michael took the costume from the cheerleader, who looked down at me with a derisive look of triumph. Michael tossed the head in the air as if it were no heavier than a softball and looked down the table.

"Hey, you," he called to one spectacularly unathletic freshman. The geeky boy looked up from his lunch tray, surprised. "Do you want to be the Wildcat this Friday?"

The geeky boy nodded excitedly, pushing up his glasses.

"Great! Here you go," Michael said. He tossed the head to the boy, who promptly fell off of his seat with the effort of catching it.

"Problem solved," Michael said, taking his chair. "Ladies." They shrieked with horror and swarmed around the boy, trying to reclaim the costume. I stole a glance at Michael. He seemed oblivious to the commotion he'd just caused.

On Valentine's Day, the entire squad decorated his locker with pink, red, and lacy white hearts, spraying the entire thing with so much perfume that we had to wheeze our way through the locker bay. But it didn't stop there. The cheerleading squad had sold singing "Cupid-Grams" for charity: a few dollars got you candy, a valentine, and a singing telegram, all delivered to your true love in class. So every hour, a scantily clad cheerleader dressed as Cupid or Venus serenaded an amused Michael, delivering professions of love from one of her teammates. By the end of the day, the Cupids had gotten increasingly hostile as Michael refused to let them sit in his lap or give him a kiss. In our last class, after finding Michael unresponsive, the frustrated messenger had simply dug around in her fake bag of arrows and slapped the other valentines down on everyone's desk, forgoing any singing. As she pulled the last letter out, her eyes narrowed.

"Who would send you a valentine?" she said acidly as she looked at me, holding the envelope between her fingers as if it were a piece of used tissue or a dead mouse. "Here." She let it flutter down to my desk and turned on her heel to stomp out of the room, forgetting to give me my candy or a song.

I looked at the red envelope. *Hope Carmichael, period 6, Mrs. Mormon,* was written in flawless cursive script across the front. I traced the silver ink and realized I didn't know what Michael's handwriting looked like.

My heart was thumping. I shot Michael a look, but I couldn't catch his eye. The class was resuming its conjugations so quickly that I shoved the envelope into my back pocket, saving it for later.

It was burning a hole in my pocket during the entire walk to our lockers and out to Michael's Charger. We were unusually quiet during the ride home. I couldn't be sure, but I thought I saw Michael darting me curious glances, his eyes deep as the sky as he watched me.

When he stopped in my driveway, he reached across my lap to open the door. I held my breath, every inch of skin tingling with the awareness of how close he was. He paused with one hand on the handle, fixing me with a deep gaze. His eyes seemed to sparkle, shifting between different shades of blue as if they were waves dancing in the sun.

"Aren't you going to open your valentine?"

I drew a shaky breath and forced a laugh. "Oh, I'm sure it's nothing. Probably a mistake."

He arched one eyebrow and grinned, a deep dimple puckering his chin. "Um-hmm. A mistake. Whatever, Carmichael."

Only then did he lift the latch, allowing me to flee from his car.

I placed the red envelope on my nightstand, where it tempted me throughout the night as I went through the forced march of environmental science, math, literature, and social studies homework. Only after I'd packed up my books and gotten into my pajamas did I allow myself to pick it up.

I sat cross-legged on my bed and drew a deep breath as I stared at it lying in my lap. Finally, I took it in my hand and ran one trembling finger along the script before flipping the envelope over to break the seal. I slid out the card—an old-fashioned lacy heart embossed with roses in shades of cream and pink—and read the verse that had been hand-lettered on the front:

I will keep you as the apple of the eye,
hide you under the shadow of my wings.

I flipped over the card. There was no signature, nothing at all. I felt my brows knitting together as I puzzled over the simple lines. They were familiar, but from where? And what did they mean?

I reached under my bed, pulling out my old Bible, and flipped quickly to Psalms. I trailed a finger across the page until I found the verses I sought:

Keep me as the apple of the eye,
hide me under the shadow of thy wings,

From the wicked that oppress me,
from my deadly enemies, who compass me about,

They are enclosed in their own fat:
with their mouth they speak proudly.

They have now compassed us in our steps:
they have set their eyes bowing down to the earth;

Like as a lion that is greedy of his prey,
and as it were a young lion lurking in secret places.

I stared at the page, bewildered. My secret admirer had sent me

Bible verses. But he'd altered it, turning it from a plea to a promise of protection. Protection from what? The only thing I seemed to need protection from was overzealous cheerleaders.

Was it a warning? My mind raced. If so, whoever had written it had expected me to recognize the verse and go to the Bible to discover the rest. But who at my school would even know I would be familiar enough with the Bible to pluck this verse out, to recognize it and find the words that came after it?

Nobody, the little voice in my head reasoned. *Whoever wrote your card probably saw the quote out of context and simply copied it out, no greater meaning intended.*

But that still left the question of who had sent the card. Could it have been Michael?

I blushed, almost ashamed to admit to myself how much I had wanted it to be from him. But why would he send me a valentine, especially one so weird? No, it couldn't have been from Michael.

Then I felt all the blood drain from my face as a more likely culprit occurred to me: my dad. How had he managed to infiltrate the cheerleaders' Cupid sale and send me a card? Anger and embarrassment rushed through me at the thought of him insinuating himself into my new life, despite all my attempts.

How stupid I was, I thought, crumpling the delicate card in my fist. I threw it across the room, disgusted at my own gullibility. Of course it had been Dad. Who else had the bad habit of tossing Bible verses around to embarrass me? Swallowing my disappointment, I turned off my light and curled up in a little ball in my bed, savoring my misery.

I did the math in my head. A little over two months until my birthday. Then I'd be sixteen. *Sixteen and never been kissed*, I thought bitterly. Kissed? I'd never so much as held hands with anybody. I punched my pillow. Well, at least Michael didn't seem to like those cheerleaders, I consoled myself. Having to hang out with them would be unbearable. With that last thought to cheer me, I drifted off to sleep.

~

The next day, Michael kept sending me meaningful looks, which I deliberately ignored. How could I explain my dad and the crazy note he'd sent? Better just to stay away from the whole topic. I managed to avoid a direct conversation during passing time and classes, but once we were at lunch, I couldn't hold him off.

"So, Hope, who was your card from?" he demanded as he steered me toward our usual table, choosing seats well removed from the rest of the crowd.

I did my best to look uninterested and shrugged. "I dunno. It wasn't signed," I said, pushing my mashed potatoes around on my tray.

"Secret admirer, eh?" Michael grinned. "C'mon, what did it say?"

He seemed way too interested in my love life. I looked at him again with suspicion. Could I have been wrong? Could it have been him after all?

I rolled the idea around in my mind as I looked at him across the table. I couldn't deny that he continued to intrigue me. He was dressed again, as always, in one of his odd, monochromatic outfits—the only thing ever changing being the exact shade of white he chose. It was a sort of hippie aesthetic that made sense, I guess, for someone who had grown up in a cult, and I had to admit it looked good on him. The white set off his glowing skin perfectly, and the way the clothes moved about him hinted at his strong, toned body and made him seem even more mysterious.

Don't kid yourself, the voice in my head spoke up.

"What are you eating?" I asked, trying to change the subject. I'd noticed he never ate the cafeteria food. Instead he packed an odd lunch of white, lumpy health food stuff that was possibly the most unappetizing thing I'd ever seen.

"Would you like to try it?" he asked politely, after watching me stare at it with revulsion for what must have been the tenth lunch period in a row. "It's just like tofu. It's really good for you."

"No thanks," I shuddered, pushing the equally disgusting lima beans the lunchroom had served around on my tray. Thank goodness he'd let the whole valentine thing drop so easily. "Did you see Dan Frasier fall asleep today in Science? It was so gross. He actually started to drool." I kept babbling on about Dan's unfortunate lapse of consciousness until I realized I was talking to myself.

"Michael?"

He wasn't paying attention. I followed his gaze. His eyes had drifted to one of the televisions mounted all around the cafeteria. Someone had changed the channel to one of the twenty-four-hour news programs. A constant scroll about refugees and violence in the Middle East crept across the bottom of the screen. Michael set his jaw, crumpling his brown lunch sack in his big, golden hands.

"Michael?" I asked again, waiting for his attention to return.

His reverie broke, and he turned to me with a sheepish grin, though his eyes still looked troubled.

"Sorry, Hope, what was that?"

"Are you interested in current events?" I asked, as politely as I could, trying to hide my annoyance.

His eyes danced with amusement. "You could say that, I guess."

Before I could ask him more, he started wiggling his eyebrows at me, making one of his patented goofy faces. "I was really just looking for the basketball scores. How 'bout an ice cream sandwich—my treat?"

"I thought you didn't eat 'junk,'" I teased him.

"Call it research. I was thinking of writing my biology paper on the eating habits of the American teenage girl. I am in awe of your calorie consumption. I just plan to watch. Maybe capture it on my iPhone."

I grabbed the crumpled bag out of his hands and threw it in his face, laughing.

~

I couldn't figure out why he had picked me, but for the first time ever in my life, I had a friend. And he was a friend with whom everything seemed effortless, a friend with whom I didn't have to pretend to be dumb, a friend with whom I could talk about important things instead of the latest program on TV. Between that and being practically faceless in my new school, I was in a state of bliss.

But something was going wrong. By the start of my third week in school, Michael seemed distant. He was preoccupied. In every class, he seemed to be sneaking peeks at papers he had tucked inside his books, rapidly shoving them inside his backpack as soon as class was over. Over the course of the week he became increasingly short tempered. By the time Friday rolled around, he was like a caged lion. His entire body was tense, his face looked drawn and tight around the eyes, and even the slightest question from me would cause him to snap.

"What's wrong?" I asked as the final bell rang and we spilled out toward the locker bays, wondering what I'd done to upset him. I didn't have much experience with friends, so I was sure it was my fault. "Can you tell me what I've done?"

"It's not about you, Hope. Just leave it alone," he sighed, his frustration palpable as he twirled the combination to his locker.

"Problems, Michael?" A dry voice interrupted our conversation.

We both turned. It was the dark-looking boy who had stared at me during the first week of school. He was surrounded by the same pack of friends who'd been fighting that day. Even the obnoxious boy from the bus was there. Only now, he wasn't the only one paying attention to me. Everyone's eyes were fully focused on us like a pack of wolves surrounding stray sheep.

"Nothing I can't handle, Lucas," Michael said smoothly. I noticed he had placed a protective arm across me. I was suddenly aware of just how tiny I was next to him. His skin felt strangely warm.

"Hmmm. I must have been mistaken, then. You just seem like maybe you need a little *getaway*, you know, to take care of some business." He dripped the words from his mouth, as if he was trying to insinuate something. "What about you, Hope? Cat got your tongue?"

I stared at the boy. Suddenly, my mouth felt like it was full of sawdust. I gulped nervously, my hand unconsciously drifting to my neck to cover my Mark before I answered.

"How do you know my name?"

He laughed with a cold and detached sort of amusement. "It's a public school, Hope. Everybody knows everything. We know all about you."

A feeling of dread washed over me. Did they? My body felt hot and sweaty, but I resisted the urge to reach up and wipe my brow, not wanting them to see how nervous they were making me.

Michael scoffed, his blue eyes flashing with anger. "Leave us alone, Lucas. There's nothing to know and nothing to do."

"We'll see about that," Lucas purred. His dark eyes shimmered with barely contained excitement. "You know me. I always seem to find some sort of trouble to make."

"Make it somewhere else," Michael retorted, grabbing my wrist roughly as he slammed his locker shut. "Come on, Hope, let's go."

He charged through the crowd of boys, pulling me in his wake. They barely seemed to give way; I was painfully aware of the press of their bodies as we cut through.

I didn't realize I was holding my breath until we were already out on the sidewalk.

"How do you know him?" I asked in a shaky voice, struggling to keep up with Michael.

"I don't," he said curtly, staring straight ahead and continuing to drag me along relentlessly.

"But he made it sound like—"

"Hope, I told you before, just leave it alone!" His voice had an edge to it that was a clear warning. I swallowed my questions and followed meekly as he led me toward the buses.

"Michael, we're going the wrong way; your car—"

He drew up short. I stumbled right into him, spilling my book bag out onto the sidewalk. He threw down my arm, bent over, and furiously began to shove things back into the bag.

"You're taking the bus today," he said without looking at me.

I rubbed the spot where he had gripped my wrist; it already ached. "But, Michael, why are you—"

"Hope, I can't babysit you every minute!" he practically yelled at me as he stood up. Out of the corner of my eye, groups of students came to a standstill to watch. "I have stuff to do. Here, take your bag." He shoved it roughly at me. "Now get on your bus," he said, pushing me toward the narrow door.

And before I could say anything, he stalked off toward the student parking lot.

I stood frozen, painfully aware of the whispers and stares. Slowly, I turned toward the bus and climbed the first few steps. As I did, I heard someone calling after me in a mocking tone.

"Have a nice weekend, Hope!"

I looked over my shoulder just in time to see the bus doors close on Lucas, a look of smug satisfaction on his face.

Back in my room, I threw myself on my bed, alternating between burying my face in and then punching the heap of pillows piled at the headboard.

I ran through my memories of the last few weeks and could find nothing, *nothing* that I had done that could have even remotely set off a reasonable human being.

I sat bolt upright in my bed.

How dare he treat you like that? said the voice inside my head.

Seriously, who did he think he was, all Mr. Nice and then *wham*! Dropping me like a bad smell just because he was in a pissy mood?

I kicked my sneakers off and let them fly across the room. They landed with a satisfying *thump!* against my closet door.

And how could he have lied to me that he didn't know Lucas? Clearly, the two had a history. But how could they have when Michael was new to the school, too? Why couldn't he just tell me the truth?

"Aarrgh!" I yelled in frustration, falling back on my bed.

I heard a soft knock at my door.

"Hope, may I come in?"

I groaned and rolled over. I had forgotten that my mom was already home. Consultant hours were unpredictable. Sometimes, like today, she'd show up in the middle of the day. I'd managed to get by her without too much conversation when I got off the bus, but apparently her Mom Radar was on alert.

"Sure, Mom," I answered, straightening out the bedcovers and fluffing the pillows.

She slid in through the door, a look of mild alarm spreading across her face as she scanned for damage. "Is everything okay? It sounded like you fell."

"Just me throwing my shoes, Mom. Sorry about that."

She frowned slightly and tilted her head, her eyebrows forming a distinct question mark.

I sighed. I'd already learned that she was hard to hide things from. I chalked it up to her MBA and consultant training.

"Michael was just being a jerk today, that's all."

I watched her carefully choose her words as she sat down on the bed and plucked at some imaginary lint. "Michael, that new boy with whom you've become friends?"

"Yes, though the way he's been acting this week you'd think I'd set his pet bunnies on fire or something. He's been so moody, Mom! And he won't tell me what I did. It's so unfair."

"What makes you think it's something you did?" Mom asked me, looking me straight in the eye. "Did you do something wrong, Hope?"

"No!" I protested, clutching one of the pillows tight to my chest. "I've racked my brain, Mom. All I can think of—"

I stopped, not even wanting to say it out loud.

"Go on," Mom urged.

". . . is that he's tired of me. I mean, who am I, right? Just some hick girl from Alabama. He's probably gotten bored of me."

My body sagged, my head drooping to my chest as I thought about this possibility. It seemed to be the only thing that made sense.

Mom gently lifted my chin so she could look me in the eye. "Hope, did Michael try to avoid you? Did he move his seat in class, or try to eat with someone else at lunch?"

"No," I admitted grudgingly.

"Have you gotten too clingy, maybe thinking of him as more than a friend?"

"No!" I protested, my cheeks burning. "It's not like that, Mom! We're just friends."

I saw her lips twitch.

"It's not funny!" I shouted, burying my face in another pillow.

"Oh, Hope, honey, I'm not laughing at you, I promise. It just seems to me that you are awfully unfamiliar with teenage boys. They go through their moods and then some, just like the rest of us do. And if I understand the situation as you've described it, he might have an awful lot of pressure on him, having to fend for himself. From what you say, it doesn't seem to me like he is trying to end your friendship. Whatever it is, he'll get over it. Just give him his space. You'll see; when Monday rolls around, I bet everything will be back to normal."

I sat up again, looking at her skeptically.

"Really?"

"Really."

"But why'd he have to be so mean, Mom? It makes me so *angry*!"

"I don't know, Hopie," she said, using her old nickname for me while she smoothed out my hair. "But when I get angry I like to take it out on my rowing machine." She glanced across my room to the treadmill she'd bought, sitting forlorn and forgotten in the corner, strewn with rejected clothing. "You haven't even touched your treadmill. It's been weeks," she noted in a neutral tone.

I felt my chin rise defensively. "I've been busy."

She skewered me with one of her looks again. "Hope, I know you love to run. Is there something about this treadmill you don't like? It still has the tags dangling from it. I could return it if you aren't going to use it."

I fought against myself but couldn't keep from blurting my response. "It's just, just . . . the only reason I ran on a treadmill is Dad wouldn't let me run outside. Ever."

The air was still as she considered this new information, her face a carefully composed mask.

"What do you mean?"

I didn't want to add to my father's long list of apparent parenting failures, but there was no way I could get out of this one.

"He thought it was too dangerous for me to be alone. So I couldn't even walk myself to school, let alone go outside for a run."

For a split second I saw beneath her composed veneer, saw the shock and anger she felt toward my dad. But just as quickly, it was gone. I knew then that I could never tell her about the Cupid-Gram Dad had sent me—she would seriously lose it. So I stayed silent until she stood up, brushed off her slacks, and moved quietly to the door. She made one parting shot as she left me to brood in my room.

"Well, nothing's stopping you now."

~

I stretched out on the front steps, eyeing the little cul-de-sac with a bit of trepidation. Of course, my mother was right. It was unfortunate that Dad had kept me under lock and key. But that was all over now, and I hadn't even taken advantage of the fact.

"No time like the present," I muttered to myself, starting up my favorite running mix on my iPod as I left the steps.

A thousand little things underscored how different it was to be outside instead of tied to a machine. The feel of pavement, unforgiving beneath my feet. The sharp air that prickled, icy, as I breathed it in. The drop in temperature when I came under the shade of a stand of tall pines. The wind slicing through my fleece.

At first, with every step I imagined I was squashing Michael's face with my foot. But eventually I gave myself to the music, my footfalls synching with the rhythm. Slowly, my stress melted away as I focused on my breathing. By the time I turned the corner off the main loop, I was singing along with my iPod at full voice, doing little hand jive moves when the spirit took me, as if the road was my own private stage.

I had never felt so free.

I suppose I looked funny to any neighbors who happened to look out their window. But I didn't care. I was running, really running, without some stupid program on a machine to tell me how fast or how long to run.

I kept running past the familiar streets and into others I'd never been on. They all looked comfortingly the same. What was that phrase Mom had used once? Safe as houses. Everybody here is safe as houses.

But no sooner had I thought this than I began to get a funny feeling that I was not alone.

I slowed down to a trot to look over my shoulder, but I could see nothing.

Unsettled, I started running again, darting a backwards glance every few yards. The safe little neighborhood suddenly felt threatening, the dark windows in the empty houses glaring at me like angry eyes. I picked up the pace.

I had made it back to the main loop, and now the sun was hanging low in the February sky. *Only a little ways left to go*, I thought to myself, trying to forget that the last bit went through an unfinished part of the neighborhood that had been left open as a preserve.

My unease deepened as I strode forward. The road was curvy here, swallowed at every bend by spindly pines that swayed in the stiff wind. My pace became more cautious. It was starting to hurt to breathe in the cold air, and my side was aching. I didn't want to stop. I wanted to get home and out of this cold, but my body was not cooperating. I dragged myself over to the curb and bent over, wheezing while I tried to work the knot out of my side.

Everything around me was silent. I couldn't even hear any approaching cars. Everyone else seemed tucked away inside their warm houses. I was alone, in the woods.

But I still felt that I wasn't quite alone. The feeling grew stronger and stronger, and even as I regained my breath, I could feel my heart thumping faster and faster.

Don't look up, the little voice in my head whispered.

And suddenly there was a rush of a thousand wings all about me. I grabbed my head, covering my ears against the shrieking and cawing that seemed everywhere. All I could see was a wall of black—I was spinning and turning, and everywhere black shapes darted in and out until I lost my balance and fell against the curb.

I huddled in a ball, pulling my hat tighter and squeezing my eyes shut against the confusion. Then, just as suddenly, everything went quiet once again. All I could hear was my ragged breath until a voice rang out.

"Hope, is that you?"

I opened one eye to peek. A flood of relief washed over me, quickly chased by irritation. "Michael!" I called out, my voice shaky. "What are you doing here?"

He was dressed in a white hooded sweatshirt and running tights.

I felt my heart rate slow as he made his way toward me, a look of concern clouding his face. My feeling of irritation grew—I didn't need anybody's help. Couldn't my own body cooperate instead of acting like it was glad to see him?

"Did you see that?" he asked, gesturing behind him toward the horizon.

"What?"

"That murder of crows. It just swarmed out of nowhere, like an enormous black cloud," he continued, his suspicious eyes scanning the sky.

"Murder? Crows?" I repeated, still not sure what had happened. "Oh."

He was directly over me. I looked up to see him reaching one gloved hand down to me. I paused before letting him pull me up, trying not to think too much about the way the tights highlighted every muscle in his legs.

"I must have scared them," I said, dusting off my legs and letting my fingers probe the sensitive spot where I'd landed on the curb. I winced. I was going to get a big bruise, for sure.

"You were *in* that?" he asked, his eyes narrowing. In the waning light, the blue of his irises seemed to fade into a steely gray.

I shrugged. "I guess. No big deal." I tried to be nonchalant about it. I didn't want him to know how freaked out I'd been. I stepped forward, gingerly. "Though it was kind of weird. I didn't hear anything at all and then, boom, they were everywhere."

He looked up at the sky, speculating.

"I'm walking you home," he said, his chin set.

"Suit yourself," I harrumphed, pretending not to care, but annoyed at him for his unexplained about-face.

We set out, him slowing his pace to match me as I hobbled

along. We walked in silence, my resentment hanging around us like the heavy air of a Georgia summer.

"What are you even doing here?" I asked, my voice accusing, when I couldn't take the silence any longer. "This isn't even close to your house. And I thought you had things to do."

He didn't rise to the bait; his eyes remained steadfastly focused on the road ahead. "I took care of them for now." There was a long pause. "And I needed a run to clear my head. I didn't plan to find you."

His words stung. "Well, don't put yourself out, then." The retort flew out of my mouth before I had time to think.

He sighed as we trudged up the last hill, the silence resettling uncomfortably around us. At the top of my cul-de-sac, he pulled up short. The sun had fully set now, and under the light shed by the corner streetlamp his blond hair seemed to shine with a halo.

He took a step, reaching out as if to touch me, but then he dropped his hand, as if he thought better of it.

"It must be hard running with all that hair in your face," he said softly.

I refused to answer him, but couldn't stop my hands from sneaking up to wrap my hair safely round my neck.

He stood there awkwardly, waiting for me for what seemed like forever. Finally, he sighed.

"I guess I'll see you around," he said, turning away.

I stood in the little puddle of light, watching him run away until he was just a little speck of white, gliding away in the dark. As I turned toward my house, I noticed something under my shoe.

A feather. It shone dark as coal under the glow of the streetlight.

I picked it up, surprised I hadn't noticed it stuck to my shoe before. I twirled it around in my fingers. It spanned the length of my hand and was stiffer than I imagined a feather should be. And the odor it gave off was odd: like sulfur, or the smell of electricity building up before a storm.

You shouldn't touch it. It's not clean.

Shrugging at the nagging voice in my head, I threw the feather into the gutter and went in to nurse my wounds along with my hurt pride.

four

Michael didn't show up for school on Monday. Or Tuesday. Or Wednesday. By the time Thursday rolled around, I was in a seriously bad mood and more than a little hurt. He'd disappeared without even telling me. I had a weird case of road rash around my wrist—apparently from my fall during the bird swarm—that wouldn't seem to heal. Everywhere I turned, that boy, Lucas, seemed to be, leering at me with a crazy look in his eyes. And meanwhile, my afternoons had turned into sheer torture: now that I was forced to ride the bus again, Bus Boy had decided to single me out for special attention.

But none of that was why I was so upset. I was lonely. It was one thing to be the odd girl out in Alabama, where I'd always been left to my own devices. It was entirely another thing here, now that I'd gotten used to Michael being constantly at my side. I was painfully aware of the empty desk right next to mine in virtually every class. And the girls who'd been so slighted by Michael's refusal to be smitten now jeered at me and talked behind my back, which made me feel even more alone.

I slid into my Contemporary Issues class, thinking of all the ways I was going to blow Michael off when he finally dared to show his face.

"Okay, class, today we are going to start working on your research papers. As a reminder, this will comprise fifty percent of your grade. Remember"—Mr. Bennett paced around our desks, enjoying one of the few precious moments of rapt attention he would get—"this will be about a current issue that is challenging our society, your views on it, and your recommendations for addressing it. And, to introduce some 'real world' dynamics, you must work in pairs or small groups."

The room broke into the chaos of sliding chairs and people shouting across the room to claim a partner. Mr. Bennett struggled to regain his command of the class amid the squeals of delight and fist bumping.

"Your first task," he bellowed over the cacophony as he walked through the aisles. "Your first task is to review this list of suggested topics and choose one. By the end of this period, you and your partner must submit your choice and outline a preliminary set of research questions."

I tuned out the rest of his instructions as he dealt the worksheets out. My classmates fell upon the lists, laughing, happy for the excuse to chat the hour away. It only made me feel Michael's absence more acutely, which made me angry all over again.

Around the room, people were paired off, heads together. I looked around, hoping to see a friendly face, anyone who was also looking for a partner.

Just one other person remained. Tabitha.

Tabitha was intimidating. She had all the trappings of a goth: shockingly spiked hair, kohl-rimmed eyes, piercings all over her ears and face, and black boots with platforms so high she probably could have looked Michael in the eye. The truth was, she scared me more than a little. I'd noticed that while most of the other black kids in school kept to themselves in pretty tight cliques, they all steered clear of her—as did everyone else.

Now, Tabitha skewered me with a look of wry amusement, one heavily penciled brow arching high in a question as she swept her long bangs out of her deep mocha face. "I guess since lover boy split, it's you and me, huh?"

I felt my cheeks turning red. "He's not my boyfriend," I protested.

"Whatever," she snorted, grabbing her notebook up in her shiny black fingertips. The chains dangling from her belt rattled as she hopped off her desk toward me. "What d'ya say, partner?"

She cleared her throat and tapped her thick-soled toes on the floor, reminding me that she was waiting for my answer.

"I guess so."

"I hope you've got more in you than 'guess so,' because this paper has got to kick ass," she smirked, stomping over to take the seat next to me. "I already know what we should write about," she asserted, flopping the list of topics down in front of me. "Look."

I followed her pointed finger to the topic she had circled. *Child slavery.*

"Atlanta has become a hub for human trafficking," she enthused, leaning in to convince me. "Just like it is for drugs and illegal immigration. Kids get kidnapped and end up in all sorts of bad situations. Lots of organizations are trying to intervene, churches and nonprofits and even the FBI, and there are shelters for kids that get rescued. We could even interview them. I heard all about it at church last Sunday."

She was moving too fast for me and I blurted out the first thing that popped into my head.

"You go to church?"

She drew herself up in her seat, staring coldly at me. "Don't you judge me by how I look, little miss. I happen to be a PK."

"PK?" I was bewildered.

"Preacher's kid. We're expected to rebel," she pronounced, gesturing elaborately around her clothes and face. "But in the end, we all come around. Or so I've been told," she smirked. "And I'm no dummy, either. I'm making a 4.0. You could do a lot worse than to have me as your research partner." She crossed her arms, dark tattoos peeking out from under her cuffs, and wiggled her foot impatiently.

I nibbled the eraser on the tip of my pencil, reappraising the situation.

"What about this topic," I said lamely, pointing to *recycling*. "Or this one?"

She snorted again. "Really? You want to write about video games and Facebook?" She started gathering up her things. "You and everyone else in here, probably. If you want to make a difference in something real, research these kids. It's my one condition for being your partner."

She was standing now, looming over me with one hand on her hip. I had the sinking feeling of being bulldozed. Somewhere deep inside me something was shifting. Old fears—fears I didn't even know I had—were coming to the surface. Could I face my own history and all these feelings that I might not be able to keep locked away?

You'll regret it, the little voice in my head said.

"I don't think I have any choice," I muttered, looking up from my chair, feeling for all the world like a child being browbeaten by a babysitter.

She beamed at me. "I knew you'd do it. Why don't we meet after school to work out our research plan?"

~

Tabitha turned out to be right. The topic was fascinating, and Atlanta really did have a problem. I tried to block out my unease by focusing on the facts.

"Look at this," I said, pointing out the results of my latest web search. "This article says that the Georgia Bureau of Investigation has started making more human trafficking raids than raids on marijuana or cocaine shipments."

"Hmmm," she mumbled, reading over my shoulder. In the quiet of the school's media center, she had slipped on a pair of thick cat-eye glasses, giving her an odd middle-aged-lady look. "Only thing outpacing it is meth lab raids."

She shoved a piece of paper at me. "Here's the list of organizations I was able to find. They're all downtown. Do you think your parents will let you go?"

"To do what?" I asked, swiveling in my chair to face her, unsure of where the conversation was headed.

"To meet some of the girls," she said, never skipping a beat. "We'll be sure to get an A if we do original research and not just regurgitate all this stuff on the Internet."

I paused. I was sure my mother wouldn't care, would probably in fact encourage me to go. But I wasn't sure I could do it. Even though I couldn't remember it, my own abduction had shaped my life so much. The idea of talking to someone who had experienced it too—and so recently—made me think twice.

Tabitha's eyebrow arched above the rim of her glasses, a skeptical look I was beginning to recognize.

"You can't possibly be scared of going to talk to them," she demanded, hands on hips.

"No!" I protested, perhaps a little too strongly.

"Then it's settled," she said smugly. "I'll call around and see what we can set up." She stared down at her boots, reaching down to rub out an imaginary scuff while she tried to hide her self-satisfied smile. "You just clear it with your parents, and I'll take care of the rest."

"Do you always get your way?" I asked, somewhat in awe.

"Only when I'm right," she smiled with a wink, sweeping up her books and heading out the door.

I looked at the books and papers strewed about our study carrel and sighed. It seemed as if I might have to get used to being the one to clean up after Tabitha's big ideas and the mess that followed. I began tidying up, separating the books and magazines into piles for reshelving.

I looked at the clock. I still had time to kill before I could catch the extracurricular bus home. Idly, I typed my homepage into the browser and scanned the news. Celebrity gossip, another big company merger. There was nothing of interest until at the bottom of the page, I spied a link labeled "Miracle in Africa." I clicked through. Some Ethiopian refugees were claiming that a miraculous light from Heaven had suddenly appeared and rescued them from the middle of a firefight between two warlords. The locals said it was the seventh or eighth time they'd seen the light.

As I was reading, the slow prickle of someone's eyes on me worked its way up the back of my neck. I turned, half hoping it was Michael coming to see me. My heart fell. There in the stacks stood Lucas, eyeing me speculatively. I flushed, and he grinned, one eyebrow arching as if he knew exactly what I had been thinking. Hurriedly, I grabbed my things and abandoned the carrel, my fingers drifting up to touch my Mark and ward off his gaze.

~

After a week of work, we'd learned it wasn't going to be as easy as we'd thought to set up the interviews with the human trafficking victims. Tabitha was persistent, but every place she called protested in the name of client privacy. We sat around my kitchen table, staring at the big red circle Tabitha had made on our research plan.

"We're already behind," she moaned. "If we can't get anyone to talk to us, I don't know what we'll do."

Mom muted her phone. She had an uncanny ability to follow a conference call and keep up with our conversation. Without turning from the presentation on her computer screen, she interjected, "I have a client on the board of Street Grace. Do you want me to call her and ask her for help?"

Tabitha squealed with delight, clapping her hands like a child. "Oh, Mrs. Carmichael, could you? That would be so awesome."

"I'd be happy to, Tabitha. It sounds like a good cause, at any rate," she said, carefully eyeing me.

Tabitha didn't notice the look as she bounded across the kitchen to give me a hug. "Your mom is the best. I'm going to make you dinner as a thank-you, Mrs. C. Is that okay?"

Mom looked surprised. "Sure, Tabitha, as long as you clear it with your parents. And don't forget about the technology risk; it is the biggest challenge facing this venture."

Now it was Tabitha's turn to look confused.

"Conference call," I mouthed to her, pointing at the phone as I headed into the pantry. Tabitha followed behind me and began rummaging through the shelves.

"Your mom seems pretty cool," she said, turning packages this way and that. "What about your dad?"

"He's not here. They've been apart for a long time," I said, paying an inordinate amount of attention to the nutrition label on a box of spaghetti.

She plucked some olives and capers from a corner and blew the dust off the jars. "This will do. You ever cook?" she asked me, pulling the spaghetti out of my hands.

"I'm more of the take-out type," I shrugged.

She flipped her long bangs—today, streaked neon green—back as she turned and left the pantry. "My father taught me to cook when I was little. I do dinner for the whole family every Friday. You should come over this Friday. We can go out after. A bunch of us were talking about going to Stone Mountain after dark. It'll be fun. And you can sleep over."

"Isn't Stone Mountain closed at night?" The doubt in my voice hung in the air but Tabitha plowed right through it.

"Live a little," she said. "Besides, don't you want to meet the people responsible for this?" She laughed, twirling around the kitchen with her arms full of the dinner groceries, and I had to smile.

~

All Friday my stomach was in knots. Sneaking into Stone Mountain Park, in and of itself, would have been enough to put me on edge. Tabitha had met all my queries about who was going and what we would do with a vague, "You'll see." And now, I found myself seated at the Franklin family dinner table at the start of my first ever sleepover.

I made a mental note not to call it a "sleepover"—it sounded so babyish—and refocused my attention on the five pairs of eager brown eyes staring at me.

With the exception of Tabitha, the Franklins were astonishingly clean-cut. Mrs. Franklin sat at the foot of the table in a starched white shirt and pearls, her straightened hair done in a flip that seemed right out of the sixties. Dr. Franklin, at the head of the table, wore a green polo shirt and looked freshly shaved. The dark brown skin on both of their faces was smooth and unmarked by worry. They both looked impossibly young to have four children.

"Stop gawking at Hope," Tabitha scolded as she placed a platter full of crab cakes on the table with a flourish that made the leather and chain bracelets on her wrist jingle. The flouncy gingham apron she sported looked ridiculous against her hot pink pants and black T-shirt. Her three younger brothers, carbon copies of their father, giggled and squirmed in their seats.

"It looks wonderful, Tabitha, thank you," her father beamed as Tabitha took her seat next to me. "Shall we say grace?" Everyone else's heads immediately snapped down, eyes closed, hands clasped, while I looked on, bewildered. I looked back at Dr. Franklin, who was frowning at the top of Tabitha's head. "Matthew 7:13," he continued, nodding at me to join them.

As I closed my eyes, Tabitha's youngest brother, Sam, began to intone in his tiny voice, "Enter ye in at the strait gate: for wide is the gate and broad is the way that leadeth to destruction, and many there be which go in thereat."

"Amen," everyone added gravely. That is, everyone but Tabitha.

When I looked up from my folded hands, she was scowling at her father, who had a smug look on his face. "Romans 3:23," she said, her chin lifting defiantly.

"Colossians 3:20," Dr. Franklin retorted, peering down the table at us over his glasses.

"Nice, Dad," Tabitha said, her voice dripping with sarcasm as she reached across the table for a corn muffin.

Dr. Franklin laughed. "Just my little Friday night reminder

before you two go out to join the festivities." Bowls and platters began to pass around as everyone filled their plates.

"How much trouble can we get into at a youth group social, Daddy?" Tabitha sweetly replied, kicking me under the table when I started to correct her.

"Besides, Tabby looks scary," Tabitha's brother David said, grinning wickedly. "No boys are going to talk to her."

"David," warned Mrs. Franklin, a smile tugging at the corners of her mouth. "Tabitha is just expressing herself."

"And I will be more than happy if no boys talk to her," added Dr. Franklin. "Now, Hope, we are counting on you to be a good influence and keep Tabby out of trouble." He looked at me over a forkful of salad.

"Sir?" I said, with a grin. "I don't think there is much risk of Bible-quoting teenagers going astray. First Corinthians, chapter ten—"

"Verse thirteen," Tabitha added triumphantly, finishing for me with a flourish of her napkin and then smiling at me gratefully.

Not a good idea to start sparring with a biblical scholar. The voice in my head reprimanded me so clearly that I looked around, thinking surely someone else must have heard it.

The Franklins' forks hovered mid-air. The boys eyed the scene with delight, shoveling in their food and watching the biblical repartee as if it were a heated tennis match.

"Well, then," Mrs. Franklin said after a long pause, her eyes sparkling with amusement as she set down her fork and tried to repress a grin. "I believe Hope has a point, dear."

"How did you come to know the Holy Book so well, Hope?" Dr. Franklin pinned me with a curious stare while Tabitha smiled to herself, taking in a bite of macaroni and cheese. "It's very unusual these days. Unless you come from a family of clergy, that is."

"Uh," I said, squirming uncomfortably, regretting that I'd spoken up. "I went to Catholic school before I moved back to Dunwoody. And my dad is kind of religious."

He looked at me, full of speculation. "Interesting. But I take it you're not?"

I looked at Tabitha for help, but she just shrugged.

"Um. I'd say I have more of an academic interest." My face burned with embarrassment. I didn't want to get into my belief—or lack thereof—with a minister. I certainly couldn't explain the heightened sense of antagonism I felt toward religion without getting into my entire confusing past with my father.

"I see," Dr. Franklin mused. "But let's take this piece of scripture. If we take the full context of Corinthians—"

"Daddy," Tabitha moaned, rolling her eyes.

Mrs. Franklin nodded to the boys, who were squirming in their seats, silently dismissing them. They threw down their napkins and dashed away.

"Roger," she said firmly as she rose from her own seat, beginning to clear the table. "I don't think the girls want to engage in theological debate right now. I believe they need to get ready for their night out. Girls?"

Tabitha beamed at her mother.

"Can we help you clear, ma'am?" I asked.

"House rules," she responded with a smile. "The cooks get the night off. Dr. Franklin and I will clean up."

Dr. Franklin grumbled in his seat as we scraped our chairs away from the table. "Bested by two teenagers," he muttered.

"Like father, like daughter," Mrs. Franklin laughed as we ran upstairs to Tabitha's room.

Her door was covered with dark posters, dramatic Keep Out

signs, and caution tape. As I swung the door open and crossed the threshold into her room, I let out an involuntary gasp at what I saw.

"What?" Tabitha crossed her arms defensively, jutting one bony hip out.

"It's just so . . . pink," I said, unable to keep a straight face. The room was a six-year-old's fantasy: rainbows, unicorns, and every sweet pastel you could imagine. Clearly her "self-expression" had been stopped short of a redecorating budget. "The princess wallpaper is definitely you."

She scowled. "Make all the fun you want. I just haven't had time to redo it."

"I see that," I said, spinning around to take it all in. The posters of goth and emo bands looked wildly out of place next to the "Hang in There!" kitten calendar.

She ignored me, throwing open her closet doors. It was a bipolar closet: starched and preppy good-girl clothes on one half, lots of black and neon on the other. She roughly shoved the J. Crew half to one side, muttering "Sunday stuff." Then she began whipping through the dark side of her closet, looking for who-knows-what.

"Aha!" she declared, pulling out a T-shirt that looked like it had been ripped to shreds and holding it up against my chest. "This will be perfect on you."

"Uh, what's wrong with what I have on?" I asked, looking down at my layered tee and polo shirt. I nervously fingered the fringe on my scarf.

"Bo-ring," she judged, rolling her eyes. "Don't you want to try something different for a change?"

"But nobody is going to see it anyway," I protested, pushing the shirt away, "since we're going to have our jackets on."

She tossed her hair back, impatient with me. "At least let me do your makeup and hair, then," she said, throwing down the shirt and dragging me into her bathroom.

Before I could protest she'd plopped me down on a stool and started rummaging through drawers, pulling out tubes and bottles and all sorts of things I didn't even know how to use. For all of her studied antisocial behaviors, she sure cared about fashion.

This is not going to turn out well, I thought, sighing inwardly.

She stepped behind me to take an appraising look in the mirror. "You have good bone structure. We just need a little drama, a little edge. Here, let's get this hair out of the way," she said, sweeping my long hair back with both hands.

"No!" My hands flew back to stop her, but it was too late. My hair was tucked high on my head in a tie, and she'd flicked away the scarf I'd wrapped around my neck. I tried to cover myself, but she swatted my hands away.

My whole body stiffened. Her jaw fell open as she stared at the back of my neck. I watched her in the mirror as she stared for a long time, cocking her head to one side, eyes narrowing, as she tried to work out this new development.

"Hope, you little devil," she said, eyeing me with new respect as she jumped up onto the counter. "Pretending to be Miss Goody Two-Shoes when all along you have a big old tattoo on the back of your neck." She peered closer and rubbed her thumb against my Mark, hard. "And it's a real one, too—not even I have the guts to do that. What else do you have going on that I don't know about?" She started pawing at me and my clothes with curiosity. "More tattoos? Piercings?"

"There's nothing else," I said, rushing the words out as I pushed away her hands and tried to create some distance between us. "And it's not what you think," I said, my face burning. "Please, believe me."

“What is it then? I’m all ears,” she demanded, crossing her arms and laughing at my discomfort.

My mind raced, trying to find an easy way out. “It’s hard to explain.” I stuck my chin out, my body daring her to continue.

“I bet it is,” she said, arching a brow. “And not just any tattoo, either. Aramaic and Greek! That must have been some highbrow tattoo parlor you went to.”

My mind stumbled over what she’d just said. “It’s Greek?” I said, bewildered that after all this time, someone seemed to know what my Mark was.

She gave me a searching look. “*Part* of it is Greek. Symbolic ancient Greek, to be precise. See this pattern along the edges? It’s called a Greek key. They used it in ancient Greek architecture. The rest of it is letters. It’s written vertically and is a bit blurry, but I’m pretty sure it’s Aramaic. I think it spells ‘key,’” she said, coming back behind me to trace the symbols down my vertebrae. “Or maybe ‘guardian of the key’? *Natchurat kleedah*,” she pronounced carefully, her tongue thick as she attempted the ancient language. She was engrossed in studying the markings, like a scholar poring over her books. “Though why anyone would go to such lengths to label themselves a ‘key’ is beyond me.”

She studied the design intently again, and then looked up at me in the mirror. “Please tell me you didn’t just choose this because it looked pretty. And you had to have chosen it—no parlor is going to offer something like this on its normal menu.”

She cocked her eyebrow and waited for my answer.

“I didn’t choose it.”

Her other eyebrow shot up. “So someone else chose it for you? That doesn’t sound like you.”

My hands crept back up to touch the spot she’d just traced, my mind racing. “I didn’t know it meant anything. Are you sure?”

"My dad taught me some Aramaic when I was little. He had to learn ancient languages in seminary. We could show him—"

"No!" I didn't even allow her to finish speaking before I'd ruled it out. It was bad enough that she'd seen it.

She knotted her eyebrows together, trying to puzzle me out. "Is this why you're always wearing those turtlenecks and scarves? Why are you so touchy about it? It *is* sort of pretty, in a totally geeky kind of way."

Don't tell her anything, said the little voice in my head.

I sat in silence, staring at the faded white linoleum of her bathroom. How could I explain to her that the Mark had just shown up on me? How could I tell her without having to go through the whole story of my abduction? Would she even believe me if I told her how my parents had tried again and again to get it removed, subjecting me to countless hours of pain, only to have the thing show up again, fresh and dark, only hours later?

Finally she let out a long sigh.

"Fine. I'll keep your secret, though I have to say you're totally overreacting." She tossed my scarf back in my lap. I wound it around my neck as if I was binding up an open wound.

The price for Tabitha's silence was giving her a complete free hand with my makeup. We turned up at Stone Mountain looking like two ghouls straight from the gates of Hades. She'd streaked my dark hair in hot pink and somehow managed to make it hang halfway across my face, drawing attention to my eyes, which glittered in pools of coal made by eyeliner and black shadow. A thin layer of pale foundation made me look sickly and glow in the dark.

"I look ridiculous," I said, pointing to my North Face jacket. "Goths don't wear fleece."

She shrugged as she stomped ahead, dragging me in her wake. "It's emo, not goth," she shot back over her shoulder. "And you could have changed your clothes."

We skirted the stream of people coming through the high wooden gates of the park and headed for the woods. Many people gave us frightened looks and steered their children away, making Tabitha chuckle. The twinkling lights inside the park disappeared as we strode into the trees.

"Where are we going?" I called after her.

"We're cutting around to the hiking path. We're supposed to meet near the summit."

"The summit?" I stopped in my tracks. "What are we going to do up there? And won't it be cold?"

She turned and stood in the darkness of the trees, shining a flashlight in my eyes so that I winced. "Are you coming or not?" The sharpness of her tone told me how frustrating she'd found me this evening. Without waiting for my answer, she turned and kept walking away from me in her tall, black boots.

"Okay," I said meekly, walking swiftly to catch up. I had to stay on good terms with her, at least until our project was finished.

The path was clearly marked, winding around the base of the mountain through the trees. Nobody else was in sight, but just in case, Tabitha drew a finger over her lips, telling me to be quiet. We veered away from the noise of the park until all I could hear was the wind whistling through the pines. The further we walked, the darker it became as the parking lot lights faded out of sight.

We came to a clearing, the intersection of two trails. To our left, the mountain stood in a heap. Bald granite twinkled as the beam from Tabitha's flashlight danced across the surface. The path seemed to go straight up.

"C'mon, let's go," she urged, starting up the trail.

The hike seemed interminable in the dark. The naked rock was marked with a faded yellow line, but the range of the flashlight was limited, leaving us with the eerie feeling of walking into space, with no signs or landmarks along the way to let us know how far we'd gone. We scrabbled over rocks and pebbles rolling down the trail, our shoes slipping on the slick surface. Periodically, we'd enter into a small stand of windswept trees or underbrush, or we'd pass an emergency telephone posted on a pole along the trail. Other than that, there was nothing: no buildings, no animals, and no people. Every now and then I thought I heard an owl or some other sort of bird screeching, but I could never convince myself it was more than just the wind. If I took my eyes off the trail, all I could see was black. But I could only do so for an instant, at the risk of slipping and falling.

The further we got, the chattier Tabitha became, returning to her normal know-it-all self. "You know, it's not really just granite," she said, randomly shifting the conversation to the geology of the mountain. "It's partly quartz monzonite. That's why it's so pretty."

I huffed back at her, catching my breath after a particularly steep portion of trail. "Is there anything you don't know about?"

"Nope," she said, turning back to grin at me. "At least not that I'll admit."

"How much longer?" I complained. It seemed like we'd been climbing for an hour.

"Shhhh. I hear voices."

We rounded a bend and looked up a few hundred yards to where a permanent shelter stood along the trail. A group of kids were already huddled around a small bonfire near the shelter. Others straddled benches, deep in conversation. The chatter built as we climbed closer.

"Hey, Tabitha! You made it!" An older boy, his hair swept into a temporary mohawk by a shellacking of gel, spotted us and started scrambling down the hill. "Give you a hand?"

Tabitha's face broke open in a smile. "I told you I'd come," she said, reaching out her hand. His hand swallowed her tiny one as he hoisted her up over the last big boulder.

"Who's your friend?"

"This is Hope," she said, leaving me to scrabble up the rock by myself. "She's new in town, and I thought it might be fun for her to come, too. It's okay, right?" She twisted a piece of her hair and nibbled it nervously. She was seriously into this boy.

"Hope, I'm Tony." Under all his makeup, he had a nice smile. "You girls thirsty?"

"After that climb, are you kidding me?" Tabitha playfully punched him in the arm. "I'm dying. What do you have?"

"You'll see," he said mysteriously, leading us over to the bonfire. The flickering light from the fire cast weird shadows across the faces of the assembled crowd, making their pale skin and liberal doses of black eyeshadow appear truly sinister. They were all dressed like Tabitha, some in dog collars and chains with weird sets of locks hooked onto their belts and boots that looked like they came off of storm troopers. All of them seemed much older than me or Tabitha.

"Where do you know these kids from?" I whispered to Tabitha, but she silenced me with a stare, mouthing behind Tony's back, "Don't embarrass me!"

"Hey, guys, let's get these girls something to drink. What d'ya say?"

They began jostling each other, trying to get into some big

coolers, and I realized that almost everyone here was a boy. Someone pressed a plastic tumbler into my hands. I took a cautious sip and nearly choked on the bitter taste of liquor. I spat it out behind my back, being careful that nobody could see. For a split second, I thought I heard familiar harsh laughter—Lucas. I whirled around to confront him, but there was no one there.

Tabitha was holding her tumbler, laughing and flirting with Tony. As soon as I could interrupt, I pulled her away.

"Tabitha, where are all the other girls?" I whispered, a note of anxiety creeping into my voice.

"I'm sure they are around here somewhere," she said, her voice trailing off as she looked around and came to the same realization.

"Tabitha," I said urgently, trying to pull her away from the fire, "how well do you know these people?"

"I know Tony well enough!" she snapped, pulling her arm away from me. "It's fine. Everything is fine."

"But they gave us alcohol—"

"So don't drink it!" she spat, exasperated, through her clenched jaw. Over her shoulder she saw Tony watching us intently. She dragged me a little ways further, lowering her voice to a whisper. "Listen, if you don't want to stay here, go hike up the rest of the way," she said, her head inclining back to the trail. "I'll be here when you realize how silly you're being."

I didn't like the idea of leaving her alone here, and told her so.

She gave my hand a firm squeeze. "Tony's dad and my dad go way back. He won't let anything happen to me. And it will take you twenty, thirty minutes tops to hike up and back. You can go up and see the famous view of Atlanta. I'll be here when you get back. I promise, we can go then."

I looked at her doubtfully, prompting her to cross her hands over her heart in an exaggerated X.

"Scout's honor," she declared, leaving her hands to rest on her hips.

I looked down at the tops of my sneakers. "You think I'm being ridiculous, don't you?"

"I think it's sweet that you are so careful," she said firmly. "Not just with yourself, but with me, too." I lifted my eyes to hers, and saw that she was telling me the truth. "You are a bit sheltered, Hope. Not everything or everyone is what they look like on the outside. God knows I'm living proof of that. But trust me—I don't mind having a friend who is willing to speak up to look out for me." Her eyes were fierce with pride and I felt a surge of pleasure as I realized she already considered me a friend. "It may be misplaced this time, but it's something I value. Now, go. I'll see you in half an hour."

I shuffled over to the last leg of the trail, grasping the metal railing. *Was I being too cautious?* I asked myself. *It doesn't matter*, I realized. *Whether you are right or not, she doesn't want you to spoil her fun.* Out of respect for my new friend, then, I'd have to give her some space. I reached for the flashlight and then my heart sank. My pocket was empty; Tabitha had been the last one to carry it. I looked back to where she stood, hoping to catch her eye, but she was engrossed, flirting and laughing with Tony.

Oh, well, I thought. *Off I go.*

The climb was a lot steeper than the earlier parts of the trail, but even so, it took me only about fifteen minutes to make it to the top. As I crested the mountain, the bitter wind whipped around me and I hugged my sides, willing my fleece to keep me warm.

Careful now, my inner voice cautioned me as I stepped forward onto the bare rock.

The top of the mountain was dark, but it didn't matter. The entire crazy quilt of lights that comprised the Atlanta skyline at night spread out before me, twinkling and sparkling as if against a backdrop of black velvet, giving the entire surface of the mountain a shimmery glow.

"It's beautiful," I murmured to no one, entranced by the dancing lights.

I was all alone, the massive expanse of stone laid out before me. I felt insignificant compared to the mountain and the sky, overcome by a rush of wonder. Giggling, I stuffed my hands in my pockets and began to skip across the surface, sliding effortlessly around the pits and cracks that pocked its surface, spinning and twirling past the cable car station and concession stand. All my earlier concerns melted away. I walked over to the edge, the caution area marked off by a low-slung cable, and let a gulp of brisk air chill my lungs.

In the distance, a crack of lightning lit up the sky, a distant rumbling of thunder following on its heels. Then another, and another. All around me, the lightning seemed to dance, snaking vines and sheets of fire, alternating as they circled the city. I had never seen so many storms, and if I closed my eyes, I could almost feel the electricity throbbing through the sky, leaving the smell of sulfur in its wake. Soon a soft rain enveloped me.

I was alone with nature's majesty, the party and my argument with Tabitha forgotten. Up on that mountain with only the weather as my companion, I had nothing to fear, nothing to hide. I let the wind rush about me, my hair swirling about me, for once not worrying who could see.

A solitary hawk swooped into my view, following the wind as it twirled and glided through the night sky. For a moment, it almost seemed as if our eyes met.

"Beautiful," I whispered again, watching it trace an arc against the flashing skies. The voice inside my head cautioned: *Don't hawks hunt during the day?* But the thought quickly passed as I became entranced with its flight.

The hawk swooped lower and lower, and then it rose up to make a lazy circle high above me. I turned around to watch its progress, admiring the ease with which it cut through the winds. Closer and closer it came, now in a straight line. And then, as I heard its eerie screech, I realized it was flying right at me, diving toward my head.

Shocked, I started to back away, stumbling over the forgotten cable and landing with a thump. The bird kept coming, sending me scrambling backwards on my hands and heels over the hard rock and scrabbling to avoid the attack.

It swerved right in front of me, disappearing from my vision. But I could hear its angry shrieking as it circled back for another try.

"Get away!" I cried out, looking blindly into the night to find it. Too late, I heard it screaming from above. Instinctively, I jumped to my feet and tried to bat it away from my head, but I lost my footing on the slippery rock.

I was rolling down the cliff face, bouncing off of rocks. I tried to slow my fall, grabbing wildly about me for anything, anything at all, but I was falling too fast and my hands came up empty. I hit something sharp and then, suddenly, I was free-falling, no longer touching the rock, the white mass of the mountain shrinking away from me as I fell into the night sky.

I always thought it was a cliché when people said that your life flashes before your eyes in the moments before your death, but there mine was, playing out like a movie in reverse right before me. I saw my night with Tabitha and the Franklins; the anonymity of my new school; the thrill of my first time running outdoors. The years of loneliness and repeated embarrassments at the hands of my father in Alabama. My mom and dad, fighting about what they should do with me. And looming in front of me, a stranger in a motel room. Not the one who'd kidnapped me, but the one who'd saved me. He faced away, his broad shoulders squared, every muscle tensed, a stark presence that flamed bright against the dingy walls of the room that my memory had almost erased.

When he turned to face me, I gasped in recognition.

"Michael!"

Suddenly, the force of what felt like a brick wall knocked the wind out of me. Stunned, everything in my body seemed to shut down.

Everything was dark. I was conscious only of the fact that the rush of wind had slowed to a rhythmic breeze. A slow warmth seemed to suffuse my body.

My brain struggled to make sense of what was happening. *So this is what it feels like to die*, I thought, waiting for the pain.

But the pain didn't come. Instead, my mind drifted away into nothingness. I felt a gentle tickling against my nose and face as I seemed to bob in a current of air, going up and down in steady rhythm. I turned away from the chill wind, burrowing my face deeper into the warmth, and sighed.

Where am I? my brain suddenly demanded.

It doesn't matter. Just sleep, a different voice came back, just as insistently.

I was starting to get hot. I turned over in languorous ease, trying to push away from the heat, and felt strong hands tighten their grip on me. Startled awake by the sudden movement, I opened my eyes.

Below me, I could see the rooftops of Atlanta.

And they were moving.

With my feet dangling over them.

The wind was rushing by me, whipping my hair around so that I could barely see. But out of the corner of my eye, I could see that the great rhythmic beating was coming from a pair of gigantic, snowy wings. Confused, I tried to turn around, but muscle-bound arms squeezed me even tighter.

"Quit wiggling or I may drop you," a voice warned, and I looked up.

For the second time that night, I gasped in recognition. And then, mercifully, everything went dark.

five

I was groggy. I pushed my face deeper into my pillow, my mind already slipping back to the bliss of sleep. Something tickled at my lip, and I reached my fingers up to rub at my face.

Feathers, I thought, plucking them away absently.

Feathers!

My eyes flew open and I bolted up. I was in my own bed. At home. Safe.

It didn't really happen.

But then I spun around and pressed my back against the headboard.

There, sitting in the corner, was Michael.

He was hunched over, holding his head in his hands, but even as self-contained as he was, he seemed to dwarf everything in my room. I sucked in my breath and he stirred.

"Good. You're awake," he said, lifting his head to eye me warily. "I was beginning to get worried."

He uncoiled his body, rising to his feet without effort. Every muscle rippled, and I felt my breath catch in my throat as I scanned his body, looking for evidence of what I'd seen the night before. The only thing unusual I could find was his hair, which had seemed to somehow grow overnight so that his bangs now fell rakishly into his face. The shadow of a beard was emerging on his jaw, and dark shadows under his eyes bore witness to his sleepless vigil. He looked like a man—an incredibly handsome, incredibly tired man. But I knew what I had seen.

I clutched at the hem of my comforter, unable to stop staring.

"You," I began, but I couldn't bring myself to say the words.

"Yes?" he asked, carefully, as if testing the waters. He stood unmoving in the corner, waiting for me to continue.

"You saved me," I stated quietly. It was the simplest way to put it. I dropped my eyes and plucked at some imaginary lint.

"You shouldn't have been up there," he said softly.

I raised my eyes, defiant. "You shouldn't have—I mean, couldn't have been, either. But you were."

A shadow of worry clouded his eyes so that the sparkling blue turned to stormy gray. He moved toward me and I shrank back against the headboard, my body betraying my fear and confusion.

He stopped short, looking as if I'd slapped him in the face. Quickly, his face became a mask and he shrugged.

"Well, it was a good thing I was, or you would have fallen off the mountain. As it was, you almost got hypothermia," he blustered. "You were barely conscious when I found you."

A rush of anger swept through me. I leaned forward, accusing him. "I didn't *almost* fall off the mountain. I *did* fall. And you didn't *find* me. You caught me. *In the air*."

"Don't be ridiculous," he scoffed, his voice full of bravado. But in his eyes, I could see fear—the fear of being known. His eyes searched mine, questioning.

"Don't lie to me," I whispered, unable to sustain his gaze. I picked at the hem of my comforter. "I can take almost anything, but not that."

When I looked up again, he was rooted in the same place. He looked torn. Lost.

"I know," he said, his jaw taut. He balled his giant hands into fists. As he saw my eyes wander over them, he willed himself to relax and slowly unfurled his fingers. "I shouldn't even be here now. But I can't help myself."

"Who are you?" I whispered, pity and fear stabbing me through the heart.

"If I tell you, things will never be the same for you," he whispered, pleading with me.

You don't have to do this. You can go back to ignorance if you say the word.

I paused, considering the lure of the promise made by the voice in my head, but only for a moment. "Tell me," I asked, brushing aside the warning as I looked Michael in the eyes. "Please."

Michael cocked his head to the side as if listening to someone, and then he sighed. "I have no choice." Then, when the only sound I could hear was my own ragged breath, he raised himself up so that he seemed to fill the entire room.

"I am the One," he began in a whisper. "The first to worship humankind. The defender of the People of God, scourge of the Evil, protector of the Innocent. I guided Adam and Eve out of Paradise so that they should live. I spoke to Moses from the burning bush and delivered his soul to the hands of Righteousness. I argued before the Lord so that the waters would not wipe humanity from the face of the Earth. I brought the wrath of the heavenly hosts upon the Fallen Ones so that they were cast forever from the Gates of Heaven."

His voice had turned into a quiet roar, the rush of a thousand voices joining his so that it sounded like music.

"I am the Prince of Light, the Captain of the Army of God, defender of Israel, judge and escort to just souls, eternal enemy of Satan and his powers. I am He Who Is Like God."

His eyes were closed now, and his entire being seemed to glow. A gentle wind swirled about him, tousling his hair and clothes.

"I am Michael, Archangel."

The wind and light died down, leaving him standing before my bed. I clutched the sheets about me, stunned.

All the denials I'd ever made about God—the walls I'd built up to defend myself against my father's crazy rantings—all of it came crashing into dust as Michael's words sunk in. I thought about everything I knew about angels, which filled all of thirty seconds. Didn't angels come to people when they were dying? Or with messages and tasks from God? What did that have to do with me?

Then I thought about all the time I had spent with Michael. All of it was a lie.

"You've been lying to me this whole time," I whispered, the accusation in my voice unmistakable. "Pretending to be my friend."

He hung his head, unable to answer.

"Why?" I asked suddenly.

He opened his eyes and looked at me with sadness.

"Why what?"

"Why are you here? What do you want from me?"

He looked confused himself. "I am sworn to protect the innocent. Usually this means intervening in the affairs of man when something horrific is threatening to happen."

"Like those refugees on TV."

"Yes," he said, startled that I'd made the connection. "Like those refugees."

"Is that where you went, when you went away the other week?"

"Yes," he conceded, bowing his head. "It was almost too late by the time I got there." Before I could ask more questions, he continued. "But over a decade ago, I was drawn to protect something a little bit more unusual for me—a little girl who was in danger."

Adrenaline shot through my veins. "You were there, in the motel room! I remembered your face when I was falling last night."

"Yes, I was there," he admitted, a dark look crossing his face. "I wasn't supposed to be there, but somehow you caught my attention and I . . . I had to stop that monster." His mouth twisted in anger.

"You killed him."

His eyes flashed. "I did it to protect you," he protested, his voice rising slightly as a vein started throbbing on his forehead.

"But why me?"

"I don't know." He practically spat the words, and I shrank back. My hand drifted to the back of my neck, touching my Mark like a talisman. *Did he know about it,* I wondered. *Could he tell me what it means*?

Now is not the time, the voice in my head told me, so I stayed quiet, watching Michael intently.

He began pacing across my room, every muscle taut. "It was as if I couldn't help myself. There was something about you . . . I just knew I had to intervene." He rubbed his hand across his face, looking desperate as he relived it.

"Just like my dad," I murmured. "Needing to protect me but not sure why." Michael barely acknowledged my observation as his confession poured out of him.

"God was displeased, but no harm really came of it. After all, it took barely an hour of time here on Earth. After that, I stayed away from you for a long time. I had nearly forgotten about it when the feeling returned."

"What feeling? Why was God displeased?"

He cocked his head to the side then, as if considering what to say next.

"I forget how little you know. But it cannot hurt. Not now." He threw himself down in my butterfly chair as he continued. "I am not supposed to bother myself with anything other than God's work. As young and innocent as you were—you were not for me to trifle with."

I was not sure I was following him. "You mean you had bigger fish to fry?" I asked, knotting my brows together as I puzzled it out.

He smiled wryly. "That is a good way to put it." He closed his eyes, rubbing his temples.

I bit my lip, considering all that he'd said.

"You said the feeling has returned."

He drew his lips into a hard, straight line and looked me straight in the eye.

"Yes. It has."

A pregnant silence filled the room. My heart seemed to skip a beat.

"You sent me that valentine, didn't you?"

He nodded silently. My heart raced: first with excitement that he'd been my secret admirer, and then with fear as I thought about the warnings held in the unfinished verses.

"Am I in danger?" My hand absentmindedly floated up to my neck again. Whether it singled me out for protection or harm, I could feel my Mark burning on my skin, and Michael's tale only made me more aware of it.

"If you keep doing stupid things like climbing on top of mountains in the middle of the night, then yes," he said, his wide grin suddenly breaking across his face.

It was the first glimpse I'd had of the old Michael, *my* Michael, and my heart leapt. I threw my pillow at him, but he expertly caught it in one hand. Even then, his eyes were sad.

"I'm serious," he said, the grin gone. "You can't be taking risks like that."

"I wouldn't have even been there if you hadn't disappeared, leaving me with Tabitha for my partner in Contemporary Issues," I pouted, crossing my arms. "Besides," I went on, cutting him off before he could continue with his lecture, "everything would have been fine if it weren't for that hawk."

"A hawk?" His voice had an edge to it as he echoed my words.

"It attacked me out of nowhere. That's how I fell." I shuddered as the memory of my free fall came rushing back to me, and my fingers unconsciously gripped the side of my bed.

He frowned, his brows furrowing deeply. "That's unusual. Two bird attacks."

"Two?"

"The crows. Remember?"

My fall, during my run the other day. The room seemed to spin as I made the connection.

"Do you know what's going on, Michael?" I whispered, barely able to speak.

He slumped deeper in the chair. "No. No, I'm afraid I don't. I'm not omniscient, unfortunately. I'm more the muscle than the brains of God's security operation. When there's trouble, I get pointed in the right direction and go take care of it. If I see the trouble, I jump in without waiting for an invitation. But this time, I'm not even sure where it's coming from. All I have is this sense that I should be here. With you."

We sat there in silence for a long time. My mind raced with all the questions I had for him: questions about my abduction, my Mark, my father. And of course, about him.

"How do you do it?" I finally screwed up my courage to ask.

"Do what?" he answered, distracted.

"Everything," I whispered, leaning closer to him. "How can you be a teenager? How can you fly? How do you get to where the trouble is?"

He looked miserable.

"How am I supposed to leave now?" he snapped at the air, pounding his fist into his knee.

I sank into my bedsheets, deflated. "I didn't ask you to leave," I said, uncertain and scared by his moodiness.

His face softened and he leaned gently toward me. "I wasn't talking to you. I was talking to Henri."

"Henri?"

"Your Guardian angel."

I could barely process this latest piece of news. My jaw fell open in disbelief before I managed to sputter, "My. Guardian. Angel."

He looked at my astonished face and roared with delight. "The archangel she swallows no problem. It's the invisible watchdog that makes her skeptical!"

I crossed my arms and stuck out my tongue. I hated being made fun of. Still, he'd piqued my curiosity.

"Why are you arguing with Henri?"

"He's angry with me for interfering."

I raised my eyebrows. "Say more."

A wicked grin crept across Michael's face. "He believes I have violated his rights and the order of Angels by intervening in his protection and guidance of you. If it continues, he is threatening to take it up to the courts."

I was dumbfounded. "There are courts in Heaven?"

"Oh, yes. And they will enforce the rules. By rights, only Guardian Angels can protect individuals, with very few exceptions.

Though I must say, old Henri, that they may come down on the other side of the law when they see how ineffective your methods have been." He was openly smirking now, and I could sense a faint buzzing in my mind.

I had a sudden epiphany. "Is he the voice in my head?" I asked.

"One and the same," said Michael, leaning back into his chair with satisfaction. "Oh, don't harass me. I didn't tell her, she figured it out," he spoke dismissively into the air.

"He *did* try to keep me from teaming up with Tabitha and from going to Stone Mountain," I said, trying to be helpful.

"Fat lot of good that did you," muttered Michael. In an instant, his humor had shifted; he seemed cross and was rubbing his temples again.

"Michael," I asked timidly, "why do you always have headaches?"

He stopped rubbing his temples, jerking his hands away. "You've noticed?"

"It's hard not to. Especially when they make you so moody."

The vein in his temple twitched again. "I'll try not to be moody."

"I don't care that you're moody. But I'd like to know why."

He took a deep breath and drew his hands together in his lap, as if he was afraid of what they might do. "Remember when I told you God was displeased with me?"

"Yes," I said, not sure where this was going.

"Well, this is what happens when God is displeased. You see, in all of creation, he made two great beings that are capable of holiness: angels and man. We were both intended to be in his likeness, but we have two crucial differences. Only mankind can create. We angels can only praise, protect, or destroy. We can convey. We can escort. But we can neither invent nor discover," he continued, his jaw tense. "It is forbidden."

I shuddered. The more Michael spoke, the more grave and

formal his speech became. In my mind's eye, I could see him as an ancient being, the fiery general of God's army.

"And while we both, man and angels, have free will," he continued, "God did not trust the angels with such a precious gift when he made us. Not as he trusted you," he said, a twinge of jealousy entering his voice. "We can disobey him and choose our own path, of course. That is what the Fallen Ones did. But when they fell, they learned that to be away from God was to embrace pain. For God punished their disobedience with great physical pain. The longer they strayed, the farther they strayed, the more intense the pain grew. Nothing can stop it. Nothing except their return to God."

His eyes seemed far away now. "Imagine living hundreds of thousands of years in never-ending pain. Imagine what that would do to you. If you hadn't already been wicked, you would surely go insane."

The idea of it was horrifying, especially when I realized what he was really saying.

"You're in pain," I said softly, my heart breaking for him. I slid out from beneath the covers and crept to his side. Carefully, not sure of what I'd find, I placed my hand on his arm. Through the cotton of his sleeve, it was burning hot. I realized with a start that except for the time he'd pulled me through the hallway, he'd managed never to touch me. "You're not supposed to be protecting me," I said. "That's why you had to leave."

"I had to fulfill my duties before I could return to guard you," he answered, his blue eyes like sapphires that shone with intensity. "I do not understand how protecting you could be against God's will when I feel such a strong urge to do it. Somehow it must all be in His plan."

"Why am I in danger?" I wondered to myself. "Is it related to my abduction?"

"I think so," he said.

"So my dad—with all his crazy fears for me—he's been right all along?"

Michael didn't speak but simply placed his big hand over mine. I looked deep into his eyes and seemed to lose myself in their intensity. The heat from his fingers licked at my bones and my heart skipped a beat. Silence filled the room.

"Hope?" My mother's voice jarred me back to reality. "Hope? Are you awake?"

I could hear her climbing the stairs toward my room. I pushed myself away from Michael and started fumbling around, panicking as I looked from myself, still dressed in last night's clothes, to Michael. I spun around, looking for somewhere to hide, or to hide him. But there was nowhere. I began to feel frantic, but then I heard my own voice sing out.

"What is it, Mom?"

I wheeled around and gasped. Michael was no longer there. Instead, I was staring at my own self, bleary eyed, with a face streaked by the runny remains of eye shadow and mascara.

I opened my mouth to scream but the person—it—*me*—cleared the space between us and clamped a hot hand over my mouth.

"Don't make a sound," it whispered to me urgently, pulling me tight. "It will be okay." I tried to pull away, but felt myself caught even closer in a vice-like, fiery grip.

"I was starting to think you'd never wake up. Are you feeling better? It's nearly noon, you know," my mom continued. She was on the other side of the door now. I held my breath, watching the doorknob and willing it not to turn. "Tabitha is on the phone. She sounds worried about you."

"I'm feeling much better. I'll take it in here, Mom. Thanks," the replica me responded. I felt my body weaken and fought to stay focused. *You cannot faint*, I admonished myself.

As we heard my mom's footsteps retreat back downstairs, I watched as my replica's face and body swiftly melted back into Michael's. My eyes widened and my knees began to give out.

"You're not going to scream, are you?" he asked me as he pulled me closer to his chest, his hot hand still over my mouth.

I shook my head violently. *No*.

"Do you want to talk to Tabitha, or shall I?" he continued. "I called and left a message at her house last night that you felt sick and found a ride home. I left a note to that effect for your mother, as well."

I stared up at him, shocked at how well he'd orchestrated everything.

"I can do it," I mumbled against his palm, my mind racing. He lifted his hand away then, watching me carefully for any further signs of panic. My whole body was shaking, but I leaned into him until I managed to make it over to the phone and pick up the receiver.

"I have it, Mom," I said, my voice shaky. I heard the click as she hung up the receiver on her end. "Tabitha?"

"Have you ever heard of a cell phone?" she demanded, the words rushing out of her. "I was worried sick! You were supposed to come back in thirty minutes. Tony and I spent two hours looking for you. Thank God we thought to call my parents. We were just about to call the police to search the mountain. Why didn't you just tell me you weren't feeling well? I would've taken you home." She sounded angry and hurt.

"I'm sorry," I whispered, scrambling to explain my disappearance from the mountain. "I didn't try to avoid you—I just felt so sick that I got disoriented and lost on the way down. So when I saw my friend in the parking lot, I took the ride home. I didn't even think to call you. I am so sorry. I didn't mean to worry you," I added, guilt surging through me for putting her through such trouble and for lying to her now.

Tabitha paused before answering. "No problem," she said grudgingly. "But don't you pull a stunt like that again on me." She breezed by the need for explanations, focusing instead on herself. "Thank goodness I was with Tony and that my parents like you, or it would have been much worse, believe me."

"I'm really sorry, Tabitha. I won't do it again, I promise." My knees were still shaking, so I sank down to the floor, never turning my back on Michael, who stood against the wall, watching me intently. *How did he do that? And what was he thinking now?*

"Hel-lo? Are you still listening to me?" Tabitha demanded. I snapped back to attention.

"Yeah, I'm here," I said sheepishly.

"We're still going to the shelter to do those interviews tomorrow, right?"

"Yes, for sure," I said. *Stick to your normal routine*, I thought to myself. *School work is just the thing I need. Nothing unusual to see here, folks. Pay no attention to the angel in your room.*

"Okay, I'll pick you up at one o'clock. Be ready," she warned. "And then I can tell you all about Tony." She giggled. "See ya."

"See ya," I echoed, staring back at Michael, but Tabitha had already hung up. I held the phone against my ear until it began beeping angrily at me.

"You should hang up," Michael suggested.

I slowly put the phone back in the cradle, keeping him squarely in my vision.

"I didn't mean to scare you," he said softly.

When I didn't respond, he lowered himself to the floor until he was eye level with me.

"May I come closer?" he asked quietly, gesturing toward my side. I nodded, still unable to speak.

He came so close to me that I could feel the waves of heat radiating off his body. Up close, he looked even more perfect. His golden hair shined, a lock of it falling forward onto his forehead. I fought off the urge to reach out and tuck it back in place.

"You asked me earlier how I did it. How I look like a teenager. Well, this is how. When I came to you, I chose the form that would be easiest for you to understand, but I can take the form of anyone. Would you like to see me do it again?"

I hesitated, not sure if I could handle it.

"I promise not to become anyone you know," he said, taking my hand. A surge of warmth swept through my entire body as I registered his touch. "What you need to understand is that when I do this, I really become human, at least in all respects that matter."

I looked into his eyes. They were full of kindness and concern.

"Are you ready?" he asked, still holding my hand.

I nodded once.

"Okay," he breathed, and closed his eyes.

Instantly, he began melting, his features twisting and morphing seamlessly into another person, his entire body doing the same. It was like flipping the channels on an old-fashioned television—a slight flurry of static as his features went out of focus before they sharpened, locking onto the picture. One by one, he became an old black lady; then a young boy, barely five; an elderly Native American; a teenaged girl. Person after person appeared, just for an instant; by the time my mind recognized who or what they were, he had transformed into the next person. Yet in that instant, I not only saw them, but I *knew* them—knew their histories, their loves, their sorrows, knew how special their time on this earth had been. And no matter who sat before me, the eyes were unchanging—the same sharp blue eyes, filled with kindness and grief, which belonged only to Michael.

I sat transfixed, watching the parade of people before my eyes, until slowly he faded back into himself. My Michael.

He was clutching my hand against his heart. I felt it thumping under my touch and my brain protested, almost convincing me that he was truly human. Almost.

He never broke his gaze, never moved his lips. But deep inside of me, I seemed to feel more than I heard his words, vibrating and thrumming with intensity.

I will protect you.

His unspoken promise hung in the air between us. Finally, I broke the silence.

"That was beautiful," I said, embarrassed, as if I had seen into his soul.

"I promise I won't do that again, at least not without your permission," he stated solemnly. "But I wanted you to understand."

"Thank you," I whispered, giving his hand a little squeeze. As I did, I realized my hand was starting to burn from his heat. "I'm sorry," I said sheepishly, pulling my hand away from his grasp.

He unclasped it immediately, looking remorseful. "I didn't hurt you, did I?"

I turned my palm over. It was red and sweaty, but nothing more. "No, no harm done. Besides, if you have to deal with constant headaches, I guess I can handle the equivalent of sunburn."

He grinned then, a small, satisfied smile.

"For the record," he began, counting off answers to my unspoken questions matter-of-factly on his fingers. "One: white stuff at lunch—manna. I can eat human food, but prefer not to. Two: yes, I can fly, and yes, I have wings, though not in human form. But I also can do what amounts to time travel between great distances if need be. Three: when I take human form, I can provide myself with all the accoutrements of human life. So yes, I do have a house and a real car. I even have an AmEx card. Four: I don't have to wear white, but it is kind of a tradition."

He gave me one of his patented wicked grins. "And I think it looks pretty good, don't you?"

I rolled my eyes. "You're impossible," I said. "Are all angels as pompous as you?"

He laughed out loud. "Wait until you meet Raphael. He is totally full of himself."

My eyes widened. "Am I going to meet more angels?"

His face darkened at the suggestion. "Not if I can help it. I don't want to draw any more attention to you than I already have."

I was confused. "What do you mean?"

He sprang to his feet, and I swear that for an instant he seemed to float. He stalked over to the window and looked out between the curtains toward the street.

"It's nothing, Hope. Just a feeling I have."

"But why?"

He was deliberately avoiding my gaze, pretending to find something of great interest in the cul-de-sac outside.

"I'm not going to give up," I said, a stubborn note in my voice. "You might as well tell me what's going on."

He doesn't want to tell you because it's his fault, said the voice in my head—that is, said Henri.

"What's your fault?" I prompted, silently thanking Henri for the tidbit of intelligence.

"Damn it, Henri, mind your own business!" Michael's face contorted with rage.

"He's only trying to do his job, Michael," I said, walking swiftly to his side. "I need to know what's going on. If I'm in danger, then the more informed I am, the better off I'll be."

He clenched his fists and released them, over and over, considering my words. The effort he was making to control his temper was awesome to witness. *How much pain is he really in*, I wondered, *if something so small can spin him out of control?*

"You know the story of the Fallen Angels," he said between clenched teeth. I nodded, not sure I liked where this was heading. "They are real, and they live on. Part of their punishment is that they cannot escape their own immortality. They have to go through Eternity knowing there is no redemption, always suffering the pain of separation from God."

I remembered what he had said about being driven mad by the pain, and I shuddered.

"The Fallen are everywhere," he breathed. "And they'd do anything to exact their revenge on me." He leaned protectively over me, surrounding me in the tiny alcove formed by the window and the eaves.

"I don't understand," I said.

He shoved away from me, pacing across the room.

"I was the one who forced them out of Paradise, Hope. They have waited millennia to get their revenge. Even something that appears insignificant—a young girl—might be tempting to them if it seemed to offer a way to get back at me. The fact of the matter is that I may be placing you in more danger by drawing attention to you—that is, if the wrong creatures notice."

Now it was my turn to rub my temples. I couldn't follow all this. I was starting to really believe I *was* being threatened, and maybe from more than one side.

"What were you saying about bird attacks, before?" I asked him.

He looked up from his pacing, surprised, as if he'd forgotten I was even there. Swiftly, he composed his face into a serene mask. "Nothing. It was nothing."

I stood, staring at him from across the room. The surrealism of the situation began to sink in. I looked at Michael, standing in the middle of my bedroom. With his broad shoulders, his proud stance, I couldn't imagine anything more solid, more real. Yet I knew it couldn't be so.

"Am I dreaming?" I wondered aloud.

"No," Michael said, his eyes heavy with resignation. "I didn't want to have to tell you all this. But after last night, I couldn't imagine how I could hide it from you any longer."

The rush of adrenaline that had been keeping me afloat dissipated, leaving me weak. I sank back down to the floor.

"This can't be real," I murmured, looking up at him from the floor and wondering what on earth I'd gotten myself into. "What am I supposed to do now?" I could feel a vague sense of panic rising inside me.

His mouth closed into a hard line. Swiftly, he bent over and plucked me from the floor, carrying me back toward my bed. "You're exhausted, and no wonder. Between last night and all this," he said, his blue eyes flashing with remorse, "I've worn you out."

"You must be tired, too," I said softly, seeing for the first time the fine lines etched around his eyes. "From the pain."

He stopped, staring at me in surprise. The corners of his mouth stole up before he shook his head and continued over to the bed. Carefully, he laid me down and tucked the covers around me.

I closed my eyes for a moment, luxuriating in the comfort of his kindness, trying to forget why it was exactly that I was the focus of this gorgeous boy's attention. When I opened my eyes, Michael was still hovering over me.

He paused, looking deep in thought as if carefully choosing his words.

"Your father is not crazy, Hope," he whispered to me, his lips hovering just above my ear. "In ancient times, we would have hailed him as a prophet. His vision may be fuzzy"—his familiar grin stole once more across his face—"but he is right about one thing: you are special, and you have been singled out. Whatever you've been singled out for is locked deep inside you and has been for a very long time."

Swiftly, he bent to kiss me on the forehead.

"Whatever it is, I will make sure you get a chance to find out. You can count on that."

Then he was gone.

As soon as I knew he was out of the room, I could feel myself surrender to the pull of sleep. Half-awake, I drew my fingers across the spot where his lips had touched my skin. It burned and tingled, and I sighed deeply as I remembered the heat of his touch. The feeling stayed with me even in my dreams.

six

Mom being who she was, I wasn't allowed to sleep for long. It was not a good afternoon. My entire body was black and blue from my fall, and every step I took was a painful reminder of each rock and shrub I'd bounced against. A slight heat rash had wrapped around my torso and arms where Michael had carried me last night, and the skin where he'd held my hand was shiny. I realized with a start that the rash on my wrist had been from his touch, too, rather than my fall against the curb during my ill-fated run.

What was worse, I couldn't baby myself—not if I wanted to keep my injuries hidden from my mom. I was on edge, nerves taut. I needed to escape Mom's watchful gaze and questions and sort things out on my own, so I took myself out for another run around the neighborhood.

I paused briefly at the top of the cul-de-sac, remembering Michael's warnings and words about the "bird attacks," but shook it off, desperately in need of the release.

I tried not to think too much about everything that had happened. Instead, I tried to empty out my mind, leaving no room for anything but the run itself.

The aftermath of last night's storms lay all around me in the street. Fallen tree limbs and brush littered the asphalt. The creek that wound through the neighborhood was about to burst its banks; the rain had been much fiercer here. It was at once familiar and alien, as if the secrets I'd discovered had altered nature itself; as if the things I didn't know still threatened me from the shadows. My body protested as I forced it to move. But the air was crisp and clean, even if the day was gray, so I pushed my fears and pain aside and concentrated again on the rise and fall of my knees, the rebound of my feet off the pavement. I soon fell into the rhythms and footfalls of my run, finding comfort in their sameness and letting the stiffness work its way out of my body.

I leaned into the curve as I entered the undeveloped section of my neighborhood and felt a familiar tingle—the tingle of being watched. This time, though, I wasn't afraid. I stumbled to a stop and bent over to catch my breath before I turned, a smile on my lips, to greet Michael.

The smile froze on my face as my father stepped from the woods.

Irritation and disappointment surged through my body, quickly chased by guilt. *When was the last time I'd even thought about my father, let alone seen him?* I thought. *Only to blame him for a valentine he didn't even send.*

"I hope you don't mind that I came here, Hope." He was holding his hat in his hands, looking almost penitent as he came closer to the road. He stopped at its very edge, his big hands twisting the hat.

"How did you know I would even be here?" I asked, suspiciously.

"I didn't know. But I figured that your mother would let you run outside and that if I came here, eventually I would see you."

I stared at him, stunned. Back near the trees I could see the hood of his beat-up car where he had parked it near one of the utility boxes. I cursed myself for failing to notice it earlier.

"You've been coming up here and lurking around in the woods, just in case I decide to go for a run?"

He nodded and then pursed his lips, as if the oddness of what he'd admitted had only just occurred to him. "It hasn't been that often. Just every now and then. On days when I thought you might not be in school." He looked down at his shoes and seemed to brace himself for my rejection.

In our times we would have called him a prophet. Michael's words came back to me and I suddenly felt small. After all, if my father was guilty of anything, it was of being overprotective. And maybe it wasn't really fair to blame him for everything that had happened to me in Alabama. From the time I'd been a little girl, parents had carefully steered their children away from me, almost unconsciously, as if a force field surrounded me and made it impossible for them to get close. I learned to recognize the look as they drew their kids to the other side of the playground, a mix of unabashed gawking, lurid supposition ("Are you sure she wasn't hurt?"), and schadenfreude. I'd had no best friend. I missed out on the My Pretty Princess birthday parties, had no one to braid my hair and whisper secrets and giggle about boys with me. I lived my meager existence, suffering the normal outrages of transitioning to middle school and high school like every other teen, I suppose, but with the extra burden of being an outcast—a status based on nothing more than parents' fears that somehow, if their kids got too close to me, something bad would happen to them, too.

"I won't tell Mom," I said, and his head jerked up, his eyes full of surprise. He stopped twisting his hat, a grin lighting up his face.

"Thank you, Hope."

I nodded, not sure what to say next.

My dad was first to break the silence. "I got a job, Hope."

"That's great, Dad!" My delight for him was genuine. It had been years since he'd last had a job.

"I'm night manager at the Taco Bell. You know the one, right off campus, near South College?" His voice was eager, his eyes searching for approval.

I swallowed my disappointment. It was a far cry from the engineering job he used to have, but it was a start.

He continued, oblivious to my warring emotions. "I figured I had more time now with you gone. They didn't want to hire me at first, said I was overqualified, but when I explained everything they changed their minds. They're really nice folks, Hope. They even let me take home the leftovers." He pulled a neatly folded bag out of his coat and thrust it at me.

"Aw, Dad, you shouldn't have." I took the paper bag from him, gingerly holding it away from me so as not to be overwhelmed by the grease.

He beamed again. "It's the new burrito. I bet you'll like it."

"I'll take it home for dinner tonight."

A shadow fell across his face. He seemed almost embarrassed and started mangling his hat again. "You probably shouldn't. Just in case."

Mom. I nodded swiftly, patting the bag. "I'll eat it on the way home."

I kicked some pebbles with my toe. This was the first time I'd ever had to visit my dad. It felt strange.

"So how is school?"

"School is okay," we began at the same time, and then laughed nervously at our awkwardness.

"School is okay," I repeated. "A lot of the same kind of classes." I fumbled around for something to add, the heat of a blush spreading across my face. "I ride the bus for now," I said. "Oh, and I made a new friend. Her dad is a minister, and her name is Tabitha."

"Great," Dad said, straining to smile. "That's just great."

"Dad," I burst out before I could stop myself. "Mom told me some things. Some things about when I was little. Why do you think that I am being targeted?"

He blanched and looked around nervously.

"Mom's not going to find out you told me," I rushed to explain. "I promise. I just, you know, wondered. Wondered why." I tried to keep my expression as neutral as possible so he did not feel threatened.

He looked at me warily. "You really want to know?"

I nodded vigorously. "I'm being serious. I won't argue or anything. I just want to know."

He sighed then, and his eyes suddenly became very tired. "Because I hear voices, Hope."

His words came slowly at first, but as he continued, they seemed to rush like water bursting a dam.

"They started the night we found you. Sometimes it's almost like a buzzing sound in my head. Other times they're whispers. But if I ignore them, they get louder."

Before, I would have asked him if he had tried using antipsychotic drugs to relieve his symptoms, but now I just remembered Michael's words and tried not to let what my dad had said startle me too much. I took a deep breath and asked the question I needed to ask, even though I didn't want to.

"What do they say, Dad?"

"To keep you close," he said. "I never wanted to find out what would happen if I didn't."

I felt a stab of pity for him. How horrible must it be to be the only one who believed in something so strange? To carry the guilt of my disappearance, but not be able to admit it, not even to yourself? To fear it might happen again?

"I know how this must sound," he said. "The only person I ever told was your mother." He laughed, his mouth twisting into a bitter smile. "She told her lawyer, but in court it never stood up. I'm not crazy. And I'm smart enough to know not to talk about it. And for whatever reason, your mother never pushed it. Couldn't bring herself to drive the knife in, I guess. But the thing is—"

His voice dropped, and a sudden burst of wind nearly drowned out the next thing he said.

"What did you say?" I asked sharply, not sure if I'd really heard him say what I thought. I locked eyes with him, willing him to say it. His whole body sagged with defeat as I dragged the words out of him.

"They just stopped." He seemed bewildered, lost, his hands falling to his sides as if a puppet master had suddenly cut the strings. "These last few months, the voices just stopped. It's almost as if . . . it's time. But time for what, I don't know."

A wave of unease gripped me. Michael and my father both felt some irresistible force, compelling one to guard me and the other to let me go. It couldn't be all coincidence, could it?

"They didn't even say anything when you tried to leave home. In fact, it felt like they almost wanted you to go."

I looked at my father and realized, as he stood there alone, the winds whipping about him, that he felt he'd failed me somehow.

"Thanks, Dad," I said, flinging my arms around him for a great hug. He looked down at me, surprised, as he wrapped his arms around me and patted my back.

"You're welcome, Hope." Awkwardly, as if he was afraid I would reject him again, he brought his great hand up and patted my head.

It wasn't until later, in the silence of my bedroom, that I really began to realize the implications of what he'd said.

~

I welcomed the visit to the shelter the next day; anything to distract myself. I figured between Tabitha's constant chatter and the interview itself, I would have plenty to keep me from thinking about Dad's dreams, Michael, or what any of it really meant.

By the time we got to the center, I had heard all about Tabitha's time with Tony on Friday night, as well as a vivid description of her father's sermon earlier in the morning. All the while, I kept stealing glances at the Sunday "cleaned up" Tabitha: rings and tattoos removed, face scrubbed clean, hair its normal shade and pulled back, wearing a prim sheath in sleek navy.

"I can see you," Tabitha finally threatened as we pulled into the parking lot, prompting me to hide a smile behind my gloved hand. "You're so backwards, Hope. You stare at the 'normal' girl and hang out with the freak show." She shook her head in mock disapproval. "Let's hope you do better inside," she said as she rolled her eyes.

The doors to the center were locked, and a numbered keypad, camera, and visitor's button were conspicuously visible next to the entry. We pressed the button and waited. The loudspeaker buzzed to life.

"Who to see?" a disembodied voice called out from the intercom.

"Delores Blankenship," Tabitha replied promptly. "We're Dunwoody High School students, here to interview her."

There was a long silence before the intercom crackled again. "Can you show your IDs in the camera?"

We dug in our purses and brandished them before the tiny lens.

We didn't hear the voice again, but a loud whirring signaled that the door was unlocked. We pushed our way through and entered the lobby.

The lobby filled me with hopelessness. It was windowless, lit only by long fluorescent tubes in the ceiling that gave the entire space a drab, lifeless feel. A gray steel desk was pushed up against the wall, stacks of papers spread out all over it and a steaming cup of tea as testament that someone had been there not long ago, but the desk itself was empty. Two lonely folding chairs sat in front of the desk. Everything was utilitarian and in slightly varying shades of gray or beige: the industrial linoleum flooring, the tiled wall, even the ceilings. Someone had done their best to cheer up the place, taping up posters and strategically placing plastic pots of dusty fake flowers around the room, but the attempt only underscored the drabness. A heavy door, its tiny window crisscrossed with bars, stood in one corner.

"Now what?" I asked Tabitha, but she just shrugged and started walking around, showing an inordinate amount of interest in the dated calendars and posters.

The click-clack of high heels echoed from behind the door, signaling someone's approach. We stared at the door expectantly as it swung open toward us, and we were met by a burst of color and noise.

The woman was tall and large, obviously comfortable in her own body. She'd dressed in layers of flowy knits, a mix of violets, magentas, pinks, and blues that enveloped her in warmth and light. Long chains punctuated by polished agates and stones fell in layers from her neck and jingled as she rolled through the door. The busy look was topped by a fuzzy knit beret, perilously perched on the side of her head. She overcame the entire dreary room with her presence before she'd ever opened her mouth.

"Hello, girls! I'm Delores, Street Grace's executive director. You must be Mona Carmichael's daughter?" she asked, nodding at me as, with one graceful move, she swept her reading glasses onto her nose. She did not pause for my answer. "Fantastic. I am so glad to have the opportunity to help you today. I don't know your mom, but she's a good friend of a member of our board, so I am happy to help you. I thought we'd start here, where I can give you some background information about Street Grace and tell you about the girls before we take you inside to their living quarters." She gestured to the folding chairs as she stepped behind her desk and sat down.

Tabitha nodded mutely, seemingly in awe of the energy and force that was Delores. I was just amazed that anyone had managed to get Tabitha to be quiet. We quickly took our seats as Delores launched into a speech she'd obviously given before, not that it was rote. Her passion for her cause exuded from every pore.

"Street Grace works with all sorts of women and children in need—getting them off the street, helping them prepare for employment or school. We opened our doors in 1965 and have been in service, more or less, ever since. Some of the people we serve are simply victims of homelessness. Some are runaways or women who have turned to prostitution for whatever reasons. But our recent focus has been on human trafficking—that's the work you're interested in, right?"

She paused to take a sip of her tea, the only pause since she'd started barreling through her speech. She didn't wait for us to answer before she jumped back into her story.

"In the past few years, we've seen a surge of people trafficked into Atlanta for a variety of purposes. In some cases, they've been lured from their home countries by the promise of a better life, only to find out later that they've really signed up for slavery. In other cases, they are sold by their families or outright kidnapped. In about half of all cases, the victims know the trafficker who 'recruits' them." Disgust flickered across her face as she pushed a stack of papers across her desk toward us. "I hate that term, 'recruits.' As if they had a choice."

Tabitha snatched up the papers, scanning them quickly.

"Nobody knows how many people are brought into slavery that way each year," Delores continued. "The figures are all over the place, partly because these are hidden populations and partly because our definitions are imprecise. Globally, we've heard everything from a few tens of thousands to up to thirty million men, women, and children trafficked annually. But really, nobody knows."

My eyes nearly popped out of my head to hear such great numbers.

Tabitha interrupted then. "But what about here, in Atlanta?"

Delores leaned forward, clasping her hands together. "The very things that make us a great city for trade make us perfect for human trafficking, a strong transportation system being at the top of the list. We've been listed as high as thirteenth in the world for the amount of trafficking activity in our city. Who knows how bad it really is? Our point of view is that even one person trafficked is one too many."

"What happens to them once they are here?" I ventured.

"All sorts of things, none of them wholesome," Delores admitted. "Some become domestic workers: cooking, cleaning, that kind of thing. Some do farm work or restaurant work."

"That doesn't sound so bad," Tabitha said. Delores's eyes flashed with anger.

"It doesn't sound so bad, having to work eighteen-hour days without pay? Being threatened with physical punishment, humiliation, or even worse—retribution against your family back home?"

Tabitha shifted uncomfortably in her seat, fingering her demure pearls. "I didn't mean—"

Delores slid her eyeglasses to the top of her head and sighed, closing her eyes as she sought to regain her patience. She reopened her eyes and smiled brightly, reaching across the messy desk to pat Tabitha's hand where it still rested on the stack of papers.

"No, I'm sorry, dear. Of course you didn't. You're just trying to learn. My temper just got a little away from me. There are a lot of people out there who don't see this for what it is—outright slavery. I know you meant no harm.

"And in a way, you're right. That kind of work is not the worst thing that can happen to these people. Forced prostitution or sexual slavery is the worst thing. And unfortunately, it happens frequently to the youngest and most vulnerable children who are put into this disgusting trade."

She slid another stack of papers across the desk. We held them up and realized they were photos: A black and white shot of a filthy room full of bare mattresses laid end to end so that they covered the entire floor, shackles and chains the only other visible things in the shot. A series starting with a basement trapdoor that led to a crowded room filled with girls in nothing but their underwear, their faces mercifully blurred in an ironic nod to privacy. A truck caught in some border crossing, its back opened up to show it packed with girls who stared with unseeing eyes into the flashlights wielded by their saviors. They were so . . . tiny, and not just because of their ages. Their knobby joints and their protruding ribs gave mute testament to their obvious hunger.

I could feel the sweat start to trickle down the back of my neck, felt my Mark burning into me. My nervous fingers fluttered up, touching it like a talisman to remind myself that it hadn't happened to me.

Delores's voice broke into my musing and snapped me back into reality. But instead of the voice of a confident public speaker selling her cause, I heard a voice tinged with sadness and futility.

"Ninety dollars is all it takes to buy one of these girls. Ninety. Less than the cost of an iPod. Less than the cost of a new pair of Nikes. How can anyone place so little value on a human life?"

Her voice broke, causing her to draw up short.

I tore my eyes away from the photos and caught her eyes. They were shiny, brimming with tears. But she blinked the tears away without a word and cleared her throat.

Her voice was steadier now. "You cannot underestimate what these girls have gone through. By all accounts, what they have been through is a nightmare, and many of the girls here are not sure that it is over."

I sucked in my breath, wondering how it could get any worse. "What do you mean?"

"You have to understand—most of them were terrified of their—their *owners*, for lack of a better word. To us, it might seem unfathomable that the girls didn't run away, didn't ask for help. But they were terrified. Some of them are psychologically as well as physically abused, manipulated by their pimps to believe that they are in love, and that prostituting themselves is one way of proving their love. Some are told over and over that they are not worth anything more than the horrors of "the life," as they call it, humiliated and broken down until they believe it. Many don't speak English very well and couldn't have communicated even if they had managed somehow to get away. Most of these girls are here only because someone eagle-eyed noticed them or the conditions they were living in and brought the authorities in. They live in constant fear that the system will fail them, that their owners or traffickers will find them and punish them."

She smiled a grim smile. "And sometimes, sometimes they happen to be right. When the system treats these girls like criminals, complicit in their crimes, they often get sent right back to the same sorry situation. Only now with a criminal record."

Tabitha had been silent up until now, afraid of being chastised again, but this last injustice broke through her intimidation. "That's not right!" she burst out. "Can't you stop that from happening?"

Delores just spread her arms, shrugging while smiling a knowing smile. "If the girls come to us on a prostitution bust and the DA doesn't understand the whole situation, then, no, there's nothing we can do. Except explain to the girl that we'll still be here if she can manage to get away. Again."

I looked at the picture with the mattresses again and thought of the cruelty of sending someone back to that life, especially after having raised her hopes. I offered up a silent prayer: *There but for the grace of God . . .*

"I bet they are scared," I whispered, thinking of the girls behind the heavy door.

"Like nothing else," Delores agreed. "And it spreads like wildfire. One of them gets out and the rumors start to fly. When that happens, it's all we can do to keep them here and safe. Forget about rehabilitation or training." She briskly straightened some of her papers, getting back down to business as she popped her reading glasses back to her nose. She peered at us over the rims.

"Maybe you can understand why we were reluctant to let you talk to any of them in person. But there is one girl, one who is slightly older than the others, whom we think might actually benefit from the opportunity to tell her story."

She pulled a file out of her pile and handed it to me. Tabitha kicked me under the desk, surreptitiously shooting me a sour look as she lifted the file out of my hands.

Delores tried to keep the corners of her mouth from curling up as she witnessed our exchange. "Her name is Maria Delgado. At least, that is the name she gave us and the police. She's been here for a little over a month, brought in after an FBI raid. She's been very skittish and won't give us any other information that might help her get home. We thought that she might warm to you."

I peeked into her file. "She's one of the older girls?" I asked, confused.

"Yes," Delores answered.

"But she's only fourteen!"

"Yes," Delores said in a quiet voice. "I know."

I jumped when I heard the heavy steel door slam closed behind us. Before, I'd thought it was to keep us—or any unwanted visitors who might prey on the girls—out. But after talking with Delores, I realized that to the girls, it might seem like just another way to shut them in.

The linoleum was faded and worn down from years of use. Delores led us past rows of doors down a long hall until we got to a room that had been turned into a visitation area. Deftly, Delores turned first one key and then another in the door before twisting the knob.

"You'll be locked in," she warned as she held the door open for us. "Just ring the buzzer when you're ready to go. If I don't hear from you within an hour, I'll come and check on you."

"Prison much?" Tabitha muttered under her breath. I elbowed her in the ribs.

"Thanks, Mrs. Blankenship," I said pointedly, pushing Tabitha through the doorway.

The door firmly clicked behind us, followed by the definitive snap of deadbolts falling into place. Halfway across the room, a small girl sat at a bare folding table, her hands folded primly in front of her. Two metal chairs were set up opposite.

We stared dumbly, not sure what to do. The girl blinked.

"You can sit down," she said so quietly that at first I wasn't sure she had actually spoken.

Tabitha and I looked at each other and, in silent agreement, took our seats.

We and the girl stared at one another across the table. Maria had glossy black hair that shone even under the brash light of the naked fluorescent tube above. Her skin was the soft color of caramels, stretched taut across high, graceful cheekbones. She looked fragile; it could have been the delicate bones of her hands, which she held so lightly on the table, or the way her body swam in the overwhelming folds of her donated clothes. Or maybe it was the slight shadows under her eyes. But there was a steely strength to her too, and her chocolate eyes were wary and charged with a bitterness well beyond her years.

"Mrs. Blankenship said you wanted to talk to me," she said, her English heavily accented. Almost imperceptibly, her chin lifted defiantly. "Why should I talk to you?"

Tabitha answered. "We're students, like you, and would like to feature your story in a class project."

Maria's mouth twisted. "I'm no student. And I'm not like you." She pulled her hands off the table and sat back in her chair, her eyes veiled.

I took a deep breath. This was going to be tricky. I darted Tabitha a look, silently imploring her to stay quiet while I tried. Tabitha shrugged and crossed her arms.

"Maria," I said. "Is it okay if I call you Maria?"

A look of confusion flitted across her face before she nodded.

"We want to share your story so that others know what is going on. So it won't happen to them. If that is okay with you?"

She looked at me skeptically, pulling herself into her chair. But she didn't say no. Encouraged, I continued.

"You don't have to talk about anything you don't want to. And if we can, we will help you. I'm not sure what we can do, to be honest, but we will try. I promise."

"I've heard that a lot since I came here," Maria sighed, showing tiny cracks in her mask of toughness. "Everyone here knows what is going on, but all they do is talk. No action."

"And meanwhile you're still here," I said. "That must really suck."

Her eyes widened with surprise, and then they narrowed as she sized me up. "You don't think I should be grateful?"

I gestured around the room. "It's no Hilton, I can tell you that much."

A slight grin danced across her face, and I caught my breath. When she let her guard down, she was beautiful.

"You're funny. You're also the first person to ask whether you can talk to me." She was fiddling at the buttons on her too-long sleeves now, fidgeting while she decided. Under the table I was crossing my fingers. She let her hands fall in her lap and shrugged. "Go ahead, ask your questions."

I let out my breath in relief, only then realizing I'd been holding it. Tabitha started rummaging in her backpack for her list of interview questions, but I reached across and touched her arm, stopping her. She pouted, but put the bag down, taking only her notepad and a pencil.

I looked across the table at Maria and smiled. "Why don't you just tell us about yourself and about what happened?"

Maria closed her eyes and nodded. She pulled her tiny feet up under her legs and settled even further into her seat. It was as if she was trying to make herself disappear, to hide from the memories. She started speaking without opening her eyes.

"I live just across the border from Texas, in Reynosa. You know Reynosa?"

Tabitha and I shook our heads no.

"It is a horrible place. It used to be like a war zone, but now it is dead. The cartels have taken it over. Everywhere is spies. Nothing to do if you do not help the *narcotraficantes*."

Her eyes were open now, but they were unfocused, looking only into the past.

"My mother used to have a job over the border, in McAllen. But she got sick and lost her job. And then she died."

Her eyes welled up, a solitary tear leaving a glistening trail down her golden skin. She picked absentmindedly at a scab on her hand.

"Because of the cartels they closed the bridge. Nobody could get through unless you bought off the *narcos*. My father, he had six of us to feed and no job. He hated the *narcos*; he wouldn't stoop so low. He said the Lord would provide."

We leaned in over the table when she paused.

"He was so excited. He said that someone had found me and my sister jobs working over the border as maids. They would smuggle us over. He just had to pay our way and this person and his friends would take care of the rest. We should have known it was too good to be true."

I looked at Tabitha, who nodded.

"Who was it, Maria?" Tabitha prompted softly.

"We thought he was clean," Maria spat through taut lips, her nostrils flaring with hate. "We trusted him."

"Who?" Tabitha repeated.

"*Mi tío*," she said, barely breathing the words. "My mother's younger brother."

I sucked my breath in. I heard a sharp crack and darted a look at Tabitha. She clutched the pieces of her pencil, snapped in half, in her hand.

"What happened then?" I asked, dreading what I was about to hear.

"Jimena—that's my sister—she noticed that there were only girls in the truck, but I thought it was because they were only looking for houseworkers. No man would take that job.

"We were supposed to be going to Texas, to be at our job by the time the sun was up. But the truck, it didn't stop. It just kept going. We were getting hungry and needed to stop, but they wouldn't stop. Even when we pounded on the walls, they wouldn't stop."

Her cheeks flamed red at the remembered indignity. "We had to squat in the corner and try not to soil ourselves. Jimena was so afraid she would be dirty for her new job. But I knew, then, that there was no job."

The hairs on the back of my neck stood on end. I felt trapped in the little airless room, trapped as if I were in the back of that truck with them.

"When we stopped, the man that came to get us was not the same man from Reynosa. He told us not to be afraid, that there had been a mistake, but that everything was okay now. We would get our jobs if we did not cry. He blindfolded us and took us to a big . . . shed. I don't know. It was empty and dark. Then he lined us up." Maria's voice was getting shaky. "I told Jimena not to let go of my hand, no matter what."

"Then there was a lot of noise, a lot of men talking in English. I tried, but I couldn't tell what they were saying. There were so many of them, so much shouting, all at once." She looked down at her hands. "If I had understood what they were saying then, maybe things would have turned out different."

"Don't ever think that, Maria," I whispered. "None of this is your fault."

"No?" She smiled at me, a strange, sad smile that sliced my heart through. "My mother always told me how important it was to know English. She used to make me practice every night when she came home from her job. But I stopped trying after she died."

She held my gaze as she straightened up in her chair, seeming to steel herself for what came next. My stomach clenched in anticipation.

"The men started separating us, like goats or cattle. I couldn't see; I tried to hold on to Jimena, but they were too strong. I lost her."

My heart skipped a beat.

"Maria, how old was Jimena?" I asked, unable to pull my eyes away from hers.

"Is," she answered, her eyes flashing. "Not was. She is still out there."

"How old, Maria?" Tabitha echoed.

"Ten."

Tabitha unleashed a string of curse words that in ordinary times would have made me blush. But right now, I was too stunned to care.

"After that, it didn't matter what they did to me," Maria continued in a flat voice. "Nothing mattered. I just pretended I was far away and that it was happening to someone else."

Somewhere in the back of my mind, a door opened. "Your name isn't really Maria Delgado, is it?" I asked, my voice low.

She shook her head no.

"Why won't you tell the FBI or Mrs. Blankenship your real name? Or what you told us?"

Tears welled up in Maria's eyes once again. "You don't get it. If I tell them my name and where I am from, they will send me back. And I can't go back there."

Tabitha frowned. "But why not?"

Maria gaped at us, wondering at our naïveté. "If he knew what really happened, my father would disown me. Or worse—my uncle could do it all over again. Besides, I can't leave here. Not yet."

I felt my own forehead folding into creases, puzzled. "Why not?"

Maria gripped the edge of the table and leaned in, her face intense. "Because that police raid didn't bring in my sister." My stomach sank with horror as I thought of the little girl, still out there, alone. "I have to find her before it is too late."

Maria, worn out by the retelling of her story and the effort of speaking English, collapsed back into her chair, refusing to speak any longer.

We pressed the button signaling for our release. While we waited, I tore a little slip of paper from Tabitha's notebook and scribbled my name and cell phone number on it.

"Thank you," I said, reaching across the table to press the number into Maria's hand. "If there is anything I can do, or if you ever need someone to talk to, call me."

She looked at the slip of paper with amusement. "Hope. You are just what I need now," she whispered, closing her tiny fist around the scrap. "Hope."

The locks began turning and the door swung open. When it closed again on Maria, she was still sitting in the chair, alone, clutching the paper.

seven

The next morning, I shuffled toward my locker, trying to stifle a yawn. Our interview with Maria had ignited a sense of urgency in me. I'd pored over Internet sites until long after midnight, absorbing all the information I could about her hometown and the trafficking business. Like a teller at the DMV, I mindlessly processed photo after photo, statistic after statistic, using the rote activity to keep my mind and my emotions at bay until I collapsed into my bed in exhaustion. But in my dreams—or rather, one specific dream, more like a nightmare, that I didn't want to think of right now—it was not as easy to push aside the questions that I did not want to answer. Was my father right in being so protective? Did I run from what I had thought was a prison only to find that I had run right into a trap? And what would have happened to me if Michael had not killed my kidnapper all those years ago?

Michael. The thought of him brought a complicated set of emotions right to the surface. Gratitude, surely. But resentment, too: resentment of the need to be watched, resentment of his lies, resentment and even fear of what his presence implied. And more. I blushed, not wanting to think about those other feelings.

I lifted my head and there he was, stationed at my locker. A casual observer would guess that he was lounging, but I could see the taut look of his eyes and the way his muscles seemed coiled for action. I flushed again more deeply as I took in his sleek body and thought of the warmth that had surged through my own at his touch, as well as the glimpse of physical perfection I'd had when he'd revealed himself to me.

Could it have really happened? Or was it all part of the hazy nightmares that had plagued me last night?

I smiled, nerves on edge as I began to spin my combination.

He leaned toward me nonchalantly, but his tone when he spoke was demanding. "Where were you yesterday?"

I remembered the neat stack of messages my mother had left on the kitchen counter and felt a surge of guilt, like a child who has been caught playing in her mother's makeup drawer.

"I was busy."

"Where?" he pressed. "You weren't at Tabitha's. I checked."

Indignation swelled within me, and I fumbled my combination. Frustrated, I turned to him. "You're not my father. I don't need you checking up on me."

"But it seems you do," he said, his eyes narrowing as he closed the distance between us to mere inches. "You were at home but you didn't want to be disturbed. What was so important that you couldn't talk to me, Hope?"

His stern eyes were shot through with anger. I looked away, but he gently took my chin in his fingers, forcing me to meet his gaze. "What are you hiding? Or are you just hiding from me?"

A wave of warmth began spreading from his hands, warring

with the anger that was swamping my body. Furiously, I pushed his hand away.

"Leave me alone. I don't owe you any explanations. What I do on my own time is my business, not yours." We stared each other down: him, frustrated by my vagueness, me, refusing to let him intimidate me. My cheeks were burning—whether from the lingering effects of his touch or my own fury, I wasn't sure. All I knew is that I didn't want to talk to him about Street Grace or Maria, and he couldn't push me around. The bell rang for first period and I turned to my locker with unseeing eyes. I tried my lock again with mechanical stiffness, willing him to look away. I tried the lock but it wouldn't give. I spun the numbers again—once, twice, three times—until my locker door opened. I studiously examined its contents with exaggerated interest.

Eventually, I heard him sigh. When I turned from my locker, he was gone. Out of the corner of my eye, I saw Lucas and his friends approaching. Hurriedly, I closed my own locker and headed for my class.

Why hadn't I just told Michael? As I worked over my pinch pot in art class, I turned the question over and over in my mind. Was it because I didn't want a watchdog on my tail every minute of the day? Or was I trying to build a wall to keep some distance between me and the one person who knew my deepest secret, and who knew it even better than I did? Maybe I was hiding from him after all. Or maybe I was just scared.

Frustrated, I squashed the pot with my fist. Whatever complicated reasons I had, it was going to be hard to avoid him. Our blissfully comingled schedules now loomed ahead of me like a series of traps.

The day exhausted me. In every class we shared, I diligently avoided Michael's probing eyes, pretending I could not feel them watching my every move. I hung onto each teacher's words and found endlessly fascinating tidbits of information in the footnotes of my textbooks. And I took every excuse I had to leave, running notes to the office and staying through lunch period to get extra help. But through it all, I was acutely aware of the closeness of his body.

So I was already on edge when Michael approached Tabitha and me during Contemporary Issues.

"Can I join your group?" he asked. "I was absent when we chose topics and need to catch up."

Tabitha took her time as she stacked her notebooks and folders neatly on top of each other. She crossed her hands carefully on top of the pile, examining her long black nails with feigned intensity. The new coldness between Michael and me had not been lost on her, and she was relishing putting Michael on the spot.

"You have to ask Hope," she finally said.

With that she sank back into her chair, her rows of bracelets jingling as she folded her arms across her chest. She nodded at me, letting me know it was truly up to me before skewering Michael with a look of disdain. "Go on, ask her." She crossed her feet jauntily on top of the desk and leaned back, relishing the prospect of seeing me shoot down Michael.

Michael rolled his eyes. "Fine. Hope? Can I join your group?" He flashed me that cocksure grin of his, but underneath I could see, for the first time ever, a glimpse of uncertainty. He leaned in over my desk, so close that my head swam with the scent of honey and hay that emanated from him. I took a trembling breath, unable to break his gaze.

Through the fog, my mind was screaming, *No! No! No!* Yet I couldn't bring myself to let him know how he'd gotten under my skin. How much things had changed . . . how out of balance I really was, when it came to me and him. I could barely even admit to myself that there was a part of me that was afraid of him, scared of what he was and what it meant to have him here, guarding me.

I shoved down my feelings and picked up a pen.

"Sure," I shrugged, deliberately doodling on my notebook to underscore how little I cared. "Suit yourself."

Tabitha's brow wrinkled. This was not what she'd expected. She dropped her feet to the ground. "You can't change our topic," she stated flatly, challenging Michael. "We're already too far into it."

Michael held up his hands in protest, his eyes twinkling. "Of course not. It wouldn't help me catch up if we had to start from scratch, would it?" He pulled his desk over to ours and straddled his chair. I noticed the ripple of his thighs and felt myself weaken.

"What are we writing about?" Michael asked.

"Human trafficking," Tabitha said, pushing some papers toward him. "Here's our outline and some notes I made from our interview yesterday."

Michael peered at the pages, swiftly turning them as he scanned with machinelike speed.

"You talked with an actual victim?" He lifted his head and fixed me with his gaze, boring his eyes into mine. I squirmed in my seat.

Tabitha answered for me. "She'd been kidnapped and sold as a sex slave. Her sister is still out there somewhere, probably in Atlanta."

Michael drew his lips tightly together, never breaking his gaze. "I see," he said softly. "So this is what you were doing last night. You were doing more research, weren't you?"

Tabitha didn't notice that this admission seemed significant to Michael. Instead, she squealed with glee and dove into my stack of papers. "You did more research, Hope? Let me see!"

In her enthusiasm, Tabitha kept up a running monologue, only pausing momentarily to get Michael and I to agree to her latest plans for completing the project. We agreed automatically, our eyes locked on one another's, knowing that our conversation was not over.

~

As much as I wasn't crazy about being trapped in a small car with Michael, I desperately wanted him to believe me when I said it was no big deal, that nothing was going on. He'd know I was lying if I willingly climbed the steps into the clutches of Bus Boy and his minions. So into the Charger I went, just like usual, to ride home with him after school. Before we'd even left the parking lot, I knew it was a bad decision.

"Don't you think it's a little funny?" Michael demanded, slamming the car door shut behind him with a hollow metallic thud. He didn't wait for my answer. "Of all the topics in the world, you picked the one that would dredge up your own past."

Michael's knuckles were white on the steering wheel, his anger barely in control. The car lurched forward as he put it into gear. I shrank into my seat, wishing—not for the first time—for the reassurance of a seat belt.

My chin lifted defiantly. "Tabitha picked the topic. It's just a coincidence. Besides, what happened to Maria isn't at all like what happened to me."

"Is that so?" he demanded, darting me a glance. "Then why wouldn't you tell me about it?"

I blushed, knowing he'd pinpointed the source of my own confusion. "I don't know."

"You *do* know!" he shouted, slamming his hand on the wheel.

"You know it feels wrong, is wrong. With everything that is going on, the last thing you need to be doing is putting yourself in more danger!"

"Maybe I just need to understand what could have happened if—"

"If what?" he interrupted tersely. "If I hadn't been there to stop that man? Do you really need to put yourself through that?"

I wheeled on him, not bothering to hide the fury that shook my voice.

"It's easy for you to say—you wiped him out and then put me from your mind for over eleven years. Did you ever stop to think what it was like for me, all those years? It broke up my parents' marriage, Michael. More than anything else, it defined my identity, and I can't even remember it!"

My words hung in the air.

"I didn't," he whispered gruffly, breaking the stillness.

"Didn't what?"

"Push you from my mind. Not ever."

I sucked my breath in, not sure what to say.

We rode the rest of the way home in silence, the only sound the occasional tick-tock of Michael's blinker. When he'd pulled into my driveway, he put the car into park and shook his head as if to clear it.

"Understanding this other girl won't help you remember, Hope," Michael finally said, his voice weary. "It won't change what happened."

I fumbled for the right words, all my anger gone. "I know it won't. But maybe if I can tell her story, it will help me put aside mine."

He leaned his head back and rubbed his eyes. "I don't like it."

I felt a flicker of annoyance. "Why, Michael? Why? Because you have some 'feeling' that I am in danger? But from what, God only knows. God doesn't even want you here to protect me, you said it yourself. And Henri has been totally silent. You know he wouldn't do that if I was in trouble."

Michael scoffed at my logic. "Henri's behavior means nothing. He's just pouting, trying to prove a point."

"He wouldn't do that," I pressed on. "And you know it. Even my father said that he feels I am meant to be here."

"You spoke with your father?" he asked, bolting upright and looking at me in surprise.

I nodded, trying to bury the sense of unease and inevitability that my father's admission had created in me. I ventured a smile, trying to soothe away Michael's concerns and my own fears. "You see, it makes no sense. I have nothing to be afraid of." I was arguing as much for my benefit as for his.

"I know," he said, sagging back into his seat and closing his eyes. He was as still as a statue, worry etching sharp lines into his face.

Emboldened by his admission, I unbuckled my seat belt and turned to him, brushing my fingers against his. "You don't have to protect me from my own emotions. And a research paper isn't going to put me in any physical danger," I cajoled. "I'm not saying I have to, but even if I go back to the Center, it's like Fort Knox. Nothing could get me there."

He took my hand in his and sighed. I felt a thrill. Whether it was from knowing I was winning the argument, or from the sheer pleasure of his touch, I wasn't sure.

"Promise me you won't go back there," he said quietly. "At least not without me. That's the only thing I ask."

As the warmth of his touch spread from my fingers, I gave his hand a squeeze. "I promise."

He opened his eyes then and looked at me. "That's all I can ask," he said, a sad, peculiar smile coming to his full lips. Squeezing my hand back, he released me.

~

My mother was waiting for me when I came through the door. She eyed the clock as she carefully wiped a dish.

"Seems you two had an awful lot to talk about," she said with studied indifference.

I chose my words carefully as I plopped my backpack on a counter stool. "He missed a lot of school last week. I needed to catch him up."

"Is that why he called you last night?" she asked, pointedly staring at the pile of messages still on the counter.

I swept them up and threw them in the trash, shrugging. "I guess so."

She tried to hide her grin. "He never struck me as the studious type."

I blushed. Why was I blushing all the time whenever the topic of Michael came up? Just asking the question made me blush even more deeply.

"It's not like that," I protested, the words feeling wrong on my lips, choosing that moment to dive back into my backpack.

"Like what?" flashed Mom, whom I could still see out of the corner of my eye, her grin ever widening. Then she seemed to take pity on me, changing the subject.

"You never told me how your interview went," she opened.

I pulled out my agenda and perched myself on a stool. She continued to wipe and put away dishes, waiting for my answer.

"It went well, Mom," I said, reaching for a pear out of the fruit bowl. "Thanks for setting it up."

"That's not why I'm asking, Hope, and you know it," she said, her watchful eyes on me even while staying in perpetual motion. "How are you feeling?"

I rolled my eyes. "Not you too." I didn't even bother trying to hide my exasperation as I rolled the pear around in my hands.

She stopped in her tracks, arching one brow in surprise. "You told Michael?"

Oops. I clamped my mouth shut and simply shrugged.

She skewered me with her stare. "When did this happen?"

"I dunno," I mumbled.

I could see the wheels turning in her mind as she reappraised the situation. Slowly, she nodded. "That's what you were talking about in the driveway." It was a statement, not a question.

I nodded dumbly. Her face was a mask as I waited for her reaction.

Slowly, she nodded. "That's good," she said, approvingly. She started rubbing at a dirty spot on a dish. I sighed with relief, thinking I was off the hook, but she spoke again. "You still haven't answered my original question."

"I'm fine," I said tersely, choosing that moment to bite into the pear. "I'm tired of talking about it. It's just a research paper," I continued, my mouth full.

The pear was juicy, and I slurped just enough to annoy Mom with my bad manners. She playfully swatted at me with her dishtowel.

"Stop that," she said, crossing her arms against my attempt at distraction. She pinned me with one of her patented hairy eyeball stares, refusing to give up the issue.

"Do your clients run away screaming in fear when you stare at them like that?" I demanded.

Frustrated, she sighed. "You're impossible. Well, I expect you to talk with me if it raises any issues," she commanded.

"Sheesh, between you and Michael I might as well give up on my education and lock myself away for the rest of my life," I shot back, keeping the tone light. I took one last bite of the pear before tossing the core into the bin. "I'm going up to study now." I jumped off the stool and kissed her on the cheek.

She wiped the sloppy kiss off with a look of dismay and rubbed her hands on the dishtowel. "I guess I have more in common with that boy than I thought. Off with you, then. But I mean it, missy." She shook the towel at me as she spoke. "Any flashbacks, any nightmares, anything at all, you tell me. Got it?"

"Got it," I called over my shoulder as I climbed the stairs, relieved that she would never know the truth.

I hurried to my room and closed the door firmly behind me. I leaned against it and slid down until I was sitting huddled on the floor. Would it change anything if Michael and Mom knew about my nightmare from this morning?

I turned the question over in my mind, forcing myself to go through the nightmare I'd been avoiding thinking about all day.

The dream had been confused. But it was just a dream. I was sure of it. It was full of images from Maria's story, some of them things I had never even seen for myself, some of them pictures I recognized from my Internet searches. Hungry children with big brown eyes crowding me on the streets of Reynosa. A hot, stifling truck, the air heavy with fear. Maria lined up to be inspected by a bunch of thugs, her sister clinging to her and then brutally torn away. Maria chained to a wall. And then me in her place.

But that had never happened, I reminded myself. And nothing in my dream—nothing—seemed like a buried memory clawing its way back to the surface.

It was just a dream, I said, looking at my shaking hands, willing them to stop. Just a dream.

~

I kept telling myself that in the weeks that followed, because the dream never stopped. Every night I found myself riding beside Maria on her fearsome journey from Mexico. And every night something new and insidious wove itself into the fabric of the dream, until the line between Maria and me, the difference between her story and mine, became tenuous.

As the truck pulled away from Reynosa and she leaned outside to wave goodbye to her hopeful father, I saw my father.

When her little sister turned up her face, sobbing with grief as the men pulled her away, it was my face.

As the crowd of men pressed against her, inspecting her like cattle, I recognized their eyes. I just could not place them. And then they would dissolve in a rush of wings and wind. I would feel myself flying and begin to believe that I was free, only to falter, plunging faster and faster toward the ground until I woke up in a sweat.

Night after night, I could not escape her story. My fear that something was terribly wrong, that somehow our fates were interwoven, began to mount.

I mostly escaped my mother's vigilant eyes. She had begun traveling again, and was preoccupied with a big merger project. But I could not hide the shadows under my eyes from Michael—or from Tabitha.

"Someone's been burning the midnight oil again," she commented drily as I stumbled into class and sat down next to her. Our appearances were a study in contrasts. I'd barely managed to crawl out of my bed, throwing on sweats and wrapping a long scarf around my neck. My hair was lank, its ends tucked into the scarf, carefully hiding the symbol on my neck. She, on the other hand, had carefully swept her hair into a spiky fauxhawk, complete with hot pink extensions down her back, which she had matched to her fingernails, eye shadow, and shoes. The pink stood out against her dark skin, drawing even more attention to her getup. It was ridiculously awe-inspiring.

"No time to shower," I mumbled under the noise of the teacher's lecture as I hunched into my chair. I could feel Michael's stare burning into my back. I reached up and smoothed my hair against my neck, as if somehow he could see through the wall of hair to my Mark.

Tabitha wrinkled her nose. "I didn't need to know that," she muttered back at me.

"Ladies, something you'd like to share with us?" Mr. Bennett hovered between our desks.

"We were just discussing our research paper, sir," Tabitha countered smoothly as the class snickered.

"I was just saying that I'd graded your interim submissions. Yours is good, but you still have some work to do," he intoned, sliding our paper off the top of his pile.

The class laughed as Tabitha eagerly snatched the paper and then sagged with disappointment as she began to read his notes.

"You all do." The teacher skewered the class with a withering glare. Everyone fell silent. He resumed walking the aisles, handing out papers as he went.

"You only have one week left before your final submissions. I suggest you take my feedback very seriously and focus on it during these last days. Failure to address this feedback will lower your score by a full grade."

The class groaned and Bennett smiled with spiteful glee.

"Because I am a nice man, I will give you the rest of this period to regroup. Now go to it."

Grumbling, the class soon broke apart, the noise of scraping chairs and conversation overwhelming the room.

I huddled over Tabitha. "What did he say?"

She held the pages out to me. "See for yourself."

I took the paper and began reading the chicken scratches of red ink he'd left across the front page. I was vaguely aware of Michael reading over my shoulder.

"There's a lot, but it's doable," I said, wondering where I'd get the energy to tackle all the additional research and revisions our teacher had suggested.

"There's more," Tabitha said glumly, turning the paper over. The entire back page was a sea of red. "But we can't do any of this without talking to Maria again."

"No way," Michael interjected sternly.

We both turned to face him. In the days and weeks since our talk, Michael and I had commenced a careful dance. Outwardly, everything was the same. We still spent most of our classes and lunch together; he still drove me home every day after school. But our conversations were stilted, as if he was afraid to say too much; it seemed as if an invisible force field kept him from getting too close to me. And I found it easier that way, even if the distance between us was sometimes painful. For as much as I relied on Michael's solid presence and the protection it seemed to offer, I was equally afraid of him now, and my dark, often sleepless nights had only made me more cautious. Somehow I knew that it would be best to keep the secret of my dreams from him.

I even welcomed his discreet, periodic absences. He couldn't hide the agony his disobedience to God was causing him any longer. I recognized it in the whiteness of his knuckles when he gripped the edge of his desk; the restless pacing as he waited for my slow, human body to catch up to him on the walk to his car; the grinding of his teeth as he muscled through his endless migraines. It racked me with guilt to think of him in constant pain—and to think of the people who needed him, the people who he was leaving out there to struggle, all because of me. His strain mounted and mounted until, in his most private moments, when he didn't think I was looking, he would let down his guard; then it seemed to rack his body in spasms of agony.

Only when he had reached that point would he allow himself to disappear, sometimes for days.

When he was gone, I was grateful that his pain would be lessened, feeling guilty at the role I played in his misery. I left unsaid my thanks for feeling that, just for a moment, I could breathe again. While I waited for him—and I did wait, cursing myself as I did so—I pored over the newspapers, searching for another unlikely story of rescue and redemption somewhere halfway around the world, happy for the distraction from my own worries and the feeling of Lucas's eyes, ever watchful while Michael was gone.

As far as the research paper had gone, Michael had simply followed Tabitha's instructions and tagged along, adding his contributions during the days when he was in school. As long as he didn't see any threat to my safety, he'd kept quiet. So his comment took Tabitha by surprise.

But not me. As soon as I knew what we had to do, I remembered his concerns and my promise not to go back to the shelter. I'd braced myself for his protest. But what I hadn't been prepared for was the closeness of his body, the heat I could almost feel rolling from him in waves, the catch of my heart as he voiced his concern. I leaned against the desk and took a deep breath.

"It's the only way," I said calmly, searching his eyes, willing him to understand. "We can't answer any of Bennett's questions unless we ask her directly."

He held out his hand. I passed him the papers so he could scan the comments himself.

"We'll just make it up then," he said dismissively, thrusting the papers back at Tabitha.

She looked at him in wide-eyed horror. "You can't just make up a research paper. That's *cheating*. It goes against the scholarly ethic."

"I'm just dumb muscle," he retorted, squaring off against her, arms crossed as if daring her to defy him. "I don't really care about the scholarly ethic."

Tabitha stood up, her patent platform boots bringing her eye to eye with Michael. "You listen to me," she started, pointing a finger at him.

"Hey, no need for that," I said, stepping quickly between them to interrupt her diatribe. I looked hurriedly over my shoulder to make sure Mr. Bennett was not listening in before continuing in a low voice. "We need these answers, Michael, and we need to get them the right way. But there's more than one way to do it."

"Yeah. If you don't want to go down there, we'll just do it ourselves," Tabitha interjected.

A vein throbbed in Michael's forehead. "No way. If you go, I'm going with you."

"What's wrong with you? First you don't want to go at all, now you insist on going? What, are you afraid you aren't going to get enough credit? Or do you just want to keep Hope all to yourself, keep her under your thumb?" Tabitha was gesturing wildly, her fauxhawk shaking with every move.

Michael's face burned with anger, but before he could respond, Tabitha continued. "Well, guess what? It doesn't matter what you want. Mrs. Blankenship said no men at the Center. Period." She crossed her arms in a mirror image of him and jutted out her hip, mentally declaring the case closed. "You heard her share the rules, Hope," Tabitha continued, goading Michael with her confidence. "Back me up."

I stared at the ground. When I'd made my promise to Michael, I'd conveniently forgotten about that one little rule.

"She's telling the truth," I mumbled, my hand straying to the back of my neck.

I raised my head, willing myself to meet his gaze. His eyes blazed with fury.

"Then you can't—" he began.

"We can call her," I blurted out.

My interruption stopped him short.

"What?" Tabitha asked.

"We don't have to physically go to the Center to talk to her. The Center has phones. We can just ask to speak to her on the phone."

Tabitha looked skeptical. "What if she doesn't want to?"

I cut her off, impatiently waving my hand. "Her English was great, and it's not like she's going to be out somewhere. They keep her there all the time under lock and key. All we have to do is call Mrs. Blankenship to set it up."

My logic was impeccable. I sat on the top of my desk, waiting for them to agree.

Tabitha was annoyed. She looked at our paper, now crumpled in her fist, and shoved it into a folder.

"Fine. But we're doing it right after school, because if this doesn't work, we have no other choice but to go down there." She glared at Michael. "Alone."

~

Michael and Tabitha huddled around me, oblivious to the bustle of the hallways, as I listened to the interminable ringing on the other end of the line.

"Why don't they pick up?" Tabitha breathed, tapping her foot with impatience.

"They probably don't have a full-time receptionist. It's a non-profit, remember?" I reminded her.

Finally someone picked up and transferred me to Mrs. Blankenship. I repeated the carefully rehearsed lines, promising to keep our phone call with Maria short if she would approve it. But then she responded, and my brow furrowed as my blood ran cold at what she was saying.

"I see," I said when she was done. "Well, thank you anyway, Mrs. Blankenship. And let me know if anything changes."

I closed my cell phone.

"See!" Tabitha was already crowing with triumph. "She wouldn't allow it. We're going to have to go down there after all."

"No, that's not it," I said slowly, still absorbing the news as the pit of foreboding in my stomach began to grow. "We can't talk to Maria, even if we go in person. She isn't there. She's disappeared from the Center."

eight

"We can't do nothing," I pleaded again, trying ineffectually to block Michael's access to his locker. "Please, hear me out."

It had been three days since we'd learned the news of Maria's disappearance. Tabitha argued that there was nothing we could do that the police couldn't, and was busy devising a new strategy for completing our paper. But I was still focused on finding Maria.

Michael sighed. Gently, he picked me up by the shoulders and moved me aside.

Ignoring the flush I could feel forming on my skin under the thin tissue of my T-shirt—the flush that always came when he touched me—I pressed on as he slowly opened the door and started stacking his books on the shelf.

"She told me she was going to find her sister. You know that means she is somewhere out on the street. Or worse."

"I know, Hope. But we have no way of finding her."

"We can go look for her!" Tears welled in my eyes. I couldn't stand feeling so helpless.

Michael turned and tilted my chin in his hand. I closed my eyes, trying to blink away the tears, but one lonely drop managed to trickle down my cheek. He wiped it away, his rough, hot fingertip leaving its own trail.

"I already have one errant girl to look after," he said gruffly, his voice low. "How could I possibly take on another?"

His words stung. The last thing I wanted to be was a burden to him. My eyes flew open as I began to protest, but before I could say anything, we were interrupted.

"Trouble in paradise?"

We both swung our heads to find Lucas, dressed to leave, strolling down the locker bay. Usually, Michael's watchful eyes kept Lucas far away from me, but today he'd taken advantage of our distraction. My cheeks were still burning with shame and anger at Michael's words. I pushed him away, wiping my face against my sleeve, hoping Lucas hadn't seen me cry.

"Why is it that whenever I see you two, there always seems to be some drama?" Lucas purred smoothly, moving closer. "I have to say, Michael, things always seemed much better for Hope when you were away. Wouldn't you agree, Hope?"

I stared silently at him, willing him to shut up.

"Has he been bothering you when I'm not here, Hope?" Michael addressed his question to me, but his black look was meant only for Lucas. Anyone else would have withered under its intensity, but Lucas just laughed it off.

"We just had some fun, didn't we Hopie?" I winced to hear my family's pet name for me on his lips.

"What's this?" he asked. I followed his gaze down to where I still clutched my scrawled notes that detailed everything I knew about Maria and her disappearance. Swiftly, he snatched it from my hands.

"Interesting," he drawled, artfully dodging my attempt to grab the paper back as he flipped through the pages, reading my notes. "A missing person. And not just any person—a lost little girl."

He shot Michael a speculative look, twirling the papers around in his hands, almost taunting Michael. Michael hung back, on edge, but seeming to hesitate. I wondered why he wasn't helping me get my notes back. He seemed reluctant to touch Lucas at all.

Lucas trapped my notes between his hands, looking vaguely disappointed that his attempt to provoke Michael had failed.

"Sorry I can't help you on this one," he said coolly, never taking his eyes off of Michael as he handed me back my precious information. "I can tell it has upset you."

Confused by his kindness, I mumbled a hasty thank-you and reached out to take the papers. As I did, Lucas clasped his hand over mine and turned his attention to me. Unconsciously, I shrank away from him, my hand drifting in its nervousness to cover my neck.

He laughed again. "Didn't think I had any emotions in me, eh, Hope? Even I can muster up some sympathy on occasion." He released my hand. I snatched it away and quickly put the pages back safely in my book bag. Lucas smirked to see me so discomfited. Satisfied, he twirled on his heel. "Good luck. I hope you find her," he offered over his shoulder as he walked away.

I stared after him, baffled by our exchange.

"Why does he always just turn up like that?" I muttered.

Michael's eyes were full of suspicion. "What do you mean, always?"

I cursed myself for the gaffe. Michael didn't need to know the kind of attention Lucas paid to me when Michael wasn't around. He had enough on his mind.

"Nothing," I said hastily, looking for some way to turn the conversation to my advantage. "At least he seemed to understand how important this is to me." The accusing tone in my voice was unmistakable.

Michael's jaw tightened. Barely controlling himself, he slammed his fist into his locker. When he pulled away, I could see the imprint of his knuckles in the buckled metal.

Knees trembling, I stepped backwards. Hastily, I pulled my fleece over my head. "If you can't control yourself, I think I'll walk home."

Before he could respond, I began making my way toward the exit, moving deliberately so that he wouldn't ever think I was afraid.

~

The March wind had turned biting. I pulled the collar of my fleece closer to me and eyed the sun, hanging low on the horizon, as I turned onto the dirty sidewalk.

It was a mere five miles home. I could easily cover that distance before sunset if I ran. Luckily, I didn't have many books to carry home tonight.

My books.

I groaned. In my haste to get away from Michael, I'd dropped my backpack in the locker bay. I looked at my watch and then again at the sky. The wind surged about me, whipping my hair around my head like a tornado, as if it were daring me to test my luck.

I thought of my homework and my phone, deserted in the school. Grudgingly, I turned back toward the building and began walking.

It seemed to take twice as long to cover the distance back to the school. The wind continued to fight me, seemingly coming from every direction, my hair becoming a nuisance as it flew into my face.

Of course I'd left my hat in the bag. Grimacing, I rummaged in my jacket pockets for anything to keep my hair out of my way, but I came up empty handed. The wind shrieked, and I dug my hands deeper into the pockets, trying to hurry myself along.

As the school came into view, a lone gray car with tinted windows slinked up to the stop sign in front of me and waited. It didn't signal. Nor did it pull away, even though there were no cars to stop its progress. As I came closer, the passenger window rolled down.

"I bet you came back for this," a smooth voice called out from inside the car.

Cautiously, I bent over and peered inside. There on the passenger seat sat my backpack. In the driver's seat was Lucas.

"Let me give you a ride home," he said, straining to be heard over the rumble of his engine and the roar of the wind. "You don't want to be walking home in this weather."

As if on cue, a crack of lightning shook the sky.

I looked over my shoulder at the massive gray clouds. Resigned, I reached for the door handle and eased myself into the car, asking, "How did you get my bag?"

Lucas slid my backpack down to the floor, at my feet. He smiled, showing a row of perfectly straight, white teeth.

"Would you believe me if I said I saw it when I went back to apologize to Michael?"

My eyes narrowed. "You did no such thing."

Lucas laughed and shrugged. "There's no love lost between me and Michael. That doesn't mean you and I can't be friends." He pushed a button, and the window next to me quietly closed back up.

Then, his eyes never leaving mine, he reached across my chest and pulled the seat belt forward, clicking it firmly into place. His gloved hand trailed up the belt to where it had trapped my wayward hair. He fingered it appreciatively.

I froze.

"I have to make sure you're safe and comfortable, if I'm to see you home," he said softly, loosening my hair from under the belt. He let the hair cascade through his fingers, brushing my collar away to expose my neck.

My heart was thudding so loud, I was certain he could hear it.

"When the wind caught your hair out there, it was like a corona, you know. The sun caught it for just a moment and it shone. Beautiful."

I turned to see if I could get the door open, but as I did so, with a steady, practiced hand, he deftly tucked my hair behind my ear and slid his hand down the back of my neck.

Instinctively, I pulled away, but not before I saw and heard the sharp intake of his breath. His hand stopped right over my Mark, tightening his hold.

"What's this?" he asked sharply.

When I didn't answer, he firmly gripped the base of my skull and gently pushed my face away, exposing the back of my head. With his other hand, he pushed down the collar of my fleece, giving him a full view of my neck.

I lunged back, pushing him away and swinging for his face. "Get your hands off of me, Lucas."

He leaned back in his seat, arms and palms up in a declaration of innocence, a bemused expression on his face as he easily deflected my useless blows. But there was a dark glint in his eye and his voice was rough when he next spoke.

"I can see what Michael sees in you now, Hope." He laughed, a cold, hard sound that made me shudder.

I scrabbled at the seat belt and then the door handle, desperate to get out. I stumbled away from the car, grabbing for my backpack at the last minute. Lucas made no move to stop me, leaving me to run into the falling darkness as the first rain began to come down.

nine

My cell phone rang that night, jarring me awake from a fitful sleep.

I looked at the clock glowing beside my bed. Two a.m. I groaned. It was probably a prank call or a wrong number, but it just might be my mother calling from overseas.

I swatted around my nightstand, trying to find the phone amid the tangle of teenage detritus. I knocked over the clock and a vase of flowers my mother's cleaning lady had placed in a vain effort to "prettify" my room.

There, under a book, I spied the phone, quivering with energy as it rang and rang.

I scrambled to answer it. "Hello?" I croaked. But all I heard was silence. It had rolled to voice mail.

Annoyed, I looked for the number, but it showed up as "not available." Just then, the phone jumped to life in my hand. Quickly, I pressed the tiny green button.

"Hello?" I demanded again, this time more awake as I sat up, pushing the hair out of my eyes.

"Hope?" The voice on the other end sounded tinny and far away. "Hope, is that you?"

"Who is this?" I stifled a yawn.

There was a long pause. "It's me. Maria."

I jolted awake with a rush of adrenaline, words and relief pouring out of me. "Maria? Are you okay? I've been so worried. Where are you?"

"I went for my sister, like I told you."

"Did you find her?"

"I did, but I need your help."

"What kind of help?"

There was another pause. "She has a broken leg and broken ribs. She cannot walk. I need you to come and get us."

My heart seemed lodged in my throat. "Where?"

"I'm not sure," she whispered. "I was by a big . . . how do you call it? *Camposanto*? You know, with the dead people?"

"A cemetery?"

"Sí, a cemetery. Very old. And we are hiding in a big neighborhood, lots of old houses. But the building we are in, it is not a house. It is like a factory. It is broken. Everything in it is dirty and broken. Other broken houses, too."

I racked my brain, but being new to Atlanta myself, nothing rang a bell.

"Is there anything else nearby? Any landmark?"

The silence on the other end grew as she thought. In the background, I began to hear the distinct rumbling of a train.

"Maria, is that the MARTA?"

"I don't know. What is MARTA?" she answered.

"The noise—that machine that I am hearing—is there a train nearby?"

"*Sí*," she said, lapsing into Spanish in her excitement. "*Muchos trenes cada hora*."

I heard a noise on the line from somewhere near her.

"I have to go, Hope," she whispered, a note of panic creeping into her voice. "You will come tonight?"

"I . . . yes. I will find you tonight. Watch for me. I will have my phone on."

"You will find us, Hope, I know it." Her whispered confidence heartened me.

I threw down the phone and went to my computer. A quick search turned up Oakland Cemetery. Apparently it was one of the largest cemeteries in Atlanta and extremely old, dating from before the Civil War. But the neighborhood next to it—Oakland—was far too small to be the place Maria had mentioned. Buried deeper in the text was a mention of a tornado that had ripped through Atlanta and damaged the cemetery. I clicked on that link.

My eyes raced through the text. Bingo. Cabbagetown, a historic district that had grown up around an old mill, was right next to the cemetery and had suffered extensive damage during the tornado, some of it still not repaired. Rail lines—including the MARTA commuter rail—ran along the north of the neighborhood. It had to be the spot. I jotted down the address of the cemetery entrance. It would be enough to navigate my way to the neighborhood.

Not stopping to think how I would find Maria and Jimena amid all the wreckage, I threw on some running pants and my fleece, and I tucked my hair under a baseball cap. I flew down the stairs, stopping in the kitchen to grab Ace bandages, gauze, and ice packs, and then I headed into the garage.

My mom's car, almost her only self-indulgence, sat waiting for her return. I looked at the industrial clock mounted to the garage wall. Two-thirty. I didn't have much time. Without thinking twice, I tossed my makeshift medical supplies into the front seat. Then I shimmied past the car to the tool shelf and reached behind the coffee can of nails to where Mom's spare set of keys hung.

She would never know I'd used it, I told myself as I wrapped my fingers around the key. But my stomach gave a queasy lurch when I came to the driver's side door.

I paused, unsure if what I was about to do was such a good idea.

Go. Henri's urgent voice whispered in my head. That voice, silent for all this time, was all I needed to prod me on.

Climbing behind the wheel, I scanned the dashboard. It was a lot more complicated than my dad's, full of bells and whistles I didn't know how to use.

"Wish me luck," I said softly to no one, hoping that the weeks that had passed since I'd last gone driving for "emergency preparedness" with my dad hadn't made me rusty. I turned the key in the ignition, and the engine roared to life. Slowly, I eased the Audi out of the garage, praying that Mrs. Bibeau was not a night owl. I punched the address into my mom's GPS as I inched out of the driveway, and I accelerated past the neighbors.

I had to get to Maria and her sister before it was too late.

The roads were nearly deserted, my only company the big rigs hauling their freight like the dependable army they were. I sailed through the 400 toll and into downtown, quickly finding the GPS steering me toward unfamiliar territory.

Out of the restaurants, liquor stores, and pawn shops, a clearing spotted with trees and rocks suddenly emerged. Across from it, etched against the night sky, loomed the white granite arches of the Oakland Cemetery.

I pulled the car over and parked. I was close, but in the middle of the city, it wasn't obvious where Cabbagetown lay. I cursed myself for not bringing a map with me.

I swung one leg out the door and then, with a second thought, opened up the glove compartment. *Good old Mom,* I thought as I spied the flashlight. *Always prepared.* Sliding from the car, I looked around again for any sign of an old factory, but nothing stood out. Maybe I'd notice something from inside the cemetery, I thought. I darted across the street, the slender beam of light from the flashlight my only guide.

The iron jaws of the gate were closed against intruders. I pushed at them, hoping they might be loose, but they just clanged in protest, refusing me entry. Along the brick wall, however, I found a foothold and managed to shimmy up and over. A short jump found me inside the graveyard.

A paved path rose before me, leading straight uphill through row upon row of grave markers and trees. I began to climb the rise, clutching my fleece about me. The monuments seemed to press in on me, a swarming thicket of marble and granite. I tried to ignore them but their eerie forms demanded my attention. These were no simple slabs. Tree trunks, effigies, baby lambs, artfully draped sheets and flags, Roman figures holding emblems of salvation and remembrance: all of them sparkled in the moonlight, the sheen of spent rain lending mystery to the stone, the glance of my flashlight's beam making them dance. Angels, wings spread over their dead in one last gesture of protection, mingled with the rest. I turned my collar up and continued on.

I broached the crest and gasped. From the top of the hill, I had an uninterrupted view of the cemetery, fields of graves falling away from me and spreading out at my feet like a patchwork quilt of stone. The ghostly fingers of trees, leaves long taken by the trespasses of winter, reached up into the sky, guiding my gaze to where monumental spires mingled with the skyscrapers of downtown Atlanta.

"A city of the dead," I whispered in awe. I couldn't help but feel an intruder.

I turned around, shining my meager light. A solitary train whistle split the night and I wheeled toward it eagerly. There, outlined against the moon, rose two smokestacks.

It took only a few minutes to navigate my way back to the car and then around the block to where Cabbagetown lay nestled into the city. I turned into a narrow street and pulled over. The streets were close, their tidy, plain box houses pressing right to the curb with barely any space between them. I didn't want to attract attention by driving through. I would be better off on foot, I thought, turning the engine off. The headlights extinguished themselves and the night seemed to settle even deeper into its quiet. In the moonlight, the dark pavement shone, slick from the rain that had swept through the city. I stashed all the medical supplies in my pockets. Then, flashlight in hand, I set out into Cabbagetown.

The sameness of the buildings here gave away their origin as mill town row houses. But as the neighborhood had gentrified, residents had tried to put their own individual stamp on things. Here and there, crazy artistry burst forth: sculptures forged from odds and ends that others would call junk, funky kaleidoscopes, aggressive murals that dared you to look again, gardens crisscrossed by fountains and arches and pathways that tumbled into the yards of neighbors who always seemed so close.

It would be hard to hide a secret in a neighborhood like this, I thought, with everyone on top of one another.

I shivered as a gust of wind tore through the deserted street, and I pulled my fleece closer. As I passed under a lonely streetlight, I caught a glimpse of my shadow, misshapen and lumpy from all of the things I carried with me. Unsettled, I walked faster, straining to find a building that did not look like a house or anything that looked like the aftermath of a storm.

I turned a corner, and suddenly the mill emerged, lurking beyond the row of homes. I ran toward it. As I drew closer to the dark shape, I began to make out its outline. It was not a monolithic building but a compound of sorts, bookended by two large brick structures. Fences surrounded it, gating in the buildings to protect the fancy condos that had claimed them.

My heart fell. I leaned against the fence, twining my fingers through the chain link and shaking it in frustration. This couldn't be the place. The parking lot was lushly landscaped and full of fancy cars. A pool, closed for the winter, radiated a turquoise blue. Here and there, in the dark expanses of brick, lonely lights twinkled in windows.

She'd said it was in ruins. Where else could they be?

But then, in the shadows of one of the factories, something caught my eye. A two-story warehouse or machine shed—one of the few mill buildings that had not been converted into condos—rose ahead of me, its entire roof collapsed in on one side. Even in the dark, I could see the rusted hulk of machinery inside of it. I heard the sounds of an express train rolling through town behind the factory and knew Maria and her sister had to be inside.

I rattled the chain-link fence. How to get inside? I had no better idea than to walk the length of it, hoping for a break big enough for me to slide through. Instead, I found a back entrance that someone had left open, allowing me to walk right through.

I moved in closer to the abandoned building. Supporting arches made of concrete stood skeletal in the night, leading to what seemed like the old entrance. Above me I saw grimy windows with cracked panes, but they were too high up to allow anyone to get in, let alone for someone with broken bones to get out. With the beam of the flashlight as my guide, I picked my way around broken glass, pieces of brick, and empty cans until I found two big doors. The handles were draped in chains, the padlock binding them conspicuously dangling open. A huge sign leaned up against the outer wall, screaming "Danger" in neon orange.

No kidding, I thought to myself. Moving silently, I pushed the door handle and let it swing open.

The beam of my flashlight caught dust motes as I walked in. It was like a cavern inside. Naked, rusting bolts studded the steel walls, and row upon row of abandoned machines strung together with cables and wire stood silent guard. The floor beneath me creaked as I stepped forward, turning in circles to scan the entire room.

"Maria?" I whispered. "Are you here?"

My question echoed back to me. Nothing.

Cautiously, I moved forward. A heavy rubber curtain—the kind that, as a child, seemed to smother our windshield and bury us in soap when we went through the car wash—covered the entrance to another part of the building. Grease and dust coated the rubber. Setting aside my squeamishness, I pushed through its fringe and stepped into the next room.

I was at the bottom of a decrepit metal staircase, a large expanse of open space dropping away and up from its rail. The building had a basement, something I hadn't noticed on my walk, but it was so dark and deep I couldn't see what was in it. I shone the flashlight down. The steps to the basement all seemed intact, though the metal was red and pockmarked, eroded from neglect and the elements, making it seem as delicate as lace. Gripping the rusty rail, I started my descent. The air in this part of the building was colder, and it had a funny smell I couldn't quite place, the tang of iron and something else.

I looked up and saw the gaping hole in the roof through which the stars winked.

"Maria?" The darkness seemed to swallow my voice as I called out her name once again.

Clinging to the rough, cold steel, I felt my way past a slick patch where the rain had hit the stairs until I was on a stable—albeit earthen—floor. From this vantage point, I could just make out the large bins that loomed in the dark, bins which could have held water, or grain, or gas.

I caught a whiff of the strange smell in the air and recognition flooded through me.

Sulfur.

"Maria!" I shouted her name, now, more afraid of being killed in a gas-leak fueled explosion than being caught by a bunch of criminals.

"You have to come out now. It's me, Hope." I ran through the basement, swinging my flashlight in hopes of finding her hidden in the corners as I ran through the basement. "It's not safe here, Maria. We need to move, now."

I heard a soft flutter behind me and wheeled around. "Maria?"

The darkness began to shift as the flutter grew more insistent, the lightless space where it came from growing and stretching into a mass that seemed to breathe with life. The flutter turned into a roar and the dark cloud came rushing at me until I found myself absorbed, battered by wings and claws that pummeled me into the unforgiving ground. Every time I tried to move, the cloud whirled and turned, the birds that comprised it moving together with one mind, barreling against me and pinning me down. I huddled on the dirt floor, covering my ears against the shrieking and rushing of wind.

Eventually, I realized that the blackness had subsided. The only sound was my own screaming. I stopped, gasping for breath, afraid to lift my head.

"She's not here, Hope."

The voice gripped my heart in its icy fist, striking new fear in me. I had lost my flashlight, but I didn't need it to know that it was Lucas who stood in the shadows.

I heard his step echo as he moved closer toward me, and then I heard a soft skidding sound. My flashlight rolled gently toward me, coming to a stop as it bumped against my fist. I grasped it, raising my head and scuttling back as I shone the beam wildly into the night. Lucas stepped into the ray, his eyes glittering with an emotion I didn't recognize.

"You don't seem happy to see me, Hope," he continued, smiling a taut, brittle smile. He was no longer in his customary letter jacket. Instead, he'd wrapped his body in a dark leather jacket and denim that showed his every muscle, making me realize how small I was in comparison.

I tried to speak, but all that came out was a whimpering squeak. He laughed, taking one step closer to me.

"No," I managed to splutter, trying to keep the distance between us. I found myself backed into a wall stacked full of baskets which teetered and fell about me.

Determined that he would not make me feel helpless, I glanced around for anything, anything at all that I could use as a weapon, settling for an old wooden broom. I turned it around and wielded it in front of me like a pike.

"That's no way to greet a friend," Lucas purred with his oily voice, obviously amused, and a wave of revulsion rippled through my body. "I just hope that you can be more gracious with my colleagues."

The shadows, which had retreated to the back of the basement, stirred again. I strained my eyes, and then, one by one, I began to pick out the hulking figures. Some of them I recognized as Lucas's regular posse of high school friends. Others had eyes that had haunted me in my dreams—my nightmares that, I could now see, had been but premonitions of what was to come.

"What have you done with Maria?" I asked, my voice hoarse.

"Maria?" He sneered. "Who knows what happened to your precious Maria? She was just a useful tool in our little game."

"Game?" I echoed, confused.

Lucas chuckled. "Don't tell me you don't understand what this is all about?" He clucked maternally, mocking me. "Poor Hope. Left in the dark, so innocent. Well, let me be the one to enlighten you. It's not Maria we want. It's you."

My mind reeled.

"But Maria," I protested, weakly, the pit of dread growing larger in my stomach. "She called me. She said she needed help."

Lucas's face contorted with disgust. "You humans—your minds are so weak. You fail to recognize the truth, even when it is standing before you! Here's your Maria," he spat.

His body quivered and melted, his features twisting and his body shrinking to that of a tiny, terrified Mexican girl.

"Hope, I need your help," Lucas whimpered in Maria's voice, sounding exactly like the voice on the phone.

"No," I protested weakly in denial. "No!"

The fear was too much for me. I sank forward on my knees once more, my stomach heaving. Wave after wave of nausea swept through me. I struggled to catch my breath, only to gag on my bile until finally, there was nothing left. I shivered in the dark, filthy from dirt and vomit, waiting.

I stared into the dirt and noticed, for the first time, the carpet of black feathers scattered all about me. How could I have been so blind? I cursed my naïveté, my refusal to see the signs. My mind raced, trying to find a way out. I was here, by myself, with no one aware that I was even missing. My mother wasn't due home for days. I was surrounded. Trapped. And not just by thugs—I realized—but by Fallen Ones. By the time anyone missed me, it would be too late.

Michael! I clung to the idea of him like a life raft, but no sooner had it entered my mind than I rejected it. He didn't know where I was either, and as much as he felt obligated to protect me, his powers did not extend to knowing where I was.

No, I was going to have to get myself out of this one on my own.

I braced my body and struggled to my feet. Lucas had morphed back into his own body, only now a majestic pair of jet-colored wings stretched out behind his bare torso. Even in the half-light of the abandoned building, I could see the edge of each feather, sharply etched as if chiseled into stone or steel. His muscles rippled, and the wings seemed to pulse with threatening energy. A gust of air, stirred by their great expanse, wafted toward me, and on it I smelled the telltale scent of sulfur.

I dragged my sleeve across my face, wiping the last of the vomit from my chin. I swallowed hard, my throat raw. The pain sharpened my focus. I drew my breath and spoke, my chin raising defiantly as I glowered at Lucas.

"You've been following me this whole time," I said.

Lucas shrugged, his wings beating once more. "It was entertaining enough, taunting Michael that way."

He eyed me with amusement as he began to circle. Behind his wings, his mob of shadows leered.

He continued talking as he paced. "Michael didn't tell you about us, did he? Didn't tell you we were Fallen Ones? But he knew we were stalking you. Isn't that odd, Hope? That he would keep that little detail to himself?"

I didn't answer, but he saw something in my eyes that prompted him to continue.

"Did he tell you he might be endangering you by paying you all that attention? Did you mention to him that birds had attacked you? Did you show him the feather you found, Hope, or tell him about the funny smell of the lightning that night on the mountain? He knows what those signs mean."

He was enjoying himself now, enjoying the drama of the moment, enjoying the fact that I had no choice but to give him the audience he craved. I willed myself to be still, willed my ears to close to the poison he was spewing. But still he came, winding closer and closer, until I could feel his hot breath on my face.

"You did tell him, didn't you, Hope? But Michael never told you the truth in return, did he? Does it hurt, Hope, knowing that the one you trusted was willing to put you at such risk?" He stopped circling then, inches from my face. His black wings blotted out everything else as he raised them up as if to shelter us. His eyes were greedy as he reached out with one hot hand, dragging his fingertips across my cheek in a mockery of a caress.

"Get your hands off of her."

The voice boomed and echoed in the dark, bouncing off the abandoned machines and lonely walls, magnifying its rage.

"Ah, Michael." Lucas's face broke into a radiant smile, and the dark shadows surrounding us seemed to pulse with energy. Lucas released my face with a flourish, spinning away to face the voice. "Are your ears burning? We were just talking about you."

Michael stepped from the shadows. His wings were unfurled, great shimmering white things that looked invitingly soft until, giving full expression to Michael's fury, they seemed to stretch to an even greater expanse. With a forceful pulse, they sliced the air. A maelstrom of wind whipped around me.

I let my eyes roam over the rest of him. His naked torso seemed to glow with a light that emanated from within. Every muscle seemed chiseled out of stone, taut and ready for a fight. I dragged my eyes from his broad shoulders—which showed no strain from carrying the burden of wings—to the spot where his carved abdomen disappeared inside low-slung jeans.

Weak-kneed, I dragged my eyes away to meet Michael's gaze. There, the rage I saw for Lucas melted into a look of fear and concern.

Lucas continued on, as if Michael's interruption was nothing more than an intermission to his carefully planned show. "The whole situation seemed strange to me, I must say. Was Michael—the vaunted Michael, Leader of the Host—falling for this mousy thing?" He gestured to me halfheartedly.

"You go too far, Lucas," Michael threatened, taking one step closer.

Lucas ignored him, circling once more so that I found myself trapped between the two angels.

"You always were a lover of humanity," Lucas taunted, spitting the word "humanity" as if it were a vile curse. "First to bow before Adam. The only one of us who clung to him after he was exiled from Paradise. Instead of despising it, you embraced God's mistake, set it on a pedestal, worshipped it!"

Michael's voice was cold as stone. "I save my worship for God."

Lucas's eyes rolled with rage as he squared off to face Michael. He stretched his wings, the dark veins in his arms and chest surging and straining with his movement.

"Even when mankind turned upon itself, even when Cain took the life of his own brother, you begged for them and hid them away to shield them from the Lord's rage! No, your love for humanity has been sickening to watch. So it didn't surprise me that you might finally stumble, finally fall for one of your beloved creatures." Foam flecked his lips and his hands clenched, opening and closing with impotent fury as he continued to spew his venom. "I should have known you had a darker motive."

Michael's forehead crumpled in confusion.

"The girl has nothing to do with this quarrel between us, Lucas. Let her be," Michael said, a note of uncertainty creeping into his voice.

"Nothing to do with us!" Lucas sputtered, clearing the distance between us in two quick strides. "Nothing to do with us!" he repeated, disbelief mingling with his anger. "Deny it, then, deny it!"

He grabbed my hair and brusquely twisted my neck, baring it to Michael's gaze as he dragged me toward his enemy.

"Deny you knew she bears the Mark," he challenged as he threw me to the ground at Michael's feet.

An uneasy quiet surrounded me. I could feel their gaze burning on my neck as they stared at the unwelcome stain that had tattooed itself onto my skin so many years ago.

I waited, breath held, body poised for flight, for Michael to speak.

Michael drew one deep, ragged breath. "Pick her up," he ordered, a frightening coldness in his voice.

Lucas pulled me roughly upright and pushed me away. I stumbled, trying to steady myself, and then I looked up to meet Michael's gaze. Suddenly his eyes were hard. There was no understanding or comfort there, none of the concern for me I had seen only minutes before—just rejection. The shock was like a slap in the face, but I refused to be cowed, refused to break his gaze.

"You cannot have her," Michael stated flatly, as if I wasn't even there.

"You cannot subvert prophecy, Michael," Lucas said, a mournful note touching his speech. "She is the one spoken of in the Book of Enoch."

"You don't know that for sure," Michael said without emotion, holding my gaze.

Lucas snorted derisively. "If we barcoded her, it couldn't be more obvious. Look at it. She is the Key, Michael."

When Michael didn't answer, Lucas turned his attention to me, catching my eye with a powerful thrust of his wings.

"Confused, sweetheart? Let me break it down for you.

"A long time ago, God swept the patriarch Enoch into Heaven, and for whatever reasons He had, God turned Enoch into an Angel. Once there, Enoch took it upon himself to document the world of Angels for mankind. He inscribed his book with the seven domains of the seven governing angels, their forty-nine Princes, and the entirety of the Host. Even the names of the Fallen Ones."

"I know about the Book of Enoch," I replied calmly, waiting for Michael to give some sign, waiting for Lucas to get to his point so I could somehow, finally, find a way out of here.

"Ah, but you don't, my dear. You know *of* the Book, but you do not know *about* the Book, for it has been lost to mankind. Spirited back to the Angels, where their secrets belong. Many of your kind have tried to recover it—some even claim to have seen it—but no one truly knows what it contains."

"But I know," he whispered in my ear, making me jump. He had managed to sneak right behind me and was breathing his tale quietly for effect. He folded me in his arms. Instinctively, I tried to pull away from the heat and stench of him, but his arms tightened around me like bands, restraining me. Unable to move away, I closed my eyes, trying to imagine myself anywhere else but here. But I couldn't escape the relentless progress of his words.

"And Michael knows. We know that Enoch was not just a patriarch—he was a prophet." His whisper was tantalizing, seductive, almost soothing as he spun the tale.

"We know one day, the Fallen will rise up. Their army will overpower the Host of Heaven, and finally, they will reclaim what once was theirs. Enoch foretold it, and we have seen it inscribed in his Book. It will happen. It is inevitable. Nothing can stop it. Nothing.

"For millennia we have waited, watching and yearning for our chance." His muscles were taut like bowstrings, and I could feel him quivering with anticipation. He tightened his grip upon me with one arm. I felt him reach up and part my hair reverently, breathing in its fragrance as he buried his head in it. I could feel Michael watching him do it.

"All we needed, Hope, was the Key to open Heaven's Gate, which had been so cruelly shut upon our faces."

His hand slid down my neck, and I felt the hot trail of his fingertip as it traced the design etched into my skin.

"All we needed, all this time, was you."

Shock and despair rippled through me and I felt my knees weaken, but there was nowhere to go, nowhere to fall, trapped as I was by his steely arm.

I looked desperately into Michael's eyes.

"Is it true?" I whispered, my heart begging him to deny it.

He hung his head, his golden hair hiding his eyes from mine. As Michael's wings sagged uselessly at his side, Lucas dumped me on the floor in front of him, and I wept.

ten

A train whistle sounded, snapping me out of my grief and back to the dank cellar. I lifted my eyes and squinted through the cratered ceiling into the sky, trying to find a glimpse of light, but dawn was too far off to break the darkness.

Michael stood like a statue, watching me, waiting.

When he spoke, at first I thought my ears had deceived me. But then he repeated himself, so quietly that I could have mistaken his words for the steady hum of the diesel engines idling in the train yard just beyond the factory's walls.

"You don't know what to do with her." He tried to say it in a matter-of-fact way, but a tone of triumph crept into his voice. He lifted his head, waiting for Lucas to respond.

Lucas flapped his wings impatiently. "It doesn't matter. We will figure that out soon enough. The most important thing is to keep her out of your hands."

I pushed myself up from the dank floor and stood to face him.

"Why?" I demanded. "If what you say is true, it doesn't matter where I am or who is with me. The Prophecy will be fulfilled. You yourself said it can't be avoided."

Lucas pressed his lips together in a thin, bloodless smile. "God has been known to change his mind. He stayed Abraham's hand at the altar. It might amuse him to allow one of his misguided henchmen to intervene again. I can't take that chance."

"I don't understand. What does that mean?" I demanded, my voice rising as hysteria crept in.

"Do you want to tell her, Michael, or shall I?" Lucas said smugly, gripping my arm tighter.

Michael crossed his arms in front of his massive chest, stone-faced.

"Very well," Lucas said. "Hope's a smart girl. Perhaps she can figure it out on her own." Lucas's wings unfurled, and suddenly, he was in front of me, looking me straight in the eye. "Hope, who is Michael?"

I felt as if my very life depended upon my answer. I looked plaintively over Lucas's shoulder to Michael, but he looked away. I dragged my gaze back to Lucas, willing myself not to flinch.

"God's warrior," I whispered.

"Very good," Lucas purred. "And as God's warrior, what is he sworn to do?"

"Protect the innocent," I said hesitantly, the words sounding strange on my lips. "Battle Satan and the Fallen Ones."

"Right you are," Lucas said, encouragingly, continuing to circle. "So think, Hope—and think very, very hard, for your life may depend upon your understanding. If Michael found the person who was the key to Heaven's defeat—the one by whose hand the Fallen would rise—*what would Michael do*?"

The ground seemed to shift beneath my feet as I realized the answer to his question.

"Say it, Hope," Lucas exhaled in my ear, cherishing each word as he said it, relishing my disillusionment. "What would—what *must*—Michael do?"

A sob caught in my throat. I reached up to my cheeks. They were bathed in tears.

"Say it!" Lucas bellowed, the rusted hulks of machines echoing back his command.

I gasped for air between sobs, forcing the words from my lips.

"He has to kill me," I said, choking on the words as I said them.

"Louder!" Lucas shouted with glee. "I want to hear your world falling apart. I want to hear your heart breaking! Say it again!"

I wanted to shriek my denials, tear out his eyes for having made mine see the truth. But most of all, I wanted to deny him the sight of my pain. Slowly I steeled myself, swallowing the sobs before they could escape my throat. Taking a deep breath to steady myself, I squared my shoulders and gathered my courage. Lucas, sensing my intention, stepped back and gave me space. I walked across the earthen floor to the place where Michael stood. The Archangel couldn't meet my eyes as I approached. Mustering my last ounce of strength, I raised my hand and struck him across the face as hard as I could. The red outline of my palm sat accusingly on his cheek until the flush of anger rose and spread across his entire face. His eyes flashed, his nostrils flared, and his jaw strained, but he said nothing.

"Michael has to kill me," I said derisively, my voice no longer shaking.

Lucas's slow, deliberate clapping echoed into the night. "Quite a show. I don't think I could have planned it better if I had tried." Then he gave an exaggerated yawn. "But I'm afraid I am out of time. It's time for you and me to go, Hope."

Michael's blue eyes bored into us both. "I told you, you can't have her," he said, the vein in his forehead throbbing.

Lucas feigned surprise. "Why of course, what was I thinking?" He turned to me with undue courtesy. "We'll ask Hope what she would like to do. Hope, do you want to go with me, or with Michael?"

"I want to go home," I said. "Alone."

Lucas's laughter pealed like bells. "Don't be ridiculous, child. That is something neither one of us will allow. Now make your choice. Come with me and take your chances, or go with Michael to certain death."

A train rushed by, the rhythm of its wheels on the track sounding so ordinary that I could almost forget what I was being asked to do.

"He's lying," Michael said under his breath so that only I could hear. "I won't hurt you, Hope."

"I don't have all night, Hope," Lucas called impatiently from the darkness to which he'd retreated. "Make your choice."

I turned to look at Michael. I wanted to believe him, but how could I? Michael's eyes mirrored back my own fear and regret.

I opened my mouth to speak, but he simply shook his head and stepped around me, ignoring whatever I was about to say.

"The choice is not hers to make," Michael said as he stretched his arm to the heavens. A flaming sword materialized in his grip. Tongues of fire licked about the corded muscles of his arm, but they did not burn him. He swung the sword down in a brilliant arc that lit the entire basement.

"Step aside, Hope," he muttered, his eyes locking in on Lucas.

I scuttled back into the shadows, away from the fiery spectacle. Lucas had drawn his own sword, which burned with a cooler, silvery heat. He waved his other hand in silent dismissal and suddenly the mass of black shadows that had hovered around us vanished into the night. Only Michael and Lucas remained, circling one another with swords sparking like lions waiting for the strike.

Lucas's lip curled up as he tossed his sword from hand to hand. "Both the Key and the chance to do you in with my own hand? This evening has turned out to be quite promising."

Michael's nostrils flared as he bit back his response, never taking his eyes off of Lucas.

Lucas lunged, trying to catch Michael by surprise, but Michael was ready, parrying the blow easily and moving with the grace of a dancer, not even seeming to feel the clash of metal on metal. Lucas heaved again, a great downward fall like an axe, but Michael caught him, crossing swords and hurling Lucas away in a shower of sparks. Lucas tumbled in the dirt like a rag doll and then scrambled to his feet.

Michael took the offensive, striking before Lucas had steadied himself. Lucas barely managed to raise his blade, a brilliant blaze igniting the sky as flame fell upon flame. I knew this was my chance to run, but something kept me riveted in place, forcing me to watch.

"He'll lie to you," Lucas panted at me as he broke away from Michael. He was dragging his sword behind him, the tongues of fire licking his wrist and entwining themselves around his rippling arm.

"He'll tell you he won't hurt you," Lucas said. "He'll tell you he didn't even know."

Michael lunged after him and Lucas stumbled backward, desperately trying to outrun the reach of Michael's sword until there was nowhere else left for Lucas to go.

Lucas's eyes were wild as he shouted his last words to me. "Don't believe a word he says, Hope. He loves mankind. He may even love you. But he loves God more. He'll never allow you to live, even if it breaks his own heart!"

Michael roared, a primal sound torn from his gut, as he brought the flaming sword down on Lucas's head. My hands flew to my eyes.

Then, nothing. Nothing but the sound of Michael's ragged breathing. His gasps for breath echoed about the cavernous room for what seemed like ages.

I slid two fingers apart to peek. There was no flame. No sword. No body, no evidence that Lucas had even been here. Only Michael. Ordinary Michael, teenage boy, looking for all the world as if he had done nothing more than run a hard sprint in PE.

He barely looked at me.

"Let's go," he said in a businesslike tone, striding toward the staircase.

I dropped my hands, staring after him. Run, I told myself, but my legs wouldn't move.

"Hope," Michael said, an edge to his voice as he turned to look at me, one foot already poised on the first step. "I said, let's go. You don't have a choice about this anymore."

I opened my mouth, a smart retort in mind, but all that came out was a foreign keening that made even my own hair stand on end. My hands flew up, trying to stop the sound from escaping my throat, but it just grew louder, and I began to shake.

Michael rubbed his brow. "Shock," he muttered, expecting no answer. "You're in shock."

I kept wailing. He covered the distance between us in a few strides and pulled me down to the ground, squatting next to me as he held me by the shoulders. I couldn't make myself move away from him.

"It's going to be okay," he soothed, brushing his warm thumb against my hairline. The unexpected gentleness of his gesture made me wail all the louder.

“Shhhh,” he urged. “Shhhh.” Then, carefully, he pulled me into his vast embrace. I tried to push away, but he only held me tighter until, defeated, I gave in. His impassive chest absorbed the great sobs that racked my body, his heat enveloping me and sinking down into my core. I howled against him until my throat was too sore to make any sound, and then I shook in silent agony. Slowly, slowly, my body gave up its grief, the spasms of anger and fear gradually succumbing to hiccups and sniffles.

He tilted my chin up. Through swollen eyes, I could see him inspecting me. Finally, satisfied by what he saw, he deposited me on the ground again and backed away, rising to his full height.

“Better?”

I watched him, nodding warily.

“Good,” he said, looking quickly through the broken roof at the sky. “It will be dawn soon. We need to leave here unobserved. Lucas’s crew won’t be looking for him yet, so we have the advantage.” He paused. “Do you understand what I am saying, Hope?”

I shook my head numbly. Nothing made any sense anymore.

He grunted with barely concealed impatience. “We’re running away from the city, Hope. You and me. And we need to get out of here. *Now*.”

I looked at him with disbelief as he stood over me, stretching to his full height.

“Why don’t you just kill me and get it over with,” I demanded.

His cheeks flushed. He shoved his hands deep into his pockets and kicked at the dirt.

“I don’t think that will be necessary,” he said tersely. He reached down, pulled me up by the armpits, and shoved me toward the stairs. “Now, walk.”

~

I somehow managed to stumble back through the factory. I kept darting glances into the shadows as Michael marched me back to my mother's car, looking for a chance to escape, but none came. When we stopped at the car, I wordlessly handed the keys to Michael when he held out his palm. I'd lost whatever opportunity I'd had. In the passenger seat, I pressed my cheek against the cold glass and looked at the leafless trees that had stood sentinel all night. In dawn's first blush, they seemed reassuringly normal, shrinking in the distance as we pulled away.

Normal. How could anything be normal after what had just happened? I wanted it all to go away: my aching body, my raw throat, and especially my lingering terror. I longed for the oblivion of sleep—sleep in my own bed—hoping I would wake up and find this was all a dream, that Michael was still just my normal teenage friend. But instead of turning north through the city and toward home, Michael steered the Audi away from Atlanta.

"Where are we going?" I asked, a tremor in my voice.

"To the airport," he said, offering no further information.

Ask him why, Henri urged.

Funny you should show up now, after all the fun is over, I snapped back at him in my mind. When Henri didn't rise to the bait, I sighed and shifted in my seat so I could better watch Michael.

"Why are we running away?" I demanded.

He looked at me out of the corner of his eye, deciding whether or not he should answer me. "Now that they know you are here, the Fallen Ones will hunt you down."

"So you're going to protect me?" I asked, sarcasm dripping from my voice.

"Yes," he replied coolly, never taking his eyes from the road.

"Why should I believe you?" I challenged, straining against the safety belt. "Why should I believe you when all you've done is lie to me?"

Careful, girl, the voice warned. I watched as Michael clutched the steering wheel tighter, his knuckles turning white. *He can be pushed too far.*

"I told you the truth about protecting you," Michael said. "I didn't know about the Mark."

Lucas had warned me that Michael would say that. I could barely stand knowing that Lucas had been right, could barely stand knowing that in this upside-down, mixed-up world, Lucas might actually have been on my side. I knew I was in danger, but some crazy impulse drove me on. With nothing to lose, I unleashed my anger upon Michael, almost daring him to finally turn against me.

"And now that you know? That changes everything, doesn't it? Now you're going to take me away and kill me. What are you going to do? Dump my body in some alley? Bury me in a desert somewhere? Or am I going to go up in flames and disappear like Lucas did?"

A muscle in his jaw spasmed. Michael took a deep breath through his nose, holding it for several seconds before allowing it to escape through a giant, controlled exhale. He chose his next words carefully, articulating them slowly with the effort of controlling his temper.

"If you give me a chance, I can explain it all to you. Lucas was right about many things, but he was wrong about one very crucial aspect of this . . . situation."

"I'm listening," I said, crossing my arms.

He glanced to his left, swiftly changing lanes.

"You aren't the Key. Your Mark says you are the *bearer* of the Key."

I thought back to that night at Tabitha's and remembered her translation. "What's the difference?"

"The difference is everything. Without the Key, you are harmless, and the Prophecy cannot be fulfilled."

I turned this new information over in my mind. "And Lucas didn't know this?"

The corners of Michael's mouth turned up in a sardonic grin. "His Aramaic must have been a little rusty."

I fell back in my seat, my head spinning. "So if I'm not the Key, why are we running away?"

"They *think* you're the Key. So that means two things. One: it means they will stop at nothing to reclaim you. The only way to keep you safe is to keep you moving. And two: as long as they think that *you* are the Key, it means they aren't looking for the *real* Key. Which means that if we can find it first, we can destroy it."

"Destroy it," I echoed. I let my gaze drift out the window, my mind wandering as the early morning lights of South Atlanta flashed by. I wondered if it was even possible to destroy something that had been foreseen so long ago.

"If you destroy me, then there is no Bearer. Is there?"

The question hung in the silence of the car. Michael did not answer.

"And then the Prophecy couldn't be fulfilled, either."

I didn't ask him to confirm what I already knew. Instead, I huddled in my seat, my feet tucked under me, exhaustion pushing me finally into a merciful sleep.

I finally woke up as we turned a curve and came into the airport, my head still resting against the cool window.

"What if I don't want to go with you?" I asked, looking through the glass at the airport. "What if I tell the gate agents you're taking me against my will?"

"Why wouldn't you want to go with me?" he asked—but not with his own voice. Wearily, I turned my head to see the figure of my father sitting behind the wheel of the car, looking at me with bemusement. "I'm sure your mother won't mind if we take a little trip."

My mind immediately began generating objections—violation of custody agreements, failure to procure the appropriate authorizations and paperwork—but I forced myself to stop. It was useless, and I knew it. He would find a way to take me.

Tears stung my eyes as I remembered that morning in my bedroom, the first time I'd seen him change into someone else before my very eyes.

"You promised me. You promised me you'd never do that without my permission," I said, the bitterness of his empty promise almost making me sick.

"You left me no choice," he said.

"I have no choice, either, do I," I stated, my voice expressionless. A lone tear trickled down my face and splashed onto my hand.

"No. You really don't," he echoed as he pulled my mother's car into the long-term parking lot.

After steering the Audi into an empty space, he turned to me. Inside the fleshy face of my aging father, I could see Michael's icy blue eyes. They were full of determination and not much else.

"Come with me," he asked, holding out his hand.

I stared at his hand, not sure what to do.

Go with him.

I paused. The last time Henri had urged me to go somewhere, I'd ended up in the middle of a death match between Lucas and Michael.

Go, Henri whispered again. *If he means to harm you, you will never escape him, no matter how far you run. And if he is telling the truth, it may be your only chance. Not just yours. The world's.*

I hadn't really thought about what would happen if the Fallen Ones reclaimed Heaven. Would it be the start of the Apocalypse, or something even worse? I began to shake at the gravity of my choice. Around me, a few harried businessmen and women scurried about, running to make their early morning flights, oblivious to the destruction that was hanging over their heads.

What if I chose wrong?

I looked once more into Michael's eyes within my father's face, but this time I saw something else. They seemed clear and untroubled. Even confident. *Damn him*, I thought. *Damn them all.*

I gripped the edge of my seat, trying to steady my quivering body. Slowly, still not trusting him, I clasped Michael's outstretched hand—my father's hand.

A flood of warmth ran from my fingertips and up my arm. I could feel it creeping slowly across my face and into my middle, where it made me feel funny. I looked up, hoping to find some confidence in the familiar gaze of Michael's eyes, but the stony look on his face stopped me short. Confused, I snatched my hand away.

"Where are we going?" I demanded, trying to keep the quiver out of my voice.

"Las Vegas," Michael answered, reaching into the backseat and thrusting my backpack at me.

I looked at the pack, stuffed full. With a quick glance I saw that it held a few items of clothing and toiletries. "You had planned this all along," I accused, my heart sinking.

"Not this way," he responded tersely. "And for a different reason."

He paused, waiting for my curiosity to kick in, but I kept my eyes glued on the little name tag that dangled off my backpack. I didn't want to give him the satisfaction of seeing how his betrayal had affected me.

I heard him give an exasperated sigh. Giving up, he pushed

himself out of the car and came around to my side. He opened my door, and when I didn't move he brusquely unbuckled my seat belt and pulled me out.

We were alone in the garage. Without waiting for me to follow, he stalked off toward the terminal. "If you care anything for your father, you'll do what I say."

"My father?" I asked dumbly, scurrying to catch up with him.

Michael slowed his pace, but did not stop. "We have a few days, maybe a week, until your mother arrives home and discovers you are missing. Right?"

I nodded, unsure where he was headed.

"That is a few days for us to get ahead of the Fallen; a few days for us to lay a false trail. The Key is ancient. I don't know what it is, or where it is, but I know that it is not here in North America."

I was jogging to keep up with him as we neared the lights of the terminal.

"We're going to have to leave without tipping anyone off to where we are going. If we're conspicuous enough to get picked up by all the security cameras in Vegas, we'll have the police and the Fallen focusing their time there while we get a head start."

I drew in my breath. "You mean to set my father up for kidnapping."

He shot me a sideways glance. "Your mother will believe it, won't she?"

The truth in what he said—and the injustice of it—shot me like an arrow. I remembered my father handing me a burrito from the restaurant he managed now, playing with his hat. I envisioned him being led off to jail, his wrists in cuffs.

"But it's not fair! It's not fair to him!" My voice rang out, echoing off the concrete pillars and ceiling.

Michael drew up short, gripping my arm and giving me a shake to warn me into silence. "It's the best we can do. Let the authorities figure out how your father was in Vegas at the same time hundreds of people saw him at work in Alabama. The confusion alone will buy us time."

My eyes blurred and hot tears ran down my face. My father had given up everything he had to protect me. Now, because of me, he was going to be exposed, ridiculed, and hated. Hated for something he didn't even do.

Michael loosed his grip. When he spoke, his voice was soft, almost soothing. "I promise you, Hope, he won't go to prison for this. He will spend a few days under the spotlight, but they won't be able to get around his alibi because it's real."

I sniffed a tear back. "My past. It's going to come out, isn't it?"

"Probably," Michael said. "But knowing your mother, she'll fight hard to keep it from the media."

"What if he loses his job?" I asked, knowing it was virtually guaranteed.

"Small price to pay," Michael asserted in a matter-of-fact manner.

It felt so odd, talking about my father as if he wasn't present, when it was his voice, his face, his body right here with me; it felt so odd to be treating him like a bit player when in reality this was as much his story as mine.

"Vegas will buy us time." I repeated it to myself, willing myself to believe.

"Vegas will buy us time." Through my tears, I saw the corners of Michael's mouth lift slightly. "And in Vegas, we might find Maria."

I opened my eyes wide. "She's there?" I gasped.

"The traffickers moved her there after they picked her up again. I guess they figured things were too hot to keep her in Atlanta." The vein in his forehead throbbed as he tried to contain his anger.

"That's why I went over to your house tonight. I know how important it is to you to find her. I wanted to tell you."

"But how did you—?" I broke off, unsure how to finish my sentence.

He shrugged my question off. "I figured it out the old-fashioned way and knocked some heads together. It's amazing how persuasive a little violence can be when you're dealing with street scum."

I stared at him, more confused than ever. It was important to me to find Maria. I'd thought he'd given up on her. But instead, he'd gone out of his way for her—for me.

"You came over to tell me and take me to Las Vegas to look for her?"

"No," he said emphatically, his eyes flashing. "I was going to tell you, yes. But I was never planning to take you along with me to search for her. This is not the kind of trip for a teenage girl. But when I found you and your mother's car missing, I knew something was wrong. So I came prepared," he said, gesturing to the backpack I still clutched in my hands.

"So now I'm going with you."

"Now you're coming with me."

"To look for Maria."

He squared his jaw. The effect wasn't quite the same, seeing it in my father's jowly face, but his displeasure was clear. "To lay a trail. I'm the only one who will be doing any exploration. You're going to stay put."

I was about to protest when I thought better of it. I still didn't know whether I could trust him, and it was better not to press my luck now. I could always argue my way out of it later, once we were on the ground in Las Vegas.

He lifted my chin in his hands. Another wave of heat swept through my body as he cradled my face. "The only thing I need you to do while we are there is to smile for the security cameras. You got that?"

I nodded mutely, confused and angry that even after everything that had happened, my body still responded to him; embarrassed that his touch affected me so much; and more than a little creeped out by having that reaction when, at least on the outside, it was my own dad standing there. Gross.

Michael dropped his hand away and moved into the terminal with me in tow. This early, the place was still empty. He walked briskly to the ticket counter and asked for the first flight to Vegas. The ticket agent looked at me funny and then looked Michael up and down.

"Is everything all right?" she said, looking at me pointedly. I looked down and realized that I was filthy, my clothing stained with red clay and rust from the factory.

The humiliation and fear of the night was all too fresh, and I began to waver. For a moment, I considered telling her everything. But when I played through the scene in my mind, I kept getting stuck at the part where I told her that the man beside me was not my father. Who would believe that? Even I could only tell the difference when I looked closely into his eyes. And after all, Henri had told me to go with him. Everything—including my own father's safety—might depend on that.

"She's fine. Right, honey?" Michael interjected smoothly, producing IDs and some paperwork. He handed them across the counter to the agent who shuffled through the papers one by one.

"What's your name, young lady?"

"Hope Carmichael."

"Well, Hope Carmichael, your papers seem to be in order. Including permission from your mother for you to travel with him.

And he is?" She pointedly ignored Michael, directing her questions to me.

"My father, ma'am," I answered, doing my best to look chipper. "Don Carmichael."

"Funny place for a family trip. Las Vegas."

Michael interjected before I could answer. "I have business there. It was convenient."

"Planned at the last minute, huh?" She looked at me searchingly. "I mean, it looks like he pulled you right off a playing field or something."

The agent paused as if she expected me to say something more, but when I dropped my eyes down to stare at my feet, she sighed and started mechanically processing our tickets. She seemed to stall as much as she could throughout the process, now and then looking down the grand hall to where a security guard stood, trying to catch his eye, but he was engrossed in conversation with a janitor. Finally, when she could drag it out no further, she passed Michael the tickets.

"Hope," she said, looking at my ID and looking at my face until she was sure she'd met my eyes. "It's our company policy for me to ask this if I'm not sure of the answer. Do you want to be traveling with your father today?"

Michael set his jaw, but I ignored him. "Yes, I do," I said firmly, meeting the agent's eye.

The agent bit her lip and looked down. I wasn't sure how convinced she really was. "You two have a fun trip to Las Vegas," she said at last, her eyebrows knitted together with worry as she slid my ID across the counter. Michael smoothly thanked her, guiding me away by the elbow.

In less than fifteen minutes we were through security and on the tram toward our gate. The train rattled around the curves as the mechanical voice announced each stop. Even though our car was empty, Michael stood as close to me as he could, leaning against a pole for support.

"Henri didn't show up tonight, did he?" he asked. He tried to sound casual, but I could see the interest burning intensely in his eyes.

Careful, Henri said. *I can be more helpful to you if he doesn't know I am with you.*

I tried to act surprised. "I always assumed you knew whether or not he was here," I said to Michael. "Can't you guys all see or sense each other?"

Michael shook his head. "No. We can communicate with one another, but it's kind of like walkie-talkies. If he turns off his button or chooses not to answer me, I have no idea whether or not he's even out there. I take it he is not."

I shook my head and chose my words carefully. "No. I haven't really heard from him in weeks. Probably since right after you found me on Stone Mountain. After you argued with him in my room."

Good girl.

Michael laughed a bitter laugh. "Some guardian," he sputtered, his fingers gripping and regripping the shiny steel. "To make a point about me, he goes on strike, leaving you completely exposed. As if he was in a union! I have half a mind to take him to court myself and file a complaint, have him stripped of his duties."

"You can do that?" I said, quickly calculating whether there was any way I could forestall him.

"Yes, though the heavenly bureaucracy is notoriously painful to navigate. If we had more time I would do it in a heartbeat. Maybe after we visit the Library."

"The Library? Where is that?"

The train ground to a halt, the screech of its wheels drowning out Michael's answer. The doors swung open with a hiss and the train spat us out to find our gate.

"Not where. Who," Michael repeated as we climbed the escalator. "The Library is really an Elder—a Librarian, you could call him—who keeps all the records related to Heaven. Every testament, every prophecy, every battle, every promotion or demotion. The Elder remembers it all and keeps records of it squirreled away somewhere."

"Everything?"

"Everything," Michael said emphatically. "If we have any hope of figuring out what the Key is, we've got to start with that Elder. He'll at least be able to tell us the prophecy in its entirety."

"Where is he?"

Michael smiled. "Let's just say he's off the grid."

"So, let me get this straight," I asked with a low voice as we stepped off into the concourse. "We're going to Vegas to lay a false trail that will throw off both my mom and the Fallen Ones, find Maria, visit the Elder, and—if we have time—we'll squeeze in a little lawsuit against Henri?"

Michael smiled with grim self-satisfaction. "Exactly. Only there will be very little 'we' involved in any of that. You will be staying put in the hotel."

I opened my mouth to argue with him, but he cut me off, placing one hand on each of my shoulders and pulling me in close. There was an air of expectation between us as I looked up into his eyes. I could feel his touch burning into my skin, but the heat of his gaze was even stronger. He swallowed, hard, before spinning me around in the opposite direction.

"Go in and clean yourself up," he said. "You should have a

change of clothes in your pack. And don't even think about trying to run away. I'll find you wherever you go, just like I did last night."

With that, he gave me a little shove in the small of my back, propelling me toward the restroom.

Inside, I looked at my reflection in the mirror. No wonder the ticket agent had looked at me funny. My lip was cracked, a tiny clot of blood visible in the corner. My hair was a complete rat's nest. Clay had worked its way under my nails and into my cuticles, making my hands look almost bloody. My clothes were destroyed.

I was alone in the restroom, so I stripped down and did my best with the thin paper towels to wipe myself clean. I worked a brush through my hair, the tugging and pulling of snarls and knots jolting me awake, each bit of pain making me more alert. My old clothes were too damaged to salvage so I dumped them into the trash. I rummaged in my backpack for a change of clothes, but all I came up with was a pair of gym shorts and a lame T-shirt that read, "I run like a girl."

Run, run, run, the shirt mocked me.

Every ounce of instinct I had was on fire, urging me to find a way out, to run anywhere I could to get away from Michael, but I could think of no way out. And at the same time, I felt irresistibly drawn to him; I wanted to bury my face in his chest and let him comfort me as I wrestled with the fear and disillusionment he had caused.

Was anything that had happened between us—any of our friendship—at all real? Or was I really just a pawn to him in some heavenly game of war?

Henri's voice echoed in my mind. *It's as I said. If he means to harm you, you will never escape him, no matter how far you run. And if he is telling the truth, going with him may be your only chance.*

I sighed, knowing he was right.

"You know, Henri, it's kind of creepy to spy on girls when they're changing their clothes. Especially when you're invisible."

Humph, he replied, clearly offended, and for the first time in a long time, a smile stole across my face.

I shook the wrinkles out of my T-shirt, pulled it over my head, and squared my shoulders.

"Viva Las Vegas," I muttered to myself. I gripped the edge of the white porcelain sink and stared at myself, long and hard, under the fluorescent lights.

"Hope?" I heard my father's voice calling into the restroom after me. I stared at the mirror for a moment longer before answering.

"Coming, Dad," I called back, almost choking on the words.

Picking up my bag, I whispered to the mirror, "I'm coming, Maria," saying it like a vow.

Then I went outside to meet the angel who carried my fate in his hands.

eleven

I pushed my face deeper into the pillow, the rustle of sheets reminding me where I was. I groaned. My body ached and my head throbbed with the regularity of the blinking neon signs that decorated the Strip.

Las Vegas.

We'd arrived in Las Vegas that morning. Michael had chosen one of the local haunts on Fremont Street as our base. Even though she'd been newly renovated, the old bones of the El Cortez stood as testimony that this shop was "old school." When we'd stumbled through the riot of slot machines and busy carpets to the front desk, I'd been overwhelmed.

Despite the early hour, there had been a smattering of people nursing their drinks and cigarettes as they mindlessly worked the machines. They didn't even notice us as we picked our way through the cavernous room. Only one man even looked our way, his glazed-over eyes not registering how disheveled and dirty we were despite my best efforts to scrub up in the airport bathroom, before returning to his game. It was as if we were invisible. And while the renovation meant that everything was relatively new, to me it still seemed garish and loud.

"We can't stay here," I had begged Michael quietly, pulling on his arm. I looked over my shoulder at the regulars, who seemed to be growing grayer and saggier before my very eyes. "It's too sad."

He'd sighed, pulling me out of the way of the waitress bearing down with a tray of drinks.

"We need to gamble on the Strip to get access to the traffickers," he explained quietly. "If we stay in a hotel there, though, we will never be able to let down our guard." He searched my eyes to see if I understood. "I will always have to appear like this," he whispered. "As your father. We will never be able to let down the charade. At least this way you can have some semblance of normalcy." One corner of his mouth shot up in a sarcastic grin. "As normal as you can have in Las Vegas, anyway."

I had nodded mutely. It was hard enough being here: half accomplice, half kidnapping victim. It was even weirder to look over, expecting to see a teenager, and instead see my dad. Only the blue eyes gave him away. If it was hard for me, I wondered what a relief it must be to Michael when he could finally slip out of that body, even if only for a few hours.

Then again, the person I knew as *my* Michael was just a disguise, too. Maybe it wasn't that big of a deal to him. But it was to me. So I'd gone along with his plan.

Now, in our room, I rolled over and looked around. I was grateful that when we'd checked in, he'd managed to get us booked into a newer building across the street that was not connected to the casino. The room was modern, all crisp whites and blacks with bold furniture and accents. It could have been a hotel room in Miami or New York. I could almost forget where we were and why we were here.

We'd drawn the shades against the burning sun, leaving the room shadowy. Only the faint glow from behind gave away that it was afternoon. And there, hunched over in the chair at the foot of my bed, was Michael.

I opened my eyes just a crack to look at him again. He hadn't moved. My eyes scanned him quickly: the golden hair, the impossible tan even in the dead of winter. The way even a button-down shirt clung to his broad shoulders, accentuating every muscle in his lean, perfect body.

I was mildly relieved he had reverted to his normal human appearance after being forced to travel with him posing as my father, but my relief was short-lived as I took him in. He held his head in his hands as he stared absently at the muted television, lost in thought. Images flickered across the screen: fighting in some distant country, hostages at an embassy. The deep lines etched in Michael's face and the shadows under his eyes seemed to grow deeper as he watched the chaos he was unable to stop. I felt a stab of pity, as well as one of guilt. I knew I should be afraid of him, and part of me was. But every minute he spent with me was time away from whatever God had ordained for him; time that would earn him punishment in the form of never-ending pain. It was evident from his face that the pain he was suffering—maybe all because of me—had become more intense.

I cleared my throat, waiting for him to reel his wandering mind back in before I spoke.

"You haven't slept."

He lifted his head and turned to me. For an instant, a shadow of a smile flickered across his face, and his eyes seemed to light up with pleasure as he realized I was awake. For that instant, he looked like a slightly more rumpled version of the friend I'd always known. But just as quickly, the smile disappeared and his eyes shuttered his soul from my prying eyes. We might pretend nothing had changed, but we both were kidding ourselves.

He dropped his hands and pulled himself up in the chair, filling the room.

"I needed to keep an eye on things," he answered.

"Things?"

His mouth constricted into a tight line. "You."

A wave of irritation surged through me and I pushed back the pristine white comforter, swinging to my feet.

"You wasted your time," I threw back at him. "You've made it perfectly clear what will happen if I try to run away. I don't need a guard."

He stared at me, and I remembered I had been sleeping in nothing but a long T-shirt. My face flushed. Self-conscious, I charged across the room, looking for a robe. Michael's grim chuckle floated after me.

"I'll be the judge of that. Especially now that Henri is gone, you need more looking after than ever."

Unease crept over me at his mention of Henri, my Guardian Angel, and I stopped, my hand poised over the creamy white bathrobe that hung on the back of the bathroom door.

Don't even think about telling him, Henri's warning rang in my ears.

Of course I couldn't tell Michael that my Guardian Angel was still here with me. Henri was the only one telling me the truth, I reminded myself. The only one who might be able to stop Michael from killing me to prevent the Prophecy from coming true, to prevent the Fallen Ones from overtaking Heaven.

I shook my head, trying to clear out all the loyalty and trust I had felt for Michael—feelings that filled my head like so many cobwebs—and swallowed my bitter retort. I wrapped myself in the robe and came back to settle on the edge of the bed, my arms crossed.

"Now what?" I demanded.

Michael's brow shot up but he ignored my icy tone. "The Librarian isn't far from here. If we leave now, we can get to him before nightfall and find out what we need to about our Prophecy, and the Key."

"No."

"No?" His eyes flashed, but he did not move, waiting for my explanation. I swallowed hard and kept going.

"You promised we'd look for Maria. I won't help you with the Prophecy until we've found her."

He shook his head slightly. "You don't know how long that could take. We can't put everything else at risk on the hope that we find her."

I pulled my folded arms closer to me and felt my lower lip go out in a pout. "No, you promised. Or was that just a ploy to get me on the plane without a fuss?"

He flushed with anger. I could see the little vein in his forehead throbbing, and I heard Henri whispering urgently, *Are you insane?* But I held my breath and waited for him to respond.

Michael stared hard at me, his eyes betraying nothing as we engaged in a silent test of wills. I couldn't tell what complicated calculus was going on behind his hooded eyes; all I knew was that something—some sort of desperate wish to prove to myself that I was in control of the situation—was spurring me on.

"Fine," he said, practically spitting the word. "You have no idea what you're getting into, but we'll do it your way. We'll go out right now and start trying to hunt down those traffickers."

My heart leapt a little. I hadn't expected it to be so easy.

"We'll *start*," he continued, looking at me stone-faced to be sure I understood what he meant. "We can't wait around before tracking down the Librarian, not with the Fallen on our tail. But we can get the ball rolling; see if we can make a connection. We're going to have to start at the tables. And since I can't leave you alone, you're going to have to do your part, starting with your appearance. I'll have to get the executive host to send up a few things that would be more appropriate for you to wear on the casino floor."

"Executive host?" I asked, blinking. "Appropriate?"

"If you're going to be with me downstairs, you need to look of age," he cryptically answered, "even if you're just watching me. And for our plan to work, we need to attract some attention."

He picked up the receiver to the sleek phone next to him. Before he'd even punched a button he began speaking. "Yes, thank you. I do need some help and unfortunately, I am in a bit of a rush." He watched me as he spoke. "My niece and her luggage appear to have been separated. I'd like you or one of your colleagues to pull together a selection of clothes for her; things that will be appropriate in the private salons on the Strip." He ran his eyes carefully over my body. I wanted to shrink inside my robe. "I'd say a size two. Shoes a nine. If you can choose some things now, I'll meet you to approve your choices before you bring them up. Thank you."

I stared at him, flabbergasted.

"You're just going to dress me up? Like some sort of . . . of . . . plaything? And this executive host person is going to jump just because you asked her to?"

He shrugged. "It's perfectly normal here. Las Vegas is known for exceptional service," he answered, ignoring my real point. "You'll want to freshen up before she gets here." With that, he unfolded himself from the chair and strode across the room, wordlessly letting himself out.

~

I fumed my way through a shower, letting the rhythm of the water soothe me as I watched the last of the red Georgia clay wash away from my skin and spin down the drain. Over the water, I heard the door to the room open and close, then the muffled sound of Michael directing the "executive host"—whatever *that* was—to my closet. I waited in the bathroom until the door closed again and I was sure they were both gone before turning off the water, wrapping myself in the robe again, and padding over to the closet to see what they had brought up for me.

The once-empty closet was now packed with a tight row of hangers in garment bags and the occasional paper shopping bag, all with names of designers I recognized.

"Oh, no," I murmured as I began ripping open the bags and flipping through the hangers. The little slips of tissue-thin fabric hanging there would scarcely cover me up; each one seemed worse than the last. I pushed my way through the lot, hoping to find something normal, but in vain. My Mark, I thought, panicking. None of these will cover my Mark. I delved into the shopping bags next, hoping to find something—a scarf, a sweater—anything that would cover my neck. Inside them were shoeboxes filled only with mile-high stilettos, platforms, and sandals.

There was a discreet knock at the door; Michael must have come back. I swung open the door, ready to launch into a tirade about the objectification of women. But I stopped, my mouth hanging open at the petite, suited woman standing in the doorway.

"Mr. Carmichael thought you might need some help," she said, bustling in with a cart full of makeup and weird tools behind her. "I'm Margaret. I'll be doing your hair and makeup." She paused to cast an expert gaze over me and tutted her disapproval. "A young thing like you shouldn't look so tired."

"I didn't sleep well. Nightmares," I said quietly.

She arched a well-groomed brow and gave me a knowing look. I felt myself flushing at her unspoken insinuation.

"No matter," she trilled, pushing her cart past me toward the bathroom. "We'll have you fixed up in no time."

Oh, this should be fun, Henri sniped.

I snapped my jaw shut in resignation and closed the door.

I'd managed to swallow my hurt and feigned enthusiasm for the fashion parade that had invaded my closet, finally settling for the least embarrassing of the dresses. As for the shoes, they were all death traps; I'd opted for the ones that looked the least uncomfortable. Then, I'd sat like a mannequin, swathed in my robe while Margaret did her dirty work.

What was for her only small talk felt to me like an inquisition, with me constantly on my guard lest I give something away. I'd parried her barrage of questions with vague answers, making up stories about my "uncle" that only made me bitter as I told them. I'd sat numbly as she'd plucked and waxed and subjected me to treatments I couldn't even name. I had finally lulled myself into the rhythm of her gentle touch and mindless banter when she'd taken a brush to my damp hair. I'd frozen, suddenly alert to the risk.

"I'll fix my own hair," I'd mumbled, reaching up for the brush.

"Nonsense," she'd cooed, gently swatting my hand away. "It's all part of the service. Plus, the hair is my favorite part."

She'd begun brushing, drowning out my protest with the blast of the hair dryer. I steeled myself for the inevitable as she began sweeping my hair away from my neck.

"Beautiful!" she'd squealed. She'd trailed her fingers on my bare skin and I'd flinched. "We'll have to put your hair up."

Of course we will, I'd thought as I sat numbly, pretending none of it was happening to me.

As she'd left, she'd told me Mr. Carmichael was waiting for me in the lobby.

If only it really was my dad, here to bring me safely home.

I'd managed not to look at myself too closely while Margaret had fixed me up, but I couldn't avoid the mirrors in the elevator. The fractured glimpses I caught of myself in the glass showed my hair piled high and makeup way too old for my years. My hand snaked up, nervously fingering my hair, but I stopped myself from pulling it back down to cover myself.

"We have to draw attention," I reminded myself. "For Dad." I dropped my hand and forced myself to look back into the mirror. A gold necklace splayed heavily across my collarbones. My dress was one-shouldered, with an asymmetric cut that left nothing to the imagination. I wore the hotel slippers and clutched platform sandals in my hand, not trusting myself not to trip, and I tugged at the short skirt, trying to force it to reach my knees.

I look like a little girl playing dress-up, I thought nervously. *Will I pass muster?*

No, you look like a tart, Henri added, seeming to enjoy my misery. *Which is probably the look he is going for. Just remember, there is a point to this. You have to stay on Michael's good side.*

As if I could ever forget.

I turned slightly, staring at the reflection of my Mark in the mirror. My hand drifted up, touching it as much as from habit as from self-consciousness. No point in trying to hide it now, I thought to myself. Dropping my hand, I squared my shoulders and stepped out of the elevator car, walking the short distance to the lobby with a sinking feeling in my stomach. As I saw Michael standing there, waiting for me in the guise of my father, I felt my eyes widen with surprise. He'd been magically transformed into something approaching elegant by the sharp cut and fine fabric of his suit. He didn't look at all like the father I'd grown up with.

Michael ran his eyes over me. I waited for a sign of approval, but all I got was a frown when he saw my slippers.

"You can change those in the car," he said in a cold, clipped voice as he stepped toward me and put a hand on my elbow to steer me out of the lobby. My skin sang at his touch, the familiar warmth spreading out slowly from the point where he made contact.

Embarrassment stained my cheeks and I felt the sting of tears behind my eyes as I struggled with his rejection. *Don't be stupid*, I said to myself. *This is just part of a game. It isn't for real.*

A Mercedes sat out front, waiting for us. The valet winked slyly at Michael before opening the door for me.

"Get in," Michael ordered. I tossed my shoes into the bottom of the car and maneuvered myself into the low seat, clinging desperately to the trailing fabric of my skirt to cover my legs.

I had never felt so exposed. My deepest secret—my Mark—was there on display for the whole world to see. As was my body. And the person I'd trusted most in the world, though he was sitting next to me in the front seat of a car—just like we'd been, countless times together—was more distant than ever and responsible for it all.

You asked to go into the lion's den. You wanted to take the search for Maria to the traffickers. This is the price you pay. Happy?

No, I am not happy, I answered Henri in my head. *I'm scared.*

We pulled away from the curb and sat in awkward silence for several minutes before Michael reached into his jacket pocket and tossed my cell phone into my lap.

"Tabitha's been calling you," he said, never taking his eyes from the road. "She's just as bossy as ever, but this time she has an excuse, as we've left her holding the bag for our class report."

I stared at the string of missed calls from the girl who'd become—now that Michael had done what he'd done—the closest thing I had to a best friend. Her digits repeated over and over on the screen.

"I've already called the school to excuse your absence, and your neighbor, Mrs. Bibeau," he said. "With your custody arrangements still preventing your father from contacting you and your mom on that business trip to the UK, we should have enough time to get done what we need to while we are here. Tabitha is the only one we need to deal with now, especially since she's the only one who might find it suspicious that we both are missing. Why don't you e-mail her our share of the report and let her know you're okay?"

Tabitha was my friend, and not one of Michael's favorite people. He found her pushy and nosy, and she was smart, to boot—all the more reason for him to be concerned about her suspicions now. I looked at him, confused. "You're actually going to let me communicate with her?"

His hands gripped the steering wheel more tightly. "I'm not a monster, Hope. And it makes sense. I need to keep her off the scent, especially since I know she'll be going crazy over the team project we skipped out on. Besides, my ability to impersonate you and get the right tone of 'girl talk' in an e-mail is much less than my ability to impersonate your mother excusing your absence to a harried school administrator. So, yes, I need you to e-mail her. Just keep it short. Your computer is in the back. I rigged it to use this disposable cell phone as a hotspot, so you'll be able to send a message."

I pulled the laptop out from the backseat and logged in, staring at the screen. What would keep Tabby from worrying too much and nosing into what was going on? My fingers poised over the keys, I began to type.

"Read it," Michael ordered in a clipped tone as soon as I stopped, so I did.

"Sorry Tabby—family emergency called me out of town. I will fill you in when I come back. Michael and I finished our parts; here they are. Thanks for pulling it all together for us. Owe you a Wright's cupcake?"

"That's good," Michael nodded. "That cupcake part, I wouldn't have thought of that. Add that your phone coverage isn't great, so she shouldn't worry if you don't pick up when she calls. Then you can hit send."

Irritated, I dutifully sent off the message, put my laptop in sleep mode, and leaned back in my seat.

"What are we doing that makes it necessary for me to get into this getup?" I demanded.

"I tracked the Mexican traffickers to a Chinese syndicate that is operating out of the city. Rumor has it that the leader is in town. The Chinese like to gamble in a big way and favor the casinos on the Strip that cater to them, so we have to work our way into an introduction at some place like Caesars Palace or Wynn. That means posing as a high roller and a likely trafficker to boot. This whole thing would have been much easier if I had a watchdog for you, but since Henri abandoned you, I have to keep you with me, where I can know you're safe."

He stole a glance at me.

"If I have to introduce you, I will introduce you as my niece. But by the way you're dressed, people will assume you're my girlfriend. Or, if they fall for the trap, one of my trafficked girls. I may have to treat you badly to make them buy our cover. Whatever you do, don't try anything, and don't talk. Just follow my lead and you'll be safe."

I gulped hard, not really knowing what any of this meant. "What are you trying to accomplish by attracting their attention?" I asked.

He smiled a reckless grin—a reminder that this was indeed Michael, and not some spiffed-up version of my father—as he turned the corner onto the Strip. "We want to meet the boss. To get invited to one of their private games. And," he added as he maneuvered through the throng of tourists toward the entrance to Wynn, "we want to get picked up on every security camera this place has running so your father has an alibi."

"I don't understand," I said. "How does getting on camera help my dad?"

"It was convenient for me to pose as your father as we traveled. And easier for you, I would guess. But now that we're here, we have to make sure someone sees us. When your mother realizes you are missing, the first person she will suspect is your dad. We have to make sure we place you here in a way that proves beyond a doubt it couldn't be your dad, even if I look like him. Otherwise, she and the police will spend a lot of time barking up the wrong tree, trying to pin it on him."

I looked out the window so he couldn't see my confusion. I was grateful that he was thinking ahead as to what would happen to my father, but his concern seemed so at odds with the situation. Not to mention that he made it sound like I was going to be gone for a long time. I didn't have much time to dwell on it, though, as the casino loomed into view, demanding my attention.

I gaped at the curve of the building, glowing in the setting sun, as we approached it. The crowds seemed to part for us as Michael eased under the porte cochere and smoothly shifted into park. He glanced over at me.

"Are you ready?"

I swallowed my questions and slid my feet into the sandals, nodding once. Suddenly my mouth felt dry, like it was filled with sawdust, and I didn't trust myself to speak.

"Just follow my lead," he whispered as the valet swung open our doors and helped us out of the car. Out of the corner of my eye, I saw the valet do a quick sweep of Michael. His expert eye took in the fine fabric and cut of Michael's suit, then widened slightly when he came to the shoes. He stood up a little straighter before addressing Michael.

"Welcome to Wynn, sir."

Michael nodded, the corner of his mouth lifting in mild amusement at the extra dose of respect his getup apparently earned him.

"Miss, welcome to Wynn." The valet was now speaking directly to me. "Is this your first time joining us?"

I darted a glance at Michael, unsure what to say. He inclined his head slightly.

"Yes, it is," I said.

"You'll find it is like no other property. Will you be staying at the hotel? Can we get your luggage from the back?"

"That won't be necessary," Michael cut in. "Keep the car close by, will you?" He casually slipped a hundred dollar bill into the valet's hand. The valet didn't even bother to look at it before tucking it into his pocket.

"Certainly, sir. It would be my pleasure. My colleague, Rhona, will assist you inside. Rhona, please take good care of Mr.—?"

He left the question hanging in the air.

"Carmichael," Michael answered tersely.

"Yes, of course. Mr. Carmichael and his guest. Have a good afternoon, sir. Miss."

"This way, miss," said the smartly dressed uniformed employee I took to be Rhona, trying to usher me through the arched entry. I hung back, trying to glimpse the huge chandeliers and graceful flowers painted on the canopy ceiling.

Michael placed his hand on the small of my back, pressing me forward. The warmth of his touch on my bare skin startled me.

"Let's go," he murmured, pushing me ahead.

I took advantage of the moment to whisper to him, "Why do they keep calling it 'Wynn'? Instead of '*the* Wynn'? It sounds funny."

He smirked as he leaned close to my ear. "It's what they call 'the brand.' The owner is very fussy about it, since it's his name. Watch—they try to work it into their conversation as often as they can. I bet you'll never hear them slip up."

Inside, the lobby unfolded into a long, polished corridor that seemed to wind through a small jungle. Balls of flowers swayed among the leafy trees, lending an element of fantasy to the brightly lit atmosphere. The trees formed a canopy that twinkled with white lights, leading us toward the registration desk.

"Checking in to Wynn, sir?" Rhona interrupted our thoughts with just the right mix of apology and authority, hovering at the fork in the path before us.

Michael winked at me, noting her use of the casino's name, before answering. "We don't need to register. Just the high-limit cage."

"Of course, sir. This way," Rhona said, turning us to the left. We wound through the casino, the usher peppering us with questions—where were we staying? What would we like to play? Were there other experiences we'd like to have while in Las Vegas?—and then discreetly depositing us with the cashier.

"Yes, Mario. Mr. Carmichael and his guest will be playing with us at Wynn today."

"Not her, just me," Michael cut in. "Mario, I'd like to speak with an executive host and get a marker for three million dollars."

I could feel my eyes popping out of my head, but the man behind the counter did not blink.

"Of course, sir. If you'd like to have a seat, I will have Arnaud here in a moment."

We sat down in the small lounge area, waving off the waitress who offered us drinks.

"Are you crazy?" I said, straining to keep my voice low. "We don't have money like that to spend!"

"Of course we do," Michael grinned back at me, seeming like some crazy version of my dad.

"Everything we will need will be there. Trust me." He patted my hand. "Just don't give us away."

I clamped my mouth shut in frustration and pulled my hand away, dreading what would happen when Arnaud realized we were frauds.

"Mr. Carmichael?" An elegant man reached his hand out as he approached us. Michael stood and grasped his hand. "So nice to meet you. I hear you and your—"

"My niece."

"Yes, your niece, would like to play with us today?"

Michael nodded his head in assent.

"Very well. You haven't played with us at Wynn before, I take it?"

"No."

"Do you have your credit application, or shall I print one for you now?"

Michael pulled a paper from his jacket pocket. I tried to get a glimpse of it, but all I saw were rows of numbers.

"Very good, your account and routing numbers are all in order. This will only take a moment to verify. If you'd like, you could do some shopping on the promenade, and I'll send someone to fetch you?"

"No, we are happy to wait."

"As you wish. It will be but a moment."

With that, he whisked himself away behind the façade of the cage, leaving us alone.

The seconds drained away, each moment filling me with dread. Michael sat calmly next to me, draping a proprietary arm over my shoulders. I curled my lip and shot him my most venomous look, but he simply squeezed my shoulder and leaned over as if to kiss my hair. I felt my breath catch and silently cursed my body for not getting the message that Michael was no longer to be trusted or even liked. He was the enemy. Never mind that he was helping me find Maria.

"Don't blow it, Carmichael," Michael whispered into my ear. "I need you to play along. And look up. Smile. There's a camera right above us." With that, he lifted his head, shooting me a warning look before receding back into his most blasé pose.

I scanned the ceiling but saw nothing but a sea of big, black domes.

"Where?" I whispered, my eyes never leaving the vast darkness above.

"Everywhere. They probably trained some on us the minute Arnaud left. So like I said, smile."

I gave the ceiling a good hard look, remembering what Michael had said about being caught on the surveillance camera to give my dad an alibi. Then, we sat for what seemed like hours—but that was in reality only minutes—until Arnaud reappeared.

"Everything is in order, Mr. Carmichael," he said, discreetly leaning in toward us to deliver the good news and pass something back to Michael. "You are cleared for your marker. Should you require more, I am at your service."

Michael nodded his head genteelly, as if he had expected nothing less.

"May I see to your accommodations at Wynn, sir?"

Michael raised a hand. "No need. We've arranged to stay elsewhere."

"Very well. Dinner reservations, then? Or perhaps theater tickets for the young lady?"

A curt shake of Michael's head cut Arnaud's litany off. "She won't be leaving my side. Are there any private games I can join?"

"Of course, sir. Baccarat, poker, blackjack—?"

"Poker. Pai Gau if you have it."

Arnaud's smooth forehead suddenly collapsed into worried folds like an accordion. "You wish to gamble with the Chinese, sir?"

Michael snorted. "Do I have to spell it out for you? Yes."

"Their minimums are quite high, sir."

"I think you know I am good for it, Arnaud." Michael raised an eyebrow pointedly, then slowly rose from his seat, clamping on to my arm to pull me up after him. I ignored the heat that emanated from his touch, licking me like flames.

"Can you arrange an introduction?" Michael persisted.

Arnaud bowed his head slightly, as if in defeat. "Follow me, sir."

We were whisked away through the casino and guided to a hallway that was cordoned off and kept by an attendant. He saw Arnaud and jumped to attention, straightening his jacket automatically. Arnaud whispered in his ear and the velvet rope was cleared. As we walked down the hall, light bouncing off the shiny marble, I could hear the attendant mumbling on the phone.

We made our way to an unlabeled brass elevator. The doors

swept open and we walked in. Inside, Arnaud pushed the only button available and stood before us, facing the door like a dutiful soldier.

"Mr. Carmichael. I will need to discuss this with my colleague and make the proper introductions in order to secure you entrance to the game. Unfortunately, I cannot guarantee that they will admit you, but the chances are better today than they might have been, as one of their party has already retired for the evening. When I speak with my colleague, it will help if I can share your credentials."

The elevator came to a smooth stop and the doors whisked open. Arnaud turned, waiting for Michael's answer. I found I was as eager to hear his response as Arnaud was.

"You can tell them I am from Atlanta and am an entrepreneur with interests in the shipping and personnel industries."

Arnaud tilted his head in assent and beckoned me through the door. "And the young lady?"

"You may introduce her as Miss Carmichael. All they need to know is that she is with me. And if that isn't enough, you can tell them my bank account balance."

Arnaud walked us into the lounge, depositing us before a long polished bar where several attractive young women were waiting to attend to us, and then he disappeared through a looming set of double doors.

With him gone, I shook my arm, which Michael still held like a vice.

He quickly dropped it and started to stalk the room.

I trailed behind him, politely declining the drinks proffered by the bored eye-candy. "What if we can't get in? Did you ever think of that?" I whispered. "What will we do then?"

"Relax, Hope," he said in his lowest voice. "It will work."

"But how do you know?" I pressed.

"I just do." He dug one hand into the high back of a club chair, his knuckles whitening as he kneaded the smooth leather. For a split second his face seemed to contort with a terrible wince, but just as quickly, he composed himself.

Careful.

Henri's warning reminded me that Michael was still in pain and potentially volatile. Half of me yearned to comfort him, to smooth the worry from his wrinkled forehead; the other half knew that our friendship was a sham, our search for Maria a compromise he'd made only to get me to go along with his other scheme. Better to be quiet. I sank down in the chair, waiting sullenly, resenting the entire situation.

Arnaud came through the door and beckoned to us, holding the door as we rose and crossed the room.

"Showtime," Michael breathed so that only I could hear. "If you want to find Maria, do what I say."

I opened my mouth to protest but snapped it shut as we approached Arnaud.

"And smile for the cameras," Michael hissed before sweeping me before him into the private suite.

The room was unlike any other part of the hotel I'd seen. The bright, airy, and almost whimsical public spaces had been replaced with rich velvet and silk drapes in deep gold and lacquer-bright red, and the entire room was swathed in shadow from candles and dim lights. Asian artifacts graced the walls: calligraphy, jade statues, and silk paintings that looked old and expensive. My brow furrowed as I noticed the lifelike terra cotta figures standing at attention in niches that interrupted each wall—didn't those belong in museums? I spun around, trying to take it all in, and realized the walls of the room formed a clear octagon. All the energy in the room seemed to flow to the center, beneath a ceiling that was crowned with a subtle painting of a dragon.

A row of marble columns separated us from the game: a table sunk lower in the room, down a flight of stairs. Around the room's perimeter stood a buffet line, a bar, even a massage table. A few discreet doors punctuated the silk wallpaper. Somewhere, I could hear the serene trickle of water.

"Koi pond," Michael mouthed as we moved in the shadows toward the center of the room and down the stairs.

"Mr. Carmichael," exclaimed a tanned, silver-haired man, proffering his outreached hand as he met us halfway up the stairs. "Thank you so much for joining us. Allow me to make a few introductions." The man began by gesturing toward the table.

"Mr. Chen has joined us from Hong Kong."

A short man with close-clipped hair and a slight five o'clock shadow inclined his head but made no other move. His wary eyes took us in. They seemed to narrow slightly as he lingered on me, taking me in from head to toe.

Nervously, my hand drifted to my neck, where my Mark was, and I felt myself blush. Michael drew his eyebrows sharply together, clamping his hand on my arm and staring down Mr. Chen with obvious displeasure. Mr. Chen did not break his gaze. Instead, I saw the corner of his mouth flicker up with amusement.

The silver-haired man continued his introductions, oblivious to my discomfort and the testosterone match that was already brewing.

"Mr. Tung is visiting us from Shanghai today," he said, gesturing to the much taller and younger man standing next to Chen. Mr. Tung stared stonily at Michael, paying me no attention. He was impeccably dressed, his muscle-bound body draped in clothes that showed his fine form and his long hair pulled back into a neat ponytail at the nape of his neck. “I believe he has similar business interests to yours, Mr. Carmichael.”

I could feel Michael tense, but the man did not notice and continued on with his introductions.

“We have Mr. Wak, in from Macau,” the host said. Wak seemed barely able to fit into his expensive striped suit, through which his muscles bulged. He scowled at Michael.

“And next to him is Mr. Liu. Mr. Liu has also made a permanent residence on Macau, but is a frequent guest here at Wynn.”

Liu alone smiled, opening his arms wide from where they rested on top of his slight paunch. He looked as if he’d been gambling for a while, the tails of his elegant linen shirt untucked and his whole appearance slightly rumpled.

“Welcome to our game, Mr. Carmichael. We are pleased to have you join us. And your young lady, too. She is so charming.”

I felt myself blush.

Liu continued, beaming at me solicitously. “Perhaps she will be more comfortable in the back rooms with the other young ladies?”

Michael’s grip imperceptibly tightened on my arm. “Thank you for your hospitality. I would prefer she stays here.” He broke into a grin, softening the hard look of determination in his eyes. “She’s lucky.”

Liu laughed heartily while the other men exchanged looks and slight smiles, breaking the tension in the room.

“You may need her more than you know, then,” Liu continued.

Michael did not move. “Who are they?” he said, gesturing to the men hovering in the shadows on the far side of the table.

“Mr. Jones and Mr. Rashid are executives with the casino. It is normal to have them observe when we play with such high stakes.” The tanned man looked at Michael shrewdly. “But of course you know that already.”

"I like to know names," Michael responded smoothly. "Including yours and his." He looked pointedly at the dealer who was standing at the center of the table.

"I am the host for Mr. Chen. You may call me Richard. And your dealer today is Frank." The dealer nodded as he was introduced. I saw a little bead of sweat trickle down from his forehead. "Now, shall we begin?"

Wak absentmindedly fingered a small figurine that sat next to his bankroll on the table, not even bothering to look up. "You ask too many questions."

"Richard spoke too soon. I do not think we have invited you to join us yet, Mr. Carmichael," Tung added, a note of menace creeping into his smooth voice. "You are presumptuous."

Michael shrugged, unperturbed. "Perhaps it's just as well. I'm not so sure I want to join a game of four," he said, his face unreadable. I was confused: Why wouldn't he want to join a game of four? He started turning away from the rail when Chen interrupted.

"Please, Mr. Carmichael. My friends here are hasty," he intoned in perfect English with a clipped British accent. "We had a fifth, but he was taken ill and had to leave us. But with your knowledge of our culture, perhaps you will prove to be a worthy adversary. Your presence here is lucky for us."

Michael turned back to the rail. "Of course, I hope my presence here is *un*lucky for you."

Chen snorted. "That we shall see. Please, join us." The other men at the table bit back their protests. Only Tung seemed unperturbed by Chen's pronouncement.

Michael's lips formed a hard smile of satisfaction. "Stay here," he ordered as he began descending to the table. From nowhere, an attendant appeared with a chair, giving me a seat from which to watch the entire table from above.

I watched as Michael took a spot at the end of the table. He placed his marker down, and Frank, the dealer, pushed an enormous pile of chips his way.

Frank looked once behind him to where the casino executives were standing. They gave him some signal and he sighed, straightening up. "Hundred ante, gentlemen. You know the game."

Without hesitation, Michael dropped some chips onto the felt, as did the other men. I looked at the number and color of chips and blanched. Hundred ante meant hundred *thousand* ante.

Frank wordlessly shuffled and loaded the cards into a dealing shoe. Then, without pause, he dealt the cards, his hands moving with an efficiency that could have only come from years of practice.

The men took their cards, their expressions blank. Then, play began, a complicated dance of betting, drawing, and folding that I could not follow. I felt myself leaning forward in my chair, straining to understand the game, which seemed to have boiled down to just Michael and Chen. The dealer softly called for the men to show their cards. Chen fanned his out slowly, the faintest of smiles floating across his face. Michael threw down his cards in disgust. The dealer called the hand, and Chen reached into the middle of the table, clearing the vast pile of chips.

Hundreds of thousands of dollars, gone in a matter of minutes. And then they did it again. And again.

Ten hands passed, some as quickly as the first, some drawn out like an elaborate seduction. More often than not, Liu, Wak, and Tung bowed out early, leaving Chen against Michael to battle it out. It was a cat-and-mouse game in which Chen seemed to have the upper hand.

The serving women flitted around the table, discreetly removing emptied crystal and sliding fresh drinks to the men. Wak and Liu relaxed, sipping their drinks, as they watched hand after hand fall to Chen. Tung joined them, not bothering to disguise his pleasure at each of Michael's losses. Michael's posture became more rigid with each passing hand. Even from where I sat, I could see the vein throbbing in his temple.

After the tenth hand, Michael knocked over his pile of chips in disgust.

"Quite a run of luck," he spat across the table. "Does anyone else ever win at your table?"

Chen said nothing, ignoring Michael's outburst. Tung, on the other hand, laughed out loud as the dealer swept the felt clean and prepared for the next hand. "Maybe you should be asking your girl. She doesn't seem to be helping you that much today."

I opened my mouth to protest, but Michael's glare stopped me cold. He was raging, and Tung had successfully diverted his attention to me.

"You have a point," he said quietly. "Maybe it's time you went with the other girls." He turned back to the table. "Take care of her, will you?" he said to no one in particular.

Chen looked to Tung, who nodded quickly and shouted something in Chinese to one of the serving girls, who quickly descended upon me and shooed me out of my chair. She dragged me behind her, insistently.

I looked back toward Michael, but he was ignoring me, his attention turned back to the game, absentmindedly flipping a purple chip in his hand. He'd gone to all this trouble to bring me down here in order to keep me safe, and now he was letting them take me in the back room: What was he planning?

"You must come with me now," the girl whispered in halting English. "Come, now."

I let her lead me back toward the curtains, and she whisked me through one of the artfully hidden panel doors into a maze of corridors. Silently she guided me down a short hallway, opening a nondescript door that could have been a doorway to a room in any hotel. Except for the fact that it had bolts and locks on the outside.

"Go on and wait here," she urged, pushing me through the door. I turned to ask her where she was going only to find the door slammed in my face, the sound of locks and bolts turning loud in my ears.

I turned around to confront a crowd of women—no, *girls*—staring at me. They were huddled together on the carpet and on the scant furnishings, dressed in everything from sweatpants to skimpy lingerie. They didn't speak, their big brown eyes looking at me as if I were an alien descended from a spaceship.

From beyond an open doorway, I heard a clatter of what sounded like pots and pans banging in a kitchen. Someone began shouting in Chinese. The shouting became louder until an older woman, dressed severely in a pantsuit, rounded the corner brandishing a pan. The crowd of girls turned as if one to stare at her, and then they turned back to me. One girl with a big, moon-shaped face licked her lips nervously.

I had the distinct feeling they were expecting something to happen. Maybe even wanting it.

The older woman began rapidly speaking at me in Chinese until she realized I had no idea what she was saying. She abruptly switched to English.

"What are you doing here?" she demanded, still balancing the pan in her hand.

"They sent me in here to wait. From the poker game." I shifted nervously, unsteady on my feet, and felt my fingers snake up to my Mark.

Her eyes narrowed. "Trouble, hmm? Don't cause any here. Sit down and stay away from my girls." She skewered me with her stare until I edged my way around the room and slithered down the wall to sit on the floor.

With that, she barked something in Chinese, and one of the girls hung her head and obediently followed her back into the kitchen.

The rest of the group shifted to fill in the empty space she had once occupied and turned again to stare at me. I looked them over carefully. A few of them had fresh scabs and bruises here and there. One had a black eye. They carefully avoided looking at me directly, taking every opportunity to stare at the ground or blindly look at their hands. Some of them clutched one another as if clinging to a lifeboat, but mostly they just sat, passively waiting for whatever was going to happen next.

The clatter in the kitchen resumed and I plucked up my courage to talk to the girls.

"Do any of you speak English?"

A few picked up their heads to look at me then, but no one spoke.

"English? Anyone?"

I waited for what seemed like an eternity. Eyeing the open kitchen door, I slid across the carpet, clutching at the hem of my dress as I inched closer to the huddle of girls.

"Are you being kept captive here? Please tell me. I can help you," I half-whispered, worried I might be overheard.

Nothing. I searched their faces, and they looked away as if ashamed.

"Please talk to me. I want to help."

The girl in front of me, pigtails in her hair, reached out and squeezed my hand. She put her finger to her lips and made a shushing sound to quiet me.

They're too scared to talk to you, Henri piped up. *As they should be. This is a waste of time. The sooner you get out of here, the better.*

Ignoring him, I decided to take a different tack.

"Has anyone here seen a girl named Maria? Or one named Jimena?"

A slow murmur went through the group as I scanned their faces. Excitement shot through me at the thought that they recognized those names.

One girl lifted up her hand and pointed into the kitchen.

"In there? Maria is in there?"

She didn't move, just pointed again with emphasis.

I wasn't thinking. All I knew was that if Maria was in there, I had to get her out of there, out of the clutches of the evil woman who was holding all of these girls hostage. I looked around the room, searching for anything that I could use as a weapon.

Nothing.

Suddenly, the sounds from the kitchen stopped, and everything became deathly quiet.

I stood up and tiptoed to the doorway, craning my neck around to see.

The kitchen was empty. A pot of water was bubbling away on the stove, steam rising up to make little wreaths above the pan.

Through the galley of the kitchen, I could see two doors, both closed. One was bolted again from the outside. I snuck over to it and looked: it was padlocked. I looked around the kitchen again, quickly, but could find no key. I knocked softly, careful not to draw attention, but no one answered.

Through the door I could hear the older woman screaming at someone. The sharp sound of a slap echoed through the thin door, followed by low whimpering.

The other door, though, was unlocked. I slipped in and found myself in another corridor that seemed to wind its way back toward the gambling salon. I walked a few paces, and then froze. I could hear voices coming from the other end, where the card table was, echoing against the bare marble floor. I clung to the wall, trying to listen around the corner.

"Your niece—do you have others like her?" asked a man with a clipped British accent—Chen.

There was silence. Chen continued. "Would you like others? We can make some introductions, of course, but we will need to check your connections before we proceed any further."

When I heard my father's voice—or rather, Michael's voice—responding, my heart stopped. "Ask around. You'll find nothing. I run my own operations. Clean, with plenty of money. The Mexicans have gotten sloppy in Atlanta. They're drawing too much attention from the Feds, and even the state legislature is grumbling about taking action. If you don't partner with me now, your pipeline there will go down with them."

"A dire threat, Mr. Carmichael," the man responded, chuckling. "I don't respond well to threats."

I could picture Michael shrugging off Chen's warning. "Not a threat. Just a statement of fact. You'll find me a willing and generous partner, but not a patient one. You have forty-eight hours."

Chen barked out a laugh. "Willing and generous and also bold. We will make our inquiries. If you check out, you may join us Sunday night."

"Sunday night?"

"We hold a location away from the Strip, closer to our operations. We will be playing there for much higher stakes than are possible here. If you check out, Tung will contact you to make arrangements."

I'd been listening so intently to their conversation that I'd forgotten to pay attention to what was going on behind me. Suddenly, rough hands yanked my hair and neck as a torrent of machine-gun-fire Chinese began echoing in the hall.

"Get off of me!" I screamed, flailing uselessly against my assailant.

The grip around my neck tightened, and I was whirled around and pushed up against the wall to face the older Chinese woman who'd been minding the girls. She raised her hand and struck me, never ceasing her tirade, never loosening the choke hold that was cutting off my precious oxygen. In the background, I could hear people running and shouting in the halls.

I watched her cold, angry eyes as she struck me again, a look of triumph stealing across her face as she slowly strangled me. I struggled, but I could feel the breath seeping out of me, and I started to feel dizzy. The screaming and crying all around me started to sound far away, and I felt myself falling to my knees. Slowly my vision started to fade in on itself, turning to black.

"Let her go. Now."

It was my father's voice, but not his voice. Michael. After a moment's hesitation, the woman who was strangling me let me loose. I dropped to my knees, hard on the floor. I choked for air, wheezing and coughing as I crawled about, trying to get up.

A warm hand grabbed me roughly under the shoulder and jerked me up.

"I told you, no trouble." He shook me, hard.

I looked up, still trying to catch my breath, and all I saw in Michael's eyes was anger. He hadn't let go of my arm, which burned where his fingers dug into me.

"You've embarrassed me in front of my new associates."

Over his shoulder, I could see Chen and Tung, their faces masks as they watched Michael shame me. I was furious.

"I—"

"Enough!" he shouted, and my eyes flew wide open. He'd never spoken to me like that. Never.

He wheeled me around to face the men. "I apologize for her behavior."

Chen nodded his assent and then cleared his throat. Tung took that as his cue.

"I think it is best that you and your niece leave now, Mr. Carmichael," Tung said, his expression stony.

Michael's jaw tensed. "Of course." He pushed me ahead of him, back through the hallway and the kitchen toward the main door, not caring that I stumbled. I thought I understood what he was trying to do—I hoped I understood it, anyway—or else I would have stood my ground. But I knew I had to let him humiliate me in this way. I looked around the living room. If anything, the girls looked more terrified than when I'd come in.

"Go," Michael said tersely from behind. Chen's executive host was standing at the door. He looked away, refusing to meet my eyes, and I knew that he had seen everything. He wordlessly opened the door for me, and I limped through, feeling the heat from Michael's body radiating behind me.

The door slammed behind us and Michael pushed roughly past me, grabbing my hand to drag me along.

"Michael," I whispered furiously as he rushed me down the hallway.

"Not now."

We made our way through the salon, which was eerily quiet. Wordlessly, we slipped into the elevator.

"Clean yourself up," he said brusquely. I looked at my reflection. My hair had fallen out of its intricate style, and the strap of my dress was falling down my shoulder. Big red welts had formed on my neck, welts that would be sure to turn to bruises. It wasn't worth jeopardizing our plan to find Maria to stand up to him here. Silently, I pulled all my hair loose, doing my best to straighten it with my fingers, and I pushed up the strap.

We wound our way back through the casino, Michael stalking in brooding silence the entire way. He paced angrily as we waited for the valet to bring the car, and he practically threw me into the passenger seat, slamming the door behind me.

We pulled away from the curb in a squeal of burning rubber.

I watched him out of the corner of my eye, waiting for his pretense of anger to fall away as we left the casino. But I waited in vain. His forehead was throbbing again, and his knuckles turned white as he gripped and regripped the steering wheel.

This isn't an act, Henri whispered to me urgently. *Be careful.*

I tucked my legs under me, trying to make myself as small as I could in the seat. Through my eyelashes, I watched his nostrils flare as he took deep breaths, as if he was trying to calm himself.

We rode in silence all the way back to the hotel. He pulled up to the curb and bounded out of the car, practically running over the valet as he stormed off. The valet gallantly helped me out.

"Rough night at the tables?" he asked, smiling knowingly.

I nodded quickly, embarrassed, hoping that he wouldn't notice how disheveled I was.

When I found Michael back in our room, he had transformed out of my father's guise. He'd dressed casually, in a T-shirt and jeans, and was holding my cell phone up to his ear. He ended his call with an emphatic push of the button and turned on me. His eyes were stormy, and he seemed to bite his words as he spoke to me.

"Your mother has been calling. We're running out of time, Hope, and your stunt tonight didn't help."

All of the anger I'd been holding back while in public came into my voice. "Stunt? What stunt? I was trying to find Maria, like we planned."

His eyes flashed. "Hope, there was more going on in that room than you realize. I sent you back there to keep you safe, not to snoop around."

"But those girls—"

"Those girls were exactly what we suspected," he interrupted, beginning to pace again. His T-shirt clung to his back, highlighting every bit of tension in his shoulders. "We have to be very careful, Hope. These men are dangerous. They are powerful and used to having their every whim catered to. That octagonal room? Deliberately made for them that way because eight is a lucky number in Chinese culture. Those artifacts? Probably stolen from some museum and bought on the black market.

"The only reason I got into that game is because I happened to know that four at the table is unlucky to them. The fact that I knew anything about Chinese culture intrigued Chen enough to let me into the game.

"Losing that money to him? Deliberate. Because Chen and Tung are our traffickers, Hope. Chen's the ringleader, and Tung is his goon. I need them to let their guard down with me, think they can manipulate me. And we need them to believe that I'm a trafficker, too. I can't have them thinking you disobey me. I can't have them thinking you aren't afraid of me. I can't have given them any reason to think I'm not the real deal."

He sat down abruptly on the edge of the bed and held his head in trembling hands.

See? Henri said pointedly. *See how the littlest thing can set off his rage? See how his pain is getting worse? It is because he is disobedient to God. It is because you are still alive. Tread carefully, my girl. This nonsense with the kidnapped girl has to stop. You must focus on the Prophecy before he can no longer control himself.*

"I'm sorry," I whispered.

Michael looked up, startled.

"You're sorry?"

I nodded, not sure if there was anything I could say that would make it better.

Michael took a deep breath and smiled ruefully, just enough to deepen his dimple. When he spoke again, his voice was rough.

"It is I who should be apologizing. I just need to keep you safe."

I nodded again, eager to soothe his anger. "I know. For the Prophecy."

He tilted his head and looked at me thoughtfully. "Yes," he said softly. "For the Prophecy."

I stood uncomfortably, unable to break his gaze.

"We're going to have a busy day tomorrow, so you'd best get some rest." With that he stood up and walked to the door. "I'll leave you to it."

He opened the door and paused. "Sweet dreams, Hope," he said quietly, being careful not to look at me. And then he was gone. There was a blinking light on the side table: my cell phone. He'd deliberately left it for me, and he'd left it where I'd be sure to see it.

I picked it up. He was giving me a choice.

I turned the power off and tucked it away in my backpack.

twelve

Michael roused me from bed with the rising sun, pushing the curtains roughly aside to let in the glare.

"We need to get a move on. We have a bit of a drive." He was moving about the room restlessly. I scooted back against the headboard, wondering whether he was still angry with me.

"A drive? To where?" I asked through my yawn as I rubbed the sleep from my eyes.

"We're going out to St. George. All the crazy crystal-toting people think Sedona is the spiritual center of the universe, but St. George is where we need to go. You have twenty minutes. Dress for a hike. You'll find some new clothes in the closet. I'll meet you in the car out in front."

Twenty minutes later, we were pulling away from the hotel. Michael shoved a paper bag at me. "Croissants from the Beat. And there's a latte for you, too."

My stomach growled, accusing me over the dinner I'd missed last night, and I gratefully took the bag. I looked at him cautiously, trying to gauge his mood as I stuck my nose into the bag, inhaling the scent of fresh pastry. He no longer seemed angry. In fact, the further we drove, the more visibly relaxed he became. Only the tightness around his eyes gave away the fact that he was still battling the pain.

"Thanks," I said, picking up the steaming latte from the cup holder and inhaling the fragrant aroma. "Mmm."

As soon as we were on the interstate, he abandoned the guise of my father, which seemed to cheer him even more. We were headed toward Salt Lake City, winding through desolate landscapes that seemed to scrape the blue sky. Without a cloud to be seen, the brightness was otherworldly. I fumbled for my sunglasses, wanting to drink in every aspect of the terrain as we drove.

"Why are we going to St. George? Is that where the Librarian is?"

Michael nodded. "At the dawn of Christianity, monks used to stay out in the desert, sometimes for years, trying to provoke visions and become closer to God. Their asceticism helped, of course, but there are places in deserts where the Heavens touch the earth. Those are special places where the boundaries between men and angels blur. It is in one of those places where we will find the Librarian."

"How do you know he is there?" I asked, my curiosity aroused.

Michael shrugged. "He is always there. The only question is whether he will allow himself to be found."

"You mean he might not want to help us?" I looked anxiously at Michael, but I couldn't read his eyes through his sunglasses.

"He will," Michael asserted, his jaw becoming stern. "He will."

I pulled off a piece of my flaky croissant and popped it in my mouth. A moan escaped me—I'd not realized how hungry I was. Michael laughed out loud. For a moment I remembered, sadly, the way he'd made fun of my appetite when Jessica Smythe had fallen into his arms, back when we had been friends. I pushed aside the memory and kept questioning him as I chewed.

"Why do you call him the Librarian?"

"It is an appropriate title for the one who has been appointed to document the history of the Heavens, wouldn't you say?"

I rolled this over in my mind.

"Is the Librarian Enoch?"

Michael looked over at me, a half-smile of surprise on his face. "Not much gets by you, does it?"

I was oddly pleased by his praise, and blushed. "He is the only one I've heard of writing that much about the angels."

Michael turned back to the road and continued. "Yes, the infamous Book of Enoch. Though the versions you have here on earth are false and corrupt, the ideas you have of Enoch documenting our history and of his skills as a prophet are well founded."

"What parts of the book aren't true?" I asked, curious.

Michael seemed to tense. Just for a moment, his posture became rigid.

"Most of it."

"Even the Book of the Watchers?" I asked, remembering my father's lessons about the coupling of Fallen Angels and mortal women and their ill-begotten offspring.

His jaw tensed. Staring ahead, he answered, "Nonsense. There never were Nephilim. It is not possible."

I decided to change the subject. "Why not just call him Enoch?" The moonlike scenery was a blur outside my window now, but I was too fascinated by what Michael was telling me to care.

Michael seemed to relax again. "You remember that Enoch was taken up into Heaven by God?"

"Yes," I said, impatient to hear the full story. "And he was transmuted into an angel."

"He had to renounce his human life to become angelic, and that included the renunciation of his name. Names are important. They signify more than just your lineage; they carry history and meaning in them. For him to take a new life, he had to cast away the old. Do you understand?"

I hesitated. "I think so. Sort of like how there are so many different names for Jesus in the Bible? Or how some people take new names when they are baptized or confirmed?"

"Exactly."

I crumpled the empty bag that had held my croissant, letting my attention wander to the steep canyons and scrubby vegetation passing by my window.

"Michael?" I asked absentmindedly after a few minutes of silence had passed. "Who is the Librarian documenting history for?"

"For whoever should need it," he responded vaguely.

"Like us," I said. Michael did not answer.

I nestled myself into the seat. Michael seemed so different today, almost as if yesterday hadn't happened. I was wary—he was capable of increasingly volatile mood swings—but I had to admit that I liked how relaxed he seemed. It felt comfortable, like how things were before. I eased further back into the seat, wondering what had changed to make him seem so calm.

~

Later in the morning, we pulled into an empty gravel parking lot. All around us, red and brown mountains and plateaus rose from the desert plains, their rocky surfaces dotted by fantastic formations.

"We're here," Michael announced as he turned the key in the ignition. "Snow Canyon State Park."

I squinted against the sun.

"Where do we go from here?"

"We'll have to hike in. Grab some water from the trunk and make sure you have sunscreen," he added as he slipped out the door.

Hiking. How very . . . human. And limited. You would think an Archangel could do something more impressive than that, Henri sniffed.

Shut up, Henri; it's not as if you're the one doing any actual hiking, I thought as I unfolded myself from the seat and stood outside. I stretched, feeling the dry heat that was already radiating off the desert floor. *By the way, nice of you to show up this morning.*

Oh, I've been here the whole time. Even through that dreary history lesson of Michael's.

I giggled, forgetting myself. Michael looked at me over his sunglasses from where he was rummaging in the trunk.

"Something amusing you?"

"Oh, um, no. Just remembering an old joke," I said lamely.

He arched his eyebrow quizzically, but he didn't pursue the matter any further, choosing instead to toss me a light backpack.

"This should have everything you need. I'm not sure exactly where we will find him, but I have a rough idea. You should be prepared to hike for a few hours. Think you can make it?"

"Of course," I said firmly, lifting the bag onto my back. "I definitely don't want to sit here and wait. I'm coming with you."

"Then let's go."

There was a clear trail leading straight from the parking lot. The immediate area was sandy, forcing us to wade slowly through the dunes until the path firmed up and headed into more rocky terrain.

Michael kept a swift pace, but I didn't mind. I hung back slightly, glad for once not to have to worry about him watching me, his probing eyes seeing everything I was thinking and feeling. Several times I caught myself following the movements of his sleek muscles, the way his broad shoulders tapered down to his impossibly thin waist, and I blushed, thankful yet again to be away from his watchful eyes.

For a long time, we just moved deeper into the park, cutting through rock formations until we were further and further away from the parking lot, our car just a speck in the distance.

Then we began to climb. We went through a rapid series of ascents and descents, no way around the monumental peaks that stood in our path. Despite how fit I was from running, my breath grew heavier, more labored. Michael noticed but did not pause or comment. Instead, he began a running commentary on the landscape and the history of the region, explaining the names of the strange formations, talking about the elevations and the medicinal purposes of the alien vegetation that crowded against the trail—everything and anything, anything at all to distract me from the climb.

When I thought I could climb no further, he led us through a gap in the rock into a natural amphitheater. The sandstone below our feet had been hollowed into a great depression that still held water left over from the torrential rains that had periodically swept the landscape. Tufts of hardy grass poked out here and there. Only a narrow opening at the opposite end revealed a sliver of endless blue sky. It was almost as if we were hidden inside a bowl, safe from prying eyes.

"The Mormon settlers used to drive their cattle here during droughts so that they could have water," Michael said, turning toward me at last. He reached into his backpack and pulled out a bottle of water, quenching his thirst with a long drink. I couldn't drag my eyes away from his Adam's apple, bobbing with each swallow. He finished drinking, pulling his arm across his mouth with a satisfied smack of the lips.

"Your turn," he said, offering me his bottle. I reached for it and our fingertips brushed, a lick of flame running up my arm before I snatched the bottle away.

He looked at me as if he was about to say something, and then he turned away, swinging his backpack off his shoulder and settling down onto the rock. I took a drink of the water and waited for him to speak.

"Here is as good a place as any for us to take a break," he said. "We'll wait for a bit, catch our breath. If he doesn't show up, we'll have to keep going."

That doesn't seem like a very promising plan, Henri whined inside my head.

Shhhh, I thought, though secretly I agreed with him. I leaned against the cool rock walls, getting as much of my body into the shade as I could. I had a clear view of Michael's back silhouetted against the sliver of blue ahead of us. He stretched with catlike grace, settling in to wait, basking in the fullness of the sun.

I stared at the opening in the rock, my apprehension growing with each minute that passed. But then we heard a small sound, like a scattering of gravel and sand, as something or someone shuffled toward us. A figure appeared, blocking out the sky in the opening. As he moved toward us, I could see he was old—not ancient, but old, with a flowing white beard and grizzled brown skin. He was wearing a Grateful Dead T-shirt and a brown sunhat with earflaps. He moved slowly and deliberately, leaning on two walking sticks that had plastic grips and tips that looked as if they belonged to ski poles.

Michael did not move as the man approached, but I could see his frame tense, poised for action.

"Hello, Michael." The man—the Librarian—stood above Michael, a welcoming smile on his face as he looked down.

"Hello. Were you followed?"

"Not now. But you know the Fallen are hot on your trail. It is only a matter of time," the Librarian sighed. He cast one of his walking sticks aside and offered Michael a hand. Michael took it and rose to his feet gracefully, then clasped the old man to his chest.

"It is good to see you."

"And you," the Librarian said, stepping back to look at Michael. "Though I wish it were under different circumstances."

Michael hung his head, looking momentarily defeated. "You know, then, why I come."

"Yes. There are rumors about. Nothing but rumors yet, but they did reach my ears." He straightened himself and turned his attention to me where I was seated in the shadows. "I suppose this is the girl, then?"

"Yes," Michael said, turning to me. A smile flitted across his face and he held out his hand. "Hope, come meet the Librarian of Heaven."

I scrambled to my feet and walked over. Michael placed an arm around my shoulder and shuffled me in front of him to face the Librarian's inspection.

"Turn around, girl," the old angel said, a note of affection softening his gruffness. "I must see this Mark of yours."

I turned, self-consciously. Michael gently reached around me and lifted my hair to the side to give the Librarian a full view. If the Librarian noticed how possessive the gesture was, he didn't say anything about it.

Instead, he sighed deeply. "May I?"

I nodded slightly. The Librarian placed a calloused finger on the Mark, tracing its intricate pattern down my neck. "So it is true."

"Yes," Michael said, allowing my hair to cascade back over my shoulders. "It has begun."

I turned around to face the Librarian once again. The old man was smiling sadly at me.

"I suppose you came to learn the full Prophecy," he said, shuffling himself over to sit on an outcropping of rocks. "That is what the Fallen are asking for, so I suppose you need it, too."

Michael didn't respond, but I felt his heavy hand upon my shoulder and imagined he was nodding his response. The old man took a granola bar out of a cargo pocket in his shorts and slowly started to unwrap it. He took a bite and began to speak again, pausing now and then to savor a morsel.

"I remember when the Prophecy first came to me—the uproar, the fear. I almost think they wanted me to take it back, pretend it had never happened. But of course I couldn't. When I refused to deny it, I was forced to go to court and explain myself. Being a newcomer to Heaven, of course, I had a target on me."

"I don't understand," I interrupted.

The old man eased back in his seat and chuckled, his eyes crinkling up behind his sunglasses as he remembered the controversy.

"My child, it is much the same as with your Michael here." I blushed, about to stammer he was not "my Michael," but the old man pressed on, never giving me a chance.

"The angelic host never really got over their resentment of humanity. They neither forgot nor forgave humans for usurping the favor of God Almighty, a favor they had enjoyed exclusively for millennia. The obedient ones could do nothing about it, of course, so they turned their petty feelings where they could. Michael—well, they blamed him for helping mankind, for ushering Adam and Eve out of Eden in safety, for defending Moses against Satan's prosecution, indeed, for defending man at every turn, even when man became sinful and murderous against his own.

"Just as many hated you, Michael, for being the champion of man, so they hated me for being elevated from man to angel. The speaking of the Prophecy gave them the perfect excuse to persecute me. The fact that they all feared what the Prophecy foretold only made it more urgent. They wanted to wipe it from the record, pretending like children that if they didn't see it there in front of them, if they refused to acknowledge it, it would not come to pass."

"So they took you to Court? In Heaven?" I asked.

"Yes," he chuckled. "Angels can be so petty. And their legal code is as bureaucratic as they come, too. I suppose when you have all of eternity, there is a sort of perverse pleasure in taking up so much time by resolving your disputes. Instead of finding common ground, angels tend to hoard their grievances like treasures, hardening and polishing them until they shine with the heat of the sun."

"What did they do?" I asked, urging him on.

"They sentenced me to millennia of isolation. I had to renounce myself and suffer my sentence at the very edges of Heaven." He leaned heavily into his walking sticks and rose up from the rock. "I came here. Since I was lonely for the earth and lonely for humans, my sentence has been a blessing, not the punishment they envisioned."

He walked slowly to where we stood and nodded at Michael. "I suppose you must hear it."

Michael tried to grip my shoulder, but I shrugged him off. The Librarian's mouth twitched, and I wondered if he'd noticed.

"Please," Michael said.

"Very well."

The Librarian drew himself up to his full height and pushed

his sunglasses to the top of his head, perching them on his hat brim. His eyes were closed. He took a deep breath and opened his eyes to fix me in his stare. I gasped: his eyes were milky white with blindness.

"Do you speak Aramaic, girl?" I shook my head dumbly, transfixed under his gaze. "Greek? Hebrew? No matter, I will translate it into English for you."

He spread his arms wide, as if he could capture the energy of nature and send it back out with his words. He began to speak, almost sing, his voice echoing off the rocky walls as he recited the Prophecy.

Woe unto ye who fear not the Lord;

The walls of Heaven shall be locked unto thee.

You will wail and gnash your teeth, and render thy garments, but He will hear not thy voices.

You will curse His name and seek to blot out the stars,

But still the Heavens will call to you.

Thy flames shall burn and twist, reaching for the Lord,

But He shall see naught but thy darkness.

How will you right this wrong? How will you reclaim your place at Heaven's throne?

The Key of Righteousness perverted Brother against Brother,

Child against Father, and rent the curtain of Heaven with the sins of Man and Angels' doubt.

With this Key, the Bearer shall come and the Gate shall open, spilling out Heaven's glory, and letting those desirous amongst you to ascend once more.

Woe then be unto them who stand in thy way,

For the bitterness of the Fall shall be tenfold times tenfold

And shall endure forever.

Forever. The last word bounced off the canyon, mocking us with its finality. I stood silently, waiting for Michael to speak or the Librarian to move, anything to break the solemnity that had descended upon us.

"What does it mean?" Michael demanded, frustration coloring his tone. "It doesn't make any sense. 'The Key of Righteousness'? I've never even heard of that."

The Librarian just shrugged and slid his glasses down back to his nose. "It is not mine to interpret. Just to deliver," he said, as if there was no use debating it.

"But you know," Michael retorted, pushing me away hastily to approach the old man. "You know what it means; you are probably the only one who knows what it means. You have to tell me."

The man looked over Michael's shoulder and seemed to stare straight through me. "It is not for me to interpret," he repeated. "Those for whom it was intended must determine its meaning."

Michael clenched his fist in rage. "You're impossible! I remember now why you were banished. Old fool!" With that, he stomped off through the gap in the rock, leaving me alone with the Librarian.

I was not sure what to do, but the Librarian quickly made his own intention clear. "It is good that he left us, Hope. Come. Sit with me. I would hear what you think of the Prophecy."

Surprised, I scuttled across the rock and sat at his feet.

"Go on," he urged. "Tell me your thoughts."

I hesitated. Who was I to tell a prophet what his prophecies meant? But he waited patiently for me to speak. Shyly, I cleared my throat.

"Well, it seems clear that the Fallen will rise again and take over Heaven."

He tilted his head, gravely considering my words. "Does it, now?"

"Yes," I continued, gaining confidence. "When they gain the Key to open the Gate of Heaven."

He crossed his hands over his walking stick and pondered my pronouncement. "Do you know what the Gate of Heaven is, Hope?"

I paused. "I imagine that it's not a physical gate, but something spiritual, or supernatural, that God has put in place to keep the Fallen out."

He rocked back and forth on his perch, considering my answer. "Yes, I suppose it is metaphysical in nature, something quite different than what the words may suggest. God often speaks to us in codes and metaphors, testing our understanding of Him. I suppose that is what is testing Michael's patience—he wants all the answers without the struggle of puzzling them through."

I didn't speak, knowing the Librarian was right.

"The Prophecy means for you to unravel its mysteries," he continued. "It plays on words and metaphors and analogies, just like the parables of Christ. It is a pity you do not know the old languages, or you might have greater appreciation for it. Take this word, 'Gate.' It is *thura* in the Greek, 'gate.' It is a beautiful word, do you not think?"

I nodded, not really clear where he was going with his language lesson.

"You would do well to consider this as you think it through. You must think through the special role that you and Michael have to play, for God has ordained it for you both."

He stared at me through the dark ovals of his sunglasses, and I felt a shiver run up my spine.

"Yes, words are simply names for things, and names are important." I perked up—he was echoing the same words that Michael had spoken when he told me about Enoch changing his name. "Words signify who or what we are. They tell us our past, and our destiny. Have you ever considered your own name, Hope?"

I shook my head, riveted.

"Your first name, Hope, is not so mysterious. Hope. Expectation. Belief. Faith. That much is clear. But your last name—ah! Your last name. Carmichael. Some people think it refers to a sacred place in Scotland, the hills where the first church ever dedicated to your angel, Michael, was built. Others believe that it is a corruption—a bad translation—and that in its original form, it meant *Cor* or *Coeur de Michel*. 'Michael's Heart.'"

He stopped speaking, letting the portent of his words sink in.

"Either way, it is a strange coincidence, is it not? Or, if we believe that there are no coincidences—if we believe that what we call things matters—it would seem you and Michael belong to one another, have been destined from the beginning to come together in this way."

I shifted uncomfortably in my seat as the blood rushed to my face. Were my feelings for Michael so obvious? And what did those feelings even mean, considering that he'd lied to me, all but kidnapped me, and might end up killing me? But the Librarian seemed oblivious to my discomfort and continued on.

"You must forgive his temper, my dear. He is in pain, as you know. And he is unused to company."

I was grateful for the change of subject and leaped upon it. "What do you mean?"

He sighed and gestured about him with his walking stick. "All angels work in pairs. Think of it as a buddy system of sorts to make sure they do not stray from the path. There are only two exceptions: Guardians, who have the company of the humans they keep, and Archangels, who are sent out as solitary emissaries of God's word. It is a lonely job to keep over the centuries. I am sure it makes him a bit rough around the edges." He smiled. "He might struggle with the normal feelings that come along with newfound companionship, not to mention those raging hormones that come along with a teenage boy's body." I felt my face flaming once again, but the old angel continued on, oblivious to my embarrassment. "So do not judge him harshly. He is doing the best he can."

"But Enoch," I said, finding his old, human name slipped more easily from my tongue. "Enoch—he will have to kill me. If I am the Bearer of the Key, he will have to. He will have no choice."

He knitted his brow together. "It doesn't have to end that way, Hope. But it all rests on your understanding of the Prophecy. You and Michael are not so far ahead of the ones who are pursuing you. The others will come. They know you defeated Lucas in battle. He will rally them, and they, too, will demand that I tell them what you have heard today. And no doubt they are looking for you even now."

Icy fear gripped my chest. "How can Lucas rally them? He's dead!"

He simply shook his head. "Angels are immortal, my dear. They can be beaten, but only God can wipe them from existence. Not even God's own warrior can do that. That is why the battle over humankind is so bitter. Neither side will ever give up because neither side will ever really lose."

He looked quizzically at me. "Did Michael let you think Lucas was dead?"

I nodded, confused. The Librarian seemed to read my mind.

"It was probably easier for him that way. You are a brave girl. Perhaps he needed to be sure you heeded that which you should fear."

He leaned heavily onto his walking stick, hoisting himself up from his rocky perch and reaching into his cargo pants. He pulled out a crumpled-up ball of notebook paper and handed it to me. I smoothed it out and saw ancient, foreign words scratched against the blue lines, the hastily scrawled English translation squeezed into the margins. It was the Prophecy.

That something so precious would be written on normal notebook paper seemed wrong. Suddenly, the paper felt fragile and dry. I held it in my hand, afraid that if I gripped it too tight it would crumble away, leaving me to figure out my fate on my own.

Enoch's hand lingered on mine, and he squeezed my fingers in his as he closed my hand around the paper. "You remind me of my granddaughter, do you know that? She was a brave one, too. Spirited. It's what makes me glad to see you working with Michael. You will keep him on his toes."

He patted my hand before letting it go. I felt oddly choked up, as if I was preparing to part from an old friend.

"Your roles are written, Hope. It is up to the both of you to find them." He clasped my shoulder with one of his ancient hands and squeezed. "Now go to Michael. He is beyond the rocks, and he is in need of you."

I turned around. "Over there?" I asked. I peered out through the rocks but could see nothing. I turned back to face the old man, hoping for an answer, but when I did, he was gone. All the proof I had that he had even been here with us was the grubby, worn-out piece of paper I gripped in my hand.

A shadow flitted over me and I suddenly felt chilled. I looked up, expecting to see a large cloud marring the bright blue sky. There was nothing. The cold feeling stayed with me as I went to find Michael.

~

We rode back to Las Vegas in silence. Not even Henri interrupted my thoughts as I stared at the illegible foreign words scratched across the paper I'd carefully smoothed out in my lap, comparing them to the English in the margins. A few times, I asked Michael what he thought this word or that meant, what the Key might actually be, but he seemed too lost in his own thoughts to respond.

Finally, he simply said, "It's not my strong suit, puzzling things out. Surely you must know that about me by now." He sighed, resigned, and began fiddling with the buttons of the radio.

We settled back into companionable silence, listening to whatever happened to come through the speakers. I thought about everything the Librarian had said about Michael's loneliness and about how we were here, together, because of fate. For an instant, it almost felt like we were back in Atlanta and were simply driving home after school.

Forgetting myself, I reached for his hand and he flinched, snatching his hand away from me.

I drew my hand back as if I'd been burned. Tears stung my eyes as I turned to stare out the window.

Never forget, he is the reason you are in danger, I chided myself. *Never forget.*

We passed the rest of the drive in silence, me straining as far away from him as the seat belt would allow, my eyes fixed on the unending ribbon of asphalt passing by outside my window.

As we approached Las Vegas, Michael cleared his throat. "I'll have to change back now. To your father," he added, in case I had forgotten.

"Okay," I said, refusing to look at him.

"I thought we might swing through downtown to see if we spot Maria?" He turned the statement into a question, speaking tentatively, as if he was unsure I would accept his offer of a truce, his gesture of unspoken apology.

"Sure," I said, still not moving. "Thank you."

In the twilight, we cruised the old neighborhood, driving past abandoned homes, boarded-up shops, and parking lots full of weeds. Here and there, huddled against the coming night, groups of women and girls stood waiting for some sort of relief. But their work was just starting, I knew. They would get no relief tonight.

I scanned their faces, knowing in my heart that I would not find Maria among them, just the echo of that same sadness in their eyes.

When we pulled up to the hotel, Michael idled the car.

"Let me see your phone," he demanded, holding out his hand.

"Are you going to take it away from me again?" I asked. "I haven't tried to call for help all day."

"Please don't argue with me," he said. "This is important."

I bit my lip, but I burrowed into the backpack at my feet, drew it out, and handed it to him. He checked the messages before returning it to me.

"It's a message from your mom," he said, quietly. "We'll have to get rid of your phone after you've listened to it. I should have taken care of it long ago."

He slid out of the car, leaving me to listen to the message while the valet milled about.

"Happy birthday, Hope!" Mom's cheery voice chirped from the other end. "I wanted to surprise you so I cut my trip short. I'm on my way from the airport, honey. I should be home in no time at all. Sweet Sixteen, can you believe it? Oops, here comes the customs agent. I have to turn off my phone before they confiscate it. I'll see you in a few hours. Love you!"

I listened mechanically to the automated prompts before hitting the delete key.

Happy birthday, indeed.

I walked into our room and could sense that Michael's mood, like the wind, had shifted again. I eased inside the door to find him pacing, staring stonily at the cheap cell phone he'd bought for himself.

"What's wrong?" I asked, almost afraid of what he might answer.

He wheeled at me, holding the phone out as if I knew already. "It was Tung. He said Chen is worried I don't have a handle on things, can't control you, and can't control my business. He's not sure he wants such a risky partner." He didn't wait for my response, but in frustration he threw the phone across the room, where it shattered into pieces against the wall.

I swallowed hard. If we couldn't get to Chen, we would never find Maria. And we were running out of time.

"I'm sorry," I whispered, staring at the floor. I hurried over to where the phone lay in pieces and started to pick up the shards of plastic and metal with shaking hands.

A hand on my arm stopped me. Michael squatted down next to me and took my chin in his hand, forcing me to look into his eyes. They were still Michael's eyes, even though he had changed his appearance back to that of my father. My heart beat, unable to make sense of things anymore.

"No, I'm sorry," he said, looking at me deeply. "We'll think of something." He let go and leaned back, holding out his hand. "In the meantime, give me your phone. It's too dangerous to keep it anymore. As soon as your mom discovers you missing, they'll start trying to trace it and it will lead them right here. And if I know Mona," he continued, showing his familiarity with my mother by referring to her by name, "she'll come after you full force."

He was right. I reached into the bag I had dragged in behind me, fished around for the phone, and handed it over.

He tucked the phone neatly inside his suit pocket. "I'm going to dispose of it," he said, gathering up a few things and heading for the door. "I want you to be dressed and ready to go when I get back. You'll have about an hour. Be on time."

"Dressed for what?" I asked, perplexed by his ever-shifting attitude.

"You'll see," he said, smiling enigmatically as he slipped through the door. "Hope—I want you to know that I trust you. Just don't let anyone in while I'm gone."

I sat back on my heels, watching as the door closed quietly behind him.

thirteen

"You're certainly in a chipper mood for having just come off the plane," said the large black man sitting behind the wheel, looking into the mirror at Mona in the backseat.

Mona beamed back at him. How many times had he driven her to and from the airport over the years? Too many to count. He'd seen her at her most tired and exhausted moments. She'd confided in him things she'd never dared breathe to another human being. Arthur was her friend and confidant. So she couldn't wait to talk to him now, to tell him about Hope.

"I've never been able to be with Hope for her birthday, Arthur—not since our separation, anyway." She fiddled with the buttons on her BlackBerry nervously, knowing that she couldn't have any more messages in the nanosecond since she'd last looked. "And this one's a special one, sixteen."

Arthur whistled. "Does she know what you've got planned?"

Mona shook her head. "I only just called her a bit ago to let her know I was on my way home. Everything is a surprise."

"Was she excited to hear from you?"

"She didn't answer," Mona said, shrugging. "Who knows where she is. Running? Studying?" She snorted then, chiding herself while she broke into a grin. "Probably seeing that boy, Michael, with whom she's become so taken."

"You didn't tell me she has a boyfriend. Do you approve?" Arthur peered into the mirror. He could always read Mona like a book, always knew just the right thing to ask her to get her to open up to him.

"I didn't at first," Mona admitted, tucking her BlackBerry into her handbag. "I thought she was too young. Or rather, too sheltered after all her father had put her through. But he seems to be a good influence. And she's opened up to him about everything. God knows she needs someone to talk to."

She smiled back at Arthur.

"They seem innocent enough. I don't think I've even caught them holding hands—just mooning after one another. It's nice."

Mona paused, stretching out with a great yawn. "These international flights are going to catch up with me one of these days. I'm getting too old for this."

"Keep talking, Mona. You know you'll never stop. You love it. Uh-oh," Arthur said, slowing the SUV down. "Looks like an accident ahead. You might as well get comfortable back there; I think we're going to be a while."

"Figures," Mona harrumphed, but even the massive delay looming ahead of them couldn't wipe the smile off her face. Nothing would take away the joy of being with Hope today.

The idea had come to her after she'd had to leave Hope to her own devices on her first day at Dunwoody High. She'd known then that she wanted to do something special for Hope's birthday, but she couldn't figure out what. Hope didn't care about material things; in fact, she almost seemed embarrassed by them. And the idea of a big party just seemed—off. Whatever she did, she knew it had to show effort more than expense; she had to show that it was personal and heartfelt. Intimate.

Once Hope had started running outside, Mona had found her inspiration. Just like the mixtapes of old, she'd started assembling downloads of the songs that had been her, her father's, or Hope's old favorites. Ten songs for every year of Hope's life—160 songs, songs that would mean something. Songs Hope could listen to while she was pounding the pavement, knowing that she was loved. Some of them were silly—like the old "I love you, you love me" song from Barney. Some of them were embarrassingly dated. But all of them were reminders of each stage of Hope's life.

At least, that's how Mona hoped her daughter would see it. That, plus the most decadent strawberry cake from Wright's, was what she'd planned for her daughter after taking her to dinner at the Club.

Mona started humming to herself one of the tunes she'd downloaded, and Arthur smiled. He couldn't remember the last time he'd seen her looking so happy.

The traffic eventually cleared and Arthur sped through the city, making up for lost time. It was dark by the time he pulled into her driveway. There didn't seem to be any lights on inside the house.

"Do you want me to wait for you?" he asked, knowing she would say no, like she always did.

"I'll be fine, Arthur. Thanks for the ride. I'll see you next week."

She let herself out the door, not standing on ceremony, and went to the keypad to punch in the code for the garage door. She made a point of never traveling with her keys; she was in too many places in any given week to risk losing them. The door began its slow climb, and Mona shifted her purse impatiently. She ducked under the door when it was about shoulder height, eager to get in, and then she stopped.

The garage was empty.

She turned around and walked into the driveway, looking to see if she'd missed something. She walked all the way around the curve of the drive, looking to the curb for her car.

But it wasn't there.

A brief moment of panic seized her, but then she told herself to relax, blowing out a deep breath before marching back into the garage. It wouldn't be the first time a teenager had taken a car out without permission. If that was, in fact, what had happened.

There had to be a logical explanation for it. She'd ask Hope as soon as Hope got home.

Mona entered the dark house. She'd gotten unused to coming home to this kind of emptiness, with no lights and no activity. A pang of loneliness gripped her, driving her up the stairs to see if maybe, just maybe, Hope was already home, quietly studying in her room.

She dragged her suitcase behind her and suddenly realized how bone tired she was. Every bump of the staircase her wheeled bag took seemed to jolt an ache she didn't even know she had. It didn't matter what class of service she flew; a flight from London was still a damn long time to sit still, trapped. She wasn't one for sleeping, and she used every minute of her travel time to knock out that extra memo, edit a report, or draft e-mails she could later send on to clients, and her habit of working through each flight had intensified after Hope had come to live with her. She wanted to be there for Hope, fully present, when she was at home.

She knocked on Hope's door, waiting for an answer. When none came, she swung the door open.

Hope's room was empty. Her schoolbooks were strewn haphazardly across the floor. Her closet doors were hanging open, with several shirts falling off the hangers that looked like they'd been rifled through. Hope's pajamas were in a wad on the floor, presumably exactly where she'd stripped them off, and the bed was still unmade.

Mona felt a surge of irritation as she looked at the mess. She backed out of the room, pulling the door shut behind her.

Clearly Hope had left in a hurry. *Remember, she didn't expect you back so soon*, Mona reminded herself. *And you were much worse at keeping your room clean when you were a teenager.*

She blew out a breath, trying to shake off her annoyance, and she went on to her bedroom to unpack her bags.

Thirty minutes later, she was downstairs, waiting. She picked up her phone and double-checked her texts and calls. Nothing from Hope.

She might as well make herself useful, she thought. She looked into the mail bin on the counter, quickly sorting through the newspapers and junk mail. She noticed she was short on newspapers and went out through the front door to fetch them. She almost fell into the box from Wright's.

She picked up the box, which had a delivery notice marked for today. "No answer—left at door," the notice read.

"Really, Hope," she muttered, bringing the box back into the kitchen. She lifted the lid to double-check that no critters or bugs had gotten into it. It was untouched, the beautiful "Happy Sweet Sixteen" script laid out in black against the rest of the pink icing. It was a good thing it hadn't rained.

Mona then backtracked, going outside to swipe up two *Wall Street Journal*s and check the mailbox. It was stuffed. She made a mental note to remind Hope to pick up the mail when she was out and, balancing it precariously in two arms, carried it all back inside.

More sorting. More checking messages and e-mails. She let her eyes stray over to the clock hanging on the kitchen wall. Nine o'clock.

She sighed and moved the cake into the refrigerator so the icing wouldn't melt. Her irritation had shifted to disappointment. The adrenaline and anticipation that had kept her going to this point had melted away, exhaustion—chased by a little bit of worry—taking its place.

She considered calling Hope again, but she decided against it. The last thing she wanted to do was make Hope feel like she was being monitored, as if she were at her dad's house. Mona snapped closed the lid of her laptop with a firm click and pushed away from the table.

There was nothing to do but wait. She took down a wine glass from the cupboard and reached into the wine cooler for a bottle. She pulled out a dark red, and then shook her head; that would knock her out. She replaced the bottle and looked around once more. A nice Pinot Grigio; that would do.

She poured the glass half full, holding it to the light to admire its soft greenish-yellow tone, before walking into the family room to wait. She sank into the couch, curling her feet up under her and tucking a blanket around her legs. She set the glass down on the side table and picked through the stack of magazines and books she kept meaning to get to.

"Good ol' *People* magazine," she sighed aloud to the empty room, looking at the posing celebrities and headlines shouting out the latest scandals on the cover. "Just the thing to distract me."

It wasn't ten minutes before her eyes started fluttering closed. She told herself she would just rest for a minute. Her eyes shut.

A pain in her neck woke her up. The little lamp on the side table still glowed, beating back the darkness. The magazine, still open to the page she'd been reading, was draped across her stomach. She shifted, and her joints protested.

She looked down at her watch: 5:00 a.m.

Annoyed, she pushed off her blanket and stood up, padding to the kitchen. She'd fallen asleep without arming the alarm system, which was still glowing green from the keypad. She frowned. She'd told Hope a million times to activate the alarm before she went to bed.

She went to the back door and flicked on the light switch before looking into the garage.

Still empty.

Something is not right, she thought, real unease sweeping through her. She slammed the door and started first walking, then running to the staircase.

"Hope!" she yelled as she took the stairs two at a time. "Hope, are you awake?"

In the back of her mind, she imagined Hope laughing at her for being afraid. Or chastising her for waking her up so early. But when she opened the door to Hope's bedroom, she found it just as she had left it.

She crumpled to the floor, dumbfounded. Hope was not the kind of kid who didn't come home at night. She was not the kind of kid to rebel—not against normal rules, anyway.

"There has to be a logical explanation," Mona whispered to herself. "There has to be." She pushed down the feelings of panic she remembered from when Hope had been abducted, chiding herself for being so weak.

She traced her steps back to the couch where she'd fallen asleep, and she fished her cell phone out from between the cushions. Her fingers danced over a few buttons to speed-dial Hope. It rolled right over into Hope's voice mail.

Mona's mind raced. *You can't panic*, she thought to herself. *Think, Mona. Who would know where Hope is? Who could she be with?*

Michael. But I don't know how to reach him.

She practically ran to her laptop and searched for his number and address, but came up with nothing.

Tabitha? She put that thought firmly out of her mind. She didn't want Tabitha's family to think she didn't have a handle on her own daughter.

Mrs. Bibeau? She sighed with relief. Mrs. Bibeau always kept tabs on Hope, might even have talked to her. And if she had gone with Michael, Mrs. Bibeau surely would have noticed.

She looked at the kitchen clock again. It was only 5:15. She couldn't call or go over to her neighbor's house this early, could she? She went to the front door and peeked out. The windows at the Bibeau house were still dark. She sighed, resigned, and settled in to watch the house.

The kitchen and porch lights went on at 6:30. Mona, still in the sweatpants she'd put on the night before, was at their door by 6:32. Her hand floated over the doorbell, hesitating. Somehow, it seemed more civilized to knock at this hour.

She rapped firmly on the door, praying they didn't think she was crazy.

The door swung open wide. Her neighbor was clutching the neck of her bathrobe, her hair pulled off her face.

"Mona, my goodness. You're up early." She paused, taking in Mona's disheveled appearance. "What is it, dear? You look like you've seen a ghost. Come in here," she said, clucking in her motherly way as she pulled Mona in the door.

Mona was barely inside the door when she burst out, "Do you know where Hope is?"

Mrs. Bibeau tilted her head as she considered the question. She moved to the coffeepot and poured a cup.

"What do you mean, Mona?" she drawled as she passed a cup to Mona.

Frustrated, Mona stomped her foot. *Patience*, she reminded herself. "She didn't come home last night, and I'm starting to think that she hasn't been home for a few days. She hasn't responded to my calls or texts. I was hoping you might have talked with her and know what happened."

"Oh, honey," Mrs. Bibeau soothed, ushering Mona to a chair and making her sit. "I think you must be working too hard. Of course I know where Hope is. Don't you remember? You called me and told me she was going to visit her father back in Alabama for a few days."

Mona's heart froze, but Mrs. Bibeau continued on, oblivious.

"It's so generous of you," she said. "The way y'all had worked it out in advance. All because you didn't want her to spend her birthday alone."

Mona dropped the coffee cup. It broke into shards on the tile floor, splattering coffee across the room.

"Oh, my!" Mrs. Bibeau jumped to her feet, flustered. She looked around the room, trying to remember where her mop was, her brain still clicking into gear at the early hour. "It's all right, now. Don't you worry, Mona, I'll clean that right up. You sit right there."

"I didn't call you," Mona barely whispered.

"What's that, dear?" The older woman stopped. "I didn't hear you."

"I didn't call you." Mona's voice was clear and strong, her meaning unmistakable.

"Why, of course you did. You called me just—when was it now? Just two days ago. I have it right here." She walked over to her desk.

She quickly rummaged in a little basket and perched a pair of reading glasses on her nose before leaning over the phone. "You even asked me to keep an eye on the house while it was empty. See, I'll just scroll through the numbers and find yours."

For a moment, the only sound in the kitchen was the ticking of the clock and the small beeps as Mrs. Bibeau scrolled through her calls.

"Well, that's funny," she said in a quiet voice. "I don't see your name or number here, Mona."

"Let me see," Mona said, nestling up to her neighbor and peering at the phone.

"I don't understand," Mrs. Bibeau continued. "Here are all the calls from that day. And I have all your phone numbers programmed in here. But I don't see it. Did you call me from your client's phone?"

"You don't have any international numbers here," Mona said, impatiently scanning the call log. "What time did you get this call?"

"Well, let me think. I was just back from the Ladies' Art League, and was getting ready to go to tennis. So it must have been about three o'clock?"

Mona scrolled through the calls, looking for the right time. She paused, her finger hovering over the buttons of the phone.

"Three o'clock, you said?"

"Yes, I believe so. Three o'clock."

"There's only one call at that time. And it came from Hope's cell phone."

Mrs. Bibeau leaned closer to the phone, peering through her glasses. "That can't be. I just know I talked to you."

"It wasn't me. It was Hope. Her father must have put her up to this," she said, biting the words through her anger.

"Well, I never," Mrs. Bibeau said, straightening herself up. "I never dreamed it wasn't you, Mona. I swear she sounded just like you." She clucked her tongue again, this time in disapproval. "I am just shocked, shocked, I tell you, that your husband would do such a thing. And manipulating that poor girl, too. He should be ashamed."

Mona's anger was growing from a small flame to a roaring fire. She could barely hear Mrs. Bibeau now. She moved to the door, her attention already turned to other things.

"I need to call my lawyer. I may have to ask you to speak with him. But first I need to call Don." She slammed the door behind her, already framing the conversation with her husband in her head. She could think of nothing but her sheer rage as she took up her phone.

Her hands were shaking as she dialed his number. He picked up on the third ring.

"This is D—"

"How dare you!" Mona interrupted, giving full voice to her rage. "It's bad enough you even contacted her behind my back, but to talk her into coming down with you, and lying about it!"

"Mona! Mona!" Don tried ineffectually to cut in. "Slow down. I don't know what you're talking about."

"You know damn well, Don, what I'm talking about. Put her on the phone."

"Put who on the phone?"

"Don't get cute with me, Don. I have played nice with you. All these years, I have bent over backwards, I—" Mona paused and took a deep breath. "Just put Hope on the phone."

"Hope's not here, Mona." Her husband sounded confused.

"Well, where is she?" Mona demanded.

"Isn't she in Atlanta, with you?"

There was a long silence. Mona could hear some distant radio station, background noise to their call, buzzing in her ear.

"That's not funny," she said.

"I'm not trying to be funny. She's not here."

"Tell me you haven't gone behind my back. Go on, tell me."

Don sighed, sending a trickle of static across the line. "I won't deny it. I went up there to see her, found her running one afternoon."

"I knew it!" Mona spat angrily. "I knew—"

"But that was weeks ago!" Don continued, his declaration causing Mona to break off. "I haven't seen her or talked to her in weeks. Just like the court order said."

More silence danced across the line.

"Mona, do you not know where Hope is?"

Mona didn't answer.

"Mona? Is Hope missing?"

Mona rushed her answer. "I'm sure it's nothing. I just got home early from a trip and she wasn't here."

"How long have you been back?" he demanded, a new, harder edge to his voice.

"Since last night," she admitted reluctantly.

Don muttered something under his breath. It sounded like "I knew it," but Mona couldn't be sure.

"I'm coming up there," Don declared. "I'm coming up there to help you find her."

Mona shifted gears, trying to reassert her control over the situation, as if it was just a catfight between her warring, merging clients.

"That won't be necessary," she said coolly. "I think it best you stay where you are."

"Like hell I will!" Don shouted. "This is exactly the reason I demanded custody in the first place. You're never there, Mona, you're never home. You have no idea what she's up against—"

"That's enough, Don." She cut him off abruptly, her voice husky. She didn't want to hear another repetition of his crazy conspiracy theories. She fought back the tears that threatened to well over. "You stay where you are. The police will want to talk to you."

She paused one last time, weighing whether or not she should say what she was thinking. She decided it was time, high time, she spoke her mind as far as Don Carmichael was concerned.

"You better not be hiding her," she added, her voice rough from fear and anger and exhaustion. "You better not be hiding her, because I will bring the book down on you. I will make sure they know every crazy idea running around inside that head of yours. And I will make sure you never, ever see your daughter again."

She hung up the phone, bowing her head and leaning up against the wall. How had it come to this? After all these years, all the pain and effort she had gone to, how had it come to this?

One solitary tear trickled down her cheek. She dashed it away and shook her head.

"Get it together, Carmichael," she whispered to herself. She looked about her, wondering how she had made her way down the dark cul-de-sac and come to be standing in the middle of her kitchen. Then, squaring her shoulders, she picked up the phone and swiftly dialed a number she knew by heart.

She cleared her voice as she waited through the ringing on the other end of the line. "Clayton, I'm sorry to bother you on a weekend, but are you in town today?"

She nodded as her managing partner responded.

"Good, I need to see you. In the office. I think Don has kidnapped Hope."

fourteen

For a full ten minutes after Michael left, I simply sat and stared at the hotel phone that rested on the shiny, mirrored bedside table. I could call my mom. I could call my mom and tell her everything, and she could come and rescue me.

At first, I told myself I was waiting to be sure that Michael was really gone. Then, I realized I was waiting because I knew, deep down, that there really was no point. I knew that there was no way out. Even if I reached my mom, we might be gone by the time she—or anyone else she could muster—could get here. And even if she did find me, I still wouldn't be safe. Until the Key was destroyed, I was still the Bearer. Still the one who would open up the Gates of Heaven to the Fallen Ones.

Still a threat. It was stamped there, the Mark on my neck declaring it for anyone who cared to see.

No, there was no way out, other than the path I was on. A snippet of a Robert Frost poem crept into my mind, a remnant from a barely remembered English class that seemed oddly appropriate. *The best way out is always through.*

"Right, Henri?" I said out loud, waiting for him to reassure me. But Henri didn't answer, leaving me to make the decision myself.

I heaved my body off the floor and dragged myself to the closet. A new outfit was hanging right in front of me. Jeans. A T-shirt. And a sweatshirt. I didn't know if this is what Michael had meant by "getting dressed," but I was going to beg forgiveness, not ask permission. I snatched the clothes from the closet and went, resigned, into the bathroom to get ready.

~

A soft knocking at the door woke me up. I fumbled in the cold bathwater as I jolted awake.

"I don't think even Bathsheba took as long to get ready as you have," Michael's voice said, ringing clearly through the door. My sleepy mind fumbled as I tried to come up with a snappy retort, my cheeks hot, only to be cut off by his chuckle. "There's no rush, but you can come out whenever you're ready, Hope."

I looked at the clock. I'd been in the bathroom for an hour and a half. The water had felt luxurious, stripping away the grit and grime of our desert hike. As I'd relaxed into its warmth, I'd let down my guard and slipped into the first deep rest I'd had since the night Lucas had tricked me with his phone call.

"I'll be right out," I said ruefully. I didn't really want to leave my sanctuary; I was afraid of which Michael I'd find when I crossed the threshold, my friend or my kidnapper. But I didn't have a choice. I sloshed my way out of the tub, wrapping myself in the big fluffy towel and quickly patting myself dry.

I threw on the T-shirt and jeans I'd brought in with me and

ran a comb through my hair. I looked at my reflection and made a face. The sunburn on my nose and cheeks contrasted against the bruises on my neck, which were turning a nasty shade of purple. I had white rings around my eyes from my sunglasses, and with my sopping wet hair, I bore a distinct resemblance to a waterlogged Chihuahua. Nice.

Oh, well. There was nothing I could do about it now, anyway. I squared my shoulders, preparing myself for whatever Michael could throw at me, and opened the bathroom door.

"Happy birthday, Hope," Michael said softly from across the room.

I walked through the door and caught my breath. Michael had opened the drapes, baring the night sky to us. We were far from the neon of the Strip, but a carpet of twinkling lights spread below us and up to the mountains. Michael had dimmed the room lights so that nothing would overshadow the view. In the middle of the room, an intimate table for two had been set with candles, china, and crystal.

Michael leaned against the wall, arms crossed, a look of amusement on his face as he watched my reaction. "Do you like it?" he asked intently. My heart gave a little thump.

"Like it? I love it," I breathed, still taking it all in.

His body seemed to uncoil with relief, and he walked toward me, breaking into a grin as he came to my side.

"I thought you deserved a special dinner after all you've been through. Especially for your sixteenth birthday." He casually placed his arm around my shoulders and leaned in to peck me on the cheek. "Happy birthday, Hope."

I felt my knees weaken as the warmth of his breath tickled at my ear, intensely aware of his light grip on my arm.

"I can't believe you remembered," I answered, leaning into him.

He tensed and pushed me away before removing his hands. “The phone call from your mother certainly helped.”

I stepped aside so I could pretend I was the one who’d pushed away. “I don’t know how you had the time to plan this,” I said, speaking quickly to cover up my embarrassment at his rejection.

“The magic of concierge service,” he said drily. “They do a good job here. Of course, the fact that every time you were asleep I went and dropped a hundred grand playing craps didn’t hurt.”

I felt my eyes bugging out as he mentioned the staggering sum of money. “Just how much money have you lost since we’ve been here?”

He shrugged, his mouth twisting wryly as he tried to avoid the question. “Enough to make me very popular with the management of several hotels, plus a few Chinese foreign nationals.”

I punched him playfully in the arm. “You aren’t getting away with it that easily. Seriously, tell me how much.”

He cocked an eyebrow as he decided whether or not to tell me. “A couple million,” he coolly admitted. “And I’m sure there will be more.”

My head was spinning. “So, you’re buying your way into the syndicate?”

“And into a few niceties here at our hotel, yes.”

“And you’re doing this how, again?”

He bowed neatly. “Angel financing, at your service.”

I shook my head, still unable to believe it. “It just shows up when you need it. Like that paperwork?” He nodded, so I continued. “What happens to it all when you leave again? Does it just disappear from their till, as if you’d never existed?”

He laughed out loud. “Leave it to you to ask something like that. In truth, I do not know—I’ve never stuck around to find out. Come on, let’s eat.”

He took my hand and led me to my chair, pulling it out for me and helping me to settle in. I turned to thank him again and caught my breath. The contrast in his appearance after all the time he'd posed as my father only made it harder. My body trembled as I scanned the long, lean lines of his muscular torso and legs. He was dressed in an old, broken-in pair of jeans and a soft white sweater that clung to every angle as he moved. His blond hair had somehow grown a little longer and was almost shaggy now, one stray lock hanging over his crystalline eyes.

I touched the back of the chair, steadying myself as I smiled up at him. With a flourish, he placed a napkin across my lap.

"Bon appétit," he murmured as he pulled away. I flushed, unable to speak.

I watched as he uncovered the dishes set before us. I looked with dismay as I stared at the beady eyes and claws of a huge red lobster.

"I can't eat that," I stuttered, panicking. "I don't know how to eat lobster."

I looked up from the beady eyes to see Michael silently laughing at me.

I flushed red. "Don't laugh at me! It's not funny," I pouted, pretending to be more hurt than I was, discomfited as Michael's keen eyes dissected my every reaction. "I'm not as, as experienced and worldly as you. Besides, it's disgusting."

"Oh, Hope," he teased. "There's a first time for everything. It's easy, I promise. I'll even show you how."

I crossed my arms and looked at him skeptically.

He raised one wicked brow at me and grinned again, his dimple puckering. "Based on my observation of your eating habits in the school cafeteria, I thought this might be the case. Plan B is in the warmer next to your knees."

I reached under the tablecloth and unlatched the little door I found there. I pulled out the plate that had been hidden away and breathed in the aroma of a cheeseburger and fries.

"Now this is more like it," I said, grinning from ear to ear as I made room on the table for my dinner. "I feel like I could eat a dozen of these." I twirled a fry in ketchup and popped it in my mouth.

"Such a waste," Michael said, feigning horror.

"Hey, it's my birthday, right?"

"Indeed, it is. And, as they say, to each his own. But if you don't mind, I'll stick to the lobster. Manna gets so boring after a while. Everyone should get a chance to have lobster every now and then."

He plopped one of the red beasts onto his plate and started in on the base of the claw, wrapping his big fingers around it and breaking it free with a gentle twist. I watched his sure movements, entranced.

"Some people think the claws have the most delicious meat," he said, "but you have to work for it. The most succulent meat is tucked away in these tiny crevices." He dug a tiny morsel out and dipped it in the drawn butter. "Here," he offered, holding it up to me in his fingertips. "Taste."

Obediently, I dipped my chin and nibbled the proffered taste. I closed my eyes, letting the blend of sweet and salty play across my tongue. An involuntary moan of pleasure escaped from my lips.

Michael chuckled and my eyes flew open. "I knew you'd like it," he said.

"I wasn't expecting it to be so sweet," I answered. "It smells so stinky."

He roared with laughter at me and I blushed, thinking I'd shown how unsophisticated I really was. But he was looking at me appreciatively over the candlelight.

"That's what I love about you, Hope. You aren't afraid to say what you really think. There's no pretense, no attempt to be someone you really aren't. That's rare. Especially in these times."

I looked down at my napkin, fumbling with it while I waited for some witty answer to pop into my head, but nothing came.

Why was he being so kind to me? Why now, after everything that had happened?

He's lulling you back into trusting him, Henri interrupted. *And it appears to be working, I might add.*

I closed my mind to Henri's obvious answer. My heart didn't want to hear it. Tonight, I just wanted it to be me and Michael, friends, like we had been before Lucas and my Mark complicated things.

Friends, I sternly reminded myself, when I caught him smiling across the table at me and my heart went *thump*.

"You missed me opening up the tail," he admonished, his dimpled smile making my heart race once more. "What were you thinking about?"

I blushed. "I was thinking how nice this is. To be back to normal. If I can call it that. Thank you for changing back to yourself. It's been weird being with you when you're pretending to be my dad."

He grimaced. "Trust me, I don't particularly relish going around as an overweight, middle-aged guy who still thinks Members Only is the height of chic."

"Be nice," I warned, playfully throwing my napkin at him. We laughed out loud, and I was surprised at how good it felt to laugh with him.

"But seriously," I added, trying to remind myself that things weren't normal, and that I still didn't know what Michael intended to do about me. "Why all the fuss over my birthday?"

Michael's eyes sparkled in the candlelight, as he suddenly turned serious. "You only turn sixteen once," he said, looking at me gravely.

You're lucky you made it this far, Henri muttered under his breath. I ignored the interruption and pressed my case.

"Most sixteen-year-olds would have cake and candles, not a lobster dinner."

"Don't forget the champagne," Michael retorted with a devilish look, gesturing to the fancy bucket standing next to the table. "We still haven't toasted you." He was trying to keep things light, but behind the façade I could see a sudden strain in his eyes.

"You're in more pain than ever," I said flatly. It was a statement, not a question, and I could tell from the flash of surprise that he'd been deliberately trying to keep it from me. "Nothing's changed at all, has it?" I asked him, forcing myself to ask the question.

The smile froze on his face and his eyes grew dark. "I don't know what you're talking about," he said coldly, folding his napkin deliberately and setting it aside.

A jolt of irritation shot through me and I stood up, pushing away from the table in frustration. "Stop lying to me. I'm trying to be serious, Michael. You've been treating me like a prisoner for the last two days, and now you've turned into Mr. Cheesy Las Vegas, turning on the charm for my birthday. What are you trying to do? What do you want from me? Tell me the tru—"

Before I could finish my speech, Michael pushed away from the table, sending the china and crystal flying, stalking after me. His face was crumpled with rage, his eyes as dark as storm clouds as he grabbed me by the shoulders and shook me.

"Who says I want anything? Do you think I wanted this? Any of this? To be on the run with you, fearing that the worst will come to pass?"

I bit my lip to keep from crying out. I couldn't let him know how much he was hurting me. As I tried to back away, his fingers only dug in deeper, tendrils of flame twining through my body. He pulled me closer and looked into my eyes, his own filled with wild despair.

"Every minute of every day, I have to look at you, knowing that everything depends on me making the right decision. And every time I do—the pain—"

His voice broke with emotion.

I held my breath, sure that I knew what he was going to say next. I listened as he fought to control his ragged breath, knowing that the only rational thing for Michael to do in this situation—truly the only rational thing he could do—was to take my life.

But as his breath slowed, he bent his head and rested his forehead against mine, pulling me closer and wrapping his arms around me like a desperate man clinging to a life raft in a violent storm.

"I can't imagine a world without you, Hope. I know in my very spirit that I belong to you. You draw me like nothing else on Earth ever has." He laughed roughly. "Even your name proclaims it." He lifted his head and searched my eyes. "Why would God put us together if it wasn't meant to be?"

I nervously licked my lips and fought off the urge to touch my Mark like a talisman. I couldn't bring myself to answer his question. We both knew the answer.

"Has the pain gotten worse or better since we've been here?" I asked, barely able to whisper as I returned his troubled gaze.

He looked away, unable to look me in the eye. "Worse."

"Maybe it's because we've been spending too much time looking for Maria," I suggested, not even believing the words as I said them.

He shook his head and suddenly let me go, turning to the window. "No, that's not it."

Ask him if things would be different if you weren't bearing the Mark.

I'd forgotten Henri was even here and felt myself flushing with embarrassment, then anger, as I realized he'd been spying on everything that had just happened. Still, Henri's questions usually served a purpose.

"It's not just because of the Mark, is it?" I said softly into the night.

Michael hung his head even lower. "No."

"Then what is it?" I asked, confused. "What more could there be?"

His voice was hollow and flat when he finally answered me. "Even if things weren't so complicated, we could never be together, Hope. Never."

"I don't understand."

He squared his shoulders and stared out the window intently. "It may be better for you that way."

"So you're going to keep it from me? Just like you've hidden everything all along? That's not fair, Michael."

"No, it isn't," he said, turning from the window with a twisted, bitter smile. He ran a restless hand over his face as if he could wipe away his emotions. "Nor is it fair that I might be damned for eternity for feeling as I do, but I can't help myself. I love you."

I froze, holding my breath. Shock, disbelief, even fear coursed through me in the instant it took me to realize what he'd said.

"Did you hear me, Hope?" He took my hand, holding on to it as if he was afraid I would break. "I said I love you."

"I—I don't believe you," I said, shaking my head in denial and pushing him away. "You can't love me."

He caught my arm and pulled me back against his chest. I could feel his heart thudding ominously. "What do you mean?"

My voice was thick as I answered. "You lied to me." I licked my lips and stared at him, daring him to deny it.

His hands tightened on me. "I never lied to you. Other than my identity, everything I have ever told you has been the truth. I swear."

He's just toying with you. Something to keep the boredom away while he babysits you. How could a majestic Archangel love a simple human girl?

"No," I whimpered. Henri's taunts, Michael's denials, the heat surging through my tired body; all of it was overwhelming. I didn't want to hear any of this.

You fool. If he loves you, would he have treated you the way he has the last few days?

Michael searched my eyes, refusing to let me go.

"I only did what I had to do to help you find Maria," he said, answering my—and Henri's—unspoken thoughts.

In other words, just to keep you here long enough to find the Key. Then he can get rid of you.

"No!" I shouted. Nowhere was safe. Not here, in Michael's arms, where I could almost believe he cared. Not listening to Henri's barbed words. And not out on my own, with no one to protect me, either. I struggled, confused, trying to break free of Michael's grip, but he simply tightened his hold on me. He held me there, absorbing the few blows I managed to land. When sobs began racking my body, he simply murmured softly to me until the anger drained from me, and I tired myself out. Through my tears, I saw the look of concern on Michael's face.

"You're overwrought." He tucked a stray strand of hair behind my ear and then ran his thumb over the line of my jaw. My heart started racing.

"I'm sorry, Hope. I shouldn't have said anything. Especially when you're under so much stress. It's been a long day. Maybe it would be best for you to go to bed."

Before I could protest, he swept me up in his arms. He carried me across the room to the bed, knocking the room service table out of the way. I felt so empty, so tired of it all.

If he loves you, make him prove it to you.

Henri's words insinuated themselves into my brain, the suggestion floating there while Michael laid me gently on the mattress and tucked the blankets tightly around my body.

Prove it to me?

Michael tugged the covers one last time and rested his hand on my hair.

"Some birthday, hmm?" he said ruefully. "I guess I messed that up, too."

I gulped. Here was my chance. I reached for his hand, looping my fingers into his, feeling the fluttering in my stomach that always came with his warm touch.

"My birthday's not over. You still have to give me my present."

He frowned, a shadow of gray creeping into his eyes. "But I didn't buy you anything."

I screwed my eyes shut, afraid to look at him. "What I want doesn't come from a store." I took a deep breath, gathering all my courage. "I want you to kiss me. Really kiss me, like you mean it."

It was as if the air got sucked from the room. Stifling silence pressed against my ears.

He tried to withdraw his hand, but this time I was the one refusing to let go, my grip on his fingers turning vice-like.

"If you love me, you'll do it," I insisted. Immediately, I regretted it. I sounded like a spoiled child demanding a toy. And I didn't like feeling as if Henri had manipulated me into it. I didn't want to be a pawn in their chess match. The truth was, Henri's comment just gave shape to an idea that had been there, forming under the surface ever since our trip to meet Enoch. My feelings for Michael, like the whole situation in which we'd found ourselves, had grown so complicated. I couldn't tell what was real and what was part of the dangerous game we were playing. I couldn't tell which Michael was the real one. Was it, as Enoch had intimated, teenage hormones and pain and confusion that were buffeting Michael's own emotions about? Or was it something more ominous? Were we on the same side at all? I needed to know. And I knew—I just knew—that if he kissed me he wouldn't be able to hide his real intentions toward me.

And, deep down, I really, really, really wanted to know what it would feel like.

"It's not safe," Michael said, his voice hoarse, as he cut me off.

"It's the only way I can trust you again," I said softly. I let my lashes flutter open and turned my head to face him. His face was a mask, only the telltale vein in his forehead giving any indication that he was upset. "You've been telling me I have nothing to fear from you. You told me you love me. I want to believe you, but it's so hard with this wall between us. Please."

I could see the indecision in his eyes.

"Please, Michael. I want to believe you. I really do."

His eyes bored into mine. "You don't know what you're asking."

I tilted my head, gazing up at him quizzically. "How much could one little kiss hurt?"

I could see him wavering. I turned onto my side and drew closer to him, the covers bunching around me.

"I never had a friend before, Michael. Not a true friend. It was inconceivable to me that of all the people you could have chosen to talk to in that school, you chose to be with me. To learn that it had to do with this—" I let one hand drift to my Mark. "It broke my heart. You keep insisting you didn't know, that it doesn't matter. If you kiss me, then I'll be able to tell if you're telling the truth." A fit of shyness overtook me and I lowered my eyes before continuing. "And I won't be afraid of you anymore."

He snapped his head back as if I'd slapped him. "You're afraid? Of me?"

I nodded, watching him through my lashes. Did he really not understand that?

He ran the fingers of his free hand through his hair, making it stand up on end so that it looked like some sort of crazy, scruffy halo. His body seemed to sag a little, defeated.

"I've made you afraid. But then again, you should be afraid."

I squeezed his hand. "I don't want to be afraid. Not of you. Not anymore."

The vein in his forehead throbbed. I could see him rolling it over in his mind, considering all the angles as he drew his eyebrows together.

"If you start to feel anything—odd—you must stop me. At once. You understand?"

I smiled shyly up at him. "You sound nervous."

"I've never done this before." I let go of his hand and he reached up to tuck a damp strand of hair off of my forehead.

"Never?"

He looked at me and smiled. "Never."

I was ashamed at the relief that swept through me. "Really?"

"No," he said quietly.

"I'm glad."

"If I were you, I would be more worried that I don't know what I'm doing." He bent over, leaning his forehead against mine. "I could never forgive myself if something happened to you."

His lips were achingly close to mine. His breath was soft against my skin.

I closed my eyes, unable to bear the wait.

It started off as a tender glance of his lips, so gentle that if it hadn't been for the flush of heat rising in my own lips, I might not have even known he was there. I sighed softly against him, my lips parting, and I felt his kiss become more insistent.

I gasped at the taste of him—salty and sweet—and he kissed me more deeply. I reached out for him, wanting to feel the length of his body against me, but he pulled away, dragging his lips from mine down the line of my jaw to the hollow of my neck. Every nerve ending tingled at his touch, a dazzling fire running up and down my skin, urging me on, making me want more.

"Don't stop," I whispered, finding the collar of his sweater and pulling him closer.

"Carmichael," he murmured against my lips. "You are so young."

"Shhhh," I said, letting my hands feel their way down his hard chest. Frantically, not even knowing what I was doing, I tugged his sweater away from his waistband. He moaned as I trailed a finger across his taut abdomen.

"No," he said, catching my hands in his. He drew a heavy breath. "No, Hope."

My eyes flew open. He was leaning over me, so close I could see every fleck of gold twinkling in his deep blue eyes. His chest heaved with each ragged breath he took.

I pulled a hand free and pushed a wayward lock of hair from his face, then wrapped my arm around his neck. I gazed up at him, at the undisguised look of longing on his face, and something inside of me shifted.

"I love you too, Michael."

The words slipped from me before I even knew what I was saying, hanging there between us, with only our shallow breathing to break the silence. My eyes raced to search his, afraid of what I might see.

A strange look crossed his face.

"God forgive me," he murmured as he leaned in, gathering me in his arms. His eyes flashed with defiance, and he crushed my lips under his.

My entire body was flooded with wave after wave of warmth. Somehow I'd escaped the covers, and I could feel every inch of him through the thin cotton of my shirt and jeans. Every place he touched me was like a burst of fire, leaving me shuddering, wanting more. I wanted his hands on me, wanted to explore every inch of him, wanted to give myself over to the heat.

But the pleasant warmth, the aching desire, wouldn't stop. It built and built without any hope of release, the exquisite longing inside of me turning into nothing but pain. The heat of the fire grew. It hollowed me out; it was burning me up. I tried to scream, but I couldn't. I couldn't do anything. I was melting—melting under his touch, melting away from his brilliance and heat.

"Fire." It was the only word I could get out through my labored breath, so low I wasn't sure he would hear it. I was already fading away, the pain too much to bear.

The faint smell of something burning slipped into my consciousness.

Henri? My mind reached out, waiting for a word of advice, some help, but none came—just a doubling of the pain that already seemed unbearable. Through my eyelids I could see the bright white light that was consuming me, turning me into nothing. My body began to shake, but it no longer felt as if I was connected to my arms and legs as they thrashed. Even the pain seemed to go away, replaced by emptiness as I began to drift away. My thoughts were becoming erratic as random flotsam from my life popped in and out of focus.

For one instant, everything seemed to stop.

Then I hit a wall of pain like a freight train. A shrieking wail filled my ears. I couldn't tell where it came from. I didn't care. I just needed to get away, away from the pain and the horrible smell of burnt flesh.

"Hope! Hope! Stay with me!" Michael's voice, at once stern and scared, reached out to me through the light, pulling me back to the pain. I could feel his rough hands on me, every touch stabbing me through with pain. He was jostling me, picking me up. I tried to push away—I couldn't bear his touch, couldn't bear to feel anything against me—but I couldn't even move my limbs anymore.

The sound of rushing water came out of nowhere.

Was that a brook? How did we get outside? I thought to myself.

Another blast of pain racked my body as I was plunged into ice. The coldness soothed and burned at the same time, pricking like thousands of tiny needles. The light behind my eyes was fading. Where was I? What was happening? I couldn't open my eyes.

From far away, I could hear Michael talking to me, repeating the same words over and over, but nothing made any sense. I didn't want to be here; the pain was too great. I just let myself fall into the black void of unconsciousness, happy to escape.

fifteen

Mona drummed her fingers on the conference table. She knew she had no right to be annoyed with her boss, Clayton. He was dropping everything to come in on a weekend; she shouldn't be quibbling over him being a few minutes late. But the presence of her lawyer, trying to discreetly check his watch every few minutes, kept reminding her that time was slipping away.

"Sorry, sorry," Clayton intoned with his vaguely patrician accent as the glass door to the conference room swung open. "I know I'm late, but I come bearing gifts, so hopefully you'll forgive me."

He pulled a drink carrier loaded with coffees from behind his back.

"Oh, God bless you," Mona sighed, suddenly aware of just how exhausted she was. "I so need that caffeine."

"And that's not all. I brought my friend, Special Agent Hale from the FBI. Come on in here, John."

A tall, lean man in a windbreaker strode into the room, hand outstretched. "John Hale, ma'am."

"I'm Mona Carmichael, and this is my lawyer, Arne Haverty. Thank you for coming, Agent Hale."

"Please, call me John. May I?" He gestured to a chair. Mona nodded and he sat down. Clayton took his customary seat at the head of the table and folded his hands.

"John's an expert in parental abductions. I filled him in on what I know, Mona, but I think it might be best for you to start from the beginning so that John knows what we're working with here."

Mona nodded. She hated to talk about her past with Don. Hated the whole story. But she knew Clayton was right.

Her lawyer piped up. "Everything will be considered privileged, of course."

"Of course," the agent assented. "And simply background."

With that reassurance, Mona began.

"Over ten years ago, my daughter was abducted. After a few days we recovered her, unharmed, but the whole incident marked the start of the unraveling of my marriage to Don. He became obsessed with Hope's safety—"

"Hope, that's your daughter?" John interrupted. Mona noticed he was jotting rapid notes in the little pad of paper he'd taken out of his jacket pocket.

"Yes, my daughter. She's fifteen, now. Actually, sixteen. Her birthday was yesterday." She reached into a cavernous purse and pulled a photo out of her wallet, sliding it across the table to the agent. "It's a little old."

The agent murmured his thanks and glanced at the photo. "I see the resemblance." He handed the photo back to Mona. "So, your husband—Don Carmichael, is it? He became obsessed with Hope's safety?"

"Yes. It got to the point where he couldn't hold down a job, he was so unwilling to let her out of his sight."

"Did he ever say why he was so fearful? It is a natural reaction to be more cautious after a kidnapping, but typically people don't go to that extreme."

"I don't really understand it myself. I think that because we never knew for sure who had taken her and could never confirm that the person we found burned to death at the motel where we recovered Hope really was her abductor, Don was afraid someone was still out there and that she was still at risk. He became quite religious and took that to extremes, as well."

"How long did this go on?"

"It probably went on for two years before I couldn't take it anymore. We never officially divorced, but we've been separated ever since."

"You never divorced?" John paused on that and looked with undisguised curiosity at Mona. She flushed, knowing how odd that might seem. She struggled to explain it even to herself sometimes. She looked at Clayton. A note of sadness crept into his eyes before he looked away.

Poor Clayton. Patiently waiting all this time for things to change.

"And he got custody of your daughter?" John's question interrupted her reverie.

Mona looked across the table at Clayton, willing him to look at her. Their eyes connected. So many times they'd gone over this, trying to understand what they could have done differently.

"Don managed to convince the judge that my job would take me away too much, that it wasn't a good home environment for Hope."

"And you didn't reveal what you knew about his obsessive behavior?"

Mona flushed, looking down at her hands. "At the time, I was embarrassed for him. For us. And I guess I thought that even though I couldn't live with it any longer, it was really quite harmless. I could provide for Hope's financial well-being and make sure nothing went wrong."

"Did he ever mention anything specifically linking his religion and his worries about Hope?"

Mona frowned. "No, not that I can remember. Do you think they are related?"

"Not necessarily. But there is always a chance that your husband has come up with some conspiracy theory. If you haven't heard him say anything, there's probably nothing there." He looked down at his notes and tapped his pen, thinking. "So you've been apart for a long time. And now you have custody, as Clayton told me. You came back last night and Hope had disappeared?"

Mona nodded, her heart racing with alarm as she recounted the events of last evening and this morning. "I haven't been able to reach her for at least a day. Her phone kept going straight to voice mail. Don says he doesn't have her, but it's the only thing that makes sense."

"Mona, if Don took Hope, where would he take her?" John asked.

"Back home to Alabama, I suppose."

Clayton and John looked meaningfully at one another.

"What?"

"Are you sure there is no other place he would take her? An old family home? Some place he used to live before he met you?" John pressed her.

Mona waved a hand dismissively. "He's not that creative. Besides, he's lived his whole life either here in Atlanta or in Alabama. He has no family left to speak of. I don't know where he could go. Why?"

Clayton cleared his throat. "The FBI found your car, Mona, but not in Alabama. It was in long-term parking at Hartsfield-Jackson."

"At the airport?" Mona was stunned. "That bastard. Acting all innocent, like he never left home."

"You spoke with him?" John leaned into the table, eager to hear her answer.

"Yes. I called him demanding to speak to Hope. He claimed not to have her, not to have even seen her for weeks."

"Landline or cell phone?"

"I called his mobile."

The agent broke into a grin. "We can trace his signal from your call records and track him down."

"Just like that?"

"Just like that. I just need your number and his."

"Don't you need a warrant for that?" Arne broke in, ever cautious.

"Location data is not protected in the United States. Besides, I would focus on recovering your client's daughter first, worry about admissible evidence later."

"Maybe you can locate them with Hope's phone," Mona added in. "When I called her, it went straight to her messages, but maybe that was enough of a signal to track her, too." Mona scribbled the numbers down on a piece of paper and slid it across to him. "What else? There has to be more we can do."

"We could issue an Amber Alert," John said, "but I gathered you wanted to keep this quiet if you could."

Clayton nodded. "My firm doesn't like to draw unnecessary attention to itself. And Mona would prefer this to be discreet. She is a very prominent partner, very high profile with the business press. It would be a media zoo."

"The media can help, though. Make it tough for him to hide."

"What if the car is a decoy? What if he moved it there to throw us off the trail, and he really is in Alabama?" Mona asked.

John nodded. "It's easy enough for us to check out his home, see if he's there. He might have put your daughter somewhere else, though. He has a job now?"

Mona snorted. "Yes, I guess you can call it that. His court-appointed lawyer just informed me a few weeks ago. He works in a fast-food restaurant. I think he's been there for a month, maybe two at the most."

John grinned. "That's perfect. They have cameras all over those places, plus electronic clock-ins and -outs for all employees. I can talk to the corporate security people and get them to give me the records. At least then we'll be able to eliminate possible alibis for your ex."

"Can you do that?" Arne looked distinctly nervous, pulling at his starched collar.

"Relax," John said, flashing an all-American smile. "They'll want to cooperate behind the scenes to prevent a big stink if the whole thing goes public." He turned to Mona, adopting a more serious tone. "In the meantime, I'll get my team to search flight manifests out of Atlanta for the last two days. We'll see if we turn up anyone even remotely resembling them. We'll find your girl, Mona. I promise."

"Everything quiet, John," Clayton spoke, looking troubled. "No press. Not unless we have no choice. I'll let our media relations team know, but for now, if they are asked they will respond with 'no comment.'"

He peered down the table. Mona was still in her high-backed chair, ashen.

"Mona? You okay?"

She looked up, startled, as if she was surprised to be spoken to.

"He wouldn't hurt her, would he Clayton?" Her eyes searched Clayton's for reassurance. "He might be crazy, but he still loves her. Right?"

Clayton returned her gaze and stretched his hand across the table. Mona placed her hand in his open palm. His big hand enveloped hers, giving it a squeeze. Arne and John looked away, knowing there was nothing they could say right now that would make Mona feel any better.

sixteen

I stayed wrapped in the safety of darkness for who knows how long. I was on a never-ending arc of pain, cycle after cycle stretching my body to its limit. Each time the pain reached its peak, I came close to regaining consciousness. I would hear snippets of things going on around me, enough to make out that I was still with Michael but that someone else was there with us, too. There was a faint, incessant beeping in the background. Other than that, an ominous hush seemed to fill the room.

I still couldn't open my eyes, so I tried to feel my way around to make out where I was. When I shifted, though, it felt as if rough sandpaper was scraping the skin off my bones, and I let out an involuntary moan.

"She's breaking through the morphine," I heard someone say.

"Then increase her drip. I don't want her to feel anything," Michael said tersely.

"There's only so much we can give her."

"As soon as you can, then."

"Michael?" I managed to croak.

I felt a rustle at my side, sensed him bending low near my face. "I'm right here, Hope."

"It hurts."

He didn't bother to answer me. Instead he spoke angrily to whoever was with him. "She's in pain. Do the drip now!"

There was a rush and a clatter. Then, I felt a rush of cool relief spreading through my body. The excruciating pain gave way to numbness as I drifted back into sleep, but not before wondering what on earth had happened to me.

It seemed like a long time had passed before I sensed that I was floating. The cool water of a lake lapped at my limbs, cradled and cushioned me as I drifted along. I sailed silently along, the sun giving way to the moon and stars above me, the soft lapping of the water steering me as if by magic, never stopping, taking me further away from the pain. I didn't want it to stop. I wanted to lose myself in the water, hide in the safety of its depths, but from somewhere on the shore I could hear the whispers, whispers that called me back and demanded my attention.

"All due respect, but she would be much better off in a hospital." I heard a deep sigh and a rustle of papers. "She would have better supervision, and if something went wrong—"

"We can't bring her to a hospital, Pete, and you know it," a second unfamiliar voice cut in. "This is below the radar. No records. No reports."

"But she's just a kid."

"The casino has been very good to you, Pete." The man's voice was rising, his anger barely contained. "But if you want to back out of our agreement, I can get the boss on the phone—"

"No!" Pete sounded nervous as he yelped the word. "No," he repeated in a whisper. "I'm still in. I guess I just never expected to see something like this. I mean, my God. What kind of animal does this to someone?"

"He didn't do it. Remember, he said it was an accident."

"Yeah, right," Pete said bitterly. "Some accident. He can't even tell us how it happened. There's no sign of anything—no fire, no chemicals. Who takes the time to clean things up when they are dealing with an 'accident'?"

What were they talking about? Where was I? I tried to open my eyes, but they were too heavy.

"You'll see worse before you're done. Trust me. For now, just focus on the job." There was a brief pause before he continued. When he spoke again, he seemed to be facing away from me, his voice louder as if to project out into a vast space. "Mr. Carmichael, we'll keep a nurse on duty at all times. Plan on a shift change in a few hours. You don't need to worry about any of them; they are all on the same little arrangement as Pete here."

I heard zippers, the sounds of things being put away. Pete began speaking in a carefully neutral tone. "It looks a lot worse than it is. Her burns are first- and second-degree burns. They'll be painful for a while—oddly enough, second-degree burns are notorious for the pain, and way worse than third-degree burns—but the morphine will help her through the worst of it. When the pain seems to have subsided, you can switch her to this megadose of ibuprofen. Keep her wrapped in these wet sheets until the new nurse comes. She'll be ready for some exposure to air then. No need to bandage her unless those blisters start to break open. If they do, keep her covered with this ointment. Infection is the biggest thing you need to worry about. Barring that, she should be ready to be up and about within twenty-four hours. It won't be pretty, and she'll still be in pain, but she should be mobile."

There was a slight pause, filled by the sound of a big zipper closing something shut. Pete continued. "But then, you don't need to worry about any of that. The nurses will know what to do."

"How long will it take for her to heal?" a voice I recognized pressed the doctor.

"She's lucky. The burns are intermittent across her torso and arms, and not too deep. She could be forming a new layer of skin in a few days. From there, it could take anywhere from two to five weeks longer for her to completely heal, barring any complications. It will take much longer than that, of course, for her skin to look the way it used to. If it ever does."

"Dad?" I whimpered, finally realizing to whom the familiar voice belonged. How did he get here? In the fog of medication, the idea that I was hearing Michael, posing as my father, never occurred to me. Instead, when I heard my father's voice I instinctively wanted him to protect me, just like he had when I was a little girl. I tried to reach out but my arms were weighted down, seemingly tethered to something.

"Time for a top off," Pete said, tersely. Someone approached me, blocking whatever light was shining on my face, and fiddled with something. And then I was floating away, the lake pulling me back into her depths as a wave of coolness seeped into my bones.

The next time I woke up was not so peaceful. Searing, burning pain jolted me from sleep. My eyes flew open, but there was something obstructing my vision. I flailed uselessly at my face, unable to feel anything but the agony shooting through me. I hit something hard to my right and let out a howl.

"Let me out of here! Dad!" He was here, somewhere. "Dad, I can't see!"

Strong hands grabbed me, only making the pain worse. "Calm down, sweetie," said a woman's voice. "You won't do yourself any good moving around like this. You need to rest." I struggled against the woman, but her grip on me was strong. "Just lay down and I will help you to see," she soothed. "It's just a bandage blocking your eyes, that's all."

I could feel hot tears rolling down my face. Each one stung, leaving a tiny trail of pain behind it.

"I want my dad," I blubbered, finally giving in and sagging against her.

"Shhhh. Poor thing. So confused. Of course you mean your uncle. You just stay right here and I'll go get Mr. Carmichael for you. But first close your eyes and I'll take this gauze off."

She eased me back against some pillows. Everything that touched my skin seemed scratchy. I moved as if to scratch my arm, but a firm hand stopped me. "Don't touch anything. And don't move that arm. You're attached to an IV."

I sagged back into the pillows. The hazy light suddenly gave way to full bright, and I had to blink.

"There," the nurse said, rolling up a strip of gauze in her hand. "Better, no?" She smiled at me, her plump cheeks rosy and her eyes kind. "Are you thirsty?"

I hadn't realized it, but my throat was parched. I nodded, and she handed me a plastic cup from a little table that was pulled up and over the bed in which I was lying. I gulped the cold water down, draining the glass and gasping for air when I was finished.

The nurse glanced at the bedside clock. Four o'clock, it read.

"I'll go get Mr. Carmichael. He wanted to be informed the instant you woke up. Maybe after that we can see about getting you some more medicine."

She bustled away. My eyes trailed after her as she closed the door behind her. I looked down, trying to understand why I was in so much pain. My arms and hands were wrapped in bandages. I reached up to my face, trying to touch it with the one finger that poked through the gauze, only to feel more wrappings. I prodded them and winced. Whatever was going on under the bandages wasn't good.

I looked to the side, where a long tube led to a hanging IV machine. Beyond it I recognized the distinctive black and white décor of the hotel room.

The hotel room.

I was in Vegas. And then it all came rushing back to me.

I wasn't here with my dad. I was here with Michael, and something had gone terribly wrong last night.

The quiet click of the door closing snapped me to attention. I closed my eyes.

"Are we alone?" I asked, my voice hoarse.

"Yes." It was my father's voice I heard. If I opened my eyes, I would see my father standing there. But he was not the man I needed to see.

"I don't want you to be in here looking like him. I want to see you. The you from last night."

"It's not safe," he protested. "The nurse—"

"Then lock the door," I answered. "Please, Michael. I need to see you."

I heard him turn the deadbolt in the door.

"I'm going to stay over here," he said quietly from across the room, and I let out my breath, relieved to hear his *real* voice, relieved that he'd transformed himself back.

You know that he doesn't have a real *voice, don't you?*

I smiled, and then winced at the pain of it, when I heard Henri's voice in my head. He always disappears for the trouble, but somehow he always makes it back in time to gloat during the aftermath.

"Come closer to me," I said, trying to ignore the shooting pains in my face as I spoke. "It hurts for me to talk."

In an instant I felt him at my side.

"How long have I been here?"

"Overnight. Sixteen, maybe eighteen hours now."

"What happened?" An odd sense of calm had settled over me. The pain had finally forced me into a Zen-like place, and right now nothing seemed to matter but the truth. "Please. I need to know." I opened my eyes and stared at him blankly, afraid to show any emotion at all.

His face was inscrutable. His jaw was set in a hard edge.

"What do you remember?" His eyes probed me as if looking into my soul. I let my eyelids flutter shut, trying to block out the memory of his touch, his kiss, and the spine-shattering pain that had come out of nowhere.

"Nothing," I said, opening my eyes to fix him in a cool stare.

"Nothing," he echoed with disbelief. Then he sighed and squared his shoulders, raising his head to look out the window. "I—lost control. My spirit turned too bright."

"I don't understand," I said.

He eased himself onto the bed and picked up one of my bandaged hands, holding it like a piece of delicate crystal. He peered at me intently, as if willing me to pay attention. "Remember when I explained to you who I am? That morning in your room back in Dunwoody?"

"Yes, of course," I answered, puzzled as to why he would bring that up now.

"I told you that angels are different from humans in a few very important ways."

"Like the pain when you don't follow God's will."

He nodded slowly. "Yes, like that. Do you remember the other way?" He looked away to the window again.

I racked my brain. "No, I don't. But I don't see what that has to do with what happened."

"It's at the heart of it," he said, his fist clenching as he turned to face me. His face was twisted into a bitter smile. "Remember, I told you we angels can't create. It would be more accurate to say that we can't procreate."

I looked at him for what seemed like a long time before what he was saying dawned on me. I froze in my bed, my mind unable to hold back the images of last night.

"I don't need to know about that," I said emphatically, my words rushing out of me in embarrassment as I pulled my hand away from his, grimacing with the sting of it.

"Oh, but you do," he said softly. "It's very important, Hope."

I squirmed under his gaze. "I don't want to talk about this."

"Hope."

I shook my head again, bringing my hands to my ears like the monkey that could hear no evil, ignoring the pain that stabbed through my body.

"Hope, we have to have this conversation. You can't pretend that nothing is going on here any more than I can."

"But nothing *is* going on," I whispered, screwing my eyes shut.

"Not because I don't want there to be anything."

I let his words hang in the silence.

"Hope," he said again, a note of exasperation creeping into his voice. "Hope, please, look at me."

When I didn't say anything, he simply sighed and continued.

"When I take human form, I am truly human. With every human urge, Hope." I felt his fingers on my chin as he turned up my face to look into my eyes. “Every one. What I felt last night was very real. It still is.” His fingers grazed my chin, softly, and I shuddered.

I tried to turn my face away, but he held his grip so that I couldn’t look away. I fixed him with the blankest stare I could manage, but he looked so profoundly sad that it took my breath away. I couldn’t pretend I didn’t notice, didn’t care.

“I shouldn’t have acted on my feelings. Had we not been able to stop, I would have destroyed you. Literally.”

My mind refused to accept what he was saying. “But what about the stories of the Nephilim?” I asked.

“Nephilim are childish legends,” he said softly, letting his hand fall away from my face. He absentmindedly fingered the bedspread as he continued speaking. “God ensured that it is impossible. My true nature, Hope—my angel nature—is spirit and fire. The Fire of God. It is uncontrollable. And it grows stronger with emotion. When that emotion is directed at worshipping God, it is a beautiful thing. But if it were directed in love toward a human, in the course of passion—well, it would be too intense. It would consume the other in flame. Last night, when you said just one kiss, I thought that it would be safe enough, that I might be able to escape it or even control it in my human form. But I was wrong.”

I stared at him, unable to speak. The waves of heat that coursed from his fingers through my body convinced me it was true more than did the bandages covering my wounds. Still, I clung to any shred of hope.

“How do you know?” I demanded. “How can you be sure?”

He snorted and gestured about me, letting one finger trace the line of bandages wrapped around my arm. “Just look at you. This is evidence enough.”

"It could have been something else." My chin raised an inch, defying him to prove me wrong.

A rueful smile flitted across his face. "Even injured, you are stubborn and idealistic, aren't you?"

Gently, he released my arm and looked at me with wary eyes. "You know the story of Lot's wife, looking back on Sodom and turning into a pillar of salt?" Michael continued.

I nodded, unable to speak.

"Just another instance of bad after-the-fact reportage. She was with an angel. She turned not to salt, but to ash." Michael flexed his fingers into angry fists, the bitterness returning to his face. "God intends for our love to center upon Him alone. The fire is all-consuming, except for He who commands it."

There was a long pause, during which I stared at him. Carefully, Michael lifted his hand and gingerly trailed a finger down the side of my face. "We were lucky. The burns are not too deep. Some are no worse than a bad sunburn. Other places—"

"What about the other places?" I prompted him.

"They blistered. And now they are raw. That's why we wrapped you, to keep away infection. The doctors say you will heal with a little time, and maybe you'll avoid scarring."

I hadn't thought ahead that far, to think about how I would look. I didn't like the sound of that "maybe." But now was not the time to dwell on it. I shifted so that I could face Michael and fixed him with a carefully neutral expression.

"How did you manage to get doctors here?"

He shrugged, looked away. "I suppose it's a benefit of being a high roller."

"All those nights in the casino paid off for you, I guess." I couldn't keep the note of accusation out of my voice.

He looked at me, startled. "I suppose so. The staff was very responsive when I asked for help. Apparently, they keep a few doctors and nurses on the payroll. The need for some quiet medical attention is not that uncommon here."

Too convenient, Henri hissed. *Almost as if he'd planned it.*

The suspicion that Henri planted entwined itself about my mind. Now that the idea was there, I couldn't overlook it. It seemed so obvious. A cold, calculating fury, stoked with the embarrassment of being so naïve, started taking over my brain.

"I guess I'm lucky I'm in bed and not a pillar of ash, huh?" My mouth twisted as the lame jest left my lips.

He grunted with disgust, his hands gripping the rails of the hospital bed so hard that his knuckles turned white. "It's not funny, Hope. You could have been killed. *I* could have killed you. The one thing I vowed I would never do, and I nearly did it because of my own selfishness."

He had given me the opening, so I took it.

"Why didn't you?"

I heard the sharp intake of his breath and saw the shock on his face. "You can't mean that."

Don't let him squirm away. You deserve the truth.

"It would have been easier for you. Just to let me die."

His eyes glittered brightly. He reached for me, but stopped himself. "I thought—"

"You thought what?" I replied, tapping into the hurt I hadn't even realized was there. "You thought that you could just tell me you loved me and everything would be better? That then I would ignore the impossible situation that we're in? Ignore that there is only one way this could ever end?"

"But you asked me to—"

My voice cracked as the words rushed out, cutting him off. "I asked you to do something, and you did it—without giving me the full picture of what that would mean."

I thought about how I'd pushed him, begged him even, to prove he loved me with that kiss. A strangled sound emerged from my throat as I realized that I'd only made it worse for myself. I was going to have to live for the rest of my life knowing what it was like to be touched by Michael just for that one exquisite moment before all hell broke loose. Nothing would ever possibly compare to that—my first kiss. I would have to deal with a memory of something that I would never, ever have again. Whatever sweetness I could have salvaged from that memory would be cut by the bitter realization that I would never know if Michael truly loved me—loved me so much he couldn't help himself—or if this had all been part of some sick game he'd been playing with me. My head pounded as the next, obvious conclusion fought its way to the forefront of my mind.

Before I could stop myself, I voiced the idea. "Maybe you did this on purpose."

I felt the sting of tears on my face again. I sniffed and dragged one of my bandaged arms across my face. I stared at Michael, daring him to contradict me, wanting him to contradict me, but his face was a mask. His eyes had gone dark, shutting me out.

"Perhaps it is better this way. Better for you to be wary." He sounded tired, defeated.

"Maybe it is," I agreed, turning away from him to bury my face in the pillow.

"I'll get the nurse to give you more morphine," he sighed. He stood up and made as if to go.

"Don't," I said suddenly.

He stopped. "Don't go?"

"No," I said, sitting up in the bed, trying not to wince. "Don't get the morphine. I don't want any more drugs. I need to be alert." Throughout the whole conversation, in the back of my mind, an idea had been taking shape. It was spinning and twisting and now it was coming to the forefront, demanding my attention, demanding its voice.

"Why?" he asked, puzzled.

As if you didn't have reason enough to be on your guard, Henri snorted. *Next chance he gets, he may burn you to a crisp.*

The image of my childhood abductor melted to ash in the motel bathroom, captured forever in the faded photograph pressed into my mother's scrapbook, rose unbidden in my mind. I forced myself to ignore it. Grimacing, I threw one leg over the side of the bed, preparing to push off. "I need to be alert when we go to the Chinese."

Michael looked at me, confused. I continued explaining to him as I stretched out a foot, carefully gaining my balance.

"It couldn't be more obvious. Look at me." I gestured about with my bandaged arms. "They didn't trust you because they thought you didn't have me under control, right? But now, as far as they know, you punished me for embarrassing you in front of your friends. A nice faceful of acid, right?" I hovered there, the pain suddenly intense. A wave of nausea came over me and I held my breath, waiting for it to pass, before continuing. "You show them you're tough, you show them you're in charge. You show them that you know how to take care of your own. You save face. Problem solved. We get back in."

His face folded into stony crags and he crossed his arms emphatically. "There's no way I am letting you do that."

"You don't have a choice," I hissed at him. "If you want that Key, you need me. And I want Maria. This is the only hope we have of getting back in there and finding her."

He stared at me, his hard eyes turning pleading. “You should be resting. You could get hurt.”

“I already am hurt,” I snapped at him. “It might as well be for a good reason. Besides, the doctor said I could be mobile within twenty-four hours.”

He stood, frozen at the foot of my bed, unsure.

“How do you know what the doctor said?” he asked.

“Never mind how, but I know I heard him say that. And you heard him, too. By the time we get in it will have almost been that long. So what do you say? You owe me this much, Michael.”

He waited, torn.

I hardened my heart. “If you say no, then your true intentions will be clear. No more pretending.”

Finally, he dropped his head, nodding in assent. “I'll make the call.”

seventeen

Five hours later we were driving down Spring Mountain Road. The nurse had thrown a holy fit when she'd realized that we were planning to leave the safety of our cocoon, threatening to call the doctors, but Michael had paid her off with a stack of chips he'd stashed away in a drawer. Satisfied, she'd slipped off. We were safe until morning, when the shift change was supposed to take place. Hopefully by then we'd be back.

Now we were driving through the glow of neon from the signs of endless rows of Chinese and Thai restaurants. We were in the heart of Las Vegas's tiny Chinatown, on our way to meet the men who held Maria.

Every time Michael changed lanes or swerved, my entire body screamed with pain. I was taking nothing but triple doses of ibuprofen now, trying to keep my head clear for whatever lay ahead. Each time the pain came, I breathed deeply, talking myself through it until it crested and left my aching body. Even though it hurt, it was a welcome distraction from the gaping quiet that filled the car and the ache of the distance between Michael and me, which had somehow grown even deeper. He had put on the guise of my father once more as easily as making a change of clothes, but this time I couldn't tell if the change made it easier or harder for me to be around him.

"This doesn't seem that sinister," I said in an effort to break the silence, peering out the window at the concrete sidewalks and strip malls crowding the street.

"Not unless you're looking closely. There are about two massage parlors for every restaurant—see?" Michael said, looking out the windshield and pointedly refusing to look at me. "And some awfully long lines for this time of night."

"Where are we going?"

He pushed a piece of paper at me, stretching his arm to cover the distance between our seats. "This is their private compound. There's a game there tonight."

He turned onto a side street, and suddenly we were in a neighborhood filled with bland apartment buildings and townhouses. Block after block, everything looked the same, as if it had been stamped out by some giant cookie cutter from the sky.

"Really? This is it?" I turned the paper over in my hands, thinking there had to be some mistake.

He shrugged. "I guess they like to be close to their business. And you have to admit that it is pretty inconspicuous."

He peered at the numbers mounted on the curb and pulled into the drive of a large complex, stopping at the gate. The sudden jolt and strain of my burns against the seat belt made me gasp, and he looked over at me.

"You don't have to do this, you know."

I gritted my teeth. "Yes, I do. Just get us through the gate."

Michael's mouth twisted into a frown before he punched some numbers into the keypad. The wrought iron barrier shuddered and then sprang to life, swinging wide to let us in. The car noiselessly pulled through, winding through the maze of inner streets until we reached the very back of the development.

We parked and sat, neither of us saying anything.

"I don't have much of a plan," he warned.

"I don't think we'll need one," I said with confidence. He darted me a confused look. "I just have a feeling," I said. "I think she's going to be here. Maybe she's already here now."

Michael shook his head, frowning. "I'm not feeling anything."

My curiosity got the best of me. "Do you normally feel something, then?"

His jaw tensed. "I thought I explained that before. I'm drawn to the places and people I am supposed to be helping."

I ignored his bad temper and pressed on. "Even when you're not on a mission from Heaven? Even for something like this, for Maria?"

He yanked his keys from the ignition, tucking them under the rug instead of into his pocket. "Normally. But not tonight. Get out of the car."

He was out of the car, slamming his door hard before I had a chance to ask him any more questions. I eased my way out of the passenger side, being careful not to brush my body up against anything. My bandages caught the low moon and seemed to glow in the dark. Michael was waiting for me at the foot of a set of steps.

"After you," he said, giving a curt nod of his head to indicate that I should lead the way. I edged my way up, leaning heavily on the railing, wincing as each fresh blast of pain rippled through my body. At the first landing, I paused to catch my breath.

"Do you want to go back down and wait in the car?" Michael asked.

"No," I answered from between gritted teeth. "Not on your life."

I looked up the remaining flight of stairs. A sliver of light escaped from the blinds where someone was peeking out. Whoever it was, they allowed the blinds to drop, and the stairs fell into darkness. I continued climbing, my breath growing heavier with the effort to keep moving through the pain.

Michael snorted impatiently. "I'm not sure how you being here actually helps," he muttered.

"You forget: without me here, you're shut out. You need me to get admittance to the inner sanctum." My nerves were on edge, and his constant sniping wasn't helping.

"Just don't get in the way once we're inside."

I bit back my response. He was right, of course.

I let out a deep breath as I made it to the top of the steps. "Go ahead," I said between gasps, shuffling aside to make room for Michael. He pushed past me and rapped on the door once. Twice.

We waited for what seemed like forever before the door swung open. An enormous Asian man, his hair pulled back into a topknot, glared out at us. His gigantic head pivoted around as he looked to see if we were alone.

"Who are you?" he demanded, his eyes narrowing as he took us in.

"Carmichael. With the girl, of course," he added nonchalantly.

The man gave a nod of grudging respect. "The boss is expecting you." He stepped back, gesturing at us to come through the door. "Go down this hallway. He's waiting for you there."

We heard the slam of the door and the click of locks sliding into place as we walked away. The hallway seemed to go around the perimeter of the building, its plain expanse punctuated here and there by windows that were mostly boarded up. Michael walked along, assessing it with the calculating eye of an experienced warrior. I trailed behind him, ignoring the protests of my body.

"He must have combined several units and gutted them to make them defensible," Michael muttered.

Defensible against what? I thought, but I kept the question to myself.

A dark wood door loomed ahead of us at the end of the hallway. Michael drew up short.

"Are you ready?" He peered at me intently. It was the first time he'd looked at me—I mean *really* looked at me—since I'd forced him to call the Chinese. I swayed a little, and he reached out a hand to hold me upright.

"You're not getting unsteady on your feet, Carmichael? Last chance to back out." He skewered me with a probing look. I shook my head and straightened up, looking him squarely in the eye.

He lowered his voice. "Anything I say in there is just for the act, okay?" He paused, waiting for me to answer. He looked strangely nervous. Spiderwebs of fear began spreading through me.

"Okay," I breathed, willing my muscles not to freeze up. "Let's do this."

He turned away from me and knocked on the door.

"Come in, Mr. Carmichael. Come in."

Michael turned the knob and the door swung open. He reached back and clamped his hand on my shoulder, causing me to gasp, before pulling me through the door behind him. I glanced around quickly. There was another muscle-bound man—presumably a bodyguard—next to the door where we'd come in. Other than that, I could see only Chen and a young woman who sat demurely on the arm of his chair.

"Search them," Chen commanded from where he sat. Michael spread his arms and legs out wide.

"Is this any way to treat a guest?" Michael asked in mock disappointment as the goon patted him down, swiftly checking his pockets for weapons. "I expected better, Chen."

Chen grinned. "I like you, Mr. Carmichael, but not enough to be foolhardy." He snapped something in Chinese, and the guard turned to me. Instinctively, I shrank back against Michael.

"Be careful—she's hurt," Michael growled. The bodyguard nodded his acknowledgment and swiftly moved his hands over my body. There was nowhere to hide a weapon, no telltale lumps under the bandages. Chen laughed as the man stepped away and resumed his post against the wall.

"You are such a caring man, Mr. Carmichael, to be so concerned about your young niece's welfare. Bring her here to me so that I can see the extent of her injuries."

Michael pushed me gently from behind and I walked, a little shaken, across the room to stand in front of Chen's chair.

He stood up and closed the distance between us in one long stride.

"Let me see you, my dear." We'd removed the bandages from my face to give Chen a full view. He clamped his fingers about my chin and turned me this way and that, inspecting my oozing sores. "Interesting. Turn around," he commanded, making a small circle in the air with his forefinger.

I turned around clumsily, allowing him to see the extent of the damage.

As I came back to face him, I heard him tutting. "You were very thorough, Mr. Carmichael. I cannot see you left any part of her untouched. What was it that you used? Battery acid?"

Michael cleared his throat. "My little secret."

Mr. Chen shook his head. "A painful lesson, but one that she will never forget. It is really too bad. She was such a pretty thing." He looked me over again appraisingly. "What will you do with her now?"

I could sense the anger rippling off of Michael and only hoped that Chen was oblivious enough to think it was directed at me.

"I will keep her here with me, until she is well. It wouldn't do to have her fall sick and get taken to the hospital. It would raise too many questions."

"Ah, yes, questions," Chen nodded sagely as he settled back into his overstuffed chair. "You are wise to be careful. Still, I must say I am impressed," he added, breaking back into the wide smile with which he had greeted them. "To hurt the thing you love, to teach it obedience, it is a very difficult thing."

"Who said I love her?" Michael snorted. "She's just another girl."

His words hit me hard, like a punch to my belly. Just for the act, he'd said. But in the recesses of my feverish mind, I could hear Henri hissing.

Chen held out his hands in protest. "Oh, is she not special to you then? I am so sorry, my mistake." He gestured to the girl at his side, who had not left her perch during the entire conversation. She slid off the chair and stood silently, waiting.

"No matter. What you did still shows you have discipline, that you are in control of your operation. That is very important to me in my selection of business partners, as you know. I thank you for bringing her to me so that I might see for myself."

Being talked about as if I were an object, as if I wasn't even there, was making me angry. But anger was good. Anger was something I could hold on to, something I could focus on to get me past the pain. Something to help me stand it until I could find Maria. I could tell she was here. I could sense it in the air, somehow, could feel her presence and that of her sister.

"Might I ask you another favor, Mr. Carmichael?"

"Of course."

"It would be very useful to me if my own family could see your girl here, see what happens to young ladies who get ideas in their heads and disobey. I have so many young daughters, you see, girls whom I have gone to great lengths to secure and to provide happiness for. Yet they do not always see things the same way as you or I do, do they? If I could get your niece here to go to them tonight while we get down to business, it would be most helpful."

I involuntarily stiffened. It didn't seem like a good idea to get separated. On the other hand, if Maria and Jimena were here, I would be more likely to find them with the other women.

"I do not let her out of my sight just now," Michael replied with a silky voice. "I'm sure you understand my concern for her health."

"As you wish," Chen conceded, a slight pout settling into his lips. He mumbled something in Chinese, and the girl eased herself back onto the arm of his chair, resuming her wait.

"Besides, I thought we were playing cards tonight. Where are the others?" Michael tried to steer the conversation away from me and the horrible punishment he'd supposedly meted out to me.

"They will be here in time. You are not in a hurry, are you, Mr. Carmichael?" Chen reached into his inside jacket pocket and withdrew a fat cigar. The girl swiftly flipped open a shiny silver lighter and lit the tip of the cigar for him as he sucked in. The end glowed to life as he awaited Michael's answer.

"I would rather get down to business."

"Then speak your mind. My girl will keep quiet, as I presume will yours."

Michael pushed me aside and stood, tense, before Chen. The sharply cut suit could not disguise my father's spreading middle, could not make up for the thinning hair on the crown of his head.

For a moment I panicked, knowing there was no way my father could ever negotiate his way with such an experienced and evil man. But then I breathed, chiding my tired brain for forgetting who was really standing before Chen. It was ridiculous to imagine Michael negotiating with anyone either, but that was how he wanted to play it, so that was what we were going to do.

"I want you to recognize my business interests in Atlanta."

Chen tapped his cigar into the ashtray proffered by the girl. He took a deep pull of the cigar, the embers suddenly surging with brightness, before exhaling the smoke in a long breath.

"That is not so easy. We already have relationships there. It would be bad for us if we developed a reputation for being . . . untrustworthy."

I saw Michael's fingers curl into fists. So did Chen. "There's nobody left there. I wiped them out. Surely your network confirmed what I told you."

"Yes," Chen sighed, stubbing out the cigar. He crossed his legs and leaned back into his seat, his eyes never leaving Michael. "It was most unfortunate that you did that. Because now I have to choose whether to exact revenge upon you for what you did to my partners, or whether to make you my new partner. It is not such an easy choice."

"Don't pretend you haven't already decided," Michael sneered. "You would never invite me here unless you already knew your mind."

Chen beamed at them, clapping his hands appreciatively. "That is one thing I have come to appreciate about you, Mr. Carmichael. You are so perceptive. You are a student of human nature. I bet that is what makes you so good at what you do."

Michael glowered at Chen as Chen reached up to hold the young girl's hand.

"Pei Pei, go fetch me a drink." The girl disentangled her fingers from Chen's and slid wordlessly from his side, disappearing through a door in the back.

"Yes, I have made up my mind to go into business with you, Mr. Carmichael. You are a man of your word, it would seem, and I can always use more honest men in my organization. But we will have to talk terms, no? For I do not intend to have things run as loosely as the Mexicans ran them for all these years."

Michael seemed to relax, but I was getting antsy, my body screaming its protest against standing there so long. How would negotiating a deal get Maria and Jimena back? The longer we took, the more likely it was that they would slip away. And I was certain they were here somewhere.

I could feel it.

I drew a breath, about to speak up, when Michael threw me a sharp look, warning me to stay quiet. Chen witnessed the exchange and chuckled.

"Still feisty, that one? What does she need?"

"She still needs to learn her place," Michael said coolly. "But she is tired. Perhaps a place for her to sit and rest? And we can start our discussion of terms with a request for an act of good faith. You have several girls of mine, Mexican girls that I procured. They should never have left Atlanta. I want them back."

"Mr. Carmichael, you surprise me," Chen said, leaning back to appraise both of us. The girl, Pei Pei, slipped in through the door and brought him a crystal tumbler full of smoky, gold liquid. He looked at the drink, swirling the ice cubes around and around as if mesmerized. "Though I cannot say which I find more astonishing: that you would grant kindness to this young woman by allowing her rest," he said, pausing to look derisively at me, "or that you keep such tight control over your inventory that you would bother over a small handful of girls." He paused and took a long, appreciative drink from the tumbler.

He handed the glass absentmindedly back to the girl and barked something in Chinese to his bodyguard. The man swiftly crossed the expanse of the room and leaned over, allowing Chen to whisper in his ear. He grunted his acknowledgment and moved swiftly through the back door as well, leaving us alone.

"Women have no place in our discussions of business. So I will have Pei Pei take your girl in the back to rest. She will be safe there. You have my word." He nodded to Pei Pei, never taking his eyes off of Michael. Pei Pei glided to me, lightly touching my elbow to guide me away. I jolted at her touch, surprised at the quiver of pain.

I *was* tired, I admitted to myself. Plus, if I went into the back, I might find Maria. I looked at Michael, waiting for a sign. He nodded once, his eyes unreadable, before he returned his attention to Chen.

As Pei Pei spirited me away, I could hear Chen's voice floating through the air. "Now why would a gentleman of your means care about a few miserable creatures from Mexico, eh? Tell me that, Mr. Carmichael. I am all ears."

The door closed behind us before I could hear Michael's reply.

Pei Pei was like a ghost, walking noiselessly through the deserted maze, finding doors where there seemed none, leading me deeper into the warren of rooms that comprised Chen's complex. The few questions I posed to her were met with noncommittal shrugs. Every once in a while I would see a group of people at the far end of the hallway, which was lined with bolted doors, or across a room, but they would scurry away while Pei Pei skillfully steered me in another direction, never allowing me to get close. When she finally guided me into a quiet study, I sank gratefully into the sofa, eager to rest. My skin—or what was left of it—was burning up, but Michael had all my ibuprofen. I saw Pei Pei looking at me with something that seemed like pity and followed her gaze down to my arms. My wounds were seeping now, turning the bandages a sickly yellow color.

"Shhhh." She lifted a finger to her lips. An expression of sadness, or maybe just understanding, came over her face. Then, she backed out of the room, leaving the door open a crack and leaving me alone.

It would be so easy to just fall asleep here, I thought to myself as I let my eyes drift closed. The sofa was so comfortable.

But who knows where you'd be when you woke up, Henri snapped. *Foolish girl. Get up and start looking for Maria. The sooner we get this over with, the faster we can get on with the business of finding the Key.*

He was right, and I knew it. The feeling that she was here was still strong. There had to be a way to find her. But the lull of sleep, the irresistible urge to sink into oblivion and escape the pain, proved too strong, and I could feel myself slipping away.

On the edge of sleep, I heard the fluttering of birds' wings and jolted awake. There was a commotion outside the room, something that sounded like a scuffle punctuated by weeping and machine-gun-fire shouting. I shoved myself off of the sofa and crept to the door to take a peek.

The bodyguard from Chen's room was struggling to drag something—no, someone—down the hallway. Two people, to be precise. Two girls, one much smaller than the other. And they were coming this way.

I cursed under my breath when I heard a snatch of Spanish float through the air.

It was Jimena and Maria.

I ducked back behind the door. This was my chance. I looked wildly about the room for anything I could use. Pillows, knick-knacks, an artful arrangement of books—nothing. Then my gaze landed on the heavy glass ashtray on the coffee table. I darted over and picked it up. It was hefty, heavier than it looked. It would have to do.

The sounds of struggle were getting closer now. It sounded like Maria and Jimena were putting up a good fight. I peeked out from behind the cracked door. They were within a few feet of me. The brawny man was twisted away from me, his arms entangled as he hauled Jimena by one arm and tried to drag Maria behind him, his hands clamped around her wrists like manacles.

Maria was resisting with all her might. As she pulled back on his trailing arm, she raised her gaze and saw me. Our eyes locked. Hers widened at once—not with recognition, I realized, but with horror at the condition of my face. She had no idea who I was.

But I had no time for reintroductions. I nodded at her, pulling the ashtray out from behind my back, hoping that she understood what I meant to do.

Her eyes grew steely and she nodded imperceptibly. Pulling back once more, she bared her teeth and dove against the guard's exposed arm, sinking her teeth into his flesh.

The guard shrieked, letting go of Jimena to fully turn on Maria. He bent over, trying to push her off, but she scuttled around him, refusing to let go like a dog with a bone. He raised his free hand, fist clenched as if to strike her, and little Jimena kicked him hard in the small of his back. He howled and fell to his knees, and that's when I struck.

I darted from the doorway, raising the ashtray above my head, and bore it down on him from behind.

The ashtray made a sickening thud as it slammed into his skull, a spray of blood spattering the air. Instantly, his hand flew open, releasing Maria before he slid to the floor, unconscious.

For a moment, we all stood there staring at the pool of slick, dark blood that was beginning to form under him. The only sound was our panting as we caught our breath.

From a room far away, I heard shouting.

"Is he dead?" Maria asked quietly.

I gagged as I realized the blood had spattered on me, too, and I dropped the ashtray to the floor where it broke into pieces against the marble. A wave of nausea and pain swept through me. Could I have killed him?

"It doesn't matter. We have to go," I stated flatly, dragging my eyes away from the man's body. "We don't have much time. Come with me."

I looked at Maria, but she wasn't paying any attention to me. She was gazing with concern at her little sister, who stood shaking, her back pressed up against the wall.

"Maria," I warned. "We have to go. Now."

Maria's head snapped back. She wheeled on me, placing her body between her sister and me.

"Who are you? Who told you I was Maria?" she said, her eyes narrowing.

"You did," I said as gently as I could manage between heaving breaths. "Back in Atlanta when I interviewed you at the shelter."

Dawning recognition spread across her face. "Hope?"

I nodded, still trying to catch my breath.

"But how—?" She broke off, clamping one hand over her open mouth. "*Dios*, you came after us. What happened to you?" She reached out toward me, but I shrank back, fearful that one more painful touch would push me over the edge.

"It doesn't matter. We have to go, Maria. Now." I spat the words through gritted teeth.

Maria nodded her understanding. Quickly, she stepped over the slick of blood and touched her sister's chin, turning her face up to look into her eyes. She whispered low, comforting words I couldn't understand until Jimena nodded. Maria turned, taking a deep breath.

We heard a door slam and looked up. At the end of the corridor, Pei Pei stood, a small tray of refreshments in her hands. She took us in and the tray clattered to the floor, raining a thousand shards of crystal into the hallway.

"Let's go." I grabbed Maria's hand, wincing as her tight grip in response sent a surge of pain screaming to my brain. I didn't know where we were headed, but I knew we couldn't go back. I stared down the corridor, away from Pei Pei's panicked screams and toward the direction the man had meant to take Maria and Jimena. I didn't know what I'd find waiting for us, but we had no choice.

The hallway was full of doors. "Wait." I knelt next to the unconscious man and rolled him over, trying to ignore the warm slick that surrounded him. I felt around his belt and drew out a key ring. "We need to set them free."

Maria nodded. Together we ran back to the top of the hall and squared off before the first locked door. My hands shook as I went through the keys one by one, searching for the one that would fit the bolt.

"Hurry," Maria urged.

"I'm trying," I said, gritting my teeth. Finally, the lock gave. "Get them out," I ordered Maria, not pausing as I moved swiftly to the next door, the master key in hand.

We worked the hallway, me opening locks, Maria and Jimena following in my wake, pounding on the doors and rattling doorknobs until, one by one, young girls started cautiously poking their heads out from behind their doors. A steady murmur began to build as we worked our way to the last door, the only exit from this warren. I had no sense of where we were in relation to the rest of the complex I'd been through, but it didn't seem to matter. We had to keep going.

The chatter behind us was growing louder as the girls trickled out into the hallway, realizing they were free. A few girls started wailing at the sight of the body in the hallway. Others, emboldened, started to shout, apparently trying to organize themselves. It was only a matter of time before one of the traffickers came back to salvage what they could from this mess. Still, I paused, my hand resting on the bar of the door, afraid of what I'd find on the other side.

Behind us, over the rising din, I heard a moan and turned. The hulking figure on the floor, whom we'd thought was dead, was beginning to stir.

Go. The single word from Henri was enough encouragement for me. My fatigue was forgotten as adrenaline rushed through my body and I pushed open the door. But there was only empty darkness behind it. Relief flooded me.

I was about to rush through when Maria's hand pulled me back roughly by the shoulder. I winced.

"What?" I demanded angrily, turning on her.

"Look down," she whispered. "There is a drop."

I peered into the blackness, giving my eyes a moment to adjust. She was right: the door opened into a gaping hole. Across the vastness, a few exit signs twinkled. I looked down. The drop seemed to be only five feet.

Contrite, I turned back to Maria and her sister.

"We don't have a choice. It looks like about five feet. Do you think you can make it?"

Maria shook her head. "Jimena has a sprained ankle. I don't think she can jump."

I frowned, the noises behind us growing even louder. Over the girls' shouting I could make out several deeper, angrier voices joining in with Pei Pei's shrieking.

"We'll lower her down first," I decided. "Then we'll jump down to her."

Maria nodded and translated our plan to Jimena. Jimena gulped, but hobbled obediently over to the doorway.

I motioned for her to squat down and take my arms. "Maria, hold my ankles," I said as I shimmied down onto the floor. "Go ahead," I ordered Jimena, nodding at the door. "Lower yourself down."

The raw skin underneath my bandages felt like it was being pulled away from my bones as she hung from me, her grip tightening as we lowered her to the floor. We got her nearly all the way there when I reached my limit. My ankles were just at the edge of the floor.

"I can't go any further," I spat from between my gritted teeth, willing myself not to pass out. "You need to jump the rest of the way."

She dangled there, unsure of what to do.

"Maria, tell her!" I shouted. "We don't have time for this."

"She's afraid, Hope," Maria chastised me. "Give her some credit for trying." Then she began cooing in soft Spanish, urging Jimena to go the rest of the way. At last, Jimena let go of my hands, and we heard her land softly below. Maria scrambled over me and jumped over the edge herself while I rolled onto my back, groaning.

"Hope, are you coming?" Maria's voice floated up from the darkness.

I gritted my teeth and pushed myself upright, swinging my legs over the threshold. "Break my fall," I said before sliding myself over.

I tumbled into them, their arms catching me before I fell fully onto the floor. I didn't have time to catch my breath before Maria pointed in the dim light to the doorway across the vast room. "Over there—there is an exit."

We ran, gleaming machines emerging from the shadows as we went deeper into the dark. Cars, row after row of them.

"It's a parking garage," I managed to say through gasping breaths. "We must be on the ground floor."

"No, look," Maria said as we made it to the door. "An elevator." Sure enough, a car-sized elevator loomed over the cars themselves. She pushed the door open with ease, revealing a stairwell. "Down we go."

We hurtled ourselves down, taking the corners as tightly as we could, mentally counting the floors until we reached another exit. I peeked through the glass. Nothing but streetlights.

Above us, I heard a screech of machinery as the elevator roared to life.

"Come on," I said, pushing through the door. We spilled out into a parking lot. To the left of us were the stairs Michael and I had climbed when we first arrived. And there, glowing under the streetlights like a beacon, was our car.

I ran for the car, Maria and Jimena trailing behind me. My fingers fumbled clumsily with the handle until I got the door open. I snagged the keys from under the mat, thankful Michael had thought to stash them there.

"Get in!" I screamed as I forced the engine awake. They scrambled in. I backed the car out with a roar, not waiting for them to close their doors.

Behind me, the garage door was starting its slow ascent. We were barely ahead of them.

Tires squealing, I turned out of the lot and headed for the

entrance. "Close your doors and put on your seat belts!" I ordered tersely. Fear and adrenaline had sharpened my mind, and I did not hesitate as I took each turn, driving us out of the depths of the development. The iron gates loomed ahead of me. I didn't know the code Michael had used.

"Get down and brace yourselves!" I shouted as I put all my weight against the gas pedal.

The engine surged and we headed straight for the gate. I saw everything as if in slow motion—the bars buckling, the hood crumpling from the impact. Automatically, I pulled hard on the wheel, sending us screaming through the gate and into a spin as we slingshotted off the metal bars. Then I felt myself slammed against the back of my seat.

I had forgotten about the air bags.

A hissing sound filled my ears. A puffy sea of white took up my whole field of vision and a fresh wave of pain went screaming through my body. Ignoring it, I pushed away at the bag, already deflating, trying to gain my bearings. The entire car was filled with white dust.

"Everyone okay?" I shouted, unable to see either one of them through the plastic and haze.

A small cough sounded from the rear of the car. "Okay," I heard Jimena's shaky voice call out from the back.

"I'm okay, too," Maria answered. "Can the car still drive?"

"I don't know. I hope so," I said. The engine was still running. "Help me pull the air bag away so we can try."

We scrambled against the plastic, shoving it down and away as best we could until finally I could see Maria's face. She was bleeding from a few places on her face and was already bruising around her neck.

That the Chinese had not already overtaken us was nothing

short of a miracle—one, I was sure, that came courtesy of Michael and the crowd of angry women we'd managed to unleash. With the deflated air bags cleared into the back, I pushed down the gas pedal, and the engine roared. Cautiously, I shifted into reverse to back us out of the curb where we had landed. The sound of screeching metal announced our move.

"Hang on," I said, jerking the car with a spasm back into drive. Something was dragging behind us, but amazingly, we pulled forward. I pressed on the gas, hoping we weren't too late to escape the Chinese.

I sped through the neighborhood, back toward Spring Mountain Road.

"Where are we going?" Maria asked, looking over her shoulder anxiously.

"I don't know," I muttered, thinking to myself. "We can't go back to the hotel. Not like this. Besides, they know where we were staying. If I can make it to the interstate, maybe I can lose them."

I turned hard onto Spring Mountain and began to weave in and out of the cars that were in my way. For a second, thoughts of my father flashed into my head. Who could have known that his crazy emergency driving training would be of such use?

"Who is 'we,'" Maria asked, interrupting my thoughts with a worried look. "Who are you with, Hope?"

How to explain? Better not to even try. "Just a friend. He was in there with me but we got split up."

"Shouldn't we go back for him?" she asked, her confusion evident.

"We don't have to worry about him. He can take care of himself."

"But, Hope, they are very bad men—"

"Trust me," I snapped, trying to rush through a light and make the entrance ramp. "He wouldn't want us to go back."

We flew through the light just as it turned from yellow to red. The muffler was dragging behind the car, sending up sparks and making it hard to be heard over the engine. As we accelerated down the ramp, I stole a glance at Maria, who looked hurt.

I immediately felt contrite. "It's nice of you to worry about him, but he has sort of—special training in this area. He'll be okay, I promise."

She looked doubtfully at me, but she didn't press the issue any further. I merged into the traffic, grateful it was moving so quickly. We might be sending out sparks, but we could hope to escape the notice of the police if we blended into the flow.

I let out a slow breath. I couldn't believe we had gotten away so easily. It had to be Michael's doing; he must have held the Chinese gang back long enough for us to make our escape. As the adrenaline began to ebb away from my body, the pain that it had kept at bay rolled back in. I gripped the wheel hard, my knuckles turning white.

"How is your sister?" I asked, trying to distract myself. "How did you find her?"

"When the men picked me up again in Atlanta, they put us back together. I don't think they know she is my sister. She is okay, I guess, considering."

She paused. The grating sound of metal on pavement filled our ears.

"I can't believe you came after us, Hope."

I shot a glance at her and was overwhelmed by the look of gratitude on her face. Her eyes were teary as she continued.

"If you hadn't been there tonight, if you hadn't stopped him from taking us—"

"Shhhh," I soothed. "You don't have to think about it. You're safe now."

I'd barely uttered the words when a huge slam jolted us from behind, sending the car careening against the metal rail. I gasped at the sudden jerking motion and swung hard on the steering wheel, trying to pull the car back into the lane. Horns sounded as I swerved, almost cutting off another car.

A large black sedan loomed in my rearview mirror. They'd caught up with us.

"Damn it," I muttered. "How did they find us?"

The lights of the black car seemed to grow steadily as it prepared to ram us again.

"We have to lose it, Hope! We can't go back with those men!"

"I know, I know!" I shouted, desperately looking for another gap in the traffic, another place to maneuver where they couldn't ram us. I headed onto the right shoulder, darting around the slower cars, unleashing another torrent of angry honking. The black sedan swung right behind us, never slowing.

I veered back across two lanes to the left side. I had no idea where I was going, no plan for escape. I didn't know the city. I couldn't even find my own way to the hotel if I wanted to, I thought in a panic.

The car was so close now that I could see their faces from behind the glass. The sedan was packed with several men, including the bulky guard from Chen's room and the one I'd knocked out. One of them unrolled the window of the front passenger seat and started to climb out, taking aim with a long pistol.

Maria screamed as he lowered the gun. From the backseat, I could hear Jimena muttering over and over, "*Santa Maria, ruega por nosotros—Santa Maria, ruega por nosotros—*"

I jerked the wheel to the right, cutting in front of another car. The black sedan slowed, shifted lanes, and pulled forward again as the man re-aimed.

I could see him in my rearview mirror. The barrel of his gun seemed as if it was pointed right at me. Everything seemed to slow as he grinned a wicked, satisfied smile and pulled the trigger.

I ducked instinctively, knowing that nothing could deter the bullet from its path, waiting for it to rip through my flesh and bring this chase to an end. "I'm sorry, Maria," I whispered, hoping that somehow she and her sister would still find a way to escape.

Suddenly, a shudder shook the car as something heavy landed on the trunk.

Maria and Jimena began shrieking hysterically. I heard a flurry of gunshots but nothing seemed to hit us. The trunk quaked and groaned, springing forward as whatever had landed on us jumped from our car to the traffickers' car.

I surged forward from the momentum, stepping on the gas to increase the distance between us. Looking over my shoulder, I saw a flash of sword and fire as the other car swerved off the road.

"Michael," I breathed. I should have known he wouldn't have given up on us until he knew we were safe.

A huge explosion shook us, and I almost lost control of the car. Billowing smoke raced after us and chunks of blackened metal hurtled through the sky, moving as one in a screaming arc that soon engulfed our car, dancing around us before disappearing in a flash.

"We need to get away from here," I breathed, more to myself than anyone else. I stepped on the gas again, inching it up. Eighty. Eighty-five. Ninety.

By the time we heard the sirens whining behind us, bringing emergency vehicles and police to the scene of the accident, we were miles away. We wouldn't stop driving until dawn.

eighteen

Once we'd gotten outside of Las Vegas, the buildings and signs seemed to fall away, exposing the desolate desert for what it was. The more distance we put between us and the Chinese gang, the safer I felt. I rolled down the window, gulping in the dry desert air, hoping it would overpower the pain that was reasserting itself so vigorously.

We went past at least ten outpost towns, identical in all but name. I rejected each of them, having a vague sense that we would be found there, that we would stand out from all the other desert travelers moving through. But with the gas gauge pushing empty and my nerves spent, we finally gave in and pulled into a tiny mom-and pop-motel right off the interstate. A quick search of the glove compartment had turned up a credit card emblazoned with my name, another surprise gift from Michael, no doubt. The night clerk gave us a hard look, but he grudgingly gave us the keys to a room with a view of the interstate after I had fished the credit card out of my pocket to present to him.

Once we were settled in the room, I edged over to sit on top of the air conditioning unit, one eye peeking through the curtains to watch the road. Maria and Jimena eyed me nervously. They had been curiously quiet since we'd left Las Vegas.

"I think we lost them for good," I smiled, turning back to them, the effort stretching my skin and setting every nerve ending on fire. They were staring at me in earnest now. I looked down and saw how bedraggled my bandages were, and I realized how I must look to them. A wave of fatigue washed over me again.

I started to stand, and Jimena flinched as if she was afraid of me. I froze. Slowly, I eased back into my perch.

"What's wrong?" I asked, suddenly aware of how uneasy they both seemed.

Jimena began speaking, her child's voice soft and slow as she looked at me with wonder. The Spanish words flowed together, gaining speed and volume as she spilled out what was on her mind, her eyes growing wider and wider.

I looked at Maria, raising my eyebrows and waiting.

"She thinks she saw an angel," Maria said simply. "We both do."

I sighed. "Back in Las Vegas?"

"Yes," Maria said. "On the cars, fighting the men who captured us. Was that your friend?"

I paused. They had been through so much already. I didn't have the heart or the energy to lie to them, so I just nodded mutely.

"That's how you found us?"

I nodded again.

They sat, stunned.

I leaned back into the window, the coolness of the glass giving me some relief. I closed my eyes, struggling to stay awake.

"My mother believed in angels," Maria whispered. "Maybe she sent him to help us."

I smiled, my eyes still shut, as I pondered that idea. It was much more pleasant than the reality I faced.

"Maybe she did," I agreed.

"Will he come here?" Maria asked urgently. "To find us?"

I opened my eyes, knowing we needed some sort of plan. We couldn't stay here forever. I thought through what was likely to happen back in Las Vegas: the throngs of emergency personnel, the minute investigation of the crash scene. None of it would matter to Michael, of course. He would simply evaporate into thin air, using that sixth sense of his to find us.

"Yes, I'm sure he will come to us. We just need to wait here for him. Maybe we can rest." I gestured to the two small beds that took up most of the room, eyeing them doubtfully.

Maria looked at me in awe. "Yes, we can wait for the angel to come to us," she said very seriously, and then broke into giggles. "The angel will come to us."

I smiled. "You're very tired. As am I. Let's lie down and get some rest. Who knows what will happen next."

Maria patted the bed upon which she sat, talking in rapid Spanish to her sister, who dutifully climbed up onto the bed next to her. "You take that one," Maria said to me, pointing to the empty bed. "I will keep watch now. We can switch later."

I slid under the scratchy sheets, holding my breath to keep from crying out against the pain as the rough cotton rubbed against my exposed wounds. I bit my lip. *I'll just rest here for a little bit*, I reasoned with myself as I closed my eyes, *and then maybe I can go out to get some medication and fresh bandages*. Now that I knew I had a functioning credit card, the idea of going to a drug store did not seem so impossible.

~

After resting for I don't know how long, I opened my eyes, preparing myself to get back up, and looked around. But I was no longer in the motel. I was in a long black hallway, seemingly with no end, its great length punctuated by a series of closed doors. I looked down and saw I was not in my bed; in fact, I was not lying down at all, and somehow I was free of all bandages, my smooth, pink skin glowing in the half-light that floated through the hallway from an unknown source.

You're dreaming.

Was that Henri's voice or my own? I couldn't tell, but it felt right that I was dreaming; it seemed to be the only explanation for where I found myself. I began walking down the corridor, trying each door as I reached it, but each one I found locked. Finally, one doorknob turned in my hand, and I eased the door open.

I had stumbled upon Jimena and Maria being strangled by the guard, and suddenly I realized I was back in the Chinese mafia's maze of rooms.

Their eyes pleaded with me to help them. I looked around and again spied the heavy glass ashtray. I picked it up in my hand, preparing myself to strike the guard, but this time the ashtray turned into a rock, a huge rock with a blunt face. I looked up to where they were struggling and found that the girls had vanished. Instead of the Chinese goon, I was facing a lone man, dressed strangely in some sort of shroud.

He crouched before me, shielding his head from my blow, his eyes confused and fearful. He pleaded something in a language I did not understand, but I felt my heart harden. I raised the rock and swung down hard upon his head, only realizing as I did so that the hand that held the rock was not my own, but the calloused and dirty hand of a person much bigger and much older than me. A man.

I bolted upright, gasping for breath. Suddenly I was back in the dingy motel, tangled in the coarse cotton sheets.

Just a dream, I told myself, clutching at my shirt.

You were dreaming? Henri sputtered into my consciousness. *God doesn't send you random dreams at a time like this. Tell me, Hope. What did you see?*

I pushed his intrusion away and propped myself up on one elbow to look around the room, trying to get my bearings. The room was filled with the half-light of dusk. I'd been asleep for some time. Jimena and Maria were perched on the foot of their bed, blue shadows from the television flickering over them.

Tell me, Hope. Henri pressed me, insistently.

It doesn't make any sense, I hissed at him in my mind. *Leave me alone; it was just a dream.*

I cleared my throat, turning my attention to the girls and effectively shutting down any further attempt Henri could make at conversation.

"What are you watching?" I croaked through my parched mouth, trying to push the nightmare from my mind.

Maria turned and smiled. "You're awake. Look." She walked to the television and turned up the old-fashioned knob so that I could hear. The announcer's smooth, accentless droning continued.

"The fiery crash was seen by several witnesses, though exactly what caused the crash remains unclear." The scene cut from flashing lights to a talking head, one of the witnesses. "There was some sort of chase, but then something big landed on the car that crashed. I don't know how to describe it, but I got the distinct impression it was very large."

"While investigators sift through the wreckage to identify what it was that impacted the car to cause the explosion," continued the announcer, "conspiracy theorists, including representatives from the Area 51 Club, have descended to investigate whether a UFO or some other 'alien probe' may be the culprit."

I groaned. "Do you understand what they just said?" I asked Maria.

She grinned, nodding. "They have been playing the same news story over and over all afternoon so I had time to figure it out. But wait—there is more. Listen to this."

She stopped speaking so that I could hear the anchor continue. "And in what proved to be a busy night in Las Vegas, another mysterious explosion and fire in Chinatown." The scene jumped to footage of several fire units battling a blazing inferno. I sat straight up in my bed. "A vast apartment or townhouse complex owned by Chinese businessmen went up in flames around midnight last night. In a shocking twist, scores of young women—now presumed to be victims in the illegal sex trade—were rescued and freed from the fire and are now held in custody by local police. Police are working with the FBI to determine their origins and are hoping to free the women and press charges against the perpetrators soon. No sign of the businessmen on site, though, Connie, and it looks like it will take a while before the arson squad and other crime units piece together exactly what happened."

The scene cut to another interview, this one with a worker in a shelter not unlike the one Maria had been in while in Atlanta. Maria turned the volume down again and turned back to me. "Your friend, the angel, did that."

I nodded. "Yes, I suppose he did." At that, I looked around the room. "He isn't here yet?"

Maria shook her head. "Nobody has come or called. I made sure Jimena watched while I went out." She picked up a bag and brought it over to me. "I got you some food and medicine."

I looked into the bag. Stale pastry, a bottled orange juice, and some granola bars.

"They didn't have much at the gas station," Maria said apologetically. "I hope it is okay."

I forced a smile. "Of course it is. But how did you pay for it?"

Her eyes grew wide again. "I picked up the credit card, the one with your name, and it changed to mine. So the cashier never questioned me. It was another of your angel's miracles, I think." She frowned then. "I found more bandages for you, though. And some aspirin and ointment."

"That was very thoughtful of you, thank you." I frowned a little bit, surprised at how good I felt. I pushed the bag to the side and pulled the sheets back. "I think I'll go take a look."

The girls' curious eyes followed me as I made my way to the narrow bathroom and closed the door firmly behind me. I laid out the bandages, ointment, and aspirin on the ledge behind the sink. As I did, my reflection caught my eye. My face was red, a rash of angry yellow blisters clustered along my mouth and chin, leading down my neck to where the collar of my shirt splayed open. I stared at my reflection unflinchingly.

"Time to see just how bad things are," I murmured to myself. I thought of the girls and turned on the tap in the sink. I didn't want them to hear my reaction if it was really bad.

I delicately undid one of the bandages on my arm and started unwinding it. I gasped. Though it was clear that I'd been injured, the oozing mess that had been my blistered skin was starting to dry out, a delicate layer of new skin already forming. I bent my elbow and winced—it was tight. If it healed too fast, I might not have a good range of motion. I would have to move around a lot, I supposed, so that my skin would heal properly.

"I can't believe it," I whispered, turning my arm this way and that. Swiftly, I unwrapped the bandages on the other arm to find the same. The blisters were all gone, and everywhere I looked, new, pink skin was in their place. I undid the buttons on the front of my shirt and saw the angry red marks that followed the path of what had been the collar of my T-shirt. The raw welts along my abdomen that led down toward my waistband were healing, too. I blushed, remembering the feel of Michael's hands along my midriff, the trail of his finger as he popped open the button on my jeans.

I closed my eyes and leaned against the wall of the bathroom, the cool tile soothing my skin as I tried to shake away the memory by focusing on my injuries. "I must be imagining it," I murmured to myself.

I stood up, opening my eyes to resolutely examine myself again. But I had been right. I was healing. Along the edges, some of the skin already bore the shiny, telltale look of scar tissue.

I remembered the doctor's warnings about infection. I grabbed the tube of ointment and delicately patted it onto my skin before rewrapping my bandages. I ignored the questions that were swirling about in my mind, questions I couldn't answer. Instead, I clumsily rebuttoned my shirt and stepped out of the bathroom.

"Okay?" Maria asked, looking up from the television. Jimena simply watched, her deep, dark eyes seeming to understand everything.

I nodded, unable to speak.

"See, your angel takes care of you, too," Maria beamed.

At the mention of Michael, I paused. "He should be here by now."

"Did you have a plan to come here?" Maria asked, quizzically.

I shook my head, feeling my eyebrows come together stiffly, as if the healing skin was resisting their movement.

"We didn't have a plan to meet up anywhere. He just always seems to know where to go. I hope nothing happened to him."

"What could have happened to him? He is an angel of God!" Maria practically shouted the words, giddy with the belief that all her prayers would be answered. "He will come here and take us somewhere safe. I know it."

Somewhere safe. Just where would that be?

I cleared my throat again. "Maria, where do you plan to go? Now that you have Jimena, there's no reason for you to stay in the United States, is there?"

Maria suddenly became somber. "I cannot go home. *Mi tío* is still there. We won't be safe. Maybe I can come back to Atlanta with you?"

I thought about the complicated web Michael and I had woven and of all the things we still had left to do. We couldn't take her back to Atlanta.

"We'll see," I said vaguely, hoping to figure something out by the time Michael got here.

It wasn't like Michael not to be on the scene—unless he'd gone to take care of some greater problem that demanded his attention in another part of the world. Half impatient, half afraid, I jumped to my feet and started pacing the room.

"I'm going to leave him a message," I announced to no one in particular. "I'll leave him a message where to find us, back at our old hotel. That's the only way I can think of to reach him. If he checks anywhere, it will be there."

I fished the phone book out of the nightstand, pushing away the Gideon Bible that rested on top of it. Quickly, I scanned the Las Vegas listings for our hotel and dialed out.

"I'd like to leave a message for room 305, please," I told the operator at the front desk. "Michael—I mean, Don Carmichael."

"Let me put you through directly," she answered. There was a click as she made the connection, but it rang only once before I heard Michael's voice.

"Hope? Is that you?" He sounded frantic.

"Michael!" I said, startled. "What happened? I mean, we saw what happened on the news, but why aren't you here? We've been waiting for you, and I've been worried."

There was a slight pause. "It doesn't matter. Just tell me where you are and I'll be right there." I rattled off the address that was printed on the face of the phone and he continued. "Are the girls with you? Is everyone all right?"

"Yes, we're fine. But Michael," I said, lowering my voice, "we have to get them out of here. We have to get them home, to Mexico. But I'm not sure Maria wants to go."

He sighed. "We'll take care of that when I get there." He paused again. "How are you feeling, Hope? Do you need me to bring a doctor?"

I laughed. "No, it's the strangest thing. I seem to be healing. I'm still stiff and sore, but the skin, it—well, you'll see when you get here. I don't think there is any risk of infection any longer."

I heard him sigh with relief. "I'll bring a few supplies, just in case. I should have never let you go last night. It was too dangerous, and I knew it."

I bristled, but reminded myself there was no need to argue. He *had* taken me along, and because of that, Maria and Jimena were free. "Just get here as soon as you can," I said. "We'll be waiting."

I put the old-fashioned phone back in the cradle and paused. How strange, I thought, that he needed directions to find us.

It's not so strange, snickered Henri. *Ask him about it.*

Stop annoying me, Henri, I thought, irritated that he seemed so useless, so bent on making me suspicious and doubtful because of his own jealousy. *I'm sure there's a perfectly reasonable explanation for it. At least he helped me when it counted—unlike some angels I know. Some Guardian Angel you've turned out to be.*

Suit yourself, he sniffed, and I heard no more from him.

I plopped down on the bed and drummed my fingers against the nightstand. Maria and Jimena looked at me expectantly.

"He'll be here soon," I promised, and they beamed. "We just have to wait a few more minutes."

I looked back over at the phone. A wave of longing for my mother swept over me. Michael had been so vigilant at first, and after that I'd resisted the temptation to contact her, afraid of what might happen or what she might do if she knew where I was. But now, knowing Michael was nowhere near, I felt guilty. I was sure by now she knew I was missing.

I looked over at Jimena and Maria and thought of their father; wondered if he even knew that they had ended up in so much danger.

Mom must be frantic, I thought. But I didn't trust myself to talk to her—not now, not with so much unfinished business. But there was someone else I could call, I thought, smiling to myself. Someone who would have no problem butting her nose in.

I picked up the phone and let my fingers dial the number I knew by heart.

It was the middle of the afternoon. Her phone was probably off while she sat in classes, so I wasn't surprised when it rolled to voice mail.

"Tabby, hi, it's me, Hope," I began, my voice a little shaky as I rushed through the words. "Sorry I haven't called you. But hey, I was wondering, could you do me a favor? Can you call my mom and tell her I'm okay? I think she's worried about me and, you know, she likes you so much, it would really mean a lot coming from you. Okay? I—I gotta go now. Bye."

I hurriedly put the receiver back in the cradle and stared at it. A loud knock at the door made me jump. My heart pumping, I moved away from the phone as fast as I could.

"Who is it?" I asked nervously.

"It's me, Michael."

I let out a long breath and walked to the door, throwing it open. He rushed through, his brow knitted with concern, and without thinking I threw myself into his arms, burying my face in his shoulder. His warmth seeped through me, soothing every aching muscle and joint in me. I almost didn't feel the painful catch of my skin as he pulled me close.

Too soon, he pushed me away, holding me out from him for inspection.

"You really are healing," he noted with wonder. He lifted a tentative hand, as if he would trace the blistered skin along the curve of my cheekbone, but then he checked himself, bringing his hand to rest in my hair instead. "You probably can't even tell how much better you look. I didn't know this was even possible." He tilted my chin, gently, to get a better look.

Behind me, Maria cleared her voice. I stepped away from Michael, confusion and embarrassment flooding through me.

"Michael, this is Maria and her sister Jimena." I gestured to them where they sat at the foot of their bed. Michael came through the doorway and closed the door behind him.

"I'm so glad you are safe," he said seriously. They stared up at him, wide-eyed. "You must be eager to get home."

Maria looked at me warily. "I am not sure if that is a good idea."

I reminded Michael of her fears of her uncle. His face darkened.

"I can take care of that," he said menacingly. I saw the blood drain from Jimena's face. She leaned over and whispered something to her sister.

"I don't care what he has to do," Maria spat, disdainful of her sister's fears. "He deserves whatever he gets. Who am I to judge the actions of an angel of God?"

Michael arched a brow and cocked his head, looking at me pointedly. "An angel of God?"

I shrugged. "They saw you when you attacked the car. At this point, I couldn't see the harm."

He grimaced slightly. "Oh, well. I suppose you are right. At least it makes our next move a little easier." He turned to the girls.

"Neither of you is too seriously injured, I hope?" When they shook their heads, he continued. "Then I'm taking you back to Mexico. Tonight. Get whatever things you have together. We'll leave as soon as it is fully dark."

The girls began scurrying about the room, looking for whatever meager belongings they had taken with them.

Then Michael turned to me, speaking under his breath. "You stay here and wait. When I get back we'll regroup. It will be time to turn our full attention to the Prophecy." He seemed to struggle with what to say next. "I'm not really sure where to go from here, but we'll figure it out." He reached out and took my hand in his. "Together."

I felt myself flushing as he looked at me. Questions came unbidden to my mind. Why was he being so tender with me? Why did he keep saving me? Could I really trust him? My heart told me yes, but I knew that nothing had changed. We still faced the horrible choices dictated by the Prophecy.

Don't forget—every action he takes is driven by his need to find the Key. That is all.

I pointedly ignored Henri.

"Can't I go with you?" I asked.

He shook his head sadly. "Flying with humans is always tricky business. Three of you will be a bit much. And with your injuries, I can't risk it. Not while you're still recovering. Especially since there's likely to be some trouble once I'm there."

"The uncle?" I asked, quickly surmising what he meant.

"Yes." He grinned, giving my hand a little squeeze. "Though I'm hoping the old 'lightning and thunderbolts from Heaven' routine will scare him straight without me having to do any permanent damage."

I smiled, happy to be holding his hand, happy to be in his confidences once again.

Oh, give it a rest.

I held back a laugh. *You just can't resist, can you?* I jabbed at Henri.

"What's so funny?" Michael asked sharply.

"Nothing," I said, dropping his hand and trying, I think unsuccessfully, to wipe the smile off my face. I looked over my shoulder for a distraction. "I think the girls are ready."

He nodded brusquely and began directing them. Maria translated his commands with ease. "Go down the hall to the fire escape. Climb up to the roof. You can manage that? Good. I'll be right behind you. You might as well make your goodbyes now."

He stood off to the side, making room for the girls. Jimena smiled shyly up to me. "Thank you," she said. Suddenly, she threw her arms around me, squeezing me tightly in her bony little arms. I winced, just a little, before hugging her back, hard. With a sob, she rushed past me and into the hallway.

Maria's gaze followed her sister until the door swung closed behind her. Then she turned back to me.

"I will never forget you," she said, almost whispering.

"Nor I you," I answered in response, my voice choking. "Take care of yourself, Maria."

She took my hand and gave it a squeeze.

"Please call me Ana. That is my real name, what my family calls me."

I felt the lump in my throat growing bigger.

"Ana," I whispered, squeezing her hand back. "God speed, Ana."

"And you, Hope. Wherever it is that you are going." She shot a furtive glance at Michael. "God has given you a special mission, I can tell. You will not fail."

Before I could ask her what she meant, she slipped out of my grasp and through the door, leaving me to gape after her.

Behind me, Michael cleared his throat. "Are you okay here by yourself?"

What he really wants to know is that you're not going to run off and try to escape, Henri sniped. My back stiffened. I turned back to Michael and eyed him warily.

"I won't run away, if that's what you mean," I answered.

Michael looked at me, incredulous, the vein in his forehead throbbing to life. "That's not at all what I meant," he snapped as he stepped toward me, clenching and unclenching his fists. "After all that happened last night, I would expect you to know that."

I crossed my arms, refusing to back down. "I don't know any such thing. But you can rest easy. I'll stay put. For now."

His eyebrows knotted together in fury, his eyes flashing as he came face to face with me. "You child," he spat at me as he gripped my shoulders with a ferocity I'd not yet seen from him. "You have no idea what you are saying. No idea at all the danger in which you keep putting yourself."

I shrank back against the wall, shaking. Heat surged from my shoulders, spreading like tendrils down my back. I gasped and tried to pull myself away, sure that I was about to erupt in flames.

Michael's eyes widened, and as if he was waking from a dream, he looked at me, looked at his own hands where they shook me, and let go, stepping away.

"I'm sorry," he said simply. I did not respond. Instead, I watched the vein in his forehead as it throbbed. I wondered if it was because of me, or if the pain of his disobedience was worsening.

He stared at the floor and continued talking. "There is something you should know about last night."

When I didn't respond, he continued.

"The men in the car that chased you weren't men. They were Fallen Ones."

My jaw fell open in disbelief. "But I saw the car explode! I saw the fire!"

"Yes, the car exploded, but mixed in with the shrapnel was the black flock the Fallen Ones turned to as they made their escape. I'm afraid for you, Hope." He paused, as if hesitating to tell me anything further. "I didn't defeat them so much as they seemed to give up."

My heart sank as I remembered hearing the fluttering of wings before I'd discovered the girls in the corridor, the way the shrapnel had seemed almost choreographed as it flew in a single direction out of the night sky.

"Your escape seems too easy to me. It was almost as if they sacrificed themselves for some reason. I don't pretend to understand it, but I believe they have been using Ana and her sister as bait all along. To what end, I do not know. But I fear you are still in danger."

Michael looked up, a bitter smile on his lips. His blue eyes shone as he drank in my face. "Which is worse, do you think, Hope? The harm you've had at my hands, or the harm you could have had at theirs?"

I answered him impulsively. "You never hurt me deliberately."

He pressed his lips together in a stern line. "Maybe not. But the damage was done nonetheless. And now—"

He broke off, leaving his thought unspoken as he held my gaze.

"I'd better go," he whispered. He edged past me in the narrow hallway and swung the door open.

"Be careful," he warned over his shoulder. "I'll be back as soon as I can."

nineteen

Mona jumped, startled awake in the chair where she'd collapsed.

That noise, what was it?

She looked around, trying to find the source. It was barely a scratch, it seemed. Maybe it was her imagination?

No. There it was again.

It was early morning, and she could barely make out the dim light of the rising sun through the slats in the shutters.

Something was behind them. Outside. Trying to get in.

She drew in a breath and rose up, clearing the space between herself and the window in a few strides.

There was a candelabra next to the window, an antique the decorator had somehow foisted upon her. She picked it up as she heard the scratching again. The candlestick was heavy, substantial. She was sure it could knock someone out if push came to shove.

Bracing herself, she raised the candlestick above her shoulder and pulled open the shutters.

"Don!" she exclaimed. "What on earth—?"

He was hiding in the shrubbery, bracing himself as if he expected her to leap through the glass and clobber him. In a second her mind took in his worn camouflage jacket and hiking boots, the obvious bulges where gear had been stuffed into countless pockets.

"Mona, please!" he half-whispered, half-shouted through the glass, his hands lifted in the air to show he meant no harm. "I need to talk to you. Let me in, please?"

She lowered the candelabra and set it down on the side table, taking the moment to look away and appraise the situation. Don would certainly have come alone. He had no friends to speak of. But that lack of friends meant that he'd have to leave Hope behind alone, and he wouldn't do that. Maybe she was here with him, too. Her adrenaline surged at the idea that her daughter could be nearby. Maybe this was her chance.

She scanned the room, trying to remember where she'd left her cell phone. She should really call that FBI agent and have him come over and arrest her husband.

It's too damn early for this, she thought to herself as she rubbed the narrow bridge of her nose.

"Please," Don said plainly. He wasn't wheedling; he wasn't whining. She turned back and sighed. He looked up at her with shining eyes, working his cap over and over in his hands, and she felt herself caving in, just as she always had.

"Come around to the garage," she grunted.

He beamed at her, the smile of a man who knew his purpose and had no doubts, and he stood up to his full height. Even though the house was slightly elevated above ground level, he could look at her eye to eye when he drew himself up. That was one of the things she'd always liked about him. She could wear heels and not be embarrassed to tower over him.

Irritated with herself for thinking that way, she closed the shutter on his smiling face and twitchy hands and made her way to the front hall. She looked into the mirror that hung there. Her hair was a disheveled heap on her head, one of Hope's borrowed headbands barely managing to stay in place. She licked her teeth and felt the coating of last night's wine. Grimacing, she rubbed her finger over her teeth and tried to smooth her hair into place.

"Futile," she muttered to herself, before straightening her robe. It would have to do.

She marched over to the kitchen door, opening it to reach into the garage. The big button glowed in the dark as if daring her to push it.

Be cool, Mona. She might be close by. This could be your chance. She repeated the words over and over to herself until she had regained her composure. Then her finger reached out and once, deliberately, pushed in the button. The garage door groaned to life, slowly inching up.

Don didn't wait, but darted under the half-raised door as soon as he could.

"I brought you doughnuts," he said, pushing a crumpled bag toward her as he came rushing in.

She caught it up in her hands. She could feel the heat of the doughnuts, just out of the oven, through the waxy paper. "I don't eat doughnuts anymore," she said, unsure what to do.

He brushed by her, darting a glance over his shoulder as he passed. "Sure you do. Everyone eats doughnuts. It's not like you forget how. Look. I even brought you an apple fritter, your favorite."

She peered into the bag and let the sugary sweetness waft toward her. Her mouth watered as she closed the door.

"You can't ply me with sweets, Don," she admonished, even as she started the coffee brewing.

He laughed. "You know they make them with non-saturated fat

now, or whatever it is that is supposed to be healthy. I say who cares—a doughnut is a doughnut. I don't need the government telling me how to eat."

He flopped into a chair at the kitchen table, looking for all the world like nothing unusual was going on; as if it were his home.

Which, once upon a time, it had been.

"Mona, we have to talk." He'd dropped the fake cheeriness and the pliant guise he'd worn to talk his way in. His jaw was set with a determination she remembered from long ago.

She turned her back and started the coffee grinder, trying to ignore the heat that coursed through her body. How could he be here? Here, in her kitchen, with her making him coffee? She should be screaming bloody murder at him. She pulled the fuzzy robe closer about her body, wishing she could just disappear into the ground.

Instead, she poured the water from the carafe into the coffee machine, occupying her mind by watching the water level rise. Eight cups. She pushed the start button. The light flickered to red. Finally, she turned to face him, squaring her shoulders.

"Did you bring Hope, Don?"

"You know I don't have her, Mona. That's why I came to talk to you." He leaned in conspiratorially. "People are watching me, Mona. I saw them. Yesterday." He drew a heavy arm across his face, as if he was trying to wipe away the memory.

She groaned, not even bothering to try to hide her reaction.

"What are you talking about this time?"

"I was at work. You know, at the Taco Bell? And I saw the cars. They stood out, you know? Not the typical teenager type of car. *Lincoln Town Cars*," he said, pausing dramatically between each word to underscore the significance of this detail. "The only people who have those are limo drivers and government types. And these didn't have any hack licenses." He lifted his eyebrows, expecting her to realize the gravity of the situation.

"Go on," she said, crossing her arms and sending him her best frown to show she was not amused.

With a sense of urgency, he continued, his hands gesturing wildly. "They were in with my manager," he whispered. "I waited until they came out. I saw the whole thing."

Her mind zoomed out for a moment. She imagined Agent Hale sending a team out to collect the time-clock records and videotape. She imagined they would question whoever was in charge. She groaned.

"What did you do then?" she asked, afraid of what Don might answer.

"I did what I had to do," he said, pounding his fist firmly on the worn kitchen table. "I took off. Too many coincidences. Not good. Not safe. Especially while Hope is missing. I need to be mobile if we are going to find her. I had to get out of there."

Mona began to pace, absentmindedly gnawing on a knuckle.

Don, an apparent fugitive, was sitting at her kitchen table. She darted a glance over at him and found him happily chewing away on a cruller.

"Hey, is that coffee ready yet?" he called out. Apparently even a paranoid needed his morning caffeine.

She went to the cupboard and silently pulled out a cup. "Mother of the Year," the cup proclaimed. *How ironic*, she thought. She filled the cup almost to the top and then dashed in a tiny bit of cream to cut the bitterness.

She brought the cup to Don, who accepted it gratefully with both hands. He took in the steam, and then gulped down a hot mouthful.

"Just the way I like it, Mona. Even after all this time, you remember. Thank you," he said.

She looked into his eyes and could tell he was sincere.

"Don, you shouldn't have come here," she began, bracing herself for what she knew would be an argument.

"Where else could I go?" he asked simply. He had a point, she acknowledged.

"Those men who came, they were probably with the FBI. They were probably sent to investigate you. Running away only makes you look guilty."

Don put down his coffee cup and sighed. He looked like someone who was trying to explain something simple, like nuclear physics, to a truculent child.

"But I'm not guilty. I don't know where Hope is. I've told you already."

Mona poured herself a cup of coffee and sat down across from him.

"Don, it is not that simple. You can't just say you don't know and expect everyone to believe you. There will be evidence. There will be facts that can prove or disprove what you are saying. Please," she continued, running her hand through her hair in frustration, "please try to understand. If you're innocent, it is much better for you to stay put, to stay where they can keep track of you, and to let the evidence play itself out."

Why are you doing this? she screamed at herself. *Call the police. He took her; you know he did.* But she couldn't. Not yet. She couldn't spook him. It would be better for them all if he turned himself in—or even better, brought her to Hope.

"Mona," he said, reaching out and grabbing her free hand. She froze. "The evidence will show that I am innocent. Then what will you do?"

She looked into his eyes. There was sadness there. And fear. But not guilt. Not one shade of guilt tainted the sincerity that shone from them.

Her mind faltered. *What if he was telling the truth?*

A huge abyss opened before her. She had never even contemplated a scenario where Don wasn't the culprit.

"That's not possible," she whispered, trying to pull her hand free. Don's grip only tightened.

"For years, Mona, I've been telling you. They weren't done with Hope. She's meant for something special. That Mark of hers—"

Mona disentangled her fingers, her face flushing with anger over the old craziness resurfacing. "I don't want to hear it, Don. That is a coincidence. It means nothing. We have put that behind us."

She heard herself reciting the same lines of the same argument, years and years of frustration rushing back at her, her voice on edge with the same sharp desperation. It used to be that her proclamation marked the slamming of the door on the conversation. The end. No more. But this time Don wouldn't stop.

"You never believed me, but I knew they would come back for her. I thought my job was to keep her safe, but when you asked me to move out, I realized something. I couldn't shelter her from her destiny. My job was not to stop her fate; it was to prepare her for it. To keep her safe until her time came. It was Divine Providence that we separate so that I could give myself over fully to her training."

His eyes were shining with intensity of purpose now, and she felt herself start to get a little sick.

"I was the one who taught her how to run—did you know that? I even taught her how to drive—did she tell you about that? We practiced evasive maneuvers, especially. And she knows all the books of the Bible. Almost all of them, anyway. I had her memorize things, especially from the prophets, just in case." The corner of his mouth tugged up a little as he reminisced. "She has very strong opinions about Genesis, by the way. Just like you."

Mona pushed her coffee cup away, not caring when it spilled all over the kitchen table. She stumbled from the table, hands over her ears as if she could block out Don's words, until she got as far away from him as the kitchen would allow. Still his voice followed her.

"You don't have to worry, Mona. She's ready. For years they would come to me. They came in my dreams—beautiful creatures, more beautiful than anything I had ever seen. They told me to prepare the way.

"When she wanted to come to live with you, they stopped coming. That's how I knew it was time to let her go. The police can try to find her, but they will search in vain. God's plan is in motion."

Oh my God, she thought. *What has he done with her? What is he plotting for her to do?* Her mind raced, sifting through his rantings to find any clue of where to find Hope. But there was nothing.

"Don," she said with ragged breath. "Do you really believe that? That Hope is off on some heavenly mission?"

She waited as he thought over her question.

"I do," he said simply.

"A mission to do what?" she demanded.

He stared into the dregs of his coffee cup, obviously disturbed by her question. "I don't know." He looked up from his cup, his eyes full of fear and doubt. "What if she's not ready, Mona? What if I didn't prepare her enough? What if she's in danger?"

He sat there in his ill-fitting clothing, his awkward haircut barely disguising the thinning of his hair, looking for all the world like some soft, suburban refugee playacting as a survivalist. He was the man who had had it all and walked away from everything, *everything*, to protect his daughter from whatever it was he imagined still threatened her.

At that moment, she knew she would never sway him, never get him to believe anything different, never get him to admit to anything if he had, indeed, spirited Hope away. And even as she thought it to herself, she began to doubt he could have done anything serious to Hope. Not when he seemed so hell-bent on protecting her.

Later she would give in to the guilt. She'd wanted to put the past behind her, and in doing so, she had been willfully blind to what was going on in Don's household. He had truly lost his grip on reality, and she would never forgive herself for not seeing his craziness for what it was, for chalking it up to harmless eccentricity. For trying to avoid it out of shame.

Or out of hope. Deep down, she'd never stopped wishing for things to go back to the way they were. That's why she'd never divorced him. That's why she'd never spoken up about his crazy accusations. She hadn't even put away their wedding pictures. How could she have accepted that the man she had fallen in love with all those years ago was really gone?

But she couldn't allow herself the luxury of wallowing in her guilt right now. She needed to be strong. So she had to try another tack.

She took a deep, steadying breath. "Then don't you think you ought to tell the authorities?"

Don's aura of uncertainty only deepened.

"Yes," he whispered, looking down at his hands. "I suppose I should. But they'll never believe me."

"You can't be so sure of that. If you're telling the truth, they're bound to come around to your side. And like I said, if you keep running, it just makes you look guilty."

She was prodding him now as if he were a little child, using the same tone of voice she'd used on Hope as a toddler when she was trying to convince her to take a nap. Reasoning with an unreasonable person was never a sure bet, but it was all she had right now. She looked across the vast expanse of the kitchen and gave him an encouraging smile.

"Do you believe me, Mona?"

She was caught in the tractor beam of his look as he pinned her down with his question. Her mouth was dry when she tried to answer him, and it took her several tries before she could speak.

"It doesn't matter what I think, Don. What matters is that you do the right thing. For Hope."

"Of course. For Hope," he repeated, looking down at his hands again. "For Hope." He dropped his head further, as if in acquiescence. "You'd better give me the name of the FBI agent you're working with."

Her head jerked sharply up. "What?" She felt her face flush, and saw from the look of amusement on Don's face that he already knew. "How—?"

He smiled serenely at her, his crisis of confidence now forgotten. "The angels told me all about him, too."

twenty

Once again, I pulled the curtain back from the motel window and peered outside. In the fullness of night, there wasn't much I could see. The lonely lamps that dotted the parking lot stood like beacons and cast shadows that time and again I assessed for threats. Did that shadow just move? Was there something there, waiting for me to let down my guard?

I let the curtain drop back into place and sighed as I leaned back on my uncomfortable perch. The tiny alcove by the window was not meant for sitting. The edges of the wall poked into my already tender skin. I jumped lightly down and began pacing the room.

After Michael's warning, there was no way I could let myself sleep.

My body, on the other hand, begged to differ. My bones ached, and my taut skin was now becoming itchy from the unnaturally rapid healing process.

I needed something to do, something to occupy my mind. An idle flipping of television channels found nothing but old sitcom reruns and infomercials. There was nothing abandoned in the meager closet, no hotel magazine touting local tourist traps. I rifled through the drawers and pulled out the Gideon Bible I'd rushed past earlier in the day.

It will have to do, I said to myself ruefully, as I fanned through the tissue-thin pages.

After years of my father's tutelage and the monotony of Catholic school, I could recite countless verses by heart, had no need to even look at the delicate pages and the tiny type to remember the stories and commands that unfolded between the covers of the book. Except for the book of Genesis. I frowned as the pages fell open to its opening words.

> *In the beginning, God created the heavens and the earth. The earth was formless and void, and darkness was over the surface of the deep, and the Spirit of God was moving over the surface of the waters. Then God said, "Let there be light"; and there was light.*

The little lamp next to the bed seemed to sputter and then righted itself. I eased onto the bed, plumping up the hard pillows as best I could to cushion me as I leaned back against the wall, and I settled in to read.

I'd always hated Genesis. Once you got past the dramatic creation of the world in the first chapter, it struck me as very misogynistic, what with the "Eve out of Adam" and "woman tempted" bits. Every single son of Noah named and numbered, but the women mentioned only by their roles, nameless wives and daughters who add not a whit to the story. Add to that the endless lists—this river became that river, so-and-so begot so-and-so—and it was a real snooze.

But I seemed to remember it had the story of Lot's wife, and some mentions of Nephilim. And since I didn't really know it, it might manage to keep my attention, so I dug in to read.

I was barely into it when my mind began to wander. Unconsciously I was skimming the pages, barely registering their words as I kept one ear listening for the sound of rustling wings. Had the Fallen Ones been following us all along? I thought back to our visit to Enoch. Enoch, whose name I would undoubtedly find in one of these never-ending lists in Genesis. I shuddered as I remembered the shadow that had seemed to pass over me when he'd disappeared. Had that been the Fallen, hunting me down even then?

I mindlessly turned the page, my eyes scanning without registering anything at all, when a verse caught my attention: *And it came about when they were in the field, that Cain rose up against Abel his brother and killed him.*

Brother against brother, the Prophecy had said. I scrambled up and ran to my purse, rifling through it for the piece of crumpled paper Enoch had given me for safekeeping. I smoothed it out, running my fingers hastily over my scribbled notes, looking for the translation that had been jotted in the paper's margins. Hands shaking, I traced the words as I read them aloud:

> *The Key of Righteousness perverted Brother against Brother,*
>
> *Child against Father, and rent the curtain of Heaven with the sins of Man and Angels' doubt.*
>
> *With this Key, the Bearer shall come and the Gate shall open, spilling out Heaven's glory, and letting those desirous amongst you to ascend once more.*

The Bible slipped from my hands, falling with a solid thud to the floor as last night's dream came rushing back to me. The dirty hand that lifted the rock and killed the guard-who-wasn't-a-guard—that wasn't just the confusion of my overtired brain. It was a vision of Cain killing Abel in the field. And the Key of Righteousness wasn't a key at all. It was a rock, the only weapon that someone at the dawn of time would have had at his disposal, the most likely thing a farmer would have used to strike out in jealousy against his own flesh and blood.

I fell to my knees, scrambling through the pages to find the one I needed once again. I raced through the rest of the passage. Cain was banished to wander and was sundered from his family, who rejoiced when God sent them another son to replace the one that Cain had killed. *Child against Father*. It said nothing about "Angel's doubt," but I was certain. This was the Key. We had to find the ancient weapon that Cain had used to slay Abel.

And then what? I was feeling dizzy, my head spinning as everything began to fall into place.

Then those who would, will ascend into Heaven. That's what the Prophecy ordains, Henri whispered. *You must tell Michael.*

I jumped, startled by his sudden presence in my mind.

"But if I tell him—" I left my sentence unfinished. Then he may have no further use for me. I bit my lip hard, willing myself to be strong.

He can't kill you yet. The Prophecy says the Key must be in the hands of the Bearer. Your mission is not yet finished. You must go with him to find the Key.

Yet. It was an ominous word, full of portent. Yet. I fingered the delicate markings on my neck. How odd, I thought, that this thing I have hated my whole life might be the only thing protecting me now.

"Do you know where it is?" I whispered to Henri, my voice trembling.

No. But Michael will know.

"How?"

He will know.

"But what do I do when we get there?"

I paused, waiting for Henri's advice, but he didn't respond. "Henri?"

He was gone.

"Great, just great," I grumbled. I turned back to the Bible and scanned the rest of the story, then the whole book. Nothing more about what happened to Cain other than that he went to some place called Nod and had a son. Like a zombie, I closed the book and slid it back into the drawer from which I'd taken it.

All of this would be so much easier to understand if I could jump on the Internet and search. Once again, I banged up against the harsh reality of my captivity.

I felt a hard lump in my throat. At times, it was so tempting to forget, just to pretend that Michael and I were on this quest together voluntarily. But it wasn't altogether true. And now, as we started to close in on the object of our search, it was even more important for me to remember that.

I need to sleep, I realized with a start. This might be my last chance. Tucking the paper with the Prophecy under my pillow, I huddled under the covers and willed myself into a dreamless rest.

~

When I woke up, Michael was sitting on the chair, staring at me.

I sat up like a shot, rubbing the sleep out of my eyes. "How did it go?"

He smiled, grimly. "I don't think we have to worry about Ana and Jimena's safety anymore. They'll face no more danger than that of your average young girl in that hellhole of a town." His face contorted with rage as he spat his next words. "It should be wiped off the face of the earth."

He could do that, I realized with a start. "Like Sodom."

He frowned. "Yes, like Sodom. But that is not my job—not right now, anyway." He made a great effort to wipe the anger from his face and nodded at the bed where I sat. "I take it nothing out of the ordinary came up while I was gone?"

I gulped.

What are you waiting for? Henri prodded.

I looked intently at Michael. "I didn't see any of the Fallen Ones, if that's what you mean." I chose my next words carefully, watching for his reaction. "But I think I may have figured out what the Key is."

He gaped at me, wide-eyed.

"How?"

"It doesn't matter how," I insisted—it seemed better, again, not to tell him about my dreams. My voice was rising, the words tumbling out of me as I rushed to share the secret I'd discovered. "Remember how the Prophecy talks about brother fighting against brother? And turning child against father? I think it's talking about Cain and Abel."

The color drained from Michael's face. "The rock."

I nodded excitedly. "I knew it! See, you knew what it was before I could even tell you." I dug the crumpled piece of notebook paper out from under my pillow where I'd tucked it away for safekeeping, and I smoothed it out on his lap, pointing to the relevant passages. "I don't understand it all—I mean, why would it be called the Key of Righteousness? And I don't understand how it is the rock's fault that Cain turned on Abel, but the rest makes sense. He killed his brother and turned his family against him. It has to be the rock."

Michael touched the paper as if he was afraid of it.

I looked up into his worried face. "You're not saying anything. Am I right?"

He pressed his lips together before nodding curtly. "You are correct."

I jumped up and did a gleeful dance. "I knew it!"

He eyed me warily. "This isn't some game of trivia you are playing, Hope. What you've discovered only increases the danger."

I stopped mid-strut, his words sending a chill through me. "I know," I whispered.

"I don't think you do. Please sit." He gestured toward the bed. I perched on the edge, watching the lines of worry that seemed to etch themselves into his skin before my very eyes. He smoothed out the Prophecy again, his fingers wandering over the words as if reading them again would somehow change their meaning.

"I've been so blind," he said, his hand coming to rest at last on the ancient words of the Prophecy. Without looking up, he resumed speaking.

"The rock has a very long lineage as a relic. It was the instrument of the first sin committed by mankind after leaving the Garden. Imagine that. Your race falls, and yet it is penitent and resists its nature for all that time, only to fall prey to the most heinous of crimes one could imagine.

"You rightly question why the Prophecy says the rock perverted Cain. It is an inanimate object, after all. And yet as he held it in his hand, it seemed to Cain as if it throbbed with life, as if it were speaking to him, goading him into taking what was his: the rightful place of honor that his brother, Abel, had so thoughtlessly stolen from him. And when he held it later, dripping and glistening with the life force of his brother, it almost seemed to mock him for his weakness. The rock was the instrument of his temptation, and thus it earned its status as a perversion."

"You talk about it as if you were there."

"I saw it all," he said, sorrow tingeing his voice.

I imagined him watching from afar, unable or perhaps too proud to intervene when mankind, which he had defended so mightily, proved unworthy of his faith.

He lifted his head and smiled sadly. "Just as money could be the root of all evil, this rock compelled your race down the path of its own destruction. It broke open the dam that had been so precariously built to save you from yourselves. After Cain struck down Abel, there was no hope of turning back."

I squirmed where I sat, suddenly aware of how weak he must think mankind. How disappointing we must be to him. To God.

He shrugged, as if reading my thoughts, and continued.

"The angels who resented God's creation of humanity seized upon this sin. Proof, they cried, that mankind is soiled and rotten to its very core. Proof that the cause of mankind is hopeless. Wishful thinking. The right thing to do, they declared, the righteous thing, was to wipe out man's existence on Earth before he sullied anything more in God's creation."

He paused, his eyes far away, his fingers twitching over the scroll as he remembered the ancient argument.

"But you fought for us," I whispered, the realization dawning on me suddenly.

His eyes snapped back into focus as he looked me full in the face, a look of amusement dancing across his gray visage.

"So quick with your intuition these days, aren't you? Yes, I defended you. My band held off those who would have exterminated you all, and I led Cain away to safety, where he lived out his life as an exile.

"So why is it called the Key of Righteousness?" he pondered almost to himself. "I have never heard of it referred to in that way—if I had, I would have immediately recognized it in the verses." He busied himself with refolding the paper. "I suppose it is because the self-righteous angels, consumed with jealousy, seized upon it as their proof, their justification, for that which they wished to do."

He rose slowly to his feet, his movements those of an ancient and weary soldier rather than of the young man he appeared to be. He turned to the window. "What Cain did split the angels into two camps, permanently. Many who had been obedient to God's will before that were appalled at the ugliness his creation had unleashed upon the world and chose to side with the ones who would exterminate mankind."

I crept up behind him and touched him lightly on the shoulder. "And they blamed you for stopping them."

He stiffened, but he did not shrug off my hand. "They blamed me, and they sealed their own fate as the Fallen."

He turned around, bringing himself within inches of my body. Every bit of me was vibrating with energy, longing to close the space between us, to be even closer to him. But I could not move, did not dare move. I looked up into his face, unable to breathe. His eyes were sad. Resigned.

"It all comes back to the war between you," I said.

"If they win their way back in, everything will change." As he said the words, his entire countenance changed, breaking the spell he seemed to have on me. His eyes glinted with steel and his back straightened; he was the warrior once again. "It won't be Armageddon. It will be much, much worse."

"What could be worse than Armageddon?" I whispered, numb with fear.

"Armageddon ends with the holy in Paradise. There will be no Paradise if the Fallen Ones have their way. We must find that Key before they do." He brushed past me, walking purposefully about the room, gathering up his things in a knapsack that I hadn't even noticed before. I let the shock of his words settle softly about me like folds of cloth, insulating me from the horrible reality of the danger we faced.

Don't just stand there. Ask him where it is, Henri urged, frustrated.

"What happened to it? The Key?" I breathed, trying to stay calm as I watched Michael pack. "Did you take it with you when you helped Cain escape?"

He snorted, shoving something into the bag as if he would punish it. "What would I do with that? Better to have thrown it into the sea where it would never be found." He stopped his packing and looked at me curiously. "You honestly don't know where it is?"

I shook my head. "I don't. It all kind of clicked for me last night, but knowing what the Key was is as far as I got."

Michael mumbled something under his breath and resumed shoving things into the pack with a vengeance.

"What did you say?"

"Nothing," he muttered between clenched teeth. "But to answer your question, the rock in question was seized upon by some misguided humans who wanted to preserve it. Because of my association with the incident, I have had the misfortune of having it linked to me on occasion."

"I don't understand."

His jaw tightened in frustration, and he threw his pack down onto the rumpled bed. "I expected you to be able to keep up, what with your sudden burst of insight."

I felt my face redden. "I'm sorry, but I don't think that was called for. I'm just trying to understand."

He blew out a long breath, raking his hand through his hair.

"They started treating it as a relic. Humans. They put it in shrines, toted it out for blessings and miracles and the like. Most of the time it was locked up in crypts inside churches that were dedicated to me: the defender and savior of mankind," he added bitterly.

"Then you must know where it is!"

Michael threw his arms down in frustration and looked at me. "How convenient that would be," he said, sarcasm dripping from his words. "But no, I have not been blessed with such knowledge. I haven't seen it in centuries." He walked off toward the tiny bathroom.

Panic started building inside of me; whether it was from his sudden change of mood or the feeling that we were lost once again, I wasn't sure. I trailed after him, trying to reason with him.

"When did you last see it? Maybe we can start from there."

He turned in the hallway and loomed before me. Once again, I was reminded of how small I was.

"Why must you torture me so?" The vein in his forehead was throbbing again, and I couldn't help noticing that he was gripping his hands into fists, restless, I supposed, to fight.

I took a deep breath and willed myself not to shrink back from his anger. "I'm not trying to torture you. I'm trying to help you find the Key. That's what you want, isn't it?"

He stared morosely at me before, with an effort, he relaxed and moved away from me. "It was in Turkey. Before the Crusades."

I didn't speak, but I urged him on with my eyes.

"There was a shrine there dedicated to me, built around a spring. It has been destroyed for a long time. There is nothing to see there now."

I let out the breath I hadn't known I was holding. "That's something to go on. Before the Crusades, you say?"

He nodded tersely, his body still filling up the tiny hallway. An idea popped into my head.

"Maybe it's on one of the pilgrimage routes. Maybe someone spirited it away to keep it safe, and it is in one of your churches along the way. Surely there are other churches in Turkey, where it could be hidden?"

Michael rolled the idea around in his brain, nodding slowly. "It could be. People had certainly gone to great lengths to preserve it before." He eyed me suspiciously. "This idea—it just came to you? Just like that, out of thin air?"

Henri snorted. *He doesn't like having the tables turned.*

Confused, I ignored Henri's comment. "Yes, it just seemed to make sense. Anyway, it's the only idea I have. Do you have anything better to go on?"

Michael rolled his eyes. "No. No, I do not."

He turned away and walked out into the hallway, not stopping as he stated, "Get yourself ready. We're going to Turkey."

The door slammed behind him, leaving me to wonder what I had done wrong this time.

I jumped when Henri, unbidden, answered my question. *He's afraid he has lost his gift of intuition.*

"His what?" I asked.

Michael always operates on hunches, remember? That feeling he has that guides him to be in the right place at the right time.

"Yes," I said, not understanding. "Why is he afraid he has lost it?"

God's little joke, Henri chuckled. *On the off chance someone actually survives an—ahem—inappropriate liaison with an angel, God has arranged it so that the lucky human gets a bonus prize. They drain a little bit of that angelic energy out of their lover, gaining angelic qualities at the very time they strip away what made the other special.*

"You mean—" I let my voice drift off as Henri's words sunk in.

Your miraculous healing, your sudden realization of what the Key is—those weren't accidents, Hope. You were only able to do those things because you've taken away some of Michael's powers. The very powers he relies upon to fulfill his role as Archangel.

"That's why he couldn't find us the other night," I whispered, horrified.

And that's why he has no clue where to look for the Key, Henri added. He laughed, full of spite. *Such a comeuppance for him, don't you think?*

"He must hate me," I said. I stared at the closed door, suddenly understanding the sarcasm and resentment that had driven him to stalk off. "Surely he knew this would happen before now?"

Apparently not, Henri responded. *That's what makes this so delicious. I'm actually surprised he managed to figure it out at all, but I guess he'd have to be in complete denial to miss the signs.*

"Oh, Michael," I whispered, raising my hand as if I could reach him. "I'm so sorry."

Don't be sorry. Now that he knows he cannot search for the Key without you, he has to keep you alive—at least for now. But stay on your toes. He undoubtedly will resent you. If you anger him, there is no telling what he might do.

"But, Henri, what do *I* do?" I pleaded with my Guardian, thankful that there was someone I could trust watching my back.

Stay one step ahead of him, Henri whispered. *Find the Key. And don't let him know that you know.*

twenty-one

"Mrs. Carmichael, you'd better sit down."

A surge of impatience went through Mona as she heard Agent Hale's voice. A neat stack of used paper cups sat in front of her on the table, marking the hours she had spent idling at the FBI's offices the day after Don had mysteriously arrived at her garage. She had been waiting for any news. She wasn't used to having to wait. She wasn't used to being told what to do, and it rankled her to feel so useless.

"I'm already sitting," she said drily, looking up at him where he stood in the doorway.

"Ah, yes," Hale said, shuffling through a stack of papers before turning his attention to her. "On second thought, why don't you come out here? It's probably going to be easier to show you than to try and explain it."

For a second, Mona thought her heart had stopped beating. She looked up at him, waiting for him to share whatever news he had, but instead he simply gestured toward the sea of computers that filled the large, open room. She stood up, her bones aching, and followed him out. They wound through the desks in silence.

They stopped at a large station where several agents were huddling. Giant television screens and maps filled the space around the bank of computers. Clayton was standing in the small crowd. He gave her a tiny half-smile, reaching his hand out toward her.

She sucked in her breath and looked at his hand, wondering how bad the news would be. Slowly, she placed her hand in his and he gave it a little squeeze.

"You'll want to come closer," he said quietly, pulling her in.

Mona took a deep breath and squared her shoulders. "Tell me."

Hale cleared his throat. "We aren't sure what to make of it, ma'am. But here is what we have. Your husband's phone signal establishes his location at the time of your conversation as Alabama, *here*," he said, pointing to the map, "just as he led you to believe. But the last signal we have for your daughter's phone places her *here*." His hand swung a big arc across the map, landing on the western half of the United States. "In Las Vegas."

Mona's mind came into sharp focus. "When was the signal?"

"A few days ago, presumably at the time you called. Shortly after that, the signal went dead. The phone must have been destroyed."

"So he did take her," she whispered, hardly believing it. "But not until after I talked with him."

"We thought so, too," Hale interrupted. "But it gets more complicated. When we went through security tape from the airport, we found confirmation of their departure to Las Vegas."

He picked up a remote control and pressed a few buttons. The television above her head sprang to life and a fuzzy picture started up. The shots were cut together, erratically jumping from scene to scene, but they were clear enough for her to see her daughter, filthy and disheveled, being escorted through various points—the ticket counter, security line, and gate—her husband, Don, at her side. The footage ended with them in the boarding process.

"I don't understand," Mona said sharply. "That is him, clear as day. This proves he did it."

"Look at the date and time stamp in the corner, Mona," Clayton said gently.

She looked at the digital numbers flashing in the corner, not comprehending until Clayton broke the silence once more.

"This footage is from almost a week ago. Well before you spoke with Don."

Her mind lashed out, refusing to accept what the flashing numbers were telling her. "But that doesn't mean anything. He took her there and he came back," she asserted, refusing to believe what she was hearing.

"They checked that, Mona. While they can find the credit card charges for the trip out, there are no records of him coming back from Las Vegas, not on any flight." Clayton pressed her hand, hard, as he spoke, as if willing her to think harder. She looked up at him.

"But—" her voice trailed off. "Maybe he went under a pseudonym?"

Hale shook his head. "We ran every manifest through the computer. Nothing checked out."

She didn't know what to think.

"Show her the rest," Clayton commanded. Hale nodded once, and the agent sitting at the computer began to type furiously. A second television screen sprang to life with another fuzzy image. She watched frame after frame of her husband, standing behind the counter at the Taco Bell, working the drive-thru window, talking to guests.

With a sinking feeling, she looked at the time stamp of the film and compared it to the one that was frozen in place on the airport footage. They were the same.

"That's not possible," she whispered.

They all watched as the restaurant security tapes jumped ahead one more day, then another, then another, accounting for her husband's presence for every day that Hope had been missing—except, of course, for yesterday morning, when he'd shown up at her house, and today.

Hale pointed his remote control at the television bank and the screens went black. "The time-clock data from the restaurant confirms what we see in the security tapes. He punched in and out every day. Your husband never left Alabama. Not even to come up to Atlanta."

She felt like she was floating above the scene now, not a part of it but far away, taking it all in so she could process it later when she was at a safe distance. Clayton's insistent voice pulled her back in.

"Mona, are you listening?"

"I'm sorry," she said, blinking back the tears that were threatening to come. "I was just thinking about what this all meant. You were saying?"

"There's one more video. Are you up for watching it?"

Fear gnawed at her stomach. What more could there be that they hadn't yet told her?

Ignoring the pit in her middle, she nodded. Clayton squeezed her hand again. She looked at him gratefully.

"This last one we're streaming in from our offices in Las Vegas," explained Hale. "You'll have to bear with us." The agent at the computer again typed furiously, bringing the video feed to the screen.

"This shows someone who looks like Hope walking through one of the casinos," Hale narrated. She squinted hard. It was Hope, but her daughter was dressed in clothes Mona had never seen before, and she looked way too grown up. She seemed uncomfortable, tugging at her skirt and wobbling on the high sandals she was wearing. Mona squinted again.

"Her neck. She isn't covering her Mark," she mumbled in shock, pointing at the screen. The poor resolution made it hard to see the markings themselves, but Hope's neck was clearly uncovered, her hair upswept, and she didn't seem to be attempting to shield the strange tattoo-like pattern from any stranger's gaze.

Mona leaned in closer to the monitor. At Hope's side was a man who looked like Don, but who was dressed to the nines and acting way too familiar with the environment, striding confidently between the tables. He didn't have the humble shuffle that had somehow overtaken Don's walk over the years. She watched the footage of them winding around the casino floor as Hale narrated what the FBI had learned.

"The Gaming Board has been very cooperative; they want to keep things clean now that they've gotten organized crime out of Vegas. Seems your daughter and her companion weren't staying at this hotel—they were holed up at a much quieter location off the Strip—but they did spend quite a bit of time here gambling. And not just chump change. Our suspect was a real whale."

He noticed her look of puzzlement and stopped to explain. "That's industry speak for a big-time gambler. Our guy only went to the high-limit salons and dropped quite a bit of money. You say your husband has no real resources of his own, right?"

She nodded once, never taking her eyes off the ghostly image of her daughter floating on the screen.

"Well, your husband—or whoever this is—seems to have come into some money, then. Casino management tallied his losses for us."

He handed a slip of paper to Mona. Her jaw dropped.

"There was even more at the place they were staying," Hale said. "I take it you haven't had any unusual charges to your credit cards or bank accounts?"

She shook her head mutely, unable to make sense of any of it.

Hale sighed, as if he had been holding out secret hope that Mona's finances had been wiped out, providing them with at least one clue that might link her husband to the abduction. "I didn't think you had."

He nodded to the agent who shut down the computer.

Mona stared at the place on the screen where her daughter's face had been.

"Ma'am," Hale pressed her, "is there any chance your husband has a twin? Or a brother who looks a lot like him, who might have cooperated with your husband to take Hope?"

She felt a little bile sneaking up her throat at the thought and swallowed hard to keep it down. "No. He has no siblings. At least that I know of."

"Is there any chance Hope would have gone willingly with someone?"

"No." Mona bit off her response with cold fury. Ignoring the faint humming that had taken up residence in her brain, she swung her eyes from the screen to skewer the agent. "You're wasting my time with your far-fetched scenarios. What are we waiting for? Let's go get them."

A quick look passed between Clayton and Hale. Clayton nodded.

Hale arched one eyebrow in response. "Are you sure?" he asked Clayton.

"Yes, I think it best to tell her everything," Clayton answered.

"What?" Mona demanded.

Hale threw up his hands in frustration. "We can't go after them, ma'am. It seems they checked out of their hotel in a hurry yesterday morning. That is, *he* checked out. Alone. Casino management thinks something may have happened to Hope. A doctor was called to their suite a couple of nights ago, but he won't talk. We're going to have to bring him in for questioning. But the maids found a bunch of bandages and a used IV drip in their rooms while cleaning, and a snatch of videotape shows your daughter obviously trying to shield her face."

The humming in Mona's brain grew to a steady buzz. She dug her fingernails into her palms, hard, willing herself to focus.

"The hotel kept a record of their rental car, so we are trying to track it down as we speak. And we've ordered checkpoints at every route in and out of the city," Hale concluded. "But for right now, we've hit a dead end."

Mona looked at the circle of agents, wondered if they had any idea what was really going on.

"Is my husband here?" She'd been uncomfortable with the whole fact that Don had visited her, upset by the ambivalence she felt toward him more than anything else, so she hadn't mentioned their encounter yesterday to the agents or to Clayton. She asked the question now, already knowing what they would answer.

"He turned himself in to us this morning. Quite a surprise, I must say. We thought we'd lost him in Alabama. He's in the interrogation room two floors down." The men looked at her expectantly.

"Take me to him. Now."

They rode the elevator in silence. Mona stared at the little digital readout, watching for the instant the floors changed, her mind working furiously to find the logical answer. There had to be one. There just had to be.

She was first out when the doors slid open, surging ahead of Clayton and the agents with the instincts of a homing pigeon. She came to a stop in front of a windowless room. Not waiting for permission, she reached out for the doorknob.

"Mona," Clayton said, placing a cautionary hand on her elbow. "He's pretty distraught."

"What did you expect?" she asked, her voice dripping with disdain as she shrugged off his hand. "Let me go."

She pushed her way through the door. Don sat behind a table, his head dropped over folded hands. Just the sight of him made her adrenaline surge.

"Give it up, Don," she spat, crossing the room to lean over the table. "Spare me your pious act. What have you done with our daughter?"

Don lifted his head slowly and opened his eyes. His face was dark with stubble, his face deeply etched with worry. The shadows under his eyes were almost black. She gasped.

"Good Lord, what have they done to you?"

All the fight drained out of her. He smiled weakly and reached a hand out to her. She clutched at it and settled down heavily into the chair opposite him.

"It's okay, Mona. They didn't do anything; it's just been a long day. I told them everything I know," he said, his voice wavering. "How I knew that something would happen to her in Atlanta, but that it was her time. I couldn't stop it. I only hope I prepared her for it."

A lone tear slid down Mona's cheek.

"Don, please—if you've done something with her, if you know where she is, you need to tell us now."

He shook his head, his eyes never leaving hers. "I didn't do anything, Mona. I swear to you, I didn't do anything. And I don't know where she is. I wish I did. Please believe me."

She stared at him. His eyes were troubled, full of the same concern she felt for her daughter. She thought about everything he had told her just this morning. She thought about how Don had known about the FBI agent. She sifted through the bits of evidence the agents had shared with her, how none of it added up, and she sighed.

She'd always prided herself on her analytical mind. One of the sharpest in the business, she'd been told, time and time again. Ruthless with the facts, demanding others keep up with her cold, unrelenting logic.

But today, logic told her nothing, and her heart was demanding its due.

"I believe you," she said, the words rushing out of her as if she was still afraid to say them. "Maybe I should have believed you a long time ago."

He brought his other hand around hers and squeezed tightly.

"Thank you."

Agent Hale cleared his throat behind her. "You should know that you are both considered persons of interest at this point. You'll remain so until birth records rule out Mr. Carmichael having a twin, on the one hand, and until we can explain how a notarized release with your signature, Mrs. Carmichael, came to be in the possession of our kidnapper."

Mona sucked in her breath and wheeled in her seat. "What did you say?"

Hale pressed his lips into a hard line. "The ticket agent in Atlanta confirmed Hope had your permission to travel with her father." He reached into his suit and pulled out a narrow envelope. Passing it to her, he continued. "Our handwriting experts have matched this signature to one of yours Clayton provided to us. There could be any number of explanations, but until we have a good one, you'll be a suspect."

Mona drew the paper from the envelope with shaking hands.

There, plain as day, was her signature, witnessed by a notary. She looked up, confused.

"But I—" She gulped, swinging to confront Clayton. "Clayton, you don't think—?"

He shrugged apologetically, his face a cipher, and she noticed the cold distance that had crept in between them. "Of course I don't, Mona. But it is better for us all to cooperate now. The more we cooperate, the faster we'll have Hope back."

"Of course," Mona murmured, carefully folding the letter back into the envelope and passing it back to Agent Hale.

She turned back to Don and smiled a goofy, lopsided grin, trying to make light of the situation. "Looks like we're both in the hot seat, then."

Clayton continued. "As much as I hate to say it, I think you need to go public, Mona. We don't know what we're dealing with, and it seems our perp is on the move. Your best bet of tracking him down is to get the press to pick up the story."

She nodded her assent. "I'm sorry, Clayton. I know this will be hard for the firm."

Clayton looked indignant. "Don't think twice about that, Mona. Our media relations team is already on standby. They'll try to keep the backstory out of this and keep the press focused on Hope's present-day abduction and possible injury. My concern is for her safety, and for yours." He glared pointedly at Don.

There was a meaningful pause before Clayton continued. "You should be prepared, though, for everything to come out. All it takes is one enterprising young reporter."

Hale jumped in. "We'll have to find a way to keep you safe, Mr. Carmichael. Once this is on the news, it won't matter that you have an alibi. You'll have a target painted on you. If you agree, we'll keep you in protective custody and out of the public eye."

Mona turned to Don. "Will you ever forgive me, Don? For thinking it was you?"

He smiled at her and squeezed her hands once again. "There's nothing to forgive, Mona. I just hope you can forgive me. I knew it was coming, but I still couldn't stop it."

"That's it, then," Clayton interrupted. "Mona, why don't you go home and freshen up? I'll call you when it's time."

She nodded again, unable to speak, stunned to find herself here holding Don's hands almost as much as she was by the storm they were about to unleash.

Clayton cleared his throat. "I'd be happy to see you out, Mona."

She looked apologetically at Don and gave his hand a little squeeze. "I'll see you—well, I don't know when I'll see you."

She turned in her seat and looked at the agents bunched up behind her. "Will he be at the press conference?"

Clayton didn't allow them to answer her question. "It will be better for you to appear alone. Come on, now. You need to freshen up and get yourself ready."

"I'll see you when I see you, then," she said to Don as she stood up. As she did, her back protested the uncomfortable chair and the days on edge. She rubbed the hollow of her back, realizing with a flutter of recognition that it was exactly the habit she had fallen into when she'd carried Hope. The only difference was that then, she'd rested a hand contentedly on her expanding belly.

A rush of emotions came over her, too fast for her to shove them down.

"You've had enough," Clayton said as he saw her falter, taking her by the elbow as he took control of the situation. "It's time to go."

He hustled her out the door, pushing past the nameless, faceless men in suits and toward the elevator. She looked over her shoulder at Don, wondering what they planned to do with him.

Clayton stabbed at the elevator call button. When it didn't light up, he punched at it, again and again.

"Clayton, it's here," she said softly as the doors silently slid open. She looked down to where he still clutched her arm and raised a questioning eyebrow.

He dropped her arm as if it were on fire. She began walking toward the open doors.

"Mona," he burst out, stopping her. She turned to him to find him staring at the carpet, freed hand shoved into his pocket.

"Yes, Clayton?"

He stood there, silent. She wondered in the back of her mind if the elevator was going to leave without her.

"Please don't."

She stared at him, bewildered. He lifted his eyes to meet her stare, and the pain in them made her take a step back.

"Don't let him hurt you."

She raised her fingers to her mouth, only now realizing how Clayton must have felt watching her exchange with Don.

"Oh, Clay. I'm so sorry," she said as she backed her way toward the elevator.

She heard the doors make a soft whoosh as they closed once again, cutting off her escape. Clayton. If it hadn't been for him all those years ago, she would have never made it through the labyrinth of legal issues she'd dealt with and kept her job. He'd been the one to find her the best family law counsel in the city when she didn't even know where to begin. The one who'd kept the firm's partner election committee with its demands for more, more, more at bay when she was running on empty. He'd managed to stretch the window for her election out long enough for her to get back on her feet after she'd lost Hope to Don; he'd forced some other partners to throw her a bone when she'd let her pipeline of clients run dry in the intensity of the custody battle. In some respects, she'd owed her career and her sanity to Clayton.

He had never asked for anything in return, and she'd never promised him anything. But as she looked at him now, she felt a stab of guilt. She'd never promised him anything, it was true, but she had also never told him no.

In fact, by her actions, she'd implied there was a future for them together. She'd always leaned on him. Always confided in him. She'd been ready with her excuses about why *now* was never the right time for them to embark on a more intimate relationship. First it was the tenuousness of her grip on her daily life as she adjusted to life without Hope. Then it was the awkwardness—and ickiness—of the power disparity between a junior and senior partner and what it might imply about their relationship.

Still, he'd waited, making his intentions plain to her. The years had gone by, and with them her excuses. Now, she realized, she had none left. She'd become a full senior partner, on equal footing with him; she'd been one for some time now. Until the events of the last few days, her situation with Hope and Don had settled into something that was probably as normal as it would ever get, a manageable routine with no surprises. If what had happened back in the interrogation room had finally forced her to realize that her stalling would never end, it surely must have made it plain to Clayton. If she had any doubt, all she had to do was look at the anguish on his face to know that he, too, finally saw the truth.

Her mouth seemed unnaturally dry as she struggled to find the words she needed to say. A commotion down the hall, back in the direction from which they'd just come, mercifully distracted him long enough for her to regain her composure.

"Let's go see what's going on," she said quietly, avoiding Clayton's eyes as she brushed past him.

They walked swiftly, not speaking to one another.

As they approached the investigation team's hub, Mona noticed that the typically frenetic activity level was even higher than normal. Something had happened.

"What's going on?" she asked to no one in particular, afraid of what she might hear.

"This," someone she didn't recognize answered, shoving an old-fashioned printout at her. She peered down, squinting to see the print of what she recognized as an AP newswire story.

"Triad?" she asked as she scanned the article, puzzled. She passed it to Clayton, who was hovering nearby, so he could read it, too. "What does that mean?"

It took a moment for anyone to even bother to answer her—they were too busy scurrying off to talk on their phones and peeling off into other offices. Finally one of the younger staff members—so young looking he could have been an intern—paused to explain what was happening.

"It means our girl Hope may have stumbled into an organized crime ring. Triad is nasty stuff, straight out of Asia. Gambling, extortion, prostitution—you name it; these dudes are bad. We don't know if there is a connection yet, but since she made pals with some high roller like she did, we could be on to something." He clucked his tongue like an old, gossipy woman. "Naughty, naughty."

Before Mona even realized what was happening, Clayton drew himself up to his full height, pushing his face into the young man's and shoving him in the shoulder. The flimsy wall of the cubicle shook as the startled man fell against it. Clayton grabbed him by the collar and shook him as he shouted.

"She wasn't *pals* with this fellow. She's the victim here. And she's not *your* girl, not some random runaway picked up off the street.

She's Ms. Carmichael's daughter. Remember that. Show some respect."

The young man shrank back against the wall, startled, raising his hands in the universal sign of no harm meant. "Of course, sir. We're just excited." He looked down at Clayton's hand, still twisted in his shirt collar. His face turned beet red as he realized what Clayton meant for him to do.

"I'm sorry, Ms. Carmichael. I apologize."

"Apology accepted," she said softly, her eyes locked on Clayton. When he didn't let go, she walked over and placed a hand gently on his arm. She could feel the tension in his muscles, the unspent rage.

"Clay. It's okay. You need to let him go."

Clayton shook his head as if he were waking from a dream. He abruptly let go of the young man. His face was flushed; whether it was from the exertion or from embarrassment, Mona couldn't tell. "Fine," Clayton said curtly, stepping away.

"Please, tell us what you know," Mona asked the agent before anything more could happen.

The young man smoothed out his collar and rolled his neck as if testing to see if there was any more damage beyond the damage done to his ego. Finding none, he continued.

"It seems your daughter went missing again right after some big action in Vegas—a really nasty car chase and a huge fire that swept through a whole apartment complex. The investigators on the scene found a bunch of trafficked girls at the scene of the fire. The complex is owned by these nasties." He pulled at the papers that Clayton was still clutching in his hand. "These guys are in custody because the buildings were being used for illegal sex trade activity, and local police think the cause of the fire was arson. It could be a coincidence, but then again, it might not be. We could have just had a big break."

He was trying to be respectful, mindful of Clayton's warning, but he couldn't keep the note of excitement out of his voice. "This could be huge."

"Good," Clayton finally said, taking his turn to try to smooth things over. "What else is going on?"

The man shrugged. "Ma'am," he said, looking politely at Mona, "you left your cell phone in the interrogation room. Looks like there are some messages on it."

He pointed over toward an empty cubicle.

"We thought you'd already left, so we put it over there."

"Good," Clayton repeated, still feeling awkward about his behavior. "We'll go look at that before I head over to prep my PR team—and before Mona heads home."

"Fine, I mean, that would be great, sir." The agent made his escape as quickly as he could, leaving Mona and Clayton to make their way to the cubicle.

Clayton stood over the desk inside it, staring at the standard-issue BlackBerry Mona had left behind. He picked it up and turned it over. A quiet smile crept across his face.

"You muted the ringer again," he said, flicking the button before handing her the phone.

She always did that. She'd turn it off to give something her full attention and forget she'd even done it, and then curse a blue streak when she realized she'd missed a day's worth of important calls. Today, of all days, you'd think she would have remembered to turn it back on.

Quickly, Mona scrolled through the missed calls. They were all from the same number, one she did not recognize, but that had an Atlanta area code. She hit the button to play the messages and lifted the phone to her ear to listen. After a few moments, her eyes widened.

"What is it?" Clayton said, moving even closer to her side.

"You'd better go get that agent," Mona said. "I think we have contact from Hope. She called her friend here in Atlanta."

twenty-two

"Hope, come on."

I'd been surreptitiously watching the news in the lobby of the private jet hangar. I tried not to look too interested in the story about the abducted girl, but it was hard to drag my eyes away.

My mother was standing behind a podium, flanked by one of her cronies from work and a bunch of people I didn't recognize—probably lawyers. Flashes were popping as she took questions from the eager press. Pictures of my dad and me occasionally filled the screen, while a young reporter working very hard to appear serious and earnest kept repeating that though the perpetrator bore a striking resemblance to my dad, my dad was not considered the primary suspect at this point.

"Hope." Michael's voice had an edge to it as he reminded me it was time to go.

"It's started," I said, reluctantly dragging my eyes from the screen to turn to him. He had returned to his own guise, but with a five o'clock shadow and fuller frame he looked slightly older so that he would not raise any suspicions as he rented the Citation jet and filed his flight plan to Turkey. I know he was relieved not to have to appear as my father any longer, and I drank in the sight of his lean body in the tight, faded jeans and open-collared shirt he'd carelessly thrown on, hating myself every minute I did it.

"I know," he said, holding out my backpack, seeming ignorant or indifferent to how the sight of him affected me. "It looks like we laid enough tracks to confuse them for a while."

"And to keep my dad safe," I added with an awkward smile. "Thank you."

He looked at me, apparently surprised that I would thank him. "You're welcome. Let's go."

I took the bag and hurried after him, ignoring the uncomfortable tug of my scarred skin as I moved. The healing process had begun to slow. While I was no longer in much pain, I was all but unrecognizable, my face still dotted with angry, yellow blisters, my hands and arms still wrapped in bandages. Out of the corner of my eye I saw people look away, uncomfortable and embarrassed by their own curiosity.

I pulled the hood of my sweatshirt closer to cover my face. Let them look away. It was just as well. I needed to be invisible to get where we needed to go.

Michael pushed through the doorway to the outside, where the plane stood waiting, not pausing for me to catch up. He seemed to want to put as much distance between him and me as possible. I looked back one more time at the television. The cameras had zoomed in for a close-up of my mother's face. As it moved closer, the camera caught the glint of tears welling in her eyes.

My own vision went blurry.

Hurry, Henri whispered. *You don't have much time.*

"I know," I said out loud.

I blinked my tears away. Then I turned my back on my mother's image still looming on the screen.

I wound my way through the chairs that were clustered here and there in the lounge. As I did, the low murmur from the other televisions followed me, and I began to notice the stories I'd been ignoring.

Rioters overwhelming yet another embassy. Settlers on the West Bank under attack again. Saber-rattling dictators indulging themselves while hundreds of thousands of their so-called people were shoved into camps and shantytowns, praying for something to eat and some way out of the hellhole in which they found themselves. Pilgrimage crowds, excited by who knows what, trampling over the weak—old and young alike—as they charged forward in one unstoppable wave.

The staccato beat of the reporters' bland, cookie-cutter voices followed me, accusing me with each step.

People needed Michael. But because of me, he was letting all those people suffer and die. How much longer could he stay away, when it seemed like the whole world was falling apart?

How much longer could he stand the pain?

He'd already disappeared inside the jet. I hurried after him, slipping through the door into the hot desert wind and then climbing the short stairway into the plane.

Inside, I stopped short. There were two people huddled together and talking halfway up the aisle. Neither one of them was Michael. They leaned forward, hunkered down for what appeared to be an intense conversation, their backs turned to me.

I wasn't sure—I could have been imagining it—but just beneath the surface, I thought I smelled the faintest hint of sulfur.

I hesitated, not sure what to do. But I didn't have a chance to do anything before they noticed me.

"Hope?" a familiar voice called out.

One of the two unfamiliar men wore the stylish cut of his crisp linen clothes to perfection. His bearing was erect and proud, almost haughty. The man approaching me, however—the man who'd spoken—looked like a reject from a yacht club. His wide frame was wrapped in a goofy navy blazer with straining bronze buttons, and a jaunty captain's hat was perched atop his head. His long gray hair was captured in a messy ponytail, his chin capped by a snowy white Vandyke beard.

In the end, it was the sunglasses and the cane that gave him away.

"Enoch!" I said, overjoyed to see a familiar face. "Or, I mean—Librarian!" I practically threw myself into his arms as he held them wide open for me, and then I nearly choked on the heavy dose of cologne in which he'd doused himself.

"Just Enoch, now," he said gently. Something about it seemed sad, so I decided not to pry. I was too grateful to see him to want to think about anything sad right now.

"I didn't recognize you at first," I said. "You look like you escaped from Gilligan's Island."

"My goodness, you'll about knock this old man over," he said, tossing his cane aside and wrapping his arms around me. "I thought I'd try out my copilot look for the journey. Try to look nice for the ladies. Lucky for you, I clean up well."

As he held me tight, I felt the growing knot of worry, guilt, and fear that had taken up permanent residence in my throat grow even bigger. I squeezed him tighter, hardly believing he was really there. In the short time we'd had together, Enoch had understood me. He'd taken the time to explain things to me, and that had made all the difference. So I probably shouldn't have been surprised when, as he started patting my head, I burst into tears.

"There, there," he said, making vague, comforting noises while he waited for the storm to pass. He didn't try to stop me, and I didn't try to stop. I just let all the tension of the last few days drain out of me as he held my tired body up.

When my torrent of tears slowed to a few sniffles, he pushed me away to inspect me. Carefully, he pulled the hood away from my face. I blushed. There was no way to disguise the ugly blisters that still covered my face and neck or the shiny tissue that was covering my hands. They were telltale signs of burns, and with his knowledge of angel lore, Enoch probably knew how I got them.

"I ruined your blazer," I mumbled, eyeing the sodden mess I'd left on his shoulder.

"Never mind that. I can see now I was right to come. You look like you could use a friend."

"I'm so glad you did," I said, smiling even though my voice wavered. "But why did you? Are you coming with us?" I asked.

"Michael asked me to help protect you," he said solemnly, taking my shoulders in his hands. He was peering at me through the dark lenses of his sunglasses, seeming to gauge my reaction. "What you are doing has only gotten more dangerous, now that you know what you are looking for."

"The rock," I breathed, almost afraid to say it aloud.

"Yes," he nodded. "The rock. Michael wants to be sure to keep you safe while you search for it, and I think in present circumstances he thought more help would be advisable."

Had Michael told Enoch about his own loss of powers? Could Enoch tell? I longed to pepper him with questions, but didn't dare, especially in front of the stranger.

"Besides," Enoch continued, dropping his hands from me and retrieving his cane, "things were getting a little dull in the desert. I thought it was about time I broke out of prison and showed those uppity bureaucrats a thing or two."

I giggled, imagining the courts in Heaven all abuzz now that Enoch had walked out on his sentence of exile.

"I will be coming with you for as long as I remain free," Enoch continued. "And so will my friend here. Raph, come and meet Hope."

The second man, Raph, uncoiled himself from where he'd been leaning against the airplane's wall and walked toward me. He was long and lean, like Michael, but while Michael shone with light, he seemed the epitome of darkness from the shiny ebony of his hair to the dark luster of his skin and to the deep black of his eyes, which seemed to glow from some unfathomable depth.

"Raphael," he said, reaching out his hand to me. "At your service."

Inside my head, I heard Henri start to growl. *Who let him in here?*

I stared at Raph's outstretched palm, wondering what exactly it was that Henri didn't like about him. I put my hand in Raph's and winced as he squeezed hard, either oblivious to my tender skin or callous about it.

"Um, are you *the* Raphael? As in one of the other Archangels?" I said, waiting for him to release my hand from his ironclad grip.

"The same," he said with a curt nod of his head. He let go of my hand. Despite myself, I snatched it away and began to rub the life back into it. Raph just smirked at me as he watched.

"Are you here to protect me, too?" I asked, unable to keep the note of frustration out of my voice. "Because I have been doing a pretty good job of that myself so far."

"Is that right?" Raph parried back, his smirk now growing to full-on mockery. "Is that how you ended up nearly burned to a crisp? And with a posse of Fallen Angels on your tail?"

Before I could answer, he'd turned and strutted down the aisle toward the cockpit, leaving me to look after him with my mouth hanging wide open.

Nothing but trouble, Henri opined.

"Seriously, Enoch. Is he here to protect me, or just to insult me?"

Enoch laughed. "Raphael has always been a testy one. Especially when it comes to Michael. And humans." He began walking down the aisle himself, leaning heavily onto his cane. "Come, sit with me."

I obediently followed, waiting as he eased himself down into a plush chair, and then taking the seat right next to him so that we were lounging together at a small table.

"This isn't like a normal plane," I said, finally taking in my surroundings. "It's pretty fancy."

"It's the fastest—and quietest—way for us to get you to Turkey. The luxury just comes along with the price tag."

"More angel financing, I suppose," I sighed.

"Indeed," Enoch said. "Now, Hope." He reached across the table and took my hand. "Tell me, truly—how are things between you and Michael?"

I blushed again. How could a blind man see right through me?

"Okay, I suppose."

"Really? To look at either one of you I would have assumed the opposite."

He'd given me the opening I needed. "I'm worried about him, Enoch. He's getting moodier and moodier. You know, he's in pain."

Enoch nodded gravely. "And most likely not sleeping. He is so intent on guarding you that he is likely to neglect the care of his human body. Tell me, do you think it is worsening, this pain?"

"I do," I said, grateful to have someone to confide in. "I think that is why he gets so angry with me sometimes. He's not doing his—you know, his angelic duty. He's with me, instead. He's disobeying God."

"The punishment for that is very grave. You have only to look at the Fallen Ones to see what comes of disobedience."

His words stopped me cold. I closed my eyes and inhaled, deeply. I was acclimating to the sterile air of the jet, but I was sure I could still smell the faintest hint of sulfur. I opened my eyes, leaning in to whisper to Enoch across the table, doing my best to not cough from his cologne.

"Enoch, could Michael fall? You know—become one of them?"

Enoch stretched out in his chair, contemplating the question. "Technically anyone could, my dear," he began. "If they distanced themselves from God enough so that reconciliation was impossible. If they were pushed to the point of madness from the pain. But I doubt very much that this would ever happen to Michael. Why do you ask?"

I looked around, afraid Raph—or even Michael himself—might overhear me. "I think the pain is driving him crazy. And I don't know for sure, but when I got on the plane behind him today—"

Enoch arched a brow. "Go on."

"I can't be sure. It was there, and then it was gone. But I thought I smelled sulfur. The same smell I noticed when I was attacked by the Fallen Ones before."

Enoch drew in his breath. "You smelled the scent of the Changing."

"What do you mean?"

"You noticed it before because the Fallen Ones nearby were changing their physical form. From human to bird, or vice versa, for example."

I nodded, urging him on.

"No matter how they shift shape, the evil ones leave telltale trails, like this scent. If Michael is getting closer to becoming one of them—"

He let the thought linger in the air.

"Enoch," I continued. "How would we know if he fell? Would he look any different?"

Enoch shook his head. "No. There would be no outward sign. But we would know."

"How? How did Michael know Lucas was Fallen? It seemed like he recognized him. But how can that be, when angels can change their shape at will?"

"Michael and Lucas are age-old enemies, Hope. They choose to reveal themselves to one another so that they can do battle honorably. It is like a challenge. Appearing in a recognizable aspect is almost like waving a red flag before a bull. In this particular situation, it was especially effective for Lucas to do so. He had the additional advantage of being a visible threat to you, something Lucas apparently surmised would be unbearable to Michael. Correctly, I might add. But if Lucas hadn't wanted to goad Michael, he could have appeared as anyone at all, and Michael would not have been the wiser, unless he was able to pick up the subtle signs, like the scent of the Changing. Just as we would not be able to detect directly if Michael fell."

It seemed awfully complicated, but nobody seemed to realize that Henri was still at my side, so the idea of an angel—Fallen or otherwise—staying anonymous and incognito rang true. No matter how realistic, though, the thought of Michael slipping, undetected, into the ranks of the Fallen made me sick to my stomach. Before I could dwell on it, Enoch dashed the idea away with an impatient wave of his cane.

"We must not let that happen. And it won't, I will be sure of it. You, in the meantime, must be careful not to anger him. Can you promise me that?"

I nodded solemnly.

"Good. Then there is the matter of your skin."

I snatched my hand away from his, flushing even deeper than I had before. "I don't want to talk about it, Enoch."

"I'm afraid you must," he sighed, pulling my hand back across the table into his firm grip. "It won't do for you to draw attention to yourself. Not where we are going. You must let Raph fix it."

"Fix it? What do you mean?"

"Raph is the Angel of Healing. He is a mighty warrior, to be sure, just like all the Archangels are, but his special gift is to heal those who are broken. It used to be one of Michael's gifts, too—in fact, the shrine where Michael last saw the rock was a place dedicated to his healing powers—but over time his role has shifted, and the miracle of healing has now fallen to Raph. I am sure this is why Michael asked him, specially, to come with us."

"So, Raph can magically make my skin better? As if I'd never been burned in the first place?"

Enoch squeezed my hand. "Of course. And no one will be the wiser."

I thought about it. The skin on my hand, which Enoch was still holding, was rough and shiny. I couldn't imagine it ever looking the way it had been before.

"No," I said simply.

"What do you mean, no?" Enoch asked, his head jerking sharply up so he could stare at me, blind-eyed, through his dark glasses.

"I don't want him to change my skin back."

"Why ever not, child? You could be vulnerable to infection if you go untreated. Not to mention the fact that you will draw attention to yourself everywhere you go."

"It's healing on its own," I said stubbornly. I wriggled my hand free from his grip and waved my fingers in front of his face. "See?"

He stomped his cane down with an insistent thud. "Nonsense. You're being ridiculous. You must let Raph heal you."

I crossed my arms and looked down at the table, unable to meet Enoch's stare.

"I won't."

I refused to look up, but could feel Enoch boring a hole into my head with his blind stare, silently demanding an explanation.

"I want him to have to see what he did to me every time he looks at me."

I let my words fall like a drop of water, sending ripples out into a lake. I was met with silence.

I waited, tracking the grain of the polished table with my eyes, counting the knots in the wood. I braced myself for Enoch's response, wondering what he must think of me. How could I, with so much at stake, cling to my pettiness? And yet I did, holding on to it like some precious jewel, as if I could hurt Michael through the sheer force of my will.

"Hope," Enoch eventually sighed. "This isn't some game you are playing, my dear. You, more than anyone, know the danger you place yourself in if you willfully torment Michael."

He paused, apparently waiting for me to respond. I stared harder at the tabletop and kept counting the whorls.

"Very well," he sighed. "I can see there is no sense talking to you about it now. Perhaps later, after you've had a chance to rest. For now, I will leave you to your thoughts."

I heard him struggle up from his chair and move down the aisle with the strange thumping walk that was the side effect of his use of the cane.

When I looked up, I was all by myself. Raph and Enoch had apparently joined Michael in the cockpit.

The door of the plane had been closed and the lights dimmed. I looked out the window and saw the tarmac rushing by. The plane was so smooth that I hadn't even noticed we were moving. I had barely felt the plane leave the bounds of the earth as it lifted its nose into the sky and drew up its wheels.

We were on our way, my band of protectors and me; on our way to find the hateful relic that could mean the destruction of the world—or my own death. Everything turned on my ability to guide us to that ancient rock, a rock that had caused so much pain and strife, its aftermath echoing through the ages.

To do it, I had little to count on. I had a scrap of paper shoved deep in my pocket, its words proclaiming the ancient Prophecy I had to fulfill. I had my new powers of intuition, inadvertently stolen from Michael. I had my determination to not fail. And I had a ragtag group of angels, assembled in haste at Michael's insistence. Whether they were my saviors or my jailers, I wasn't yet sure.

Even from where I sat, alone, in the back of the plane, I could feel their powerful presence, just as surely as I could still hear Lucas's taunts from that night at the factory hanging in the air, sowing doubt between Michael and me. The angels were all around me.

But I had never felt so alone.

ACKNOWLEDGMENTS

Many people have helped me along the way with this book. If the high-glamour, high-stakes world of Las Vegas gambling rings true at all, it is in large part to the counsel of Colin DeVaughan, a career veteran who advised me on the proper etiquette and treatment of "the whale," as well as clued me in on the rising influence and gambling culture of the Chinese in Las Vegas.

The details of Hope and Michael's hotel home off the Strip came to me while on a research trip where I was hosted by the amazing Tony Hsieh and his incredible team at Zappos. The hospitality with which they welcomed me was truly awe-inspiring; they shared their contacts and their favorite haunts with me, and as they talked about their plans for engaging and partnering with others to revitalize downtown Las Vegas, I came to love the spirit of the city and their dreams for it. I hope that I have captured just a bit of the magic they are creating there together.

Michael and Hope's trek through Snow Canyon closely mirrors the guided hikes I shared with my longtime friend, Rebecca Foster, on our "girls' trip" to Utah. I was certain the stunning and sometimes eerie landscape would be the perfect setting for some angelic encounters; the fact that Beck and I got to explore it together just made it more special. Thank you, Beck, for the support and love through career, writing, and other travails!

Arthur Greer, how many trips to and from the airport have we shared? You have been on the journey with me all along, and I hope you don't mind that I wrote you into this book, my tribute to you and our friendship.

I started out with the idea that Hope's childhood abduction would be the act of a stereotypical lone pedophile. In conducting my research, I stumbled onto the sad, everyday reality of human trafficking and domestic minor sexual trafficking in Atlanta, Las Vegas, and around the world. I am grateful to the many experts who have fact-checked and commented on this critical subplot, creating the opportunity for me to shine a light upon this modern-day slavery. I am particularly grateful to Cheryl DeLuca-Johnson of Street Grace (an actual nonprofit in Georgia!) for her counsel and gracious permission to use her organization's name. I would be remiss to not mention that with the help of Street Grace and many other fantastic organizations, Atlanta and the State of Georgia have been at the forefront in advocating for stronger victim rights and tougher sanctions for perpetrators of these crimes. While there are still many challenges, we are making progress.

To the amazing team at Greenleaf, and especially Jeanne, editor extraordinaire—thank you for guidance, for understanding my vision and, most importantly, for your intuitive grasp of Hope and the careful balance I was striving to create with her story.

I have deep gratitude for my amazing extended family and network of friends who read this book in its earlier editions (even when it meant—horrors—reading it on your cell phone screen!)

and urged me on to complete the story. Petra, Josselyn, Shami, Tara, Kathy, Michelle—thank you for all the support and advice you have given me. Special thanks go to my mother, Lorraine Houle, and my brother, Jake Houle, for their early and enthusiastic reading and editing of manuscripts.

Finally, Trey, Reagan, and John—thank you for letting Mom sneak some writing in, nights and weekends. I appreciate your forbearance. And to my husband, Tom—for your unflagging encouragement, ideas, critiques, space, and tech support—I couldn't have done it without you! I love you all.

ABOUT MONICA McGURK

Monica McGurk started out writing fan fiction based on Stephenie Meyer's Twilight series under the pen name Consultant by Day. She has been recognized for her prequels and alternate versions by her fans, winning the Twific Fandom "Undiscovered Gem" award for *Morning Star* in 2013. Since her fan fiction days, she has left the consulting firm at which she was a senior partner and remains a full-time business executive based in Atlanta. While this is her first novel of any sort, she has been published in the business press on numerous topics.

She is married and the mother of three children, for whom she creates elaborate bedtime stories that sometimes last for over a year.

She has already completed her sequel to *Dark Hope*, which she hopes to publish soon.

READERS GUIDE

DARK HOPE BY MONICA McGURK

Pretty fifteen-year-old Hope Carmichael returns to her mother's house in Atlanta for the first time since a court order gave custody to her over-protective religious father many years before. Her mother's frequent out-of-town business trips, the well-manicured home, and her first day at Dunwoody High grant Hope the wish she has had for so long: to be free and to make friends for the first time in her life. As *Dark Hope* unfolds, Hope catches the eye of handsome golden boy, Michael, whose interest in her is more than she could have ever wished for in her wildest dreams. Hope begins to let go of first-week jitters, and to wonder if at long last, she may have made a best friend. When Hope finds herself partnered with pierced and tattooed Tabitha on a school project, she can't help but stare at Tabitha's heavy eyeliner and streaked Mohawk hairdo. "Not everyone or everything is what they look like on the outside.

God knows it's true for me," comments Tabitha. But Hope's past is full of dark and frightening secrets and her future is about to become populated with equally dark mysteries. Hope—abducted and returned safely as a toddler—carries a mark that will link her to a host of individuals who are definitely not what they look like on the outside. Hope's story connects the powerful emotions and desires of a teenage girl with present-day human sex trafficking, the search for an ancient relic, and the battle of good and evil against a backdrop of immense and grave worldwide proportions.

QUESTIONS & TOPICS FOR DISCUSSION

What do we really know about the character of Hope herself? Is she easy to know or not? What are her likes and dislikes? What emotions motivate her? Does the fact that she was isolated as a child make her personality harder to understand?

What do we know about Mona? It's stated in the book that she had no family. It's suggested that she and Don have few friends. What in their personalities motivated them to do what they did with regard to Hope? What weaknesses did each of them have? What strengths?

Contrast Mona's appearance and lifestyle with those of Don. What does it reveal about the worlds they inhabit or what they consider important? What does it mean that they continued to stay married? How did you feel about the fact that Mona left Hope alone so soon after she arrived from Alabama or that she didn't know what Hope's favorite food was?

The book said that in school pictures, Hope's spirit had seemingly been snuffed out. What do you think was meant by this? Hope lived a very lonely childhood and it seems her parents lived lonely lives too. Does their isolation have a purpose in the story? What other characters in the book are also isolated?

How do you believe the Mark got on Hope's neck? Does it warn her of danger or provide her protection? Why is the Mark always referred to with a capital letter? Why do people outside Hope's family see the Mark as beautiful?

What do the throbbing vein in Michael's forehead and the feeling in Hope's Mark have in common?

What is the role of Henri in the book? How does Henri move the plot along? When the voice in your head speaks to you the next time, will you think of it as the voice of a guardian angel?

Does the idea that angels such as Michael and Ralph could walk among us change your view of people you meet or have met, or your idea of the world itself? After reading this book, do you know someone whom you think might be an angel?

Tabitha provides a great contrast to Hope. She has siblings, a very happy family life and a circle of support via her church. What significance is the fact that Tabitha has two personas—one for home and one for the outside world? What is the significance that she dresses so differently from her classmates and is also the perfect daughter to her loving parents? Why is it significant that Tabitha is the daughter of a preacher? Tabitha's bedroom and possessions are described in detail. Hope's are not—why?

The scenes involving domestic minor sex trafficking (DMST) and the men and girls involved in them were very dramatic. Did these scenes change your thinking about the trafficking of humans in the United States? Did you realize that these things are happening in ordinary American cities? Will this knowledge change any of your normal routines or habits? What do you think you can do to spread the word about human trafficking and try to bring it to an end?

Who do you think is at risk of being trafficked and sold into prostitution? Foreign children or native citizens? Young girls or young boys? At what ages? From what socioeconomic backgrounds? What risk factors increase the odds someone is victimized in this way? Why would a woman—such as the older Chinese woman at Wynne— cooperate in such a crime? Why would the victims—such as the Asian girls at Wynne—not try harder to escape? In what ways is Hope similar and different to the victims of DMST that she meets?

What is the significance of Michael saying that angels can neither create nor discover? How does his declaration of love for Hope provide a pivotal moment in the story?

Enoch is blind and in exile, yet is the source of knowledge. Is there significance in this?

When Mona pulls into the driveway with Hope for the first time, Hope thinks that the windows of her mother's house look sad. What do you think is the significance of observation?

There is a great deal of emphasis on names and naming in the book—for example, Michael listing out his various aliases when he reveals himself to Hope; Enoch pondering the importance of what we call things and noting the special significance of Hope's own names. What is the author trying to convey by emphasizing this point repeatedly?

The course of Hope's life was and is determined by Michael's presence in her life. By the end of the book, we learn that some of his power has been transferred to Hope as a result of the irresistible force that draws them together. Do you think Hope will eventually attain the level of power Michael possesses in this book? What does it mean if she does?

What is the significance of a heavenly being and a human being drawn together in such a physically powerful way as Michael and Hope were? What could it mean for the future of each of them? What does it say about cooperation between heaven and earth?

In many ways, this is a story about a girl struggling to define her own destiny—one that is not predetermined by her past or by fate. What are your feelings about predictions and fate, prophecies and destiny? Does Hope have a choice in how her life plays out, given the greater forces around her? Do you think the rock will be found?

AUTHOR Q&A

Q. Although Dark Hope is a work of fiction, you seem to understand the young protagonist's mind very well. Was there a particular teen-aged girl in your life or a specific event that inspired you to write the book?

MM: I have always been very attuned to women and girls' issues and the role of popular culture in shaping our expectations of young women. The initial impetus for this particular story was my own observation that many YA novels targeting teens depicted girls as victims needing rescuing, with significant amount of the action being motivated by a traditional love triangle. Often times in these books, the consequences of the decisions made by the heroine are whisked away to enable a "happily ever after" end-ing. I wanted to provide a counterpoint to that—a supernaturally infused, action-driven plot that showed a young girl struggling to define her own destiny against the backdrop of something much bigger, facing real consequences for the choices she actually makes. I wanted it to be something I would be proud to have my own daughter, who is now twelve, read; something that would send her the right message about the role she has to play in shaping her own life path.

Q. Your knowledge of the Bible seems significant. Did that knowledge lead you to the story or did the story in your head lead you to the Bible?

MM: I approach my writing like putting together a puzzle. I generally know how I am going to start and how the story is going to end and the real problem solving is to find a way to get the characters from point A to point B in a way that is consistent with their personalities as well as my message. While from my own upbringing I was familiar with many parts of the Bible, I tried to approach the story with fresh eyes, researching not just the Biblical stories but also angelic folklore from many religious traditions, including Islam and Judaism. So, I didn't start with the religious references, but they became an integral aspect of pushing the plot forward.

Q. Enoch mentions names and that the names of things and people are important. Did you pick the names of characters and places in the book for a specific reason?

MM: As far as locations go, I started in Atlanta because it is my current home and I thought it would be fun to write about it. Other locations—Las Vegas in this book, and Istanbul, Skellig Michael in Ireland, and Puy-en-Velay in France in the next book—I chose because they were places I wanted to visit, places I had been intrigued by, or places which offered something interesting in terms of a connection to the plot.

Character names were a bit different. Some were random. Some were named after people in my life—for example, Mrs. Bibeau, who bears a surname that comes from my own maternal family line. Hope's name was chosen specifically for its meaning. Choosing her name was one of the first decisions that I made as I began to write.

Q. What does the title Dark Hope *have to do with the plot of the book? Why did you choose* Dark Hope *and not just Hope?*

MM: It is called *Dark Hope* as a reference to the term "dark horse"—in other words, a little known or inconsequential person or thing that emerges to prominence and achieves unexpected success against great odds. That is what we are talking about as Hope (with Michael's help) tries to define her own fate, beat the Fallen, and save the world.

Q. How did you become interested in the trafficking of young girls in the United States?

MM: I stumbled across the facts about the modern-day slave trade and the domestic sexual trafficking of minors, in particular, as I began to research Hope's abduction story. I had originally envisioned her abduction as a random act by the proverbial disturbed pedophile. I was shocked when I learned that there is a whole modern industry of slavery and that it was going on right here, in Atlanta, where I have lived since 1998.

Q. Did your research for the book have any other impact on you?

MM: For me and for many people, I think, once you learn about the scale of the problem, you cannot look away. You feel the need to act. So I decided to learn more about the problem and to weave it into my plot. I also decided to get more directly involved—I have joined the advisory board of Street Grace; I am part of their speakers' bureau, working to educate PTAs, business leaders, church congregations, and other community leaders about the issue; and I have pledged a portion of profits from the sale of *Dark Hope* to some organizations working to eradicate this problem in the United States and globally.

Q. Do you think that the degree of human trafficking that is going on has any implications for the future of humankind?

MM: The modern slave trade is bigger, affecting more human beings than was ever the case at the height of the plantation-driven economy. As much as I love my technology, I worry that it enables us to dehumanize others and that the human trafficking problem we have today is in part a reflection of that. The flip side, though, is that technology can help us spread the word and take action. We just need enough people to not look away from the horror, but to step into it to take a stand and do what they can to help. Readers can get ideas and inspiration for how they can help on my website, www.monicamcgurk.com

Q. Was there any other significance of choosing the particular location of Enoch in the desert other than it was close to the Chinese traffickers in Las Vegas?

MM: I find that particular landscape captivating and eerie. I could easily imagine Enoch hiding in isolation in such a barren place. I wanted to convey the loneliness of the choice he has made—not just to abandon his humanity, but also to reject the pettiness of the angels.

Q. Is it a coincidence that a place where heaven meets earth is also the setting for such bad things?

MM: In choosing to do what he thought was right, Enoch placed himself at odds with the larger angel community. It is hard when your decisions cast you as an outsider, and since part of my message is about choice and consequence, it seemed fitting to emphasize this as part of Enoch's story.

Q. We know that Hope grew up as a very lonely child. The last line of the book stresses her solitude once again. Even with the love of Michael and the love of her parents, Hope feels alone. Can you explain why?

MM: I think there is nothing lonelier than loving someone but not being sure if you can fully trust them. That is the place Hope finds herself with respect to Michael at the end of the book.

Q. You make the movement of Michael between spiritual and real forms seem so natural. And the ancient Enoch seems like someone you would actually run into out in the desert. Why did you want to make the lines between angels and human so easily blurred?

MM: In Biblical stories of angel visitations, most of the time the human beings encountering angels—in their homes, on a path while traveling—never seem to recognize the angels for what they are, at least not until after the fact. The drama of the Annunciation seems more like the exception than the rule. But—and this is important—this is a choice the angels make. They can appear however they want. Why do they choose to adopt human form? Is it to be more relatable and less scary to the people they encounter? Is it because they secretly admire and even envy the humans?

Is it because they are trying to understand what it is that makes human beings tick, and why God would have embraced and elevated them so thoroughly? It is an interesting question.

Q. What is the overarching meaning that you hope the reader will take away when reading about the Prophecy?

MM: I want the reader to struggle with questions of destiny versus personal choice. Beyond that, I cannot say until readers understand the true meaning of the Prophecy, which will be revealed in the second book!

Q. Which character in Dark Hope *do you most personally identify with and why?*

MM: In some respects, Mona, simply because she is closer to my age and has the same profession I once had. I can understand the guilt she feels, trying to balance a tricky personal life with a rich professional one.

Q. Do you have a favorite character?

MM: My favorites are Tabby and Enoch. They are the most fun to write.

Q. Hope is repeatedly in dangerous situations where it's not clear she'll survive. Have you ever been in any dangerous situation from which you weren't sure you'd be able to escape? How did you escape?

MM: Not really. I have had plenty of accidents and scares, including some health scares that were pretty serious, but those things were in the hands of very capable doctors so it wasn't really a matter of escape. It was more a matter of trust and faith.

Q. What types of scenes do you find the most difficult to write?

MM: I am always a bit squeamish about love scenes. It was a struggle in my fan fiction and a bit here, too. I also paid careful attention when writing Hope—whether it be during confrontations with Michael or in her own musings—that she walk the fine line of being appropriately scared but not lean all the way into victimhood. I wanted to show a balanced and realistic view of her thought processes, reflecting the complexities of her situation, but to never compromise her strength nor her individual agency.

Q. Which was your favorite chapter or scene to write in Dark Hope?

MM: I had two favorite scenes in *Dark Hope*: the first was the interlude with Enoch. I love his character and that scene was important on many, many levels. The second was the moment in Atlanta when Hope realizes who Lucas really is and Lucas reveals the true nature of her Mark, vastly complicating her relationship with Michael. I think my next favorites were when Michael and Hope go to see Chen, after she is disfigured, and Chen's interrogation. It is fun to play around with the bad guys!

Q. Have you ever had to deal with something that set you apart from others such as Hope's Mark?

MM: Nothing that significant or physically visible. I have had moments in my professional career where I was the only woman in the room or on a leadership team, and sometimes that was very hard. But those moments thankfully belong more to the past as more and more women are succeeding in business. I think the fact that I had many aunts who were successful businesswomen in their own right helped me have the right attitude to deal with those challenges along the way.

Q. Do you have any unusual or special practices that help you to write?

MM: I like to create and listen to playlists that reflect the characters, the plot, or the mood of the book I am working on. It helps keep me motivated and focused. Readers can actually access the Spotify lists from *Dark Hope* on my website, www.monicamcgurk.com.

Q. Anything else?

MM: I also like to surround myself with visual cues—so I will print out photos and online images and tape them all over my walls while I am writing a particular scene, to make sure that the physical sense of place, of location, stays alive for me. It is a bit messy, but fun.

Q. For a story involving very ancient characters, there is plenty of technology in Dark Hope, *from Wi-Fi hot spots to iPods. Do you write on a computer or with pen and paper?*

MM: Both! I carry a Moleskine or other notebook with me to jot down ideas or little snippets of dialog on the fly. I write questions and answers to myself on my iPad in Evernote as I try to resolve particular points of motivation or plot. And I write my actual manuscripts on my laptop.

Q. Do you prefer lobster or a cheeseburger and fries?

MM: I love both but would offer a compromise: deep-fried lobster tail from Chops in Atlanta. Yum!